Extrao
MICHA
NINE DRAGONS

"The action barrels at breakneck pace . . . But what remains most interesting is the new dimension added to the character—a man who has evolved over the series of fifteen novels to become ever more interesting and real."
—*Denver Post*

"Opens with the proverbial bang . . . A thing of cool beauty, meticulously plotted, rigorously controlled . . . What gives [NINE DRAGONS] its kick are not only the frenetic action scenes but also Bosch's sorrow."
—*Chicago Tribune*

"The trip to Hong Kong is pure thriller material . . . while the Los Angeles case . . . puts a human face on the way criminal triads function in immigrant communities. There's also something quietly gripping about a case that makes us consider the hard lives of people trying to make an honest living in a tough neighborhood."
—**Marilyn Stasio**, *New York Times Book Review*

"This is Bosch at his sharpest and Connelly at his most engaging. High-voltage stuff."
—*Sunday Oregonian*

more . . .

"Unfolds with exquisite procedural details; unexpected violence; and increased insight into the stoic, jazz-loving, relentless, flawed detective . . . There's no need to have read the previous Bosch tales; but if you haven't, this one will drive you to them."
—*Columbus Dispatch*

"Entertaining . . . impossible to put down."
—*Detroit News*

"May be the most wrenching Bosch novel yet . . . the jagged intersection between a cop's personal and professional lives is a recurring theme in many crime novels, but never has it been portrayed with the razor-edge sharpness and psychological acuity that Connelly brings to the subject. And that's layered underneath the nonstop action of the novel's last half—[a] kind of full-throttle, blood-spattered narrative road race."
—*Booklist* (starred review)

"A fast-paced, emotionally devastating plotline . . . Connelly's gift as a crime writer is his ability to create empathy for his hard-case characters."
—*Houston Chronicle*

more . . .

MICHAEL CONNELLY

NINE DRAGONS

GRAND CENTRAL
PUBLISHING

NEW YORK   BOSTON

The characters and events in this book are fictitious. Any similarity to real persons, living or dead, is coincidental and not intended by the author.

Copyright © 2009 by Hieronymus, Inc.
All rights reserved. Except as permitted under the U.S. Copyright Act of 1976, no part of this publication may be reproduced, distributed, or transmitted in any form or by any means, or stored in a database or retrieval system, without the prior written permission of the publisher.

Grand Central Publishing
Hachette Book Group
237 Park Avenue, New York, NY 10017
Visit our website at www.HachetteBookGroup.com

Grand Central Publishing is a division of Hachette Book Group, Inc. The Grand Central Publishing name and logo is a trademark of Hachette Book Group, Inc.

Printed in the United States of America

Originally published in hardcover by Little, Brown and Company
First international mass market edition, April 2010

10 9 8 7 6 5 4 3 2 1

To the whole crew on Enterprise Boulevard,
Lebanon, Indiana.
Many, many thanks.

PART ONE:

Homicide Special

1

From across the aisle Harry Bosch looked into his partner's cubicle and watched him conduct his daily ritual of straightening the corners on his stacks of files, clearing the paperwork from the center of his desk and finally placing his rinsed-out coffee cup in a desk drawer. Bosch checked his watch and saw it was only three-forty. It seemed that each day, Ignacio Ferras began the ritual a minute or two earlier than he had the day before. It was only Tuesday, the day after Labor Day weekend and the start of a short week, and already he was edging toward the early exit. This routine was always prompted by a phone call from home. There was a wife waiting there with a toddler and a brand-new set of twins. She watched the clock like the owner of a candy store watches the fat kids. She needed the break and she needed her husband home to deliver it. Even across the aisle from his partner, and with the four-foot sound walls separating work spaces in the new squad room, Bosch could usually hear both sides of the call. It always began with "When are you coming home?"

Everything in final order at his workstation, Ferras looked over at Bosch.

"Harry, I'm going to take off," he said. "Beat some of the traffic. I have a lot of calls out but they have my cell. No need waiting around for that."

Ferras rubbed his left shoulder as he spoke. This was also part of the routine. It was his unspoken way of reminding Bosch that he had taken a bullet a couple years before and had earned the early exit.

Bosch just nodded. The issue wasn't really about whether his partner left the job early or what he had earned. It was about his commitment to the mission of homicide work and whether it would be there when they finally got the next call out. Ferras had gone through nine months of physical therapy and rehab before reporting back to the squad room. But in the year since, he had worked cases with a reluctance that was wearing thin for Bosch. He wasn't committed and Bosch was tired of waiting for him.

He was also tired of waiting for a fresh kill. It had been four weeks since they'd drawn a case and they were well into the late summer heat. As certain as the Santa Ana winds blowing down out of the mountain passes, Bosch knew a fresh kill was coming.

Ferras stood up and locked his desk. He was taking his jacket off the back of the chair when Bosch saw Larry Gandle step out of his office on the far side of the squad room and head toward them. As the senior man in the partnership, Bosch had been given the first choice of cubicles a month earlier when Robbery-Homicide Division started to move over from the decrepit Parker Center to the new

Police Administration Building. Most detective 3s took the cubicles facing the windows that looked out on City Hall. Bosch had chosen the opposite. He had given his partner the view and took the cube that let him watch what was happening in the squad room. Now he saw the approaching lieutenant and he instinctively knew that his partner wasn't going home early.

Gandle was holding a piece of paper torn from a notepad and had an extra hop in his step. That told Bosch the wait was over. The call out was here. The fresh kill. Bosch started to rise.

"Bosch and Ferras, you're up," Gandle said when he got to them. "Need you to take a case for South Bureau."

Bosch saw his partner's shoulders slump. He ignored it and reached out for the paper Gandle was holding. He looked at the address written on it. South Normandie. He'd been there before.

"It's a liquor store," Gandle said. "One man down behind the counter, patrol is holding a witness. That's all I got. You two good to go?"

"We're good," Bosch said before his partner could complain.

But that didn't work.

"Lieutenant, this is Homicide Special," Ferras said, turning and pointing to the boar's head mounted over the squad room door. "Why are we taking a rob job at a liquor store? You know it was a banger and the South guys could wrap it up — or at least put a name on the shooter — before midnight."

Ferras had a point. Homicide Special was for the difficult and complex cases. It was an elite squad that went after the tough cases with the relentless skill of a boar rooting in the mud for a truffle. A liquor store holdup in gang territory hardly qualified.

Gandle, whose balding pate and dour expression made him a perfect administrator, spread his hands in a gesture offering a complete lack of sympathy.

"I told everybody in the staff meeting last week. We've got South's back this week. They've got a skeleton crew on while everybody else is in homicide school until the fourteenth. They caught three cases over the weekend and one this morning. So there goes the skeleton crew. You guys are up and the rob job is yours. That's it. Any other questions? Patrol is waiting down there with a witness."

"We're good, Boss," Bosch said, ending the discussion.

"I'll wait to hear from you, then."

Gandle headed back to his office. Bosch pulled his coat off the back of his chair, put it on and then opened the middle drawer of his desk. He took the leather notebook out of his back pocket and replaced the pad of lined paper in it with a new one. A fresh kill always got a fresh pad. That was his routine. He looked at the detective shield embossed on the notebook flap and then returned it to his back pocket. The truth was, he didn't care what kind of case it was. He just wanted a case. It was like anything else. You fall out of practice and you lose your edge. Bosch didn't want that.

Ferras stood with his hands on his hips, looking up at the clock on the wall over the bulletin boards.

"Shit," Ferras said. "Every time."

"What do you mean, 'every time'?" Bosch said. "We haven't caught a case in a month."

"Yeah, well, I was getting used to that."

"Well, if you don't want to work murders, there's always a nine-to-five table like auto theft."

"Yeah, right."

"Then, let's go."

Bosch stepped out of the cubicle into the aisle and headed toward the door. Ferras followed, pulling his phone out so he could call his wife and give her the bad news. On the way out of the squad room, both men reached up and patted the boar on its flat nose for good luck.

2

Bosch didn't need to lecture Ferras on the way to South L.A. His driving in silence was his lecture. His young partner seemed to wither under the pressure of what was not said and finally opened up.

"This is driving me crazy," he said.

"What is?" Bosch asked.

"The twins. There's so much work, so much crying. It's a domino effect. One wakes up and that starts the other one up. Then my oldest kid wakes up. Nobody's getting any sleep and my wife is..."

"What?"

"I don't know, going crazy. Calling me all the time, asking when I'm coming home. So I come home and then it's my turn and I get the boys and I get no break. It's work, kids, work, kids, work, kids, every day."

"What about a nanny?"

"We can't afford a nanny. Not with the way things are, and we don't even get overtime anymore."

Bosch didn't know what to say. His daughter, Madeline, was a month past her thirteenth birthday and almost ten thousand miles away from him. He had never been directly involved in raising her. He saw her four weeks a year—two in Hong Kong and two in L.A.—and that was it. What advice could he legitimately give a full-time dad with three kids, including twins?

"Look, I don't know what to tell you," he said. "You know I've got your back. I'll do what I can when I can. But—"

"I know, Harry. I appreciate that. It's just the first year with the twins, you know? It will be a lot easier when they get a little older."

"Yeah, but what I'm trying to say here is that maybe it's more than just the twins. Maybe it's you, Ignacio."

"Me? What are you saying?"

"I'm saying maybe it's you. Maybe you came back too soon—you ever think about that?"

Ferras did a slow burn and didn't respond.

"Hey, it happens sometimes," Bosch said. "You take a bullet and you start thinking that lightning might strike twice."

"Look, Harry, I don't know what kind of bullshit that is, but I'm fine that way. I'm good. This is about sleep deprivation and being fucking exhausted all the time and not being able to catch up because my wife is riding my ass from the moment I get home, okay?"

"Whatever you say, partner."

"That's right, partner. Whatever I say. Believe me, I get it enough from her. I don't need it from you, too."

Bosch nodded and that was enough said. He knew when to quit.

The address Gandle had given them was in the

Seventieth block of South Normandie Avenue. This was just a few blocks from the infamous corner of Florence and Normandie, where some of the most horrible images of the 1992 riots had been captured by news helicopters and broadcast around the world. It seemed to be the lasting image of Los Angeles to many.

But Bosch quickly realized he knew the area and the liquor store that was their destination from a different riot and for a different reason.

Fortune Liquors was already cordoned off by yellow crime scene tape. A small number of onlookers were gathered but murder in this neighborhood was not that much of a curiosity. The people here had seen it before — many times. Bosch pulled their sedan into the middle of a grouping of three patrol cars and parked. After going to the trunk to retrieve his briefcase, he locked the car up and headed toward the tape.

Bosch and Ferras gave their names and serial numbers to a patrol officer with the crime scene attendance log and then ducked under the tape. As they approached the front door of the store, Bosch put his hand into his right jacket pocket and pulled out a book of matches. It was old and worn. The front cover said FORTUNE LIQUORS and it carried the address of the small yellow building before them. He thumbed the book open. There was only one match missing, and on the inside cover was the fortune that came with every matchbook:

Happy is the man who
finds refuge in himself.

Bosch had carried the matchbook with him for more than ten years. Not so much for the fortune, though he did believe in what it said. It was because of the missing match and what it reminded him of.

"Harry, what's up?" Ferras asked.

Bosch realized he had paused in his approach to the store.

"Nothing, I've just been here before."

"When? On a case?"

"Sort of. But it was a long time ago. Let's go in."

Bosch walked past his partner and entered the open front door of the liquor store.

Several patrol officers and a sergeant were standing inside. The store was long and narrow. It was a shotgun design and essentially three aisles wide. Bosch could see down the center aisle to a rear hallway and an open back door leading to a parking area behind the store. The cold-beverage cases ran along the wall on the left aisle and then across the back of the store. The liquor was on the right aisle, while the middle aisle was reserved for wine with red on the right and white on the left.

Bosch saw two more patrol officers in the rear hallway and he guessed they were holding the witness in what was probably a rear storage room or office. He put his brief-case down on the floor by the door. From the pocket of his suit coat he pulled two pairs of latex gloves. He gave a set to Ferras and they put them on.

The sergeant noticed the arrival of the two detectives and broke away from his men.

"Ray Lucas," he said by way of greeting. "We have one vic down behind the counter here. His name is John

Li, spelled *L-I.* Happened, we think, less than two hours ago. Looks like a robbery where the guy just didn't want to leave a witness. A lot of us down here in the Seventy-seventh knew Mr. Li. He was a good old guy."

Lucas signaled Bosch and Ferras over to the counter. Bosch held his coat so it wouldn't touch anything when he went around and squeezed into the small space behind the counter. He squatted down like a baseball catcher to look more closely at the dead man on the floor. Ferras leaned in over him like an umpire.

The victim was Asian and looked to be almost seventy. He was on his back, eyes staring blankly at the ceiling. His lips were pulled back from clenched teeth, almost in a sneer. There was blood on his lips, cheek and chin. It had been coughed up as he died. The front of his shirt was soaked with his blood and Bosch could see at least three bullet entry points in his chest. His right leg was bent at the knee and folded awkwardly under his other leg. He had obviously collapsed on the spot where he had been standing when he was shot.

"No casings that we can see," Lucas said. "The shooter cleaned those up and then he was smart enough to pull the disc out of the recorder in the back."

Bosch nodded. The patrol guys always wanted to be helpful but it was information Bosch didn't need yet and could be misleading.

"Unless it was a revolver," he said. "Then there would have been no casings to clean up."

"Maybe," Lucas said. "But you don't usually see too many revolvers down here anymore. Nobody wants to be caught in a drive-by with just six bullets in their gun."

Lucas wanted Bosch to know that he knew the lay of the land down here. Bosch was just a visitor.

"I'll keep that in mind," Harry said.

Bosch focused on the body and studied the scene silently. He was pretty sure the victim was the same man he had encountered in the store so many years before. He was even in the same spot, on the floor behind the counter. And Bosch could see a soft pack of cigarettes in the shirt pocket.

He noticed that the victim's right hand had blood smeared on it. He didn't find this unusual. From earliest childhood people touch their hand to an injury to try to protect it and make it better. It is natural instinct. This victim had done the same here, most likely grabbing at his chest after the first shot hit him.

There was about a four-inch spatial separation between the bullet wounds, which formed the points of a triangle. Bosch knew that three quick shots from close range would usually have made a tighter cluster. This led him to believe that the victim had likely been shot once and then fell to the floor. The killer had then probably leaned over the counter and shot him two more times, creating the spread.

The slugs tore through the victim's chest, causing massive damage to the heart and lungs. The blood expectorated through the mouth showed that death was not immediate. The victim had tried to breathe. After all his years working cases Bosch was sure of one thing. There was no easy way to die.

"No headshot," Bosch said.

"Right," Ferras said. "What's it mean?"

Bosch realized he had been musing out loud.

"Maybe nothing. Just seems like three in the chest, the shooter wanted no doubt. But then no headshot to be sure."

"Like a contradiction."

"Maybe."

Bosch took his eyes off the body for the first time and looked around from his low angle. His eyes immediately held on a gun that was in a holster attached to the underside of the counter. It was located for easy access in case of a robbery or worse, but it had not even been pulled from its holster.

"We've got a gun under here," Bosch said. "Looks like a forty-five in a holster, but the old man never got the chance to pull it."

"The shooter came in quick and shot the old guy before he could reach for his piece," Ferras said. "Maybe it was known in the neighborhood that the old man had the gun under the counter."

Lucas made a noise with his mouth, as if he was disagreeing.

"What is it, Sergeant?" Bosch asked.

"The gun's gotta be new," Lucas said. "The guy's been robbed at least six times in the last five years since I've been here. As far as I know, he never pulled a gun. This is the first I knew about a gun."

Bosch nodded. It was a valid observation. He turned his head to speak over his shoulder to the sergeant.

"Tell me about the witness," he said.

"Uh, she's not really a witness," Lucas said. "It's Mrs. Li, the wife. She came in and found her husband when she was bringing him in his dinner. We've got her in the back room but you'll need a translator. We called the ACU, asked for Chinese to go."

Bosch took another look at the dead man's face, then stood up and both his knees cracked loudly. Lucas had referred to what was once known as the Asian Crimes Unit. It had recently been changed to the Asian Gang Unit to accommodate concerns that the unit name besmirched the city's Asian population by suggesting all Asians were involved in crime. But the old dogs like Lucas still called it the ACU. Regardless of name or acronym, the decision to call in an additional investigator of any stripe should have been left to Bosch as lead investigator.

"You speak Chinese, Sarge?"

"No, that's why I called ACU."

"Then, how did you know to ask for Chinese and not Korean or maybe even Vietnamese?"

"I've been on the job twenty-six years, Detective. And—"

"And you know Chinese when you see it."

"No, what I'm saying is I have a hard time making it through a shift these days without a little jolt, you know? So once a day I stop by here to pick up one of those energy drinks. Five-hour boost it gives you. Anyway, I got to know Mr. Li a little bit from coming in. He told me he and his wife came from China and that's how I knew."

Bosch nodded and was embarrassed at his effort to embarrass Lucas.

"I guess I'll have to try one of those boosts," he said. "Did Mrs. Li call nine-one-one?"

"No, like I said, she doesn't have much English. From what I got from dispatch, Mrs. Li called her son and he's the one who called nine-one-one."

Bosch stepped out and around the counter. Ferras

lingered behind it, squatting to get the same view of the body and the gun that Bosch had just had.

"Where is the son?" Bosch asked.

"He's coming but he works up in the Valley," Lucas said. "Should be here anytime now."

Bosch pointed to the counter.

"When he gets here, you and your people keep him away from this."

"Got it."

"And we're going to have to try to keep this place as clear as possible now."

Lucas got the message and took his officers out of the store. Finished behind the counter, Ferras joined Bosch near the front door, where he was looking up at the camera mounted on the ceiling at the center of the store.

"Why don't you check out the back?" Bosch said. "See if the guy really pulled the disc, and look in on our witness."

"Got it."

"Oh, and find the thermostat and cool it down in here. It's too warm. I don't want that body to turn."

Ferras headed down the center aisle. Bosch looked back to take in the scene as a whole. The counter was about twelve feet long. The cash register was set up at center with an open space for customers to put down their purchases. On one side of this were racks of gum and candy. On the other side of the register were other point-of-purchase products like energy drinks, a plastic case containing cheap cigars and a lotto display case. Overhead was a wire-mesh storage box for cigarette cartons.

Behind the counter were shelves where high-end

liquors were stored, and which had to be asked for by customers. Bosch saw six rows of Hennessy. He knew the expensive cognac was favored by high-rolling gang members. He was pretty sure the location of Fortune Liquors would put it in the territory of the Hoover Street Criminals, a street gang that once was a Crips set but then became so powerful its leaders chose to forge their own name and reputation.

Bosch noticed two things and stepped closer to the counter.

The cash register had been turned askew on the counter, revealing a square of grit and dust on the Formica where it had been located. Bosch reasoned that the killer had pulled it toward him while he took the money from the drawer. This was a significant assumption because it meant that Mr. Li had not opened the drawer and given the robber the money. This likely meant he had already been shot. Ferras's theory that the killer had come in shooting could be correct. And this could be significant in an eventual prosecution in proving intent to kill. More important, it gave Bosch a better idea of what had happened in the store and what kind of person they were looking for.

Harry reached into his pocket and pulled out the glasses he wore for close work. He put them on and without touching anything leaned over the counter to study the cash register's keyboard. He saw no button that said OPEN or any other obvious indication of how to open the cash drawer. Bosch was unsure how to open the register. He wondered how the killer knew.

He straightened back up and looked at the shelves of bottles on the wall behind the counter. The Hennessy was front and center, with easy access for Mr. Li when members of Hoover Street came in. But the rows were flush. No bottle was missing.

Again Bosch leaned forward across the counter. This time he tried to reach across to one of the bottles of Hennessy. He realized that if he put his hand down on the counter for balance he would be able to reach the row and take one of the bottles easily.

"Harry?"

Bosch straightened back up and turned to his partner.

"The sergeant was right," Ferras said. "The camera system records to disc. There's no disc in the machine. It was either pulled or he wasn't recording to disc and the camera was just for show."

"Are there any backup discs?"

"There's a couple back there on the counter but it's a one-disc system. It just records over and over on the same disc. I worked Robbery way back when and we saw a lot of these. They last about a day and then it records over it. You pull the disc if you want to check something but you have to do it in the same day."

"Okay, make sure we get those extra discs."

Lucas came back in through the front door.

"ACU is here," he said. "Should I send him in?"

Bosch looked at Lucas for a long moment before answering.

"It's AGU," he finally said. "But don't send him in. I'll be right out."

3

Bosch stepped out of the store into the sunlight. It was still warm though getting late in the day. The dry Santa Ana winds were passing through the city. Fires in the hills had put a pallor of smoke in the air. Bosch could feel the sweat drying on the back of his neck.

He was almost immediately met outside the door by a plainclothes detective.

"Detective Bosch?"

"That's me."

"Detective David Chu, AGU. Patrol called me down. How can I be of help?"

Chu was short and slightly built. There was no trace of an accent in his voice. Bosch signaled him to follow as he ducked back under the tape and headed to his car. He took off his suit jacket as he went. He took the matchbook out and put it in his pants pocket, then folded the jacket inside out and put it in a clean cardboard box he kept in the trunk of his work car.

"Hot in there," he told Chu.

Bosch opened the middle button of his shirt and stuck

his tie inside. He now planned to get fully involved in the crime scene investigation and didn't want it to get in the way.

"Hot out here, too," Chu said. "The patrol sergeant told me to wait until you came out."

"Yeah, sorry about that. Okay, what we've got is, the old man who has run this store for a number of years is dead behind the counter. Shot at least three times in what looks like a robbery. His wife, who does not speak English, came into the store and found him. She called their son, who then called it in. We obviously need to interview her and that's where you come in. We may also need help with the son when he gets here. That's about all I know at the moment."

"And we're sure they're Chinese?"

"Pretty sure. The patrol sergeant who made the call knew the victim, Mr. Li."

"Do you know which dialect Mrs. Li speaks?"

They headed back to the tape.

"Nope. Is that going to be a problem?"

"I am familiar with the five main Chinese dialects and proficient in Cantonese and Mandarin. These are the two we most often encounter here in L.A."

This time Bosch held the tape up for Chu so he could go back under.

"Which are you?"

"I was born here, Detective. But my family is from Hong Kong and I was raised speaking Mandarin at home."

"Yeah? I have a kid who lives in Hong Kong with her mother. She's getting good at Mandarin."

"Good for her. I hope it will be useful to her."

They entered the store and Bosch gave Chu a quick view of the body behind the counter and then walked him to the rear of the store. They were met by Ferras and then Chu was used to make introductions to Mrs. Li.

The newly widowed woman appeared to be in shock. Bosch saw no indication that she had shed a single tear for her husband so far. She seemed to be in a dissociated state that Bosch had seen before. Her husband was lying dead in the front of the store. She was surrounded by strangers who spoke a different language. Bosch guessed she was waiting for her son to arrive, and then the tears would fall.

Chu was gentle with her and conversational at first. Bosch believed that they were speaking Mandarin. His daughter had told him that Mandarin was more singsong and less guttural than Cantonese and some of the other dialects.

After a few minutes Chu broke away to report to Bosch and Ferras.

"Her husband was alone in the store while she went home to prepare their supper. When she came back she thought the store was empty. Then she found him behind the counter. She saw no one in the store when she came in. She parked in the back and used a key to open the back door."

Bosch nodded.

"How long was she gone? Ask her what time it was when she left the store."

Chu did as instructed and turned back to Bosch with the answer.

"She leaves at two-thirty every day to pick up the supper. Then she comes back."

"Are there other employees?"

"No, I asked that already. Just her husband and Mrs. Li. They work every day eleven to ten. Closed Sundays."

A typical immigrant story, Bosch thought. They just weren't counting on the bullets coming at the end of it.

Bosch heard voices coming from the front of the store and ducked his head into the rear hallway. The forensics team from SID had arrived and were going to work.

He turned back into the storage room, where the interview with Mrs. Li was continuing.

"Chu," Bosch interrupted.

The AGU detective looked up at him.

"Ask about the son. Was he at home when she called?"

"I already asked. There is another store. It's in the Valley. He was working there. The family lives together in the middle. In the Wilshire District."

It seemed clear to Bosch that Chu knew what he was doing. He didn't need Bosch to prompt him with questions.

"Okay, we're going back up front. You deal with her and after her son arrives it might be better to take everybody downtown. You okay with that?"

"I'm fine with it," Chu said.

"Good. Tell me if you need anything."

Bosch and Ferras went down the hall and to the front of the store. Bosch already knew everybody on the forensics team. A team from the medical examiner's office had also arrived to document the death scene and collect the body.

Bosch and Ferras decided to split up at that point. Bosch would stay on scene. As lead detective he would monitor the collection of forensic evidence and the removal of the body. Ferras would leave the store and go knock on doors. The liquor store was located in a commercial area of small businesses. He would go door-to-door in an effort to find someone who had heard or seen something related to the killing. Both investigators knew this would likely be a fruitless effort but it was one that needed to be made. A description of a car or a suspicious person could be the piece of the puzzle that would eventually break the case. It was basic homicide work.

"All right if I take one of the patrol guys?" Ferras asked. "They know the neighborhood."

"Sure."

Bosch thought that knowing the lay of the land was not Ferras's true reason for taking a patrol officer with him. His partner thought he needed backup to knock on doors and visit stores in the neighborhood.

Two minutes after Ferras left, Bosch heard loud voices and a commotion coming from outside at the front of the store. He stepped out and saw two of Lucas's patrol officers trying to physically detain a man at the yellow tape. The struggling man was Asian and in his midtwenties. He wore a tight-fitting T-shirt that displayed his lean build. Bosch quickly stepped toward the problem.

"Okay, stop it right there," he said forcefully so no one would doubt who was in charge of the situation.

"Let him go," he added.

"I want to see my father," the young man said.

"Well, that's not the way to go about doing it."

Bosch stepped closer and nodded to the two patrolmen.

"I'll take care of Mr. Li now."

They left Bosch and the victim's son alone.

"What is your full name, Mr. Li?"

"Robert Li. I want to see my father."

"I understand that. I'm going to let you see your father if you really want to. But you can't until it's clear. I'm the detective in charge of this whole thing and I can't even see your father yet. So I need you to calm down. The only way you will get what you want is if you calm down."

The young man looked down at the ground and nodded. Bosch reached out and touched him on the shoulder.

"Okay, good," Bosch said.

"Where's my mother?"

"She's inside in the back room being interviewed by another detective."

"Can I at least see her?"

"Yes, you can. I'll walk you around back in a minute. I just need to ask you a few questions first. Is that okay?"

"Fine. Go ahead."

"First of all, my name is Harry Bosch. I'm the lead detective on this investigation. I'm going to find whoever killed your father. I promise you that."

"Don't make promises you don't intend to keep. You didn't even know him. You don't care. He's just another—never mind."

"Another what?"

"I said, never mind."

Bosch stared at him for a moment before responding.

"How old are you, Robert?"

"I'm twenty-six and I would like to see my mother now."

He made a move to turn and head toward the back of

the store but Bosch grabbed him on the arm. The younger man was strong but Bosch had a strength in his grip that was surprising. The young man stopped and looked down at the hand on his arm.

"Let me show you something and then I'll take you to your mother."

He let go of Li's arm and then pulled the matchbook from his pocket. He handed it over. Li looked at it with no surprise.

"What about it? We used to give these away until the economy went bad and we couldn't afford the extras."

Bosch took the matchbook back and nodded.

"I got it in your father's store twelve years ago," he said. "I guess you were about fourteen years old then. We almost had a riot in this city. Happened right here. This intersection."

"I remember. They looted the store and beat up my father. He should have never reopened here. My mother and me, we told him to open the store up in the Valley but he wouldn't listen to us. He wasn't going to let anybody drive him out and now look what happened."

He gestured helplessly toward the front of the store.

"Yeah, well, I was here that night, too," Bosch said. "Twelve years ago. A riot started but it ended pretty quick. Right here. One casualty."

"A cop. I know. They pulled him right out of his car."

"I was in that car with him but they didn't get to me. And when I got to this spot I was safe. I needed a smoke and I went into your father's store. He was there behind the counter but the looters had taken every last pack of cigarettes in the place."

Bosch held up the book of matches.

"I found plenty of matches but no cigarettes. And then your father reached into his pocket and pulled out his own. He had one last smoke left and he gave it to me."

Bosch nodded. That was the story. That was it.

"I didn't know your father, Robert. But I'm going to find the person who killed him. That's a promise I'll keep."

Robert Li nodded and looked down at the ground.

"Okay," Bosch said. "Let's go see your mother now."

4

The detectives didn't clear the crime scene and get back to the squad room until almost midnight. By then Bosch had decided not to bring the victim's family to PAB for formal interviews. After appointments were made for them to come in Wednesday morning, he let them go home to grieve. Shortly after getting back to the squad Bosch also sent Ferras home so he could attempt to repair damages with his own family. Harry stayed behind alone to organize the evidence inventory and to contemplate things about the case for the first time without interruption. He knew that Wednesday was shaping up as a busy day, with appointments with the family in the morning and results of some of the forensic and lab work coming in, as well as the possible scheduling of the autopsy.

While the canvass of the nearby businesses by Ferras had proved fruitless as expected, the evening's work had produced one possible suspect. On Saturday afternoon, three days before his murder, Mr. Li had confronted a young man he believed had been routinely shoplifting from the store. According to Mrs. Li and as translated by Detective Chu, the teenager had angrily denied ever stealing anything and drew the race card, claiming Mr. Li had only accused him because he was black. This seemed laughable, since ninety-nine percent of the store's business came from neighborhood residents who were black. But Li did not call the police. He simply banished the teenager from the store, telling him never to return. Mrs. Li told Chu that the teen's parting shot at the door was to tell her husband that the next time he came back it would be to blow the shopkeeper's head off. Li in turn had pulled his weapon from beneath the counter and pointed it at the youth, assuring him that he would be ready for his return.

This meant the teenager was aware of the weapon Li had beneath the counter. If he were to make good on his threat, he would have to enter the store and act swiftly, shooting Li before he could get to his gun.

Mrs. Li would look through gang books in the morning in an effort to find a photo of the threatening youth. If he was associated with the Hoover Street Criminals, then chances were they had his photo in the books.

But Bosch wasn't fully convinced it was a viable lead or that the kid was a valid suspect. There were things about the crime scene that didn't add up to a revenge killing. There was no doubt that they had to run the lead down and talk to the kid but Bosch wasn't expecting to close the case with him. That would be too easy and there were things about the case that defied easy.

Off the captain's office, there was a meeting room with a long wooden table. This was primarily used as a lunchroom and occasionally for staff meetings or for private discussions of investigations involving multiple detective teams. With the squad empty, Bosch had commandeered the room and had spread several crime scene photographs, fresh from forensics, across the table.

He had laid the photos out in a disjointed mosaic of overlapping images that in a whole created the entire crime scene. It was much like the photo work of the English artist David Hockney, who had lived in Los Angeles for a while and had created several photo collages as art pieces that documented scenes in Southern California. Bosch became familiar with the photo mosaics and the artist because Hockney had been his neighbor for a time in the hills above the Cahuenga Pass. Though Bosch had never met Hockney, he drew a connection to the artist because it had always been Harry's habit to spread crime scene photos out in a mosaic that allowed him to look for new details and angles. Hockney did the same with his work.

Looking at the photos now while sipping from a mug of black coffee he had brewed, Bosch was first drawn to the same things that had hooked him while he had been at the scene. Front and center were the bottles of Hennessy standing untouched in a row just across the counter. Harry had a hard time believing that the killing could be gang related because he doubted that a gangbanger would take the money and not a single bottle of Hennessy. The cognac would be a trophy. It was right there within reach, especially if the shooter had to lean over or go around the counter to grab bullet casings. Why not take the Hennessy, too?

Bosch's conclusion was that they were looking for a shooter who didn't care about Hennessy. A shooter who was not a gangbanger.

The next point of interest was the victim's wounds.

For Bosch, these alone excluded the mystery shoplifter as a suspect. Three bullets in the chest left no doubt that the intention was to kill. But there was no face shot and that seemed to put the lie to this being a killing motivated by anger or revenge. Bosch had investigated hundreds of murders, most of them involving the use of firearms, and he knew that when he had a face shot, the killing was most likely personal and the killer was someone known to the victim. Therefore, the opposite could be held true. Three in the chest was not personal. It was business. Bosch was sure that the unknown shoplifter was not their killer. Instead, they were looking for someone who was possibly a complete stranger to John Li. Someone who had coolly walked in and put three slugs into Li's chest, then calmly emptied the cash register, picked up his brass and gone to the back room to grab the disc out of the camera-recorder.

Bosch knew it was likely that this was not a first-time crime. In the morning he would need to check for similar crimes in Los Angeles and the surrounding areas.

Looking at the image of the victim's face, Bosch suddenly noticed something new. The blood on Li's cheek and chin was smeared. Also, the teeth were clean. There was no blood on them.

Bosch held the photo up closer and tried to make sense of it. He had assumed the blood on Li's face was expectorant. Blood that had come up from his destroyed lungs in his last fitful gasps for air. But how could that happen without getting blood on his teeth?

He put the photo down and moved across the mosaic to the victim's right hand. It had dropped down at his side.

There was blood on the fingers and thumb, a drip line to the palm of his hand.

Bosch looked back at the blood smeared on the face. He suddenly realized that Li had touched his bloody hand to his mouth. This meant a double transfer had taken place. Li had touched his hand to his chest, getting blood on it, and had then transferred blood from his hand to his mouth.

The question was why. Were these movements part of the final death throes, or had Li done something else?

Bosch pulled his cell and called the investigators' line at the medical examiner's office. He had it on speed dial. He checked his watch as the phone rang. It was ten past midnight.

"Coroner's."

"Is Cassel still there?"

Max Cassel was the investigator who had worked the scene at Fortune Liquors and collected the body.

"No, he just—wait a minute, there he is."

The call was put on hold and then Cassel picked up.

"I don't care who you are, I'm out the door. I just came back in because I forgot my coffee warmer."

Bosch knew Cassel lived at least an hour's commute out in Palmdale. Coffee mugs with warmers you plugged into the cigarette lighter were a must for downtown workers with long drive times.

"It's Bosch. You put my guy in a drawer already?"

"Nope, all the drawers are taken. He's in icebox three. But I'm done with him and going home, Bosch."

"I understand. I just have one quick question. Did you check his mouth?"

"What do you mean, check his mouth? Of course I checked his mouth. That's my job."

"And there was nothing there? Nothing in the mouth or throat?"

"No, there was something there all right."

Bosch felt the adrenaline start to kick in.

"Why didn't you tell me? What was it?"

"His tongue."

The adrenaline dried up and Bosch felt deflated as Cassel chuckled. Harry thought he had been on to something.

"Very funny. What about blood?"

"Yes, there was a small amount of blood on the tongue and in the throat. It's noted in my report, which you will get tomorrow."

"But three shots. His lungs must've looked like Swiss cheese. Wouldn't there be a lot of blood?"

"Not if he was already dead. Not if the first shot blew up the heart and it stopped beating. Look, I gotta go, Bosch. You're on the sked tomorrow at two with Laksmi. Ask her these questions."

"I will. But I'm talking to you now. I think we missed something."

"What are you talking about?"

Bosch stared at the photos in front of him, his eyes moving from the hand to the face.

"I think he put something in his mouth."

"Who did?"

"The victim. Mr. Li."

There was a pause while Cassel considered this and probably also considered whether he had missed anything.

"Well, if he did, I did not see it in the mouth or throat.

If it was something he swallowed, then that is not my jurisdiction. It's Laksmi's and she'll find it—whatever it is—tomorrow."

"Would you make a note so she'll see it?"

"Bosch, I'm trying to get out of here. You can tell her when you come for the cut."

"I know, but just in case, make a note."

"Fine, whatever, I'll make a note. You know nobody's gettin' overtime around here anymore, Bosch."

"Yeah, I know. Same over here. Thanks, Max."

Bosch closed the phone and decided to put the photos aside for the time being. The autopsy would determine if his conclusion was correct, and there was nothing he could do about it until then.

There were two plastic evidence envelopes that contained the two discs that had been found next to the recorder. Each was in a flat plastic case. Each case was marked with a date scribbled with a Sharpie. One was marked 9/01, exactly a week earlier, and the other was dated 8/27. Bosch took the discs over to the AV equipment at the far end of the meeting room and put the 8/27 disc into the DVD player first.

The images were contained on a split screen. One camera angle showed the front of the store, including the cash register counter, and the other was on the rear of the store. A time and date stamp ran across the top. The activities in the store ran in real time. Bosch realized that, since the store was open from 11 A.M. to 10 P.M., he had twenty-two hours of video to watch unless he used the fast-forward button.

He checked his watch again. He knew he could work

through the night and try to solve the mystery of why John Li had put these two discs aside or he could go home now and get some rest. You never knew where a case would take you and rest was always important. Added to that, there was nothing about these discs that suggested they had anything to do with the murder. The disc that had been in the machine had been taken. That was the important one and it was gone.

What the hell, Bosch thought. He decided to watch the first disc and see if he could solve the mystery. He pulled a chair over from the table, set himself up in front of the television and moved the playback speed to four times real time. He figured it would take him less than three hours to knock off the first disc. He would then go home, get a few hours sleep and be back at the same time as everybody else in the morning.

"Sounds like a plan," he said to himself.

5

Bosch was roughly dragged out of sleep and opened his eyes to see Lieutenant Gandle staring down at him. It took Harry a moment to clear his head and understand where he was.

"Lieutenant?"

"What are you doing in my office, Bosch?"

Bosch sat up on the couch.

"I...I was watching video in the boardroom and it got so late it wasn't worth going home. What time is it now?"

"Almost seven but that still doesn't explain why you're in my office. When I left yesterday, I locked my door."

"Really?"

"Yes, really."

Bosch nodded and acted like he was still clearing his head. He was happy he'd put his picks back in his wallet after he'd opened the door. Gandle had the only couch in RHD.

"Maybe the office cleaners came by and forgot to lock it," he offered.

"No, they don't have a key. Look, Harry, I don't mind

people using the couch to sleep. But if the door is locked, it's for a reason. I can't have people opening my door after I've locked it."

"You're right, Lieutenant. You think maybe we can get a couch out in the squad?"

"I'll work on it but that's not the point."

Bosch stood up.

"I get the point. I'm going back to work now."

"Not so fast. Tell me about this video that kept you here all night."

Bosch briefly explained what he had seen when he spent five hours viewing the two discs through the middle of the night and how John Li had unintentionally left behind what looked like a solid lead.

"You want me to set it up for you in the conference room?"

"Why don't you wait till your partner's here. We can all look at it together. Go get some coffee first."

Bosch left Gandle and walked through the squad room. It was an impersonal maze of cubicles and sound barriers. It whispered like an insurance office and the truth was, it was so quiet that at times Bosch had trouble concentrating. It was still deserted but would now start to fill up quickly. Gandle was always the first man in. He liked to set the precedent for the squad.

Harry went down to the cafeteria, which had opened at seven but was empty because the bulk of the police department's personnel were still working out of Parker Center. The move to the new Police Administration Building was progressing slowly. First some detective squads, then administrators and then the rest. It was a soft opening and the building would not be formally dedicated for another two months. For now it meant there were no lines in the cafeteria but there wasn't a full menu either. Bosch got the cop's breakfast: two doughnuts and a coffee. He also picked up a coffee for Ferras. He ate the doughnuts quickly while putting cream and sugar in his partner's cup and then took the elevator back up. As expected, when he got back to the squad his partner was at his desk. Bosch put one of the coffees down in front of him and walked over to his own cubicle.

"Thanks, Harry," Ferras said. "I should have known you'd be here before — hey, you wore that suit yesterday. Don't tell me you've been working all night."

Bosch sat down.

"I got a couple hours on the lieutenant's couch. What time are Mrs. Li and her son coming in today?"

"I told them ten. Why?"

"I think I've got something we need to pursue. I watched the extra discs from the store's cameras last night."

"What did you find?"

"Grab your coffee and I'll show you. The lieutenant wants to see it, too."

Ten minutes later Bosch was standing with the remote control in front of the AV equipment while Ferras and Gandle sat at the end of the boardroom table. He cued the disc marked 9/01 to the right spot and then froze the playback until he was ready.

"Okay, our shooter took the disc out of the recorder, so we have no video of what happened in the store yesterday. But what *was* left behind were two extra discs marked

August twenty-seven and September one. This is the disc from September one, which happens to be one week prior to yesterday. You follow?"

"Follow," Gandle said.

"So what Mr. Li was doing was documenting a tag team of shoplifters. The commonality between these two discs is that on both days these same two guys come in and one goes to the counter and asks for cigarettes while the other goes down the liquor aisle. The first guy draws Li's attention away from his partner and the camera screen he had behind the counter. While Li's getting smokes for the guy at the counter the other guy slides a couple flasks of vodka into his pants, then takes a third to the counter for purchase. The guy at the counter pulls his wallet, sees he left his money at home or whatever and they leave without making a purchase. It happens on both these days with them alternating their roles. I think that is why Li kept the discs out."

"You think he was trying to make a case or something?" Ferras asked.

"Maybe," Bosch said. "If he got them on film he'd have something to give the police."

"This is your lead?" Gandle said. "You worked through the night for this? I was reading the reports. I think I like the kid Li pulled the gun on better than this."

"This is not the lead," Bosch said impatiently. "I'm only telling you the reason for the discs. Li pulled the discs out of the camera because he must have known those two guys were up to something and he wanted to preserve the record of it. Inadvertently, he also preserved this on the September first tape."

Bosch hit the playback and the image started to move. On the split screen both camera angles showed the store was empty except for Li behind the counter. The time stamp at the top showed that it was 3:03 P.M. on Tuesday, September 1.

The front door of the store opened and a customer entered. He waved casually to Li at the counter and proceeded to the rear of the store. The image was grainy but it was clear enough for the three viewers to tell the customer was an Asian man in his early thirties. He was picked up on the second camera as he went to one of the cold cases at the rear of the store and selected a single can of beer. He took it forward to the counter.

"What's he doing?" Gandle asked.

"Just watch," Bosch said.

At the counter the customer said something to Li and the store owner reached up to the overhead storage rack and pulled down a carton of Camel cigarettes. He put them on the counter and then put the can of beer into a small brown bag.

The customer had an imposing build. Though short and squat, he had thick arms and heavy shoulders. He dropped a single bill on the counter and Li took it and opened the cash register. He put the bill in the last slot of the drawer and then counted several bills out as change and handed the money across the counter. The customer took his money and pocketed it. He put the carton of cigarettes under one arm, grabbed the beer and with his remaining free hand pointed a finger like a gun at Li. He pumped his thumb as if shooting the gun and then left the store.

Bosch stopped the playback.

"What was that?" Gandle asked. "Was that a threat with the finger? Is that what you've got?"

Ferras didn't say anything but Bosch was pretty sure his young partner had seen what Harry wanted them to see. He backed the video up and started to replay it.

"What do you see, Ignacio?"

Ferras stepped forward so he could point to the screen.

"First of all, the guy's Asian. So he's not from the neighborhood."

Bosch nodded.

"I watched twenty-two hours of video," he said. "This was the only Asian who came into the store besides Li and his wife. What else, Ignacio?"

"Watch the money," Ferras said. "He gets back more than he gives."

On the screen Li was taking bills out of the cash register.

"Look, he puts the guy's money in the drawer and then he starts giving him money back, including what the guy gave him in the first place. So he gets the beer and smokes for free and then all the money."

Bosch nodded. Ferras was good.

"How much does he get?" Gandle asked.

It was a good question because the video image was too grainy to make out the denominations on the currency being exchanged.

"There are four slots in the drawer," Bosch said. "So you've got ones, fives, tens and twenties. I slowed this down last night. He puts the customer's bill in the fourth slot. A carton of smokes and a beer, we assume that is the slot for twenties. If that is the case, he gives him a one, a five, a ten and then eleven twenties. Ten twenties if you don't count the one the customer put in first."

"It's a payoff," Ferras said.

"Two hundred thirty-six dollars?" Gandle asked. "Seems like an odd payoff and you can see there's still money in the drawer. So it was like a set amount."

"Actually," Ferras said, "two *sixteen* if you subtract the twenty the customer gives in the first place."

"Right," Bosch said.

The three of them stared at the frozen screen for a few moments without speaking.

"So, Harry," Gandle finally said. "You got to sleep on this for a couple hours. What's it mean?"

Bosch pointed to the time stamp on the top of the screen.

"This payoff was made exactly one week before the murder. Three o'clock on Tuesday a week ago. This Tuesday at about three Mr. Li gets shot. Maybe this week he decided not to pay."

"Or he didn't have the money to pay," Ferras offered. "The son told us yesterday that business has been way down and opening the store in the Valley has nearly bankrupted them."

"So the old man says no and gets popped," Gandle said. "Isn't that a bit extreme? You kill the guy and as they say in high finance, you've lost your funding stream."

Ferras shrugged.

"There's always the wife and the son," he said. "They'd get the message."

"They're coming in at ten to sign statements," Bosch added.

Gandle nodded.

"So how are you going to handle this?" he asked.

"We'll put Mrs. Li with Chu, the guy from AGU, and Ignacio and I will talk to the son. We find out what it's about."

Gandle's usually dour expression brightened. He was pleased with the progress of the case and the lead that had surfaced.

"Okay, gentlemen, I want to know," he said.

"When we know," Bosch said.

Gandle left the meeting room, and Bosch and Ferras were left standing in front of the screen.

"Nice going, Harry. You made him happy."

"He'll be happier if we clear this thing."

"What do you think?"

"I think we have some work to do before the Li family gets here. You check with the lab and see what they've got done. See if they're finished with the cash register. Bring it over here if you can."

"What about you?"

Bosch turned the screen off and ejected the disc.

"I'm going to go have a talk with Detective Chu."

"You think he held something back on us?"

"That's what I'm going to find out."

6

The AGU was part of the Gang and Operations Support Division, from which many undercover investigations and officers were directed. As such the GOSD was located in an unmarked building several blocks away from the PAB. Bosch decided to walk because he knew it would take longer to get his car out of the garage, fight the traffic and then have to find another place to park. He got to the front door of the AGU office at eight-thirty, pressed the buzzer but nobody answered. He pulled his phone, ready to try to call Detective Chu, when a familiar voice came from behind him.

"Good morning, Detective Bosch. I wasn't expecting to see you here."

Bosch turned. It was Chu, arriving with his briefcase.

"Nice hours you guys get to keep over here," Bosch replied.

"Yeah, we like to keep it light."

Bosch stepped back so Chu could open the door with a card key.

"Come on in."

Chu led the way to a small squad room with about a dozen desks and a lieutenant's office on the right. Chu went behind one of the desks and put his briefcase down on the floor.

"What can I do for you?" he asked. "I was already planning to come by RHD at ten when Mrs. Li comes in."

Chu started to sit down but Bosch stayed standing.

"I got something I want to show you. Do you guys have an AV room here?"

"Yeah, this way."

The AGU had four interview rooms at the back of the squad room. One had been converted to an AV room with the standard rolling tower of television stacked on top of DVD. But Bosch saw that the stack also had an image printer and that was something they didn't have yet in the new RHD squad room.

Bosch handed Chu the DVD from Fortune Liquors and he set it up. Bosch took the remote and fast-forwarded the playback to 3 P.M. on the time stamp.

"I wanted you to take a look at this guy who comes in," he said.

Chu watched silently as the Asian man entered the store, bought a beer and a carton of cigarettes and got the big return on his investment.

"Is that it?" he asked after the customer left the store.

"That's it."

"Can we play it again?"

"Sure."

Bosch replayed the two-minute episode, then froze the playback as the customer turned from the counter to leave. He then played with it, making slight advances on

the playback, until he froze it on the best possible view of
the man's face as he turned from the counter.

"Know him?" Bosch asked.

"No, of course not."

"What did you see there?"

"Obviously, a payoff of some kind. He got much more
back than he gave."

"Yeah, two hundred sixteen on top of his own twenty.
We counted it."

Bosch saw Chu's eyebrows rise.

"What's it mean?" Bosch asked.

"Well, it probably means he's triad," Chu said matter-
of-factly.

Bosch nodded. He had never investigated a triad murder before but he was aware that the so-called secret societies of China had long ago jumped the Pacific and now
operated in most major American cities. Los Angeles,
with its large Chinese population, was one of the strong-
holds, along with San Francisco, New York and Houston.

"What makes you say he's a triad guy?"

"You said the payoff was two hundred sixteen dollars,
correct?"

"That's right. Li gave the guy his own money back. He
also gave him ten twenties, a ten, a five and a one. What's
it mean?"

"The triad extortion business relies on weekly payments from small shop owners seeking protection. The
payment is usually one hundred eight dollars. Of course,
two sixteen is a multiple of that. A double payment."

"Why one oh eight? They charge tax on top of the

tax? They send the extra eight bucks to the state or something?"

Chu did not register the sarcasm in Bosch's voice and answered as if lecturing a child.

"No, Detective, the number has nothing to do with that at all. Let me give you a brief history lesson that hopefully will give you some understanding."

"By all means," Bosch said.

"The creation of the triads goes back to the seventeenth century in China. There were one hundred thirteen monks in the Shaolin monastery. Buddhist monks. Manchu invaders attacked and killed all but five of the monks. Those remaining five monks created the secret societies with the goal of overthrowing the invaders. The triads were born. But over the centuries, they changed. They dropped politics and patriotism and became criminal organizations. Much like the Italian and Russian mafias, they engage in extortion and protection rackets. To honor the ghosts of the slaughtered monks, the extortion amounts are usually a multiple of one hundred eight."

"There were five remaining monks, not three," Bosch said. "Why are they called triads?"

"Because each monk started his own triad. *Tian di hui*. It means 'heaven and earth society.' Each group had a flag in the shape of a triangle symbolizing the relationship between heaven, earth and man. From that they became known as the triads."

"Great, and they brought it over here."

"It's been here a very long time. But they didn't bring it over. Americans brought it over. It came with Chinese labor brought to build railroads."

"And they victimize their own people."

"For the most part, yes. But Mr. Li was religious. Did you see the Buddhist shrine in the storage room yesterday?"

"I missed that."

"It was there and I talked to his wife about it. Mr. Li was very spiritual. He believed in ghosts. To him, paying the triad might have been like making an offering to a ghost. To an ancestor. You see, you are an outsider looking in, Detective Bosch. If all you knew from day one was that part of your money went to the triad just as simply as money goes to the IRS, then you would not view yourself as a victim. It was simply a given, a part of life."

"But the IRS doesn't put three slugs in your chest when you don't pay."

"Do you believe that Li was murdered by this man or the triad?"

Pointing at the man on the screen, Chu was almost indignant in asking the question.

"I believe it is the best lead we have at the moment," Bosch countered.

"What about the lead we developed through Mrs. Li? The gangbanger who threatened her husband on Saturday."

Bosch shook his head.

"Things don't match up there. I still want her to look at the books and ID the kid but I think we are spinning our wheels there."

"I don't understand. He said he would come back and kill Mr. Li."

"No, he said he would come back and blow his head

off. Mr. Li was shot in the chest. It wasn't a crime of rage, Detective Chu. It doesn't fit. But don't worry, we'll run it down, even if it's a waste of time."

He waited for Chu to respond but the younger detective didn't. Bosch pointed to the time stamp on the screen.

"Li was killed at the same time on the same day of the week. We have to assume that Li made regular payoffs. We have to assume that this man was there when Li was killed. I think that makes him the better suspect."

The interview room was very small and they had left the door open. Bosch now stepped over and closed it, then looked back at Chu.

"So tell me you didn't have any idea about this yesterday."

"No, of course not."

"Mrs. Li didn't say anything about making payments to the local triad?"

Chu stiffened. He was much smaller than Bosch but his posture suggested he was ready for a fight.

"Bosch, what are you suggesting?"

"I'm suggesting that this is your world and you should have told me. I found this by accident. Li kept that disc because there's a shoplifter on it. Not because of the payoff."

They were now facing each other less than two feet apart.

"Well, there was nothing before me yesterday that even suggested this," Chu said. "I was called out there to translate. You didn't ask me my opinion about anything else. You deliberately shut me out, Bosch. Maybe if you had included me, I would have seen or heard something."

"That's bullshit. You're not trained as a detective to

stand there with your thumb in your mouth. You don't need an invite to ask a question."

"With you I thought I did."

"And what's that supposed to mean?"

"It means I watched you, Bosch. How you treated Mrs. Li, her son . . . me."

"Oh, here we go."

"What was it, Vietnam? You served in Vietnam, right?"

"Don't pretend you know anything about me, Chu."

"I know what I see and I've seen it before. I'm not from Vietnam, Detective. I'm an American. Born right here, like you."

"Look, can we just drop this so we can get on with the case?"

"Whatever you say. You're the lead."

Chu put his hands on his hips and turned back to the screen. Bosch tried to back his emotions down. He had to admit Chu had a point. And he was embarrassed that he had been so easily pegged as someone who had come back from Vietnam with a racial prejudice.

"All right," he said. "Maybe the way I dealt with you yesterday was a mistake. I'm sorry. But you're in now and I need to know what you know. No holding back."

Chu relaxed too.

"I just told you everything. The only other thing I was thinking was about the two hundred sixteen."

"What about it?"

"It's a double payment. Like maybe Mr. Li missed a week. Maybe he was having trouble paying. His son said business was bad there."

"And so maybe that's what got him killed."

Bosch pointed to the screen again.

"Can you make me a hard copy?"

"I would like one myself."

Chu moved to the printer and pushed a button twice. Soon two copies of the image of the man turning from the counter were printing.

"Do you have mug books?" Bosch asked. "Intelligence files?"

"Of course," Chu said. "I will try to identify him. I will make inquiries."

"I don't want him to know we're coming."

"Thank you, Detective. But, yes, I assumed that."

Bosch didn't respond. It had been another misstep. He was having a hard time with Chu. He found himself unable to trust him, even though he carried the same badge.

"I would also like to get a print of the tattoo as well," Chu said.

"What tattoo?" Bosch asked.

Chu took the remote from Bosch and tapped the rewind button. He eventually froze the picture at the moment the man was reaching his left hand out to take the cash from Mr. Li. Chu used his finger to trace a barely visible outline on the inside of the man's arm. Chu was right. It was a tattoo, but the marking was so light on the grainy image that Bosch had completely missed it.

"What is that?" he asked.

"It looks like the outline of a knife. A self-administered tattoo."

"He's been in prison."

Chu pushed the button to make prints of the image.

"No, usually these are done on the boat. On the way across the ocean."

"What does it mean to you?"

"Knife is *kim*. There are at least three triads that have a presence here in Southern California. *Yee Kim, Sai Kim* and *Yung Kim*. These mean Righteous Knife, Western Knife and Brave Knife. They are offshoots of a Hong Kong triad called Fourteen K. Very strong and powerful."

"Over here or there?"

"Both places."

"Fourteen K? Like fourteen-karat gold?"

"No, fourteen is a bad-luck number. It sounds like the Chinese word for death. *K* is for kill."

Bosch knew from his daughter and his frequent visits to Hong Kong that any permutation of the number 4 was considered bad luck. His daughter lived with his ex-wife in a condominium tower where there were no floors marked with the numeral 4. The fourth floor was marked *P* for parking and the fourteenth was skipped in the way the thirteenth floor was skipped in most western buildings. The floors in the building that were actually the fourteenth and twenty-fourth contained the residences of English speakers who did not hold the same superstitions as the Han — the Chinese people.

Bosch gestured to the screen.

"So you think this guy could be in one of the Fourteen K spin-offs?" he asked.

"Perhaps yes," Chu said. "I will begin to make inquiries just as soon as you leave."

Bosch looked at Chu and tried to read him again. He

believed he understood the message. Chu wanted Bosch out of there so he could go to work. Harry stepped over to the DVD player, ejected the disc, and took it.

"Stay in touch, Chu," he said.

"I will," Chu responded curtly.

"As soon as you get something, you give it to me."

"I understand, Detective. Perfectly."

"Good, and I'll see you at ten with Mrs. Li and her son."

Bosch opened the door and left the tiny room.

7

Ferras had the cash register from Fortune Liquors on his desk and had run a wire from its side into the side of his laptop. Bosch put the photo printouts down on his desk and looked across at his partner.

"What's happening?"

"I went over to forensics. They were through with this. No prints other than the victim's. I'm just getting into the memory now. I can tell you the take for the day up until the murder was under two hundred bucks. The victim would have had a hard time making a payment of two hundred sixteen dollars, if that's what you think happened."

"Well, I've got some stuff on that to tell you. Anything else from forensics?"

"Not much. They're still processing every—oh, the GSR on the widow came back negative. But I guess we were expecting that."

Bosch nodded. Since Mrs. Li had discovered her husband's body, it was routine to test her hands and arms for gunshot residue to determine if she had recently discharged a firearm. As expected, the test came back negative for GSR. Bosch was pretty sure she could now be scratched from the list of potential suspects, even though she was barely on it in the first place.

"How deep is the memory on that thing?" Bosch asked.

"It looks like it goes back a whole year. I ran some averages. The gross income on that place was slightly less than three thousand a week. You figure in overhead and cost of goods, insurance and stuff like that, and this guy was lucky if he was clearing fifty a year for himself. That ain't no way to make a living. Probably more dangerous down there doing what he did than being a cop on those streets."

"Yesterday the son said business was down lately."

"Looking at this, I don't see where it was ever up."

"It's a cash business. He could have pulled money out of it in other ways."

"Probably. And then there was the guy he was paying off. If he was handing him two bills and change a week, that would add up. That would be ten grand off the top on an annual basis."

Bosch told Ferras what he had learned from Chu and that he was hoping the AGU could come up with an ID. They both agreed that the focal point of the investigation was shifting toward the man in the grainy printout from the store's surveillance camera. The triad bagman. Meanwhile, the possible gangbanger who had argued with John Li the Saturday before his murder still needed to be identified and interviewed, but the contradictions between the crime scene and an anger/revenge-type killing put that lead into second position.

They went to work on the statements and other

voluminous paperwork that accompanied every murder investigation. Chu arrived first at ten o'clock, making his way right to Bosch's desk unannounced.

"Yee-ling isn't here yet?" he asked by way of greeting.

Bosch looked up from his work.

"Who's Yee-ling?"

"Yee-ling Li, the mother."

Bosch realized he had not known the full name of the victim's wife. This bothered him because it was an indication of how little he really knew about the case.

"She's not here yet. You come up with anything over there?"

"I checked through our photo albums. Didn't see our guy. But we're making inquiries."

"Yeah, you keep saying that. What exactly does 'making inquiries' mean?"

"It means that the AGU has a network of connections within the community and we will make discreet inquiries about who this man is and what Mr. Li's affiliation was."

"Affiliation?" Ferras asked. "He was being extorted. His affiliation was that he was a victim."

"Detective Ferras," Chu said patiently. "You are looking at it from the typical western point of view. As I explained to Detective Bosch this morning, Mr. Li may have had a lifelong relationship with a triad society. It is called *quang xi,* in his native dialect. It has no direct translation but it has to do with one's social network, and a triad relationship would be included in that."

Ferras just stared at Chu for a long moment.

"Whatever," he finally said. "Over here I think we call

that bullshit. The vic had lived here almost thirty years. I don't care what they call it in China. Over here it's extortion."

Bosch admired his young partner's adamant reaction. He was contemplating joining the fray, when the phone on his desk rang and he picked it up.

"Bosch."

"This is Rogers downstairs. You've got two visitors, both named Li. They say they have an appointment."

"Send them up."

"On the way."

Bosch hung up.

"Okay, they're on their way up. This is how I want to play this. Chu, you take the old lady into one of the interview rooms and go over her statement and have her sign it. After she signs it I want you to ask her about the payoff and the guy on the video. Show her his photo. And don't let her play dumb. She's got to know about it. Her husband had to have talked about it."

"You'd be surprised," Chu said. "Husbands and wives wouldn't necessarily talk about this."

"Well, do your best. She could know a lot whether she and her husband talked about it or not. Ferras and I will talk to the son. I want to find out if he's paying protection at the store up in the Valley. If so, that could be where we grab our guy."

Bosch looked across the squad room and saw Mrs. Li enter but she was not with her son. She was with a younger woman. Bosch raised his hand to draw their attention and waved them over.

"Chu, who is this?"

Chu turned around as the two women approached. He didn't say anything. He didn't know. As the two women got closer Bosch saw that the younger woman was in her midthirties and attractive in an understated, hair-behind-the-ears sort of way. She was Asian. She was dressed in blue jeans and a white blouse. She walked a half step behind Mrs. Li with her eyes cast down on the floor. The initial impression Bosch got was that she was an employee. A maid pressed into service as a driver. But the deskman downstairs had said they were both named Li.

Chu spoke to Mrs. Li in Chinese. After she responded, he translated.

"This is Mr. and Mrs. Li's daughter, Mia. She drove her mother here because Robert Li is delayed."

Bosch was immediately frustrated by the news and shook his head.

"Great," he said to Chu. "How come we didn't know there was a daughter?"

"We didn't ask the right questions yesterday," Chu said.

"You were the one asking questions yesterday. Ask Mia where she lives."

The young woman cleared her throat and looked up at Bosch.

"I live with my mother and father," she said. "Or I did until yesterday. I guess now I live with just my mother."

Bosch felt embarrassed that he had assumed she spoke no English and she had heard and understood his annoyed response to her showing up.

"Sorry. It's just that we need all the information we can get."

He looked at the other two detectives.

"Okay, we are going to need to interview Mia. Detective Chu, why don't you continue with the plan and take Mrs. Li into an interview room to go over her statement. I will talk with Mia and, Ignacio, you wait for Robert to show up."

He turned back to Mia.

"Do you know how long your brother is delayed?"

"He should be on his way. He said he was going to leave the store by ten."

"Which store?"

"His store. In the Valley."

"Okay, Mia, why don't you come with me, and your mother can go with Detective Chu."

Mia spoke in Chinese to her mother and they proceeded toward the bank of interview rooms at the back of the squad. Bosch grabbed a yellow legal pad and the file containing the print off the camera video before leading the way. Ferras was left behind.

"Harry, you want me to start with the son when he gets here?" he asked.

"No," Bosch said. "Come and get me. I'll be in room two."

Bosch led the victim's daughter to a small, windowless room with a table in the middle. They sat down on either side of it and Bosch tried to put a pleasant expression on his face. It was hard. The morning was starting off with a surprise and he didn't like surprises coming up in his murder investigations.

"Okay, Mia," Bosch said. "Let's start over. I am Detective Bosch. I am assigned as lead investigator on the case involving the murder of your father. I am very sorry for your loss."

"Thank you."

She had her eyes cast down to the tabletop.

"Can you tell me your full name?"

"Mia-ling Li."

Her name had been westernized with her given name first and the family name last. But she had not taken a wholly western name like her father and brother. Bosch wondered if this was because the men were expected to integrate into western society while the women were held back from it.

"When is your birthday?"

"February fourteenth, nineteen eighty."

"Valentine's Day."

Bosch smiled. He didn't know why. He was just trying to start the relationship over. Then he wondered if they even had Valentine's Day in China. He moved on with his thoughts and did the math. He realized that while she was still very attractive, Mia was younger than she looked, and only a few years older than her brother, Robert.

"You came here with your parents? When was that?"

"In nineteen eighty-two."

"You were only two."

"Yes."

"And your father opened the store then?"

"He didn't open it. He bought it from someone else and he renamed it Fortune Liquors. Before, it was called something else."

"Okay. Are there any other brothers or sisters besides you and Robert?"

"No, just us."

"Okay, good. Now, you said you have been living with your parents. For how long?"

She looked up briefly and then back down.

"My whole life. Except for about two years when I was younger."

"Were you married?"

"No. What does this have to do with who killed my father? Shouldn't you be finding the killer?"

"I'm sorry, Mia. I just need to get some basic information and then, yes, I will be out there looking for the killer. Have you talked to your brother? Did he tell you I knew your father?"

"He said you met him one time. You didn't even really meet him. That's not knowing him."

Bosch nodded.

"You're right. That was an exaggeration. I didn't know him but because of the situation we were in when I . . . met him, I feel like I sort of knew him. I want to find his killer, Mia. And I will. I just need you and your family to help me wherever you can."

"I understand."

"Don't hold anything back, because you never know what might help us."

"I won't."

"Okay, what do you do for a living?"

"I take care of my parents."

"You mean at home? You stay home and take care of your parents?"

Now she looked up and right into his eyes. Her pupils were so dark it was hard to read anything in them.

"Yes."

Bosch realized he might have crossed into a cultural custom and standard he knew nothing about. Mia seemed to read him.

"It is tradition in my family for the daughter to care for her parents."

"Did you go to school?"

"Yes, I went to university for two years. But then I came home. I cook and clean and keep the house. For my brother, too, though he wants to move to his own place."

"But as of yesterday, everybody was living together."

"Yes."

"When was the last time you saw your father alive?"

"When he left for work yesterday morning. He leaves about nine-thirty. I made him his breakfast."

"And your mother left then, too?"

"Yes, they always go together."

"And then your mother came back in the afternoon?"

"Yes, I make the supper and she comes for it. Every day."

"What time did she come home?"

"She came home at three o'clock. She always does."

Bosch knew that the family home was in the Larchmont area of the Wilshire District and at least a half-hour drive from the store. The direct route would have been on surface streets the whole way.

"How long before she took the supper and went back to the store yesterday?"

"She stayed about a half hour and then she left."

Bosch nodded. Everything was jibing with the mother's story and the timing and everything else they knew.

"Mia, did your father talk about anybody at work he was afraid of? Like a customer or anybody else?"

"No, my father was very quiet. He didn't talk about work at home."

"Did he like living here in Los Angeles?"

"No, I don't think so."

"Why?"

"He wanted to go home to China but he couldn't."

"Why not?"

"Because when you leave you do not come back. They left because Robert was coming."

"You mean your family left because of Robert?"

"In our province you could only have one child. They already had me and my mother would not put me in the orphanage. My father wanted a son and when my mother became pregnant, we came to America."

Bosch did not know the specifics of China's one-child policies but he was aware of them. It was a population containment plan that resulted in a higher value being placed on male births. Newborn females were often abandoned in orphanages or worse. Rather than giving up Mia, the Li family had left the country for the USA.

"So your father wished all along he could have stayed and kept his family in China?"

"Yes."

Bosch decided that he had gathered enough information in this regard. He opened the file and removed the printout of the image from the store camera. He placed it in front of Mia.

"Who is that, Mia?"

Her eyes narrowed as she studied the grainy image.

"I don't know him. Did he kill my father?"

"I don't know. You sure you don't know who he is?"

"I'm sure. Who is he?"

"We don't know yet. But we'll find out. Did your father ever talk about the triads?"

"The triads?"

"About having to pay them?"

She seemed very nervous about the question.

"I don't know about this. We didn't talk about it."

"You speak Chinese, right?"

"Yes."

"Did you ever hear your parents talking about it?"

"No, they didn't. I don't know about this."

"Okay, Mia, then I think we can stop now."

"Can I take my mother home?"

"As soon as she's finished talking to Detective Chu. What do you think will happen with the store now? Will your mother and brother run it?"

She shook her head.

"I think it will be closed. My mother will work in my brother's store now."

"What about you, Mia? Will anything change for you now?"

She took a long moment to consider this, as if she had not thought about it before Bosch had asked.

"I don't know," she finally said. "Perhaps."

8

Back in the squad room, Mrs. Li had already finished her interview with Chu and was waiting for her daughter. There was still no sign of Robert Li, and Ferras explained that he called and said he could not get away from his store because his assistant manager had called in sick.

After escorting the two women out to the elevator alcove, Bosch checked his watch and decided there was still time to get out to the Valley and speak to the victim's son and then get back downtown for the scheduled 2 P.M. autopsy. Besides, he didn't need to be at the medical examiner's office for the preliminary procedures. He could roll in late.

It was decided that Ferras would stay behind to work with forensics on the return of evidence gathered the day before. Bosch and Chu would go out to the Valley to talk to Robert Li.

Bosch drove his Crown Vic with 220,000 miles on the odometer. The air conditioner worked but just barely. As they got closer to the Valley the temperature started rising and Bosch wished he had taken his suit jacket off before getting in the car.

Along the way, Chu spoke first and reported that Mrs. Li signed her statement and had nothing new to add to it. She had not recognized the man from the store video and claimed to know nothing about paying off the triad. Bosch then relayed what little information he had gleaned from Mia-ling Li and asked Chu what he knew of the tradition of keeping an adult daughter home to care for her parents.

"She's a *chin*derella," Chu said. "Stays home and does the cooking and cleaning, stuff like that. Almost like a servant to her parents."

"They don't want them to get married and leave the house?"

"No, man, it's free labor. Why would they want her to get married? Then they'd have to hire a maid and a chef and a driver. This way they get them all and don't have to pay."

Bosch drove silently for a while after that, thinking about the life Mia-ling Li lived. He doubted anything would change with the death of her father. There was still her mother to care for.

He remembered something relating to the case and spoke again.

"She said the family would probably close the store now and just keep the one in the Valley."

"It wasn't making any money, anyway," Chu said. "They might be able to sell it to somebody in the community and make a little bit."

"Not much for almost thirty years there."

"The Chinese immigrant story is not always a happy one," Chu said.

"What about you, Chu? You're a success."

"I'm not an immigrant. My parents were."

"Were?"

"My mother died young. My father was a fisherman. One time his boat went out and it never came back."

Bosch was silenced by the matter-of-fact way Chu had told his family tragedy. He concentrated on the drive. Traffic was rough and it took them forty-five minutes to get to Sherman Oaks. Fortune Fine Foods & Liquor was on Sepulveda just a block south of Ventura Boulevard. This put it in an upscale neighborhood of apartments and condominiums below the even more upscale hillside residences. It was in a good location but there didn't seem to be enough parking. Bosch found a spot on the street in front of a fire hydrant. He flipped down the visor, which had a card clipped to it showing a city vehicle identification code, and got out.

Bosch and Chu had worked out a plan during the long ride up. They believed that if anyone knew about the triad payoffs besides the victim, it would be the son and fellow shop manager, Robert. Why he would not have told the detectives about this the day before was the big question.

Fortune Fine Foods & Liquor was something completely different from its counterpart in South L.A. This store was at least five times bigger and it was brimming with the high-end touches that befit its neighborhood.

There was a do-it-yourself coffee bar. The wine aisles had overhead signs displaying varietals and world regions of wine, and there were no gallon jugs stacked at the end.

The cold cases were well lighted with open shelves instead of glass doors. There were aisles of specialty foods and hot and cold counters where customers could order fresh steaks and fish or precooked meals of roast chicken, meatloaf and barbecued ribs. The son had taken his father's business and advanced it several levels. Bosch was impressed.

There were two checkout stations and Chu asked one of the women behind them where Robert Li was. The detectives were directed to a set of double doors that led to a stockroom with ten-foot-high shelves against all the walls. To the far left was a door marked OFFICE. Bosch knocked and Robert Li promptly answered the door.

He looked surprised to see them.

"Detectives, come in," he said. "I am so sorry about not getting downtown today. My assistant manager called in sick and I can't leave the place without a supervisor. I'm sorry."

"It's okay," Bosch said. "We're only trying to find your father's killer."

Bosch wanted to put the kid on the defensive. Interviewing him in his own surroundings put him at an advantage. Bosch wanted to bring some discomfort to the situation. If Li was on the defensive he'd be more forthcoming and willing to try to please his interviewers.

"Well, I am sorry. I thought all I needed to do was sign my statement, anyway."

"We have your statement but it's a little more involved than signing papers, Mr. Li. It's an ongoing investigation. Things change. More information comes in."

"All I can do is apologize. Have a seat, please. I'm sorry the space is so tight in here."

The office was narrow and Bosch could tell it was a shared office. There were two desks side by side against the right wall. Two desk chairs and two folding chairs, probably for sales representatives and job interviews.

Li picked up the phone on his desk, dialed a number and told someone he was not to be disturbed. He then made an open-hands gesture, signaling he was ready to go.

"First of all, I'm a little surprised that you are working today," Bosch said. "Your father was murdered yesterday."

Li nodded solemnly.

"I am afraid that I have been given no time to grieve for my father. I must run the business or there will be no business to run."

Bosch nodded and signaled to Chu to take over. He had typed up Li's statement. As he went over it with Li, Bosch looked around the office. On the wall over the desks were framed licenses from the state, Li's 2004 diploma from the business school at the University of Southern California and an honorable-mention certificate for best new store of 2007 from the American Grocers Association. There were also framed photos of Li with Tommy Lasorda, the former manager of the Dodgers, and a teenage Li standing at the steps of the Tian Tan Buddha in Hong Kong. Just as he had recognized Lasorda, Bosch recognized the one-hundred-foot-high bronze sculpture known as the Big Buddha. He had once journeyed with his daughter to Lantau Island to see it.

Bosch reached across and straightened the cockeyed frame of the USC diploma. In doing so he noticed that Li had graduated from the school with honors. He thought for a moment about Robert going off to the university and getting the opportunity to take his father's business and turn it into something bigger and better. Meantime, his older sister dropped out of school, came home and made the beds.

Li asked for no changes to his statement and signed the bottom of each page. When he was finished he looked up at a wall clock hung over the door and Bosch could tell he thought they were done.

But they weren't. Now it was Bosch's turn. He opened his briefcase and removed a file. From it he took the photo print of the bagman who had collected money from Li's father. Bosch handed it to Li.

"Tell me about this guy," he said.

Li held the printout in both hands and knitted his eyebrows as he looked at it. Bosch knew that people did this to show they were earnestly concentrating, but it usually was a cover for something else. Bosch knew that he had probably taken a call in the last hour from his mother and had known that he might be shown the printout. However Li responded, Bosch knew he would not be truthful.

"I can't tell you anything," Li said after a few seconds. "I don't recognize him. I've never seen him."

He handed the printout back to Bosch but Harry didn't take it.

"But you know who he is, don't you."

It wasn't really said as a question.

"No, actually, I don't," Li said, mild annoyance in his voice.

Bosch smiled at him but it was one of those that carried no warmth or humor.

"Mr. Li, did your mother call you and tell you we would be showing you that picture?"

"No."

"We can check the phones, you know."

"So what if she did? She didn't know who it was and neither do I."

"You want us to find the person who killed your father, right?"

"Of course! What kind of question is that?"

"It's the kind of question I ask when I know somebody is holding something back from me and that it—"

"What? How dare you!"

"—could be very useful to my investigation."

"I am holding nothing back! I don't know this man. I don't know his name and I have never seen him before! That is the goddamn truth!"

Li's face grew flushed. Bosch waited a moment and then spoke calmly.

"You might be telling the truth. You might not know his name and maybe you've never seen him before. But you know who he is, Robert. You know your father was making payoffs. Maybe you are, too. If you think there is any danger involved in talking to us, then we can protect you."

"Absolutely," Chu chimed in.

Li shook his head and smiled like he couldn't believe the situation he had found himself in. He started breathing heavily.

"My father just died—he was killed. Can't you leave me alone? Why am I being badgered? I'm a victim here, too."

"I wish we could leave you alone, Robert," Bosch said.

"But if we don't find the party responsible, there's nobody else who will. You don't want that, do you?"

Li seemed to compose himself and shook his head.

"Look," Bosch continued. "We have a signed statement here. Nothing you tell us now has to go beyond this room. No one will ever know what you tell us."

Bosch reached over and ticked the printout with his finger. Li was still holding it.

"Whoever killed your father took the disc out of the recorder in the back but left the old discs. This guy was on it. He took a payment from your father at the same time and on the same day a week before the murder. Your father gave him two hundred sixteen dollars as a payoff. The guy is triad and I think you know it. You have to help us out here, Robert. There's nobody else who can."

Bosch waited. Li put the printout on the desk and rubbed his sweating palms down the thighs of his blue jeans.

"Okay, yes, my father paid the triad," he said.

Bosch breathed slowly. They had just made a big step. He wanted to keep Li talking.

"For how long?" he asked.

"I don't know, all his life — all my life, I guess. It was just something he always did. To him, it was part of being Chinese. You paid."

Bosch nodded.

"Thank you, Robert, for telling us this. Now, yesterday you told us that with the economy and everything, things were not going so well at the store. Do you know, was your father behind on his payments?"

"I don't know, maybe. He didn't tell me. We didn't see eye to eye on that."

"What do you mean?"

"I didn't think he should pay. I told him a million times. This is America, Pop, you don't have to pay them."

"But he still paid."

"Yeah, every week. He was just old school."

"So you don't pay here?"

Li shook his head but his eyes darted to the side a moment. An easy giveaway.

"You do pay, don't you?"

"No."

"Robert, we need the—"

"I don't pay, because he paid for me. Now I don't know what will happen."

Bosch leaned closer to him.

"You mean your father paid for both stores."

"Yes."

Li's eyes were cast down. He rubbed his palms on his pants again.

"The double payment—one oh eight times two—was to cover both stores."

"That's right. Last week."

Li nodded and Bosch thought he saw tears welling in his eyes. Harry knew the next question was the most important one.

"What happened this week?"

"I don't know."

"But you have an idea, right, Robert?"

He nodded again.

"Both stores are losing money. We expanded at the wrong time—right before the downturn. The banks get the government bailout but not us. We could lose everything. I told him...I told my father we couldn't keep paying. I told him we were paying for nothing and we were going to lose the stores if we didn't stop."

"Did he say he would stop making the payments?"

"He didn't say that. He didn't say anything. I thought that meant he was going to keep on paying until we were out of business. It was adding up. Eight hundred dollars a month is a lot in a business like this. My old man, he thought if he found other ways..."

His voice trailed off.

"Other ways of what, Robert?"

"Other ways of saving money. He became obsessed with catching shoplifters. He thought if he stopped the losses he'd make a difference. He was from a different time. He didn't get it."

Bosch leaned back in his chair and looked over at Chu. They had broken through and gotten Li to open up. It would now be Chu's turn to move in with specific questions relating to the triad.

"Robert, you have been very helpful," Chu said. "I want to ask you a few questions in regard to the man in the photo."

"I was telling the truth. I don't know who he is. I never saw him before in my life."

"Okay, but did your father ever talk about him when, you know, you were discussing the payments?"

"He never used his name. He just said he would be upset if we stopped the payments."

"Did he ever mention the name of the group he paid? The triad?"

Li shook his head.

"No, he never—wait, yes, he did once. It was something about a knife. Like the name came from a kind of knife or something. But I don't remember it."

"Are you sure? That could help us narrow it."

Li frowned and shook his head again.

"I'll try to remember it. I can't right now."

"Okay, Robert."

Chu continued the interview but his questions were too specific and Li continually answered that he didn't know. All that was okay with Bosch. They had made a big breakthrough. He saw the case coming together with a stronger focus now.

After a while Chu finished up and passed the baton back to Bosch.

"Okay, Robert," Harry said. "Do you think the man or men your father was paying will now come to you for the money?"

The question prompted a deep frown from Li.

"I don't know," he said.

"Do you want protection by the LAPD?"

"I don't know that either."

"Well, you have our numbers. If someone shows up, cooperate. Promise him the money if you have to."

"I don't have the money!"

"That's the point. Promise him the money but say it will take you a day to get it. Then call us. We'll take it from there."

"What if he just takes it out of the cash registers? You told me yesterday that the cash drawer was empty in my father's store."

"If he does that, let him and then you call us. We'll get him when he comes back the next time."

Li nodded and Bosch could see he had thoroughly spooked the young man.

"Robert, do you have a gun in the store?"

It was a test. They had already checked gun records. Only the gun in the other store was registered.

"No, my father had the gun. He was in the bad area."

"Good. Don't bring a gun into this. If the guy shows up, just cooperate."

"Okay."

"By the way, why did your father buy that gun? He had been there for almost thirty years and then six months ago he buys the gun."

"The last time he was robbed, they hurt him. Two gangbangers. They hit him with a bottle. I told him if he wouldn't sell the store, then he had to get a gun. But it didn't do him any good."

"They usually don't."

The detectives thanked Li and left him in his office, a twenty-six-year-old who somehow seemed a couple decades older now. As they walked through the store Bosch checked his watch and saw it was now after one. He was starving and wanted to grab something before heading to the medical examiner's office for the autopsy at two. He stopped in front of the hot case and zeroed in on the meatloaf. He pulled a service number out of the dispenser. When he offered to buy Chu a slice, he said he was a vegetarian.

Bosch shook his head.

"What?" Chu asked.

"I don't think we could make it as partners, Chu,"

Bosch said. "I don't trust a guy who doesn't eat a hot dog every once in a while."

"I eat tofu hot dogs."

Bosch cringed.

"They don't count."

He then saw Robert Li approaching them.

"I forgot to ask. When will my father's body be released to us?"

"Probably tomorrow," Bosch said. "The autopsy is today."

Li looked crestfallen.

"My father was a very spiritual man. Do they have to desecrate his body?"

Bosch nodded.

"It's a law. There's an autopsy after any homicide."

"When will they do it?"

"In about an hour."

Li nodded in acceptance.

"Please don't tell my mother this was done. Will they call me when I can have his body?"

"I'll make sure they do."

Li thanked them and headed back to his office. Bosch heard his number called by the man behind the counter.

9

On the way back downtown Chu informed Bosch that after fourteen years on the job he had yet to witness an autopsy and didn't care to change course. He said he wanted to get back to the AGU office to continue efforts to identify the triad bagman. Bosch dropped him off and then headed over to the county coroner's office on Mission Road. By the time he checked in, gowned up and got into suite 3, the autopsy of John Li was well under way. The coroner's office performed six thousand autopsies a year. The autopsy suites were tightly scheduled and managed and the medical examiners didn't wait for late-arriving cops. A good one could knock off a surgical autopsy in an hour.

All of this was fine with Bosch. He was interested in the findings of the autopsy, not the process.

John Li's body was lying naked and violated on the cold stainless-steel autopsy table. The chest had been opened and the vital organs removed. Dr. Sharon Laksmi was working at a nearby table where she was putting tissue samples on slides.

"Afternoon, Doctor," Bosch said.

Laksmi turned from her work and glanced back at him. Because of the mask and hair cap Bosch was wearing, she could not readily identify him. Long gone were the days when the detectives could just walk in and watch. County health regs required the full protection package.

"Bosch or Ferras?"

"Bosch."

"You're late. I started without you."

Laksmi was small and dark. What was most noticeable about her was that her eyes were heavily made-up behind the plastic shield of her mask. It was as if she realized that her eyes were the only feature people saw behind all the safety garb she wore most of the time. She spoke with a slight accent. But who didn't in L.A.? Even the outgoing chief of police sounded like he was from South Boston.

"Yes, sorry. I was with the victim's son and it ran kind of long."

He didn't mention the meatloaf sandwich that had cost him some time as well.

"Here's what you are probably looking for."

She tapped the blade of her scalpel on one of four steel specimen cups lined up to her left on the counter. Bosch stepped over and looked down into them. Each held one piece of evidence extracted from the body. He saw three deformed bullets and a single bullet casing.

"You found a casing? Was it on the body?"

"In it, actually."

"*In* the body?"

"That's right. Lodged in the esophagus."

Bosch thought of what he had discovered while looking

at the crime scene pictures. Blood on the victim's fingers, chin and lips. But not on his teeth. He had been right about his hunch.

"It appears you are looking for a very sadistic killer, Detective Bosch."

"Why do you say that?"

"Because either he shoved a casing down your victim's throat or the ejected casing somehow landed in his mouth. Since the latter would be a million-to-one shot, I would go with the former."

Bosch nodded. Not because he subscribed to what she was saying. But because he was thinking of a scenario Dr. Laksmi hadn't considered. He thought he now had a bead on what had happened behind the counter at Fortune Liquors. One of the ejected casings from the shooter's gun had landed on or near John Li as he lay dying on the floor behind the counter. Either he saw the shooter collecting the casings or knew they might be valuable evidence in the investigation of his own murder. With his last moment Li had grabbed the casing and tried to swallow it, to keep it from the shooter.

John Li's final act was to attempt to provide Bosch with an important clue.

"Did you clean the casing, Doctor?" he asked.

"Yes, blood had backed up into the throat and the casing acted like a dam, keeping most of it out of the mouth. I had to clean it to see what it was."

"Right."

Bosch knew that the possibility of there being fingerprints on the casing were negligible, anyway. The explosion of gases when a bullet was fired almost always vaporized fingerprints on the casing.

Still the casing could be useful in determining a match to a weapon if the recovered slugs were too damaged. Bosch looked down into the evidence cups containing the slugs. He immediately determined they had been hollow points. They had mushroomed upon impact and were badly deformed. He could not tell if any of them would be useful for comparison purposes. But the casing was most likely a good solid piece of evidence. The marks made by the weapon's extractor, firing pin and ejector could be useful in identifying and matching the gun if it was ever found. The casing would link the victim to the gun.

"You want to hear my summary and then be on your way?" Laksmi asked.

"Sure, Doctor, run it down."

While Laksmi gave a preliminary report on her findings, Bosch grabbed clear plastic evidence envelopes off a shelf over the table and bagged the slugs and casing separately. The casing looked like it had come from a 9 millimeter round but he would wait for confirmation from ballistics on that. He marked each envelope with his name as well as Laksmi's and the case number and then lifted his splatter gown and put them in his coat pocket.

"The first shot was to the upper left chest, the projectile piercing the right ventricle of the heart and impacting the upper vertebrae, severing the spinal cord. The victim would have immediately dropped to the floor. The next two shots were to the right and left lower sternum. It is impossible to place an order on these two shots. Right and left lobes of the lungs were pierced and the projectiles lodged in the back musculature. The result of the three shots was instant loss of cardiopulmonary function and subsequent death. I'd say he lasted no more than thirty seconds."

The report on the spinal cord damage seemingly put in jeopardy Bosch's working theory of the victim intentionally swallowing the bullet casing.

"With the spinal cord damage, could he have had any hand and arm movement?"

"Not for very long. Death was almost instantaneous."

"But he wasn't paralyzed, right? In those last thirty seconds, could he have picked up the casing and put it in his mouth?"

Laksmi considered the new scenario for a few moments before answering.

"I believe he would have indeed been paralyzed. But the projectile lodged in the fourth thoracic vertebra, cutting the cord there. This would have certainly caused paralysis but it would begin at that point. The arms could still function. It would be a matter of time. As I said, his body would have ceased function inside a minute."

Bosch nodded. His theory still worked. Li could have quickly grabbed the casing with his last strength and put it in his mouth.

Bosch wondered if the shooter knew this. He most likely had to move around the counter to look for the casings. In that time Li could have grabbed one of them. Blood found underneath Li's body indicated that it had been moved. Bosch realized that it most likely occurred during the search for the missing shell.

Bosch felt a growing excitement. The casing was a significant evidence find, but the idea that the shooter had made a mistake was even greater. He wanted to get the evidence over to Tool Marks and Ballistics as soon as possible.

"Okay, Doctor, what else is there?"

"There's something you might want to look at now rather than wait for the photos. Help me turn him."

They moved to the autopsy table and carefully rolled the body over. Rigor mortis had come and gone and the procedure was easy. Laksmi pointed to the ankles. Bosch moved down and saw that there were small Chinese symbols tattooed at the back of Li's feet. It looked like either two or three symbols were on each foot, located on either side of the Achilles tendon.

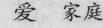

"You photographed these?"

"Yes, they'll be in the report."

"Anybody around here who can translate these?"

"I don't think so. Dr. Ming might be able to but he is on a vacay this week."

"Okay, can we slide him down a bit so I can hook the feet over the edge and take a picture?"

She helped him move the body down the table. The feet went over the edge and Bosch positioned the ankles right next to each other so the Chinese symbols were in a line across. He reached under his gown and pulled out his cell phone. He switched it to camera mode and took two photos of the tattoos.

"Okay."

Bosch put the phone down and they turned the body back over and moved it back up into place on the table.

Bosch took off his gloves and threw them into the medical waste receptacle, then picked his phone up and called Chu.

"What's your e-mail? I want to send you a photo."

"Of what?"

"Chinese symbols that were tattooed on Mr. Li's ankles. I want to know what they mean."

"Okay."

Chu gave him his department e-mail. Bosch checked his camera work and sent the clearest photo to him, then put the phone away.

"Dr. Laksmi, is there anything else I need to know here?"

"I think you got it all, Detective. Except there's one thing that maybe the family will want to know."

"What's that?"

She gestured to one of the organ bowls she had spread across the work counter.

"The bullets only brought about the inevitable. Mr. Li was dying of cancer."

Bosch stepped over and looked into the tray. The victim's lungs had been excised from the body for weighing and examination. Laksmi had opened them up to probe the bullet tracks and both lower lobes were dark gray with cancerous cells.

"He was a smoker," Laksmi said.

"I know," Bosch said. "How long do you think he had?"

"Maybe a year. Maybe longer."

"Can you tell whether this had been treated?"

"It doesn't look like it. Certainly no surgery. And I see no signs of chemotherapy or radiation. It may have been undiagnosed at this point. But he would have known soon enough."

Bosch thought about his own lungs. He had not smoked in years but they say the damage is done early. Sometimes in the mornings his lungs felt heavy and full in his chest. He'd had a case a few years before that resulted in his being exposed to a high-level dose of radiation. He'd cleared medical on it but always sort of thought or hoped that the blast had knocked down anything that might be growing in his chest.

Bosch took out his cell phone again and once more put it on camera function. He leaned over the bowl and shot a photo of the ravaged organs.

"What are you doing?" Laksmi asked.

"I want to send it to somebody."

He checked the photo and it was clear enough. He then sent it off in an e-mail.

"Who? Not the family, I hope."

"No, my daughter."

"Your daughter?"

There was a tone of outrage in her voice.

"She needs to see what smoking can do."

"Nice."

She said nothing else. Bosch put his phone away and checked his watch. It was a double display watch that gave him the time in L.A. and Hong Kong—a present from his daughter after too many miscalculated middle-of-the-night phone calls. It was just past three o'clock in L.A. His daughter was fifteen hours ahead and sleeping. She'd get up for school in about an hour and would get the photo then. He knew it would bring a protest call from her but even a call like that was better than none.

He smiled at the thought of it and then refocused on the work. He was ready to get moving again.

"Thank you, Doctor," he said. "For your records, I'm taking the ballistic evidence over to forensics."

"Did you sign for it?"

She pointed to a clipboard on the counter and Bosch found she had already filled out the chain-of-evidence report. Bosch signed the line acknowledging he was now in possession of the evidence listed. He headed toward the autopsy suite's door.

"Give me a couple days on the hard copy," Laksmi said.

Meaning the formal autopsy report.

"You got it," Bosch said as he went through the door.

10

On the way to forensics Bosch called Chu and asked about the tattoos.

"I haven't translated them yet," Chu said.

"What do you mean, did you look at them?"

"Yeah, I looked at them but I can't translate them. I'm trying to find somebody who can."

"Chu, I saw you talking to Mrs. Li. You translated for her."

"Bosch, just because I speak it doesn't mean I can read it. There are eight thousand Chinese symbols like these. All my schooling was in English. I spoke Chinese at home. Never read it."

"Okay, then is there somebody there that can get me a translation? It is the *Asian* Crimes Unit, isn't it?"

"Asian *Gang* Unit. And, yes, there are people here who can do it, but they don't happen to be here right now. As soon as I have it I will call you."

"Great. Call me."

Bosch hung up. He was frustrated by the delay. A case

had to move like a shark. It could never stop its momentum because that could be fatal. He checked his watch for the time in Hong Kong, then pulled to the curb and sent the photo of the ankle tattoos to his daughter in an e-mail. She would get it on her phone—right after she saw the photo of the lungs he had sent her.

Pleased with himself, Bosch pulled back into traffic. He was becoming more and more adept at digital communication thanks to her. She had insisted that they communicate on all modern levels: e-mail, text, video—she had even tried unsuccessfully to get him onto something called Twitter. He insisted in return that they also communicate the old-fashioned way—verbal conversation. He made sure their phones were covered by international call plans.

He made it back to the PAB a few minutes later and went straight to the Tool Marks and Ballistics unit on the fourth floor. He took his four plastic evidence bags to a technician named Ross Malone. His job was to take bullets and casings and use them to attempt to identify the make and model of the firearm they came from. Later, in the event that a gun was recovered, he would be able to match the bullets to it through ballistic testing and analysis.

Malone began with the casing, using a set of tweezers to take it from its packaging and then hold it under a high-powered magnifying glass with a lighted rim. He studied it for a long moment before speaking.

"Cor Bon nine-millimeter," he said. "And you're probably looking for a Glock."

Bosch was expecting him to confirm the size of the

round and identify the brand but not to name the make of weapon that had fired the bullet.

"How do you know that?"

"Take a look."

Malone was on a stool in front of the magnifying glass, which was attached to an adjustable arm anchored to the worktable. He moved it over slightly so Bosch could look over his shoulder. He was holding the back end of the casing into the light and magnification. Bosch could read the words *Cor Bon* stamped into the outer edge of the cap. At center was a depression made when the gun's firing pin had struck the primer, firing the bullet.

"You see how the impression is elongated, almost rectangular?" Malone asked.

"Yeah, I see it."

"That's Glock. Only Glocks have the rectangle because the firing pin is rectangular. So you are looking for a nine-millimeter Glock. They have several different models that would apply."

"Okay, that helps. Anything else?"

Malone pulled the glass back over in front of him and turned the bullet casing underneath it.

"You have clear extractor and ejector marks here. You bring me the gun and I think I'll be able to match it."

"As soon as I find it. What about the slugs?"

Malone put the casing back in its plastic bag and one by one took out the slugs and studied them under the glass. He looked at each one quickly before putting it down. He then went back to the second one and took another look. Then he shook his head.

"These aren't much use. They're not in good shape.

The casing is going to be your best bet for comparison. Like I said, you bring me the weapon, I'll match it up."

Bosch realized that John Li's last act was growing in importance. He wondered if the old man could have known just how important it was turning out to be.

Bosch's quiet contemplation prompted Malone to speak up.

"Did you touch this casing, Harry?"

"No, but Dr. Laksmi at the ME's sprayed blood off it with water. It was found inside the victim."

"Inside? That's impossible. There's no way a casing could—"

"I don't mean he was shot with it. He tried to swallow it. It was in his throat."

"Oh. That's different."

"Yeah."

"And Laksmi would have been gloved up when she found it."

"Right. What's up, Ross?"

"Well, I was thinking. We got a flyer about a month ago from latents. It said they were getting ready to start using some new state-of-the-art, electro-something-or-other method of raising prints on brass casings, and they were looking for test cases. You know, to get it into court."

Bosch stared at Malone. In all his years of detective work he had never heard of fingerprints being raised on a casing that had been fired in the chamber of a gun. Fingerprints were made of oils from the skin. They burned up in the millisecond of explosion in the chamber.

"Ross, you sure you're talking about spent casings?"

"Yeah, that's what it said. Teri Sopp is the tech over there handling it. Why don't you go see her?"

"Give me back the casing and I will."

Fifteen minutes later Bosch was with Teri Sopp in the SID's latent fingerprints lab. Sopp was a senior examiner and had been around nearly as long as Harry. They had an easy comfort with each other but Bosch still felt he had to finesse the meeting and lead Sopp to the water.

"Harry, what's the story?"

It was how she always greeted Bosch.

"The story is I caught a case yesterday down south and today we recovered a single bullet casing from the shooter's gun."

Bosch raised his hand, holding out the evidence bag with the casing in it. Sopp took it, held it up and squinted as she studied it through the plastic.

"Fired?"

"Yup. I know it's a long shot but I was hoping maybe there'd be a print on it. I don't have much else going on the case at the moment."

"Well, let's see. Normally, you'd have to wait your turn but seeing how we go back about five police chiefs..."

"That's why I came to you, Teri."

Sopp sat down at an examination table and, like Malone, used a pair of tweezers to pull the casing from the evidence bag. She first fumed it with cyanoacrylate and then held it under an ultraviolet light. Bosch was watching over her shoulder and had the answer before Sopp voiced it.

"You have a smear here. Looks like somebody handled it after it was fired. But that's all."

"Shit."

Bosch guessed that the smear had most likely been left on the casing when John Li grabbed it and put it in his mouth.

"Sorry, Harry."

Bosch's shoulders sagged. He knew it was a long shot, or maybe a no shot, but he was hoping to convey to Sopp how much he had counted on getting a print.

Sopp started to put the casing back into the evidence envelope.

"Tool Marks look at this yet?"

"Yeah, I just came from there."

She nodded. Bosch could tell she was thinking about something.

"Harry, tell me about the case. Give me the parameters."

Bosch summarized the case but left out the detail about the suspect they had pulled out of the surveillance video. He made it sound like the investigation was almost hopeless. No evidence, no suspect, no motive other than common robbery. *Zip, nada, nothing.*

"Well, there's one thing we might be able to do," Sopp said.

"What's that?"

"We'll be putting a bulletin out by the end of the month on this. We're gearing up for electrostatic enhancement. This might be a good first case for us."

"What the hell is electrostatic enhancement?"

Sopp smiled like the kid who still had candy after you were all out.

"It's a process that was developed in England with the Northamptonshire police by which fingerprints can be raised on brass surfaces such as bullet casings by using electricity."

Bosch looked around, saw an empty stool at one of the other workstations and dragged it over. He sat down.

"How's it work?"

"Okay, here's the deal. When you load bullets into a revolver or a magazine for an automatic, it is a precise process. You hold each bullet between your fingers and you push it in. You apply pressure. It would seem like a perfect setup for leaving prints, right?"

"Well, until the gun is fired."

"Exactly. A latent print is essentially a deposit of the sweat that builds between the grooves of your fingerprint. The problem is, when a gun is fired and the casing is ejected, the latent print usually disappears in the explosion. It's rare that you pull a print off a spent shell, unless it belongs to the person who picked it up off the ground after."

"All this I know," Bosch said. "Tell me something I don't know."

"Okay, okay. Well, this process works best if the gun is not immediately fired. In other words, for this process to be successful, you need a situation where maybe the bullet was loaded into the gun but then allowed to sit in there for at least a few days. The longer, the better. Because if it's sitting in there, the sweat that forms the latents is reacting with the brass. You understand?"

"You mean there's a chemical reaction."

"A microscopic chemical reaction. Your sweat is made up of a lot of different things but mostly sodium chloride—salt. It reacts with the brass—corrodes it—and leaves its mark. But we just can't see it."

"And the electricity lets you see it."

"Exactly. We run a twenty-five-hundred-volt charge through the casing, dust it with carbon and then we see it. We've run several experiments so far. I've seen it work. It was invented by this guy named Bond in England."

Bosch was growing excited.

"Then, why don't we do it?"

Sopp spread her fingers in a calming gesture.

"Whoa, hold on, Harry. We can't just do it."

"Why not? What are you waiting for, a ribbon-cutting ceremony with the chief or something?"

"No, it's not that. This kind of evidence and procedure has not been introduced in a California court yet. We're working with the district attorney on protocols and nobody wants to go out with this for the first time on a case where it's not a slam-dunk. We have to think of the future. The first time we use this process as evidence will set the precedent. If it's not the right case, we'll blow it and it would really set us back."

"Well, maybe this is the case. Who decides that?"

"It's first going to be up to Brenneman to pick the case and then he'll take it to the DA."

Chuck Brenneman was the commander of the Scientific Investigation Division. Bosch realized that the process of choosing the first case could take weeks, if not months.

"Look, you said you guys in here have been experimenting with it, right?"

"Yeah, we have to make sure we know what we're doing."

"Good, then experiment with this casing. See what you come up with."

"We can't, Harry. We're using dummy bullets in a controlled experiment."

"Teri, I need this. There might be nothing there but then again, the killer's print might be on that shell. You can find out."

Sopp seemed to realize that she had been cornered by someone who was not going to go away.

"All right, listen. The next set of experiments is not scheduled till next week. I can't promise anything but I'll see what I can do."

"Thanks, Teri."

Bosch filled out the chain-of-evidence form and left the lab. He was excited about the possibility of using the new science to possibly get the killer's print. It almost felt to him as if John Li had known about electrostatic enhancement all along. The thought sent a different kind of electricity down Bosch's spine.

As he stepped out of the elevator on the fifth floor he checked his watch and saw that it was time to call his daughter. She would be walking down Stubbs Road to the Happy Valley Academy. If he didn't get to her now he would have to wait until after school was out. He stopped in the hallway outside the squad room, pulled his phone and hit the speed dial. The transpacific call took thirty seconds to connect.

"Dad! What's with the picture of a dead person?"

He smiled.

"Hello to you, too. How do you know he's dead?"

"Um, let's see. My dad investigates murders and he sends me bare feet on a steel table. And what is this other picture? The guy's lungs? That is so gross!"

"He was a smoker. I thought you should see that."

There was a moment of silence and then she spoke very calmly. There was no little girl in her voice now.

"Dad, I don't smoke."

"Yeah, well, your mother told me you smell like smoke when you come home from hanging out with your friends at the mall."

"Yeah, that might be true, but it's not true that I smoke with them."

"Then who *do* you smoke with?"

"Dad, I don't! My friend's older brother hangs out sometimes to watch over her. I don't smoke and neither does He."

"He? I thought you said your friend was a her."

She said the name again, this time putting a heavy Chinese accent on it. It sounded like *He-yuh*.

"He is a her. He is her name. It means 'river.'"

"Then why don't you call her River?"

"Because she's Chinese and so I call her by her Chinese name."

"Must get like Abbott and Costello. Calling a she He."

"Like who?"

Bosch laughed.

"Never mind. Forget the lungs, Maddie. If you tell me you don't smoke, I believe you. But that's not why I'm calling. The tattoos on the ankles, could you read them?"

"Yes, it's gross. I have a dead guy's feet on my phone."

"Well, you can delete it as soon as you tell me what the tattoos mean. I know you study that stuff in school."

"I'm not going to delete it. I'm showing my friends. They'll think it's cool."

"No, don't do that. It's part of a case I'm working and nobody else should see it. I sent it to you because I thought you could give me a quick translation."

"You mean in all of the LAPD you don't have one person who can tell you? You have to call your daughter in Hong Kong for such a simple thing?"

"At the moment, that's about right. You do what you have to do. Do you know what the symbols mean or not?"

"Yes, Dad. They were easy."

"Well, what do they mean?"

"It's like a fortune. On the left ankle the symbols are *Fu* and *Cai,* which mean 'luck' and 'money.' Then on the right side you have *Ai* and *Xi,* which is 'love' and 'family.'"

Bosch thought about this. It seemed to him the symbols were the things that were important to John Li. He had hoped that these things would always walk with him.

Then he thought about the fact that the symbols were located on either side of Li's Achilles tendons. Perhaps Li had placed the tattoos there intentionally, realizing that the things he hoped for also made him vulnerable. They were also his Achilles' heel.

"Hello, Dad?"

"Yeah, I'm here. I'm just thinking."

"Well, does it help? Did I crack the case?"

Bosch smiled but immediately realized she couldn't see this.

"Not quite but it helps."

"Good. You owe me."

Bosch nodded.

"You're a pretty smart kid, aren't you? How old are you now, thirteen going on twenty?"

"Please, Dad."

"Well, your mother must be doing something right."

"Not much."

"Hey, that's no way to talk about her."

"Dad, you don't have to live with her. I do. And it's not so much fun. I told you when I was in L.A."

"She's still seeing somebody?"

"Yeah, and I'm yesterday's news."

"It's not like that, Maddie. It's just that it's been a long time for her."

A long time for me, too, Bosch thought.

"Dad, don't take her side. To her I'm just in the way all the time. But when I say, fine, I'll live with Dad, she says no way."

"You should be with your mother. She's raised you. Look, in a month I'll be coming over for a week. We can talk about all of this then. With your mother."

"Whatever. I gotta go. I'm here at school."

"All right. Say hello to He the she for me."

"Funny, Dad. Just don't send me any more pictures of lungs, okay?"

"Next time it will be a liver. Or maybe a spleen. Spleens photograph real nice."

"Daaaadd!"

He closed the phone and let her go. He thought about what had been said during the conversation. It seemed to him that the weeks and months between seeing Maddie were getting more difficult. As she became her own person and grew more bright and communicative, he loved her more and missed her all the time. She had just been out to L.A. in July, taking the long flight for the first time

on her own. Barely a teenager and already a world traveler, she was wise beyond her years. He'd taken off work
and they'd enjoyed two weeks of doing things together,
exploring the city. It had been a wonderful time for him
and at the end it was the first time she had ever mentioned
wanting to live in Los Angeles. With him.

Bosch was smart enough to realize that these senti-
ments were expressed after two weeks of full-time attention from a father who began each day by asking what she
wanted to do. It was far different from the full-time commitment of her mother, who raised her day after day while
making a living for them. Still, the toughest day Bosch
had ever had as a part-time father was the day he took his
daughter back to the airport and put her on the plane to fly
home alone. He half expected her to bolt and run, but she
got on under protest and then was gone. He'd felt a hol-
lowness inside ever since.

Now his next vacation and trip to Hong Kong wasn't
scheduled for another month and he knew it was going to
be a long, tough wait until then.

"Harry, what are you doing out here?"

Bosch turned. His partner, Ferras, was standing there,
having come out of the squad room, probably to use the
restroom.

"I was talking to my daughter. I wanted some privacy."

"She all right?"

"She's fine. I'll meet you back in the squad."

Bosch headed toward the door, putting his phone back
in his pocket.

11

Bosch got home at eight that night, coming through the door with a to-go bag from the In-N-Out down on Cahuenga.

"Honey, I'm home," he called out as he struggled with the key, the bag and his briefcase.

He smiled to himself and went directly into the kitchen. He put his briefcase down on the counter, grabbed a bottle of beer out of the refrigerator and went out to the deck. Along the way he turned on his CD player, leaving the sliding door open so the music could mingle on the deck with the sound of the 101 Freeway down in the pass.

The deck was positioned with a northeasterly view stretching across Universal City, Burbank and on to the San Gabriel Mountains. Harry ate his two hamburgers, holding them over the open bag to catch drippings, and watched the dying sun change the colors of the mountain slopes. He listened to "Seven Steps to Heaven" off Ron Carter's *Dear Miles* album. Carter was one of the most important bassists of the last five decades. He had played with everybody and Bosch often wondered about the stories he could tell, the sessions he'd sat in on and the musicians he knew. Whether on his own recordings or on somebody else's, Carter's work always stood out. Harry believed this was because as a bassist he could never really be a sideman. He was always the anchor. He always drove the beat, even if it was behind Miles Davis's horn.

The song now playing had an undeniable momentum to it. Like a car chase. It made Bosch think about his own chase and the advances that had been made through the day. He was satisfied with his own momentum but uncomfortable with the realization that he had moved the case to a point where he was now reliant on the work of others. He had to wait for others to identify the triad bagman. He had to wait for others to decide whether to use the bullet casing as a test case for their new fingerprint technology. He had to wait for somebody to call.

Bosch was most at home in a case when he was pushing the action himself, setting the track for others to follow. He wasn't a sideman. He had to drive the beat. And at this juncture he had pushed it just about as far as he could. He started thinking about his next moves and the options were few. He could start hitting Chinese-owned businesses in South L.A. with the photo of the triad bagman. But he knew it would likely be an exercise in futility. The cultural divide was wide. No one would willingly identify a triad member to the police.

Nevertheless, hc was prepared to go that route if nothing else broke soon. It would at least keep him moving. Momentum was momentum, whether you found it in music or on the street or in the beat of your own heart.

As the light started to disappear from the sky, Bosch

reached into his pocket and pulled out the book of matches he always carried. He thumbed it open and studied the fortune. Since the night he first read it he had taken it seriously. He believed that he was a man who had found refuge in himself. Over time, at least.

His cell rang as he was chewing his last bite. He pulled the phone and checked the screen. The ID was blocked but he answered anyway.

"Bosch."

"Harry, David Chu. You sound like you're eating. Where are you?"

His voice was tight with excitement.

"I'm at home. Where are you?"

"Monterey Park. We got him!"

Bosch paused for a moment. Monterey Park was a city in the east county where nearly three-quarters of the population was Chinese. Fifteen minutes from downtown, it was like a foreign country with impenetrable language and culture.

"Who have you got?" he finally asked.

"Our guy. The suspect."

"You mean you got an ID?"

"We got more than an ID. We got him. We're looking right at him."

There were several things about what Chu was saying that immediately bothered Bosch.

"First of all, who is *we*?"

"I'm with the MPPD. They IDed our guy off the video and then took me right to him."

Bosch could feel the pulse pounding in his temple. No doubt, getting the ID of the triad bagman—if it was legit—was a big step in the investigation. But everything else he was hearing wasn't. Bringing another police department into the case and moving in on the suspect were potentially fatal mistakes and should never have been even considered without the lead investigator's knowledge and approval. But Bosch knew he couldn't go off on Chu. Not yet. He had to stay calm and do his best to contain a bad situation.

"Detective Chu, listen closely to me. Did you make contact with the suspect?"

"Contact? No, not yet. We were waiting for the right moment. He's not alone right now."

Thank God for that, Bosch thought but didn't say.

"Has the suspect seen you?"

"No, Harry, we're across the street."

Bosch let out some more air. He was beginning to think that the situation might be salvageable.

"Okay, I want you to hold where you are and tell me what moves you've made and where exactly we're at. How did you get to Monterey Park?"

"The AGU has a strong relationship with Monterey Park's gang detail. Tonight after work I took by the photo of our guy to see if anybody recognized him. I got a positive ID from the third guy I showed it to."

"The third guy. Who was that?"

"Detective Tao. I'm with him and his partner right now."

"Okay, give me the name you got."

"Bo-Jing Chang."

He spelled the name out.

"So the last name is Chang?" Bosch asked.

"Right. And according to their intel, he's in *Yung Kim*—Brave Knife. It fits with the tattoo."

"Okay, what else?"

"That's it at the moment. He's supposedly a low-level guy. All these guys have real jobs. He works at a used-car lot here in MP. He has been here since 'ninety-five and has dual citizenship. No arrest record—over here, at least."

"And you got a twenty on him right now?"

"I'm watching him play cards. Brave Knife is mostly centered here in MP. And there's a club here where they like to get together at the end of the day. Tao and Herrera took me."

Bosch assumed Herrera was Tao's partner.

"You said you're across the street?"

"Yeah, the club's in a little strip mall. We're across the street. We can see them in there playing cards. We can see Chang with the binoculars."

"Okay, listen, I'm coming out there. I want you to back away until I get there. Move at least another block away."

There was a long pause before Chu responded.

"We don't need to move back, Harry. If we lose track of him he might get away."

"Listen, Detective, I need you to back away. If he gets away, that will be on me, not you. I don't want to risk him seeing a police presence."

"We're across the street," Chu protested. "Four lanes."

"Chu, you're not listening. If you can see him, then he can see you. Back the fuck away. I want you to move at least a block down the street and wait for me. I'll be there in less than thirty minutes."

"This is going to be embarrassing," Chu said in a near whisper.

"I don't care what it is. If you'd handled this the right

way, you would've called me the moment you had an ID on the guy. Instead, you're out there cowboying my case and I'm going to stop it before you fuck things up."

"You've got it wrong, Harry. I called you."

"Yeah, well, I appreciate that. Now back away. I'll call when I'm close. What's the name of the place?"

After a pause Chu answered in a sulking voice.

"It's called Club Eighty-eight. It's on Garvey about four blocks west of Garfield. Take the ten out to—"

"I know how to get there. I'm on my way."

He closed the phone to end any further dispute and debate. Chu was on notice. If he didn't back off or control the two Monterey Park officers, then his ass would belong to Bosch in an internal complaint process.

12

Harry was out the door within two minutes. He drove down out of the hills and then took the 101 back through Hollywood into downtown. He hooked up with the 10 and headed east. Monterey Park was another ten minutes in light traffic. Along the way Bosch called Ignacio Ferras at home, apprised him of what was happening and offered him the opportunity to meet up in Monterey Park. Ferras declined, saying it might be better if one of them was fresh in the morning. Besides, he was knee-deep in the forensic analysis of the financial aspects of the case, trying to determine how bad business had gotten for John Li and how badly he might have been entrenched with the triad.

Bosch agreed and closed the phone. He had expected his partner to decline the invitation. His fear of the streets was becoming more and more evident and Bosch was just about out of time, waiting for him to come around. But Ferras seemed to go out of his way to find work that could be done inside the squad room. Paperwork, computer runs and financial backgrounding had become his specialties. Oftentimes Bosch had to recruit other detectives to go outside the building with him, even for simple assignments like interviewing witnesses. Bosch had done his best to give Ferras time to recover, but the situation had reached a point where he had to consider the victims who were not getting what they should get. It was hard to conduct a relentless investigation when your partner was tethered to a desk chair.

Garfield was a main north–south corridor and he got a full view of the city's commercial district as he headed south. Monterey Park could easily pass for a neighborhood in Hong Kong. The neon, the colors, the shops and the language on the signs were geared toward a Chinese-speaking populace. The only thing missing were the towers rising high above. Hong Kong was a vertical city. Monterey Park was not.

He turned left on Garvey and pulled his phone to call Chu.

"Okay, I'm on Garvey. Where are you?"

"Come down and you'll see the big supermarket on the south side. We're in the lot. You'll pass the club on the north side before you get here."

"Got it."

He closed the phone and kept driving, his eyes scanning the neon on the left side. Soon he saw the red *88* glowing above the door of a small club with no other demarcation on it. Seeing the numeral rather than hearing the spoken number from Chu prompted a realization. It was not the address of the place. It was a benediction. Bosch knew from his daughter and his many visits to Hong Kong that 8 was a lucky number in Chinese culture.

The numeral symbolized infinity—the infinity of luck or love or money or whatever it was you wanted in life. Apparently, the members of Brave Knife were hoping for double infinity by putting 88 over their door.

As he drove by he could see light behind the front plate-glass window. The slatted blinds were turned open slightly and Bosch could see about ten men either sitting or standing around a table. Harry kept going and three blocks later pulled into the parking lot of the Big Lau Super Market. He saw a government-model Crown Victoria at the far end of the lot. It looked too new to be LAPD and he figured Chu was riding with the MPPD. He pulled into the space next to it.

Everybody put their windows down and Chu made introductions from the backseat. Herrera was behind the wheel and Tao was riding shotgun. Neither of the Monterey Park officers was close to thirty years old but that was to be expected. The small cop shops in the outlying cities around Los Angeles acted as feeder departments for the LAPD. The cops signed up young, got a few years' experience and then applied to the LAPD or the L.A. County Sheriff's Department, where carrying the badge was seen as more glamorous and fun and the added experience gave them an inside edge.

"You IDed Chang?" Bosch asked Tao.

"That's right," Tao said. "I pulled him over on an FI stop six months ago. When Davy came around with the photo, I remembered him."

"Where was this?"

While Tao spoke his partner kept his eyes on Club 88

up the street. Occasionally, he raised a pair of binoculars to check out people going or coming more closely.

"I ran across him in the warehouse district down at the end of Garvey. It was late and he was driving a panel van. Looked like he was lost. He let us look and the van was empty but I figure he was going to make a pickup or something. A lot of counterfeit goods go through those warehouses. It's easy to lose your way in there because there's so many of them and they all look the same. Anyway, the van wasn't his. It was registered to Vincent Tsing. He lives in South Pasadena but he's pretty well known to us as a member of Brave Knife. He's a familiar face. He has a car lot here in MP and Chang works for him."

Bosch understood the procedure. Tao had pulled the van over but with no probable cause to search it or to arrest Chang, he was reliant on Chang's volunteerism. They filled out a field interview card with information he provided and checked the back of the van after being given permission.

"And what, he just volunteered that he was in the Brave Knife triad?"

"No," Tao said indignantly. "We noted his tattoo and the ownership of the vehicle. We put two and two together, Detective."

"That's good. Did he have a DL?"

"He did. But we already checked that address tonight. It's no good. He moved."

Bosch glanced back at Chu in the backseat. This meant that if the address on Chang's driver's license had been correct, they probably would have already encountered the suspect without Bosch.

Chu looked away from Bosch's stare. Bosch checked himself and tried to stay cool. If he blew up on them, he would lose all cooperation and the case would suffer for it. He didn't want that.

"You have the shake card with you?" he asked Tao.

Tao handed a 3 × 5 card out the window and across to Bosch. Harry put the overhead light on and read the information handwritten on the card. Since field interviews had been challenged repeatedly over the years by civil rights groups as unwarranted shakedowns, the information forms filled out by officers were universally referred to as "shake cards."

Bosch studied the information on Bo-Jing Chang. Most of it had already been relayed to him. But Tao had conducted a very thorough field interview. There was a cell phone number written on the card. It was a watershed moment.

"This number is good?"

"I don't know about now—these guys dump phones all the time. But it was good then. I called it right on the spot to make sure he wasn't fucking with me. So all I can tell you is that it was good back then."

"Okay, we have to confirm it."

"You're just going to call the guy up and say, how ya doin'?"

"No, you are. Block your ID and call the number in five minutes. If he answers, tell him you've got a wrong number. Let me borrow the binocs and, *Davy,* you come with me."

"Wait a minute," Tao said. "What are we doing fucking with the phones?"

"If the number's still good we can go for a wire. Give

me the glasses. You call while I'm watching and we confirm, get it?"

"Sure."

Bosch handed the shake card back to Tao and took the binoculars in return. Chu got out of their car, came around to Bosch's ride and got in.

Bosch pulled out onto Garvey and headed toward Club 88. He scanned the parking lots, looking for a place to get close.

"Where were you parked before?"

"Up there on the left."

He pointed to a lot and Bosch turned in, circled around and killed the lights as he pulled into a space that was facing Club 88 across the street.

"Take the glasses and see if he answers his phone," he told Chu.

As Chu zeroed in on Chang, Bosch studied the entire view of the club, looking for anyone who might be looking out the window in their direction.

"Which one is Chang?" he asked.

"He's at the left end, next to the guy in the hat."

Bosch picked him out. But he was too far away for Harry to make any confirmation of Chang as the man in the video from Fortune Liquors.

"You think it's him or you just going with Tao's ID?" he asked.

"No, it's a good ID," Chu said. "It's him."

Bosch checked his watch. Herrera should've made the call. He was growing impatient.

"What are we doing, anyway?" Chu asked.

"We're building a case, Detective. We confirm that

number, then we get a warrant for a wire. We start listening to him and we find things out. Who he talks to, what he's up to. Maybe we hear him talk about Li. Maybe we don't and we spook him and we see who he calls. We start closing in. The point is, we take our time and do it right. We don't ride in on horses, shooting up the town."

Chu didn't respond. He kept the binoculars locked on his eyes.

"Tell me something," Bosch said. "Do you trust those two guys, Tao and Herrera?"

Chu didn't hesitate.

"I trust them. You don't?"

"I don't know them, so I can't trust them. All I know is that you took my case and my suspect and showed everything all around that police department."

"Look, I was trying to make a break in the case and I did. We got the ID."

"Yeah, we got the ID and hopefully our suspect doesn't find out about it."

Chu lowered the binoculars and looked at Bosch.

"I think you're just pissed because it wasn't you."

"No, Chu, I don't care who makes the break as long as it's handled right. Showing my cards to people I don't know is not my idea of good case management."

"Man, don't you trust anybody?"

"Just watch the club," Bosch responded sternly.

Chu put the binoculars back up as instructed.

"I trust myself," Bosch said.

"I just wonder if this is something to do with me and Tao. Whether that's the issue."

Bosch turned toward him.

"Don't start that shit again, Chu. I don't care what you're wondering. You can go back to AGU and stay the hell out of my case. I didn't call you out in the first—"

"Chang just took a call."

Bosch looked at the club. He thought he saw the man Chu had identified as Chang with a phone to his ear. He then dropped his arm.

"He put it away," Chu said. "The number's good."

Bosch backed out of the space and started back to the supermarket.

"I still don't know why we're fucking around with a phone number," Chu said. "Why don't we just go pick the guy up? We got him on tape. Same day, same time. We use it to break him."

"And what if he doesn't break? We're left with nothing. The DA would laugh us right out the door if we went in with just that tape. We need more. That's what I'm trying to teach you."

"I don't need a teacher, Bosch. And I still think we can turn him."

"Yeah, go home and watch some more TV. Why the fuck would he say a single word to us? These guys are told from day one, you get popped, you say nothing. If you go down, you go down and we'll take care of you."

"You told me you never worked a triad case before."

"I haven't but some things are universal and this is one of them. You get one shot at these cases. You have to do it right."

"Okay, so we do it your way. What's next?"

"We go back to the parking lot and cut your friends loose. We'll take it from here. It's our case, not theirs."

"They're not going to like that."

"I don't care if they like it or not. That's the way it's going to be. You figure out a way of letting them down nice. Tell them we'll bring them back in when we're ready to make a move on the guy."

"Me?"

"Yeah, you. You invited them in, you invite them out."

"Thanks, Bosch."

"Any time, Chu. Welcome to homicide."

13

Bosch, Ferras and Chu sat on one side of the meeting table across from Lieutenant Gandle and Captain Bob Dodds, commander of the Robbery-Homicide Division. Spread across the polished surface between them were the case documents and photographs, most notably the shot of Bo-Jing Chang from the Fortune Liquors security camera.

"I'm not convinced," Dodds said.

It was Thursday morning, just six hours after Bosch and Chu had ended their surveillance of Chang, with the suspect going to an apartment in Monterey Park and apparently retiring for the night.

"Well, Cap, you shouldn't be convinced yet," Bosch said. "That's why we want to continue the surveillance and get the wire."

"What I mean is, I'm not convinced it's the way to go," Dodds said. "Surveillance is fine. But a wire is a lot of work and effort for long-shot results."

Bosch understood. Dodds had an excellent reputation as a detective but he was now an administrator and about as far removed from the detective work in his division as a Houston oil executive is from the gas pump. He now worked with personnel numbers and budgets. He had to find ways of doing more with less and never allowing a dip in the statistics of arrests made and cases closed. That made him a realist and the reality was that electronic surveillance was very expensive. Not only did it take double-digit man hours to carefully draft a fifty-plus-page affidavit seeking court permission, but once permission was granted, a wiretap room had to be staffed twenty-four hours a day with a detective monitoring the line. Often a single-number tap led to other numbers needing to be tapped and under the law each line had to have its own monitor. Such an operation quickly sucked up overtime like a giant sponge. With the RHD's OT budget seriously down because of economic constraints on the department, Dodds was reluctant to give any of it up for what amounted to an investigation of the murder of a south side liquor store clerk. He would rather save it for a rainy day — a big-time media case that might come up and that would demand it.

Dodds, of course, would not say any of this out loud but Bosch knew, just as everyone else in the room knew, that this was the issue the captain wrestled with and which left him unconvinced. It had nothing to do with the particulars of the case.

Bosch took one last shot at convincing him.

"This is the tip of the iceberg, Captain," he said. "We're not just talking about a liquor store shooting. This is just a doorway. We could take down a whole triad before this is over."

"Before this is over? I retire in nineteen months, Bosch. These sorts of things can last forever."

Bosch shrugged.

"We could call in the bureau, go partners. They're always up for an international case and they've got money to spend on wiretaps and surveillance."

"But we'd have to share everything," Gandle said, meaning the spoils of the bust. Headlines, press conferences, everything.

"I don't like the idea of doing that," Dodds said as he held up the photo of Bo-Jing Chang.

Bosch threw in his last card.

"What if we did it without overtime?" Bosch asked.

The captain was holding a pen in his hand. It probably reminded him of his authority. He was the one who signed off on things. He twiddled it now as he considered Bosch's unexpected question but quickly shook his head.

"You know I can't ask you to do that," he said. "I can't even know about that."

It was true. The department had been sued so many times for unfair labor practices that no one in administration would ever give even tacit approval to detectives working off the clock.

Bosch's frustration with budgets and bureaucracy finally got the best of him.

"Then, what do we do? Bring Chang in. We all know he's not going to say a word to us and the case will die right there."

The captain wiggled his pen.

"Bosch, you know what the alternative is. You work the case until something breaks. You work the witnesses.

You work the evidence. There's always a link. I spent fifteen years doing what you're doing and you know there is always something. Find it. A wiretap is a long shot and you know it. Legwork is always the better bet. Now, is there anything else?"

Harry felt his face growing red. The captain was dismissing him. What burned was that deep down Bosch knew Dodds was right.

"Thanks, Captain," he said curtly and stood up.

The detectives left the captain and the lieutenant in the conference room and convened in Bosch's cubicle. Bosch threw a pen he was carrying down on his desk.

"Guy's an ass," Chu said.

"No, he's not," Bosch quickly said. "He's right and that's why he's the captain."

"Then, what do we do?"

"We stay with Chang. I don't care about overtime and what the captain doesn't know won't hurt him. We watch Chang and we wait for him to make a mistake. I don't care how long it takes. I can make a hobby of it if I have to."

Bosch looked at the other two, expecting them to decline to participate in a surveillance that would likely go beyond the bounds of the eight-hour day.

To his surprise, Chu nodded.

"I already talked to my lieutenant. I'm detached to this case. I can do it." Bosch nodded and at first considered that he had been wrong to be so suspicious of Chu. His next thought, however, was that the suspicion was valid and that Chu's commitment to stay with the case was just a means of remaining close to the investigation and monitoring Bosch.

Harry turned to his partner.

"What about you?"

Ferras reluctantly nodded and gestured toward the conference room across the squad room. Through the glass wall, Dodds could be seen still talking with Gandle.

"You know they know this is what we're doing," he said. "They're not going to pay us and they leave it to us to either step up or let it go. It's not fucking fair."

"Yeah, so?" Bosch said. "Life isn't fair. Are you in or out?"

"I'm in, but with a limit. I've got a family, man. I'm not sitting on surveillance all night. I can't do it—especially for nothing."

"All right, fine," Bosch said, even though his tone communicated his disappointment with Ferras. "You do what you can. You handle the inside work and Chu and I will stay with Chang."

Noting Bosch's tone, Ferras put a mild protest in his own tone.

"Look, Harry, you don't know what it's like. Three kids...you try selling it at home. That you're going to sit in a car all night watching some triad guy and your paycheck is going to look the same no matter how many hours you're gone."

Bosch put his hands up as if to say *enough said*.

"You're right. I don't have to sell it. I just have to do it. That's the job."

14

From behind the wheel of his own car, Bosch watched Chang as he performed menial chores at Tsing Motors in Monterey Park. The car lot had formerly been a 1950s-style gas station with two garage bays and an attached office. Bosch was parked a half block away on busy Garvey Avenue and was in no danger of being made. Chu was in his own car half a block past the car lot in the other direction. Using their personal cars for the surveillance was a violation of departmental policy but Bosch had checked with the motor pool and there were no undercover vehicles available. The choice was to use their unmarked detective cruisers, which might as well have been painted black and white for all the camouflage they offered, or to break policy. Bosch didn't mind breaking policy because he had a six-CD stack in his car. Today he had it loaded with music from his latest discovery. Tomasz Stańko was a Polish trumpeter who sounded like the ghost of Miles Davis. His horn was sharp and soulful. It was good surveillance music. It kept Bosch alert.

For almost three hours they had watched their suspect

handle his mundane duties on the lot. He had washed cars, greased tires to make them look new, even taken the one prospective customer on a test drive of a 1989 Mustang. And for the past half hour he had been systematically moving each of the three dozen cars on the lot to new positions in an effort to make it appear that the inventory was changing, that there was sales activity and that business was good.

At 4 P.M. "Soul of Things" came out of the stack and Bosch couldn't help but think that even Miles would grudgingly give Staňko his due. Harry was following the groove with his fingers on the steering wheel when he saw Chang go into the small office and change his shirt. When he stepped out he was finished for the day. He got into the Mustang and drove by himself off the lot.

Bosch's phone immediately buzzed with a call from Chu. Harry killed the music.

"You got him?" Chu asked. "He's moving."

"Yeah, I see."

"Heading up to the ten. You think he's done for the day?"

"He changed his shirt. I think he's done. I'll take the lead and then you be ready to move up."

Bosch followed five car lengths behind and then caught up as Chang headed west on the 10 toward downtown. He was not going home. Bosch and Chu had followed him the night before to an apartment in Monterey Park — also owned by Vincent Tsing — and had watched the place for an hour after the lights had gone out and they felt comfortable with the belief that he was in for the night.

Now he was heading into L.A. and Bosch's instincts

told him he was carrying out triad business. He sped up and passed by the Mustang, holding his cell phone up to his ear so Chang wouldn't get a look at his face. He called Chu and told him he was now on point.

Bosch and Chu continued to trade off the point while Chang connected to the 101 Freeway and headed north through Hollywood toward the Valley. Traffic bogged down in the rush-hour crunch and following the suspect was easy. It took Chang nearly an hour to get up to Sherman Oaks, where he finally exited on the Sepulveda Boulevard ramp. Bosch called Chu.

"I think he's going to the other store," he told his surveillance partner.

"I think you're right. Should we call Robert Li and warn him?"

Bosch paused. It was a good question. He had to decide whether Robert Li was in danger. If so, he should be warned. But if he was not in danger, a warning could blow the whole operation.

"No, not yet. Let's see what happens. If Chang goes into the store, we go in with him. And we'll step in if things go wrong."

"You sure, Harry?"

"No, but that's how we'll play it. Make sure you make the light."

They held the connection. The light at the bottom of the ramp had just turned green. Bosch was four cars behind Chang but Chu was at least eight.

Traffic moved slowly and Bosch crept along, watching the light. It turned yellow just as he hit the intersection. He made it but Chu wouldn't.

"Okay, I got him," he said into the phone. "No worries."

"Good. I'll be there in three minutes."

Bosch closed the phone. Just then he heard a siren from directly behind him and saw flashing blues in the rearview.

"Shit!"

He looked ahead and saw Chang proceeding south on Sepulveda. He was four blocks from Fortune Fine Foods & Liquor. Bosch quickly pulled to the curb and hit the brake. He opened his door and jumped out. He was holding his badge up as he approached the officer on the motorcycle who had pulled him over.

"I'm on a surveillance! I can't stop!"

"Talking on a cell phone is illegal."

"Then write it up and send it to the chief. I'm not blowing a surveillance for this."

He turned around and went back to his car. He bulled his way back into the traffic and looked ahead for Chang's Mustang. It was gone. The next traffic signal turned red and he was stopped again. He banged the heel of his hand off the steering wheel and started wondering if he should call Robert Li.

His phone buzzed. It was Chu.

"I'm making the turn. Where are you?"

"I'm only a block ahead of you. I got pulled over by a motor cop for talking on a cell phone."

"That's just great! Where's Chang?"

"Somewhere up ahead. I'm moving now."

Traffic was slowly moving through the intersection. Bosch wasn't panicked because the road was so glutted with vehicles that he knew Chang could not have gotten too far ahead. He stayed in his lane, knowing that he might draw attention in Chang's mirrors if he started jockeying between lanes and cars to move up.

In another two minutes he got to the major intersection of Sepulveda and Ventura Boulevard. He could see the lights of Fortune Fine Foods & Liquor a block further down Sepulveda at the next intersection. He did not see Chang's Mustang anywhere in front of him. He buzzed Chu.

"I'm at the light at Ventura and don't see him. He might already be there."

"I'm one light back. What do we do?"

"I'm going to park and go in. You stay out and look for his car. Buzz me when you see either him or the car."

"You're going right to Li?"

"We'll see."

As soon as the light turned green Bosch pinned the accelerator and jumped into the intersection, nearly broadsiding a red-light runner. He cruised up the next block and took a right into the market's parking lot. He didn't see Chang's car or any open parking spaces other than the one clearly marked for handicapped motorists. Bosch pulled through the lot into the alley and parked behind a trash bin with a NO PARKING sticker on it. He jumped out and trotted back through the parking lot to the market's front door.

Just as Bosch was going through the automatic door marked ENTER, he saw Chang coming out the door marked EXIT. Bosch raised his hand and brushed it through his hair, blocking his face with his arm. He kept going and pulled his phone out of his pocket.

He walked between the two checkout counters. Two women, different from the ones the day before, stood at the cash registers waiting for customers.

"Where's Mr. Li?" Bosch asked without stopping.

"In the back," said one woman.

"His office," said the other.

Bosch called Chu as he was walking quickly down the main aisle to the back of the store.

"He just walked out the front door. Stay with him. I'll check on Li."

"Got it."

Bosch disconnected and pocketed the phone. He followed the same route to Li's office as he had the day before. When he got there, the office door was closed. He felt adrenaline burst inside him as he reached for the knob.

Bosch pushed the door open without knocking and found Li and another Asian man sitting at the two desks. They were in a conversation that abruptly stopped when the door came open. Li jumped up and Bosch saw immediately that he was physically unharmed.

"Detective!" Li exclaimed. "I was just about to call you! He was here! That man you showed me was here!"

"I know. I was following him. Are you all right?"

"Just scared, that's all."

"What happened?"

Li hesitated for a moment to gather his words.

"Sit down and calm down," Bosch said. "Then you can tell me. Who are you?"

Bosch pointed at the man seated at the other desk.

"This is Eugene, my assistant manager."

The man stood up and offered his hand to Bosch.

"Eugene Lam, Detective."

Bosch shook his hand.

"You were here when Chang came in?" he asked.

"Chang?" Li responded.

"That's his name. The man in the photograph I showed you."

"Yes, Eugene and I were both here. He just walked into the office."

"What did he want?"

"He said I had to pay the triad now. He said my father was gone and I had to pay now. He said he would come back in one week and I had to pay."

"Did he say anything about your father's murder?"

"He just said that he was gone and now I had to pay."

"Did he say what would happen if you didn't pay?"

"He didn't have to."

Bosch nodded. Li was right. The threat was implicit, especially after what had happened to Li's father. Bosch was excited. Chang's coming to Robert Li widened the possibilities. He was attempting to extort Li and that could lead to an arrest that could ultimately lead to a murder charge.

Harry turned to Lam.

"And you witnessed this—everything that was said?"

Lam was clearly hesitant but then nodded. Bosch thought that maybe he was reluctant to be involved.

"You did or you didn't, Eugene? You just told me you were here."

Lam nodded again before responding.

"Yes, I saw the man, but . . . I don't speak Chinese. I understand a little bit but not that much."

Bosch turned to Li.

"He spoke to you in Chinese?"

Li nodded.

"Yes."

"But you understood him and it was clear he was telling you that you had to start making weekly payments now that your father is gone."

"Yes, that was clear. But..."

"But what?"

"Are you going to arrest this man? Will I have to appear in court?"

He was clearly scared of the possibility.

"Look, it's too early to tell whether this ever even leaves this room. We don't want the guy for extortion. If he killed your father, that's what we want him for. And I am sure you will do what you need to do to help us put your father's killer away."

Li nodded but Bosch could still see the hesitation. Considering what had happened to his father, Robert clearly didn't want to cross Chang or the triad.

"I need to make a quick call to my partner," Bosch said. "I'm going to step out and make it, then I'll be back in here."

Bosch left the office and closed the door. He called Chu.

"You got him?"

"Yes, he's heading back to the freeway. What happened?"

"He told Li he had to start making the payments his father had been making. To the triad."

"Holy shit! We've got our case!"

"Don't get too excited. A case of extortion maybe—and that's only if the kid cooperates. We're still a long way from a murder charge."

Chu didn't respond and Bosch suddenly felt bad about raining on his excitement.

"But you're right," he said. "We're getting closer. Which way is he headed?"

"He's in the right lane for the southbound one oh one. It looks like he's in a hurry. He's tailgating the guy in front of him but it's not doing him any good."

It looked like Chang was heading back the way he had come.

"Okay. I'm going to talk to these guys a little longer and then I'll clear. Call me when Chang stops somewhere."

"'These guys'? Who else besides Robert Li?"

"His assistant manager. Eugene Lam. He was in the office when Chang came in and told Li how things were going to be. Only, Chang was speaking Chinese and Lam only knows English. He won't be a good witness other than to place Chang in the store's office."

"Okay, Harry," Chu said. "We're on the freeway now."

"Stay with him and I'll call you as soon as I clear," Bosch said.

Bosch closed the phone and went back into the office. Li and Lam were still at their desks, waiting for him.

"Do you have video surveillance in the store?" he asked first.

"Yes," Li said. "Same system we have in the south end store. Only we have more cameras in this location. It records in multiplex. Eight screens at once."

Bosch looked up at the ceiling and the upper walls.

"There is no camera in here, right?"

"No, Detective," Li said. "Not in the office."

"Well, I'm still going to need the disc so we can prove Chang came back here to see you."

Li nodded hesitantly, like a boy being pulled onto the dance floor by somebody he didn't want to dance with.

"Eugene, would you go get the disc for Detective Bosch?" he said.

"No," Bosch said quickly. "I need to witness you pulling the disc. Chain of evidence and custody. I'll go with you."

"No problem."

Bosch spent another fifteen minutes in the store. He first watched the playback of the surveillance video and confirmed that Chang had come in and made his way back to Li's office, then left after three minutes off camera with Li and Lam. He then collected the disc and returned to the office to go over Li's account of what happened with Chang one more time. Li's reluctance seemed to grow with Bosch's more detailed questioning. Harry began to believe that the murder victim's son would eventually refuse to cooperate with a prosecution. Still, there was another positive aspect to this latest development. Chang's attempted extortion could be used in other ways. It could provide probable cause. And with probable cause Bosch could arrest Chang and search his belongings for evidence in the murder, whether Li eventually cooperated with a prosecution or not.

As he walked out the store's automatic door, Bosch was excited. The case had new life. He pulled his phone and checked on the suspect.

"We're all the way back to his apartment," Chu said. "No stops. I think he might be in for the night."

"It's too early. It's not even dark."

"Well, all I can tell you is that he booked it home. He pulled the curtains closed, too."

"Okay. I'm heading that way."

"You mind picking me up a tofu dog on the way, Harry?"

"No, you're on your own there, Chu."

Chu laughed.

"Figures," he said.

Bosch closed the phone. Chu had obviously caught the case excitement, too.

15

Chang didn't come out of his apartment until nine Friday morning. And when he did, he was carrying something that immediately put Bosch on high alert.

A large suitcase.

Bosch phoned Chu to make sure he was awake. They had split the overnight surveillance into four-hour shifts, each man taking a sleeping stint in his car. Chu had the four-to-eight sleep shift but Bosch hadn't heard from him yet.

"You awake? Chang's making a move."

Chu still had sleep in his voice.

"Yeah, what move? You were supposed to call me at eight."

"He put a suitcase in his car. He's running. I think he was tipped."

"To us?"

"No, to buying shares of Microsoft. Don't play stupid."

"Harry, who would tip him?"

Chang got into the car and started backing out of his space in the apartment complex parking lot.

"That's a good goddamn question," Bosch said. "But if anybody has the answer it's you."

"Are you suggesting I tipped off the subject of a major investigation?"

Chu's voice carried the requisite outrage of the accused.

"I don't know what you did," Bosch said. "But you put our business out all over Monterey Park, so now it's who knows who could've tipped this guy. All I know right now is that it looks like he's splitting town."

"All over Monterey Park? Are you just making this shit up?"

Bosch followed the Mustang north out of the parking lot, staying a block back.

"You told me the other night that the third guy you showed Chang's photo to over there made the ID. Okay, so that's three guys and they all have partners and they all have roll calls and they all talk."

"Well, maybe this wouldn't have happened if we didn't tell Tao and Herrera to back off like we didn't trust them."

Bosch checked his mirror for Chu. He was trying not to let his anger distract him from the tail. They couldn't lose Chang now.

"Move up. We're heading to the ten. After he gets on, I want you to switch off with me and take the lead."

"Got it."

Chu's voice still held anger. Bosch didn't care. If Chang had been tipped to the investigation, then Harry would find out who had made the call and he would burn them to the ground, even if it was Chu.

Chang got on the westbound 10 Freeway and soon Chu

passed Bosch to take the lead. Bosch glanced over and saw Chu flip him the bird.

Bosch moved over a lane, dropped back and made a call to Lieutenant Gandle.

"Harry, what's up?"

"We've got problems."

"Tell me."

"The first one is that our guy put a suitcase in his trunk this morning and is on the ten heading toward the airport."

"Shit, what else?"

"It looks to me like he was tipped, maybe told to get out of town."

"Or maybe he was told all along to split after he clipped Li. Don't go off the deep end on that, Harry. Not until you know something for sure."

It annoyed Bosch that his own lieutenant wasn't backing him, but he could deal with it. If Chang had been tipped and somewhere along the line the cancer of corruption was in the investigation, Harry would find it. He was sure of that. He let it go for now and concentrated on the choices that involved Chang.

"Do we take Chang down?" he asked.

"You sure he's flying? Maybe he's making a delivery or something. How big's the suitcase?"

"Big. The kind you pack when you're not coming back."

Gandle sighed as he put on his plate yet another dilemma and decision to be made.

"Okay, let me talk to some people and I'll get back to you."

Bosch assumed that would be Captain Dodds and possibly someone in the district attorney's office.

"There is some good news, Lieutenant," he said.

"Holy shit, imagine that," Gandle exclaimed. "What good news?"

"Yesterday afternoon we tailed Chang to the other store. The one our victim's son runs in the Valley. He extorted him, told the kid he had to start paying now that his old man was gone."

"What, this is great! Why didn't you tell me this?"

"I just did."

"That gives us probable cause to arrest."

"To arrest but probably not prosecute. The kid is a reluctant witness. He would have to come in to make the case and I don't know if he'll hold up. And either way, it's not a murder charge. That's what we want."

"Well, at the very least, we could stop this guy from getting on a plane."

Bosch nodded as the beginning of a plan started to form.

"It's Friday. If we hold on to him and book him late in the day, he wouldn't get a hearing till Monday afternoon. That would give us at least seventy-two hours to pull a case together."

"With the extortion being the fallback position."

"Right."

Bosch was getting another call beeping in his ear and he assumed it was Chu. He asked Gandle to get back to him as soon as he had run the scenario by the powers that be.

Bosch took the other call without looking at the screen.

"Yeah?"

"Harry?"

It was a woman. He recognized the voice but couldn't place it.

"Yeah, who's this?"

"Teri Sopp."

"Oh, hi, I thought it was my partner calling. What's up?"

"I just wanted you to know I convinced them to use the casing you gave me yesterday in the testing program for electrostatic enhancement. We'll see if we can raise a print off it."

"Teri, you're my hero! Will that be today?"

"No, not today. We're not going back to that till next week. Probably Tuesday."

Bosch hated to ask for a favor when he had just been given a favor, but he felt he had no choice.

"Teri, is there any way it can be done Monday morning?"

"Monday? I don't think we'll get to the actual application un—"

"The reason is, we may have our suspect in jail before the end of the day. We think he's trying to leave the country and we might need to arrest him. That will give us till Monday to make the case, Teri. We're going to need everything we can get."

There was a hesitation before she responded.

"I'll see what we can do. Meantime, if you arrest him, bring me down a print card so I can make the comparison as soon as I have something on this end. If I have something."

"You got it, Teri. Thanks a million."

Bosch closed his phone and searched the freeway in front of him. He saw neither Chu's car—a red Mazda

Miata — nor Chang's silver Mustang. He realized he had fallen far behind. He hit Chu on speed dial.

"Chu, where are you?"

"South four oh five. He's going to the airport."

Bosch was still on the 10 Freeway and saw the 405 interchange up ahead.

"Okay, I'll catch up."

"What's happening?"

"I've got Gandle making the call on whether we take Chang down or not."

"We can't let him go."

"That's what I say. We'll see what they say."

"You want me to get my boss involved?"

Bosch almost responded by saying he didn't want to bring another boss into the mix with the possibility that there was a leak in the pipe somewhere.

"Let's wait and see what Gandle says first," he said diplomatically instead.

"You got it."

Bosch hung up and worked his way through traffic in an effort to catch up. When he was on the overpass that took him from the 10 to the 405, he was able to pick out both Chu's and Chang's vehicles half a mile ahead. They were caught in the slowdown where lanes merged.

Switching off lead two more times, Bosch and Chu followed Chang to the LAX exit at Century Boulevard. It was now clear that Chang was leaving the city and they were going to have to stop him. He called Gandle back and was put on hold.

Finally, after a long two minutes Gandle picked up.

"Harry, whadaya got?"

"He's on Century Boulevard four blocks from LAX."

"I haven't been able to talk to anybody yet."

"I say we take him down. We book him for murder and worst-case scenario is on Monday we file on him for extortion. He'll get bail but the judge will slap no travel on it, especially after him trying to leave today."

"Your call, Harry, and I'll back you."

Meaning it would still be Bosch who had made the wrong call if by Monday everything fell apart and Chang waltzed out of jail a free man able to leave L.A. and never come back.

"Thanks, Lieutenant. I'll let you know."

Moments after Bosch closed his phone Chang turned right into a long-term parking lot that provided a shuttle service to all airport terminals. As expected, Chu called.

"This is it. What do we do?"

"We take him. We wait till he parks and he has that suitcase out of the trunk. We take him down then and we'll get a look in the suitcase with a warrant."

"Where?"

"I use this lot when I go to Hong Kong. There are endless rows and shuttle stations where they come pick you up. Let's get in there and park. We act like we're travelers and we get him at the shuttle station."

"Roger that."

They hung up. Bosch was in the lead at the moment, so he entered the lot directly behind Chang, taking a ticket out of an automatic feeder. The arm rose and he pulled through. He followed Chang down the main parkway and when Chang turned right into a tributary road Bosch kept going, thinking Chu would follow and take the right.

Bosch parked in the first space he saw, then jumped out and doubled back on foot to where Chang and Chu had turned. He saw Chang one lane over, standing behind the Mustang and struggling to pull his big suitcase out of the trunk. Chu was eight cars past him and parked.

Apparently realizing he would look suspicious without luggage in a long-term lot, Chu started walking toward a nearby shuttle stop, carrying a briefcase and a raincoat like a man on a business trip.

Bosch had no props to disguise himself with, so he moved down the center of the parking rows, using the vehicles as cover.

Chang locked his car and lugged the heavy suitcase to the shuttle stop. It was an old piece of luggage without the wheels that are almost standard on all sizes these days. When he got to the shuttle stop, Chu was already standing there. Bosch cut behind a minivan and came out two cars away. This would give Chang little time to recognize that the approaching man should have luggage in the long-term lot.

"Bo-Jing Chang," Bosch said loudly as he got close.

The suspect jerked his body around to look at Bosch. Up close, Chang looked strong and wide, formidable. Bosch saw his muscles tense.

"You're under arrest. Please place your hands behind your back."

Chang's fight-or-flight response never had a chance to kick in. Chu stepped behind him and expertly clipped one cuff to his right wrist while grabbing hold of the left wrist. Chang struggled for a moment, more in response to the surprise than anything else, but Chu cuffed the other wrist and the arrest was complete.

"What is this?" Chang protested. "What I do?"

He had a strong accent.

"We're going to talk about all of that, Mr. Chang. Just as soon as we get you back to the Police Administration Building."

"I have flight."

"Not today."

Bosch showed him his badge and ID, and then introduced Chu, making sure to mention that Chu was from the Asian Gang Unit. Bosch wanted to get that percolating in Chang's head.

"Arrest for what?" the suspect asked.

"The murder of John Li."

Bosch saw no surprise in Chang's reaction. He saw him physically go into shut-down mode.

"I want lawyer," he said.

"Hold on there, Mr. Chang," Bosch said. "Let us tell you about your rights first."

Bosch nodded to Chu, who produced a card from his pocket. He read Chang his rights and asked if he understood them. Chang's only response was to ask for a lawyer again. He knew the drill.

Bosch's next move was to call for a patrol unit to transfer Chang downtown, and a tow truck to take his car to the downtown police garage. Bosch was in no hurry at this point; the longer it took to transport Chang downtown, the closer they were to 2 P.M., the cutoff time in felony arraignment court. If they delayed Chang from getting into court, he could be secured as a guest of the city jail through the weekend.

After about five minutes of standing in silence while

Chang sat on a bench in the shuttle stop's shelter, Bosch turned and gestured to the suitcase and spoke to him conversationally, as if the questions and answers didn't matter.

"That thing looks like it weighs a ton," he said. "Where were you going?"

Chang said nothing. There was no such thing as small talk when you were under arrest. He stared straight forward and did not acknowledge Bosch's question in any way. Chu translated the question and got the same non-response.

Bosch shrugged his shoulders like it didn't matter much to him whether Chang answered or not.

"Harry," Chu said.

Bosch felt his phone vibrate twice, the signal that he had received a message. He signaled him a few yards away from the shelter so they could talk without Chang hearing.

"What do you think?" Chu asked.

"Well, it's clear he isn't going to talk to us and has asked for a lawyer. So that's that."

"So what do we do?"

"First of all, we slow things down. We take our time getting him downtown and then we take our time booking him. He doesn't call his lawyer till he's been processed and with any luck that won't be till after two. Meantime, we get warrants. His car, suitcase and his cell phone, if he has it on him. After that, we hit his apartment and his place of work. Wherever the judge lets us go. And we hope like hell we come up with something like the gun by noon Monday. Because if we don't, he's probably going to walk."

"What about the extortion?"

"It gives us PC but it won't go anywhere if Robert Li doesn't step up."

Chu nodded.

"*High Noon,* Harry. That was a movie. A western."

"I never saw it," he said to Chu.

Bosch looked down the long row of parked cars and saw a patrol car make the turn toward them. He waved.

He pulled his phone to check the message. The screen said he had received a video from his daughter.

He would have to check it later. It was very late in Hong Kong and he knew his daughter should be in bed. She was probably unable to sleep and expecting him to respond. But he had work to do. He put the phone away as the patrol car stopped in front of them.

"I'm going to ride in with him," he said to Chu. "In case he decides to say something."

"What about your car?"

"I'll get it later."

"Maybe I should ride with him instead."

Bosch looked at Chu. It was one of those moments. Harry knew it would be better for Chu to make the ride with Chang because he knew both languages and he was Chinese. But it would mean Bosch would be ceding some control of his case.

It would also mean he was showing trust in Chu, just an hour after pointing the finger of blame at him.

"Okay," Bosch finally said. "You ride with him."

Chu nodded, seeming to understand the significance of Bosch's decision.

"But take the long way," Bosch said. "These guys

probably work out of Pacific. Go by the division first, then call me. I'll tell you there's a change of plans and we're going to book him downtown. That ought to add an extra hour to the ride."

"Got it," Chu said. "That'll work."

"You want me to drive your car in?" Bosch asked. "I don't mind leaving mine here."

"No, it's okay, Harry. I'll leave mine and come get it later. You wouldn't want to hear what I've got on the stereo, anyway."

"The musical equivalent of tofu hot dogs?"

"To you, probably, yeah."

"Okay, then I'll take mine."

Bosch told the two patrol officers to put Chang in the back of the patrol car and to load the suitcase into the trunk. Harry then got serious with Chu.

"I'm going to put Ferras to work on search warrants for Chang's property. Any admission from him will help with the PC. Him telling us he had a flight is an admission that goes to his fleeing. Try to make him slip up like that when you're riding in the back with him."

"But he already said he wants a lawyer."

"Make it conversational. Not an interrogation. Try to find out where he was going. That'll help Ignacio. And remember, stretch everything out. Take the scenic route."

"Got it. I know what to do."

"Okay, I'm going to wait here for the tow truck. If you get to the PAB ahead of me, just put Chang in a room and let him stew. Make sure you turn the video on—Ignacio can show you how. You never know, sometimes these guys sit for an hour in a room by themselves and they start confessing to the walls."

"Got it."

"Good luck."

Chu slipped into the back of the patrol car next to Chang and closed the door. Bosch slapped his palm twice on the roof and then watched the cruiser pull away.

16

It was almost one by the time Bosch got back to the squad room. He had waited for the tow truck and then taken his time coming in, stopping at the In-N-Out near the airport for a hamburger on the way. He found Ignacio Ferras in place in his cubicle, working on his computer.

"Where are we at?" he asked.

"I'm almost done with the search warrant app."

"What are we going for?"

"I have one affidavit going for the suitcase, the phone and the car. I take it that the car is at the OPG?"

"Just towed it in. What about his apartment?"

"I called the DA's help line and told the woman what we were doing. She suggested two waves. These three first and then we hopefully come up with something that will give us the PC for the apartment. She said the apartment was a stretch with what we have now."

"Okay, you got a judge waiting on this?"

"Yeah, I called Judge Champagne's clerk. She's getting me in as soon as I'm ready."

It sounded like Ferras had things in order and moving along. Bosch was impressed.

"Sounds good. Where's Chu?"

"Last I knew he was in the video room, watching the guy."

Before joining Chu, Bosch stepped into his cubicle and dropped his keys on his desk. He saw that Chu had left Chang's heavy suitcase there and had bagged the suspect's other possessions and left them all on the desk. There were evidence bags holding Chang's wallet, passport, money clip, keys, cell phone and airline boarding pass, which he had apparently printed at home.

Bosch read the boarding pass through the plastic and saw that Chang had an Alaska Airlines ticket for a flight to Seattle. This gave Harry pause because he was expecting to learn that Chang had been headed to China. Flying to Seattle didn't exactly sell an allegation of attempting to flee the country to avoid prosecution.

He put the bag back down and picked up the bag containing the phone. It would have been easy for him to quickly open the phone and scan the call log for the numbers of Chang's associates. He might even find a call from a number belonging to a Monterey Park cop or Chu or whoever had tipped Chang off to the investigation surrounding him. Maybe the phone had e-mail or texts on it that would help them build the murder case against Chang.

But Bosch decided to play by the rules. It was a gray area and the department and DA's office had both issued directives telling officers to seek court approval before viewing data contained in a suspect's phone. Unless, of course, permission was granted by the suspect. Opening the phone was treated the same as opening the trunk of a car on a traffic stop. You had to do it correctly or whatever you found in that trunk might be taken out of the case by the courts.

Bosch put the phone down. It might contain the key to the case but he would wait for Judge Champagne's approval. Just as he did so, the phone on his desk buzzed. The caller ID display said XXXXX, meaning it was a call transferred over from Parker Center. He picked up.

"This is Bosch."

There was no one there.

"Hello. This is Detective Bosch, can I help you?"

"Bosch . . . you can help yourself."

The voice was distinctly Asian.

"Who is this?"

"You do yourself the favor and you back off, Bosch. Chang is not alone. We are many. You back the fuck off. If not, there will be consequences."

"Listen to me, you—"

The caller had hung up. Bosch dropped the phone into its cradle and stared at the empty ID screen. He knew he could go over to the communications center at Parker and pull up the number the call had come from. But he also knew that someone calling to threaten him would have blocked their number, used a pay phone or a throwaway cell. They would not be so stupid as to use a traceable number.

Instead of worrying about that, he concentrated on the timing of the call and its content. Somehow, Chang's triad associates knew already that he had been picked up. Bosch rechecked the boarding pass and saw the flight was scheduled to take off at eleven-twenty. That meant the plane was still in the air and it couldn't be that someone waiting in Seattle for Chang would know he wasn't on the plane. Nevertheless, Chang's people somehow knew that he was in the hands of the police. They also knew Bosch by name.

Once again dark thoughts entered Bosch's brain. Unless Chang was meeting a fellow traveler at LAX or was being watched all the while Bosch was watching him, the evidence once more pointed to a leak inside the investigation.

He left the cubicle and walked directly back to the video center. This was a small electronics alcove between the RHD's two interview rooms. The IRs were wired for sight and sound and the space in the middle was where suspects could be observed on the recording equipment.

Bosch opened the door and found both Chu and Gandle in the room watching Chang on the monitor. Bosch's entrance made it crowded.

"Anything?" Bosch asked.

"Not a word so far," Gandle said.

"What about in the car?"

"Nothing," Chu said. "I tried to get a conversation going and he just said he wanted a lawyer. That killed it."

"Guy's a rock," Gandle said.

"I looked at his plane ticket," Bosch said. "Seattle doesn't help us, either."

"No, I think it does, actually," Chu said.

"How?"

"I figured he was going to fly to Seattle and go across the border to Vancouver. I have a contact in the RCMP and he was able to check passenger lists for me. Chang's booked on a flight tonight from Vancouver to Hong Kong. Cathay Pacific Airways. It clearly shows he tried to leave quickly and deceptively."

Bosch nodded.

"Royal Canadian Mounted Police? You get around, Chu. Nice work."

"Thanks."

"Did you tell this to Ignacio? Chang's attempt to smoke his trail will help with the PC for the search warrant."

"He knows. He put it in."

"Good."

Bosch looked at the monitor. Chang was sitting at a table with his wrists now handcuffed in front of him to an iron ring bolted through the center of the table. His massive shoulders looked ready to burst the seams of his shirt. He was sitting ramrod straight and staring dead-eyed at the wall directly across from him.

"Lieutenant, how long are you comfortable with us stalling this before we book him?"

Gandle looked concerned. He didn't like being put on the spot with something that could later hit him in the face with blowback.

"Well, I think we're stretching it. Chu told me you already gave him the scenic tour coming in. You wait too much longer and a judge might take issue with it."

Bosch looked at his watch. They needed another fifty minutes before allowing Chang to call his lawyer. The booking process involved paperwork, fingerprinting and then the physical transfer of the suspect to jail, at which point he would be given access to a phone.

"Okay, we can start the process. We just keep taking it slow. Chu, you go in and start filling out the sheet with him. If we're lucky he won't cooperate and that will just take up more time."

Chu nodded.

"Got it."

"We don't put him into a cell until two at the earliest."

"Right."

Chu squeezed between the lieutenant and Bosch and left the room. Gandle started out after him but Bosch tapped him on the shoulder and signaled him to stay. Bosch waited until the door was closed before speaking.

"I just got a phone call. A threat. Somebody told me to back off."

"Back off what?"

"The case. Chang. Back off everything."

"How do you know the call was even about this case?"

"Because the caller was Asian and he mentioned Chang. Said Chang was not alone, that I needed to back off or there would be consequences."

"You try to trace it? You think it's serious?"

"A trace would be a waste of time. And as far as the threat goes, let them come. I'll be waiting. But the point is, how did they know?"

"Know what?"

"That we picked up Chang. We pull him in and then within two hours one of his asshole buddies from the triad calls up and tells me to back the fuck off. We've got a leak, Lieutenant. First Chang is tipped, now they know we grabbed him. Somebody's talking to—"

"Whoa, whoa, whoa, we don't know that, Harry. There could be explanations."

"Yeah? Then how do they know we have Chang?"

"Could be a lot of reasons, Harry. He had a cell phone. Maybe he was supposed to check in from the airport. Could be anything."

Bosch shook his head. His instincts told him otherwise. There was a leak somewhere. Gandle opened the door. He didn't like this conversation and wanted to get out of the room. But he looked back at Bosch before leaving.

"You better be careful with this," he said. "Until you have something like this nailed down, you be very careful."

Gandle closed the door behind him, leaving Bosch alone in the room. Harry turned to the video screen and saw that Chu had entered the interview room. He sat down across from Chang with a pen and clipboard, ready to fill out the arrest form.

"Mr. Chang, I need to ask you some questions now."

Chang did not answer. He showed no recognition in his eyes or body language that he had even heard the question.

Chu followed this with a Chinese translation but again Chang remained mute and motionless. This was no surprise to Bosch. He left the interview room and went back out to the squad, still feeling anxious and upset about the phone-call threat and Gandle's seeming lack of concern about it or the leak that had to have spawned it.

Ferras's cubicle was empty now and Bosch assumed he

had already left with the search warrant application for his appointment with Judge Champagne.

Everything was riding on the search warrant. They had Chang on the attempted extortion of Robert Li—if Li agreed to file a complaint and testify—but weren't even close on the murder. Bosch was left hoping for a daisy chain. The first search warrant would yield evidence that would support further search warrants and they would lead to the grand prize—the murder weapon—hidden somewhere in Chang's apartment or workplace.

He sat down at his desk and thought about calling Ferras to see if the judge had signed the warrant, but he knew it was too soon and that Ferras would call the minute he got the permission for the searches. He pushed the heels of his palms into his eyes. Everything about the case was on hold until the judge signed. All he could do was wait.

But then he remembered he had gotten the video message from his daughter earlier and had not looked at it. He knew his daughter would be long asleep by now—it was after 4 A.M. Saturday in Hong Kong. Unless she was at a sleepover with friends, in which case she might be up all night but wouldn't want her father calling in, anyway.

He pulled out his phone and opened it. He was still getting used to all the techno bells and whistles on it. On the last day of his daughter's most recent visit to L.A. they had gone to the phone store and she had selected his-and-her cells, choosing a model that would allow them to communicate on multiple levels. He didn't use it much for e-mail but he knew how to open and play the thirty-second videos she liked to send. He saved them all and often played them over again.

Bo-Jing Chang temporarily faded away. Concern about the leak receded. Bosch had a smile of anticipation on his face when he pushed the button and opened her latest video message.

17

Bosch stepped into the interview room and left the door open. Chu was in midquestion but stopped and looked up at the intrusion.

"Is he not answering?" Bosch asked.

"Won't say a word."

"Let me give it a try."

"Uh, sure, Harry."

He stood up and Bosch moved to the side so he could leave the room. He handed Bosch the clipboard.

"Good luck, Harry."

"Thanks."

Chu left, closing the door behind him. Bosch waited a moment until he was sure he was gone, then moved swiftly around behind Chang. He slammed the clipboard off his head and then grabbed him around the neck with his arms. His rage grew uncontrolled. He locked his arms tightly in the choke hold long outlawed by the department. He felt Chang tense as he realized his air intake had been cut.

"Okay, motherfucker, the camera's off and we're in

a soundproof room. Where is she? I will kill you right here if—"

Chang reared up from his seat, pulling the anchor bolt of the cuff ring right through the top of the table. He smashed Bosch back against the wall behind them and together they fell to the floor. Bosch kept his grip and cinched it even tighter. Chang fought like an animal, using his feet against one of the anchored legs of the table as leverage and he repeatedly smashed Bosch back into the corner of the room.

"Where is she?" Bosch yelled.

Chang was making grunting sounds but showing no sign of losing power. His wrists were cuffed together but he was still able to swing his arms together back over his head like a club. He was going for Bosch's face at the same time he was using his body to crush Harry into the corner.

Bosch realized that the choke hold wasn't going to work and that he had to release and attack. He let go and caught Chang's wrist on one of his backward swings. He shifted his weight and turned the blow to the side. Chang's shoulders turned with the shift in momentum and Bosch was able to get on top of him on the floor. Bosch raised his hands together and brought down a hammer blow on the back of Chang's neck.

"I said, Where is—"

"Harry!"

The voice came from behind him. It was Chu's.

"Hey!" Chu yelled into the squad room. *"Help!"*

The distraction allowed Chang to rise up and get his knees under his body. He then pushed up and Bosch was thrown into the wall and then down to the floor. Chu jumped on Chang's back and was trying to wrestle him to the ground. There were running steps and soon more men squeezed into the tiny room. They piled onto Chang, roughly pinning him to the floor with his face smashed into the corner. Bosch rolled away, trying to catch his breath.

For a moment everyone was silent and the room filled with the sounds of all of the men gasping for breath. Lieutenant Gandle then appeared in the open doorway.

"What the hell happened?"

He leaned forward to look down through the hole in the top of the table. The bolt had obviously not been properly reinforced underneath. One of many kinks that were sure to surface in the new building.

"I don't know," Chu said. "I came back to get my jacket and all hell was breaking loose."

All eyes in the room turned to Bosch.

"They've got my daughter," he said.

18

Bosch stood in Gandle's office. Not still. He couldn't stand still. He paced back and forth in front of the desk. The lieutenant had told him twice to sit down but Bosch couldn't do it. Not with the terror growing inside his chest.

"What's this about, Harry?"

Bosch pulled his phone and opened it.

"They have her."

He pushed the play command on the video program, then handed the phone to Gandle, who had sat down behind his desk.

"What do you mean, 'They have—'"

He stopped as he watched the video.

"Oh, Jesus...Oh, Je—Harry, how do you know this is real?"

"What are you talking about? It's real. *They have her and that guy knows who and where!*"

He pointed in the direction of the interview room. He was pacing more quickly now, like a caged tiger.

"How do you do this? I want to see it again."

Bosch grabbed the phone and restarted the video.

"I need to get in there with him again," Bosch said as Gandle watched. "I need to make him tell—"

"You're not going anywhere near him," Gandle said without looking up. "Harry, where is she, Hong Kong?"

"Yes, Hong Kong, and that's where he was going. It's where he's from and it's where the triad he's in is based. On top of that, they called me. I told you. They said there were consequences if—"

"She doesn't say anything here. Nobody says anything. How do you know it's Chang's people?"

"It's the triad! They don't have to say anything! The video says it all. They have her. That's the message!"

"Okay, okay, let's think this through. They have her and what's the message? What are you supposed to do?"

"Let Chang go."

"What do you mean, let him just walk out of here?"

"I don't know. Yeah, kick the case somehow. Lose the evidence or, better yet, stop looking for the evidence. Right now, we don't have enough to hold him past Monday. That's what they want, for him to walk. Look, I can't just stand in here. I have to—"

"We have to get this to forensics. That's the first thing. Have you called your ex to see what she knows?"

Bosch realized that in his immediate panic upon seeing the video, he had not called his ex-wife, Eleanor Wish. He had first tried to call his daughter. Then when he got no answer he had immediately gone to confront Chang.

"You're right. Give me that."

"Harry, it's got to go to forens—"

Bosch leaned across the desk and grabbed the phone out of Gandle's hand. He switched over to the phone program and hit a speed dial for Eleanor Wish. He checked his watch while he waited for the call to go through. It was almost 5 A.M. Saturday in Hong Kong. He didn't understand why he wouldn't have already heard from Eleanor if their daughter was missing.

"Harry?"

The voice was alert. She had not been dragged from sleep.

"Eleanor, what's going on? Where's Madeline?"

He walked out of Gandle's office and headed toward his cubicle.

"I don't know. She hasn't called me and doesn't answer my calls. How do you know what's going on?"

"I don't but I got a...a message from her. Tell me what you know."

"Well, what did her message say?"

"It didn't say anything. It was a video. Look, just tell me what's going on there."

"She didn't come home from the mall after school. It was Friday, so I let her go with her friends. She usually checks in about six and asks for more time, but this time she didn't. Then when she didn't come home I called and she wouldn't answer my call. I left her a bunch of messages and I got really angry. You know her, she probably got angry back and she didn't come home. I've called her friends and they all claim not to know where she is."

"Eleanor, it's after five in the morning there. Did you call the police?"

"Harry..."

"What?"

"She did this once before."

"What are you talking about?"

Bosch dropped heavily into the seat at his desk and huddled down, holding the phone tight against his ear.

"She stayed with a friend all night to 'teach me a lesson,'" Eleanor said. "I called the police then and it was all very embarrassing because they found her at her friend's. I'm sorry I didn't tell you. But she and I have been having problems. She's at that age, you know? She acts much older than she really is. And it seems like she doesn't like me very much right now. She talks about wanting to live in L.A. with you. She—"

Bosch cut her off.

"Listen, Eleanor, I understand all of that but this is different. Something's happened."

"What do you mean?"

Panic flooded her voice. Bosch recognized his own fear in it. He was reluctant to tell her about the video but felt he now had to. She needed to know. He described the thirty seconds of video, leaving nothing out. Eleanor made a high-pitched keening sound that only a mother could make for a lost daughter.

"Oh my God, oh my God."

"I know, but we're going to get her back, Eleanor. I—"

"Why did they send it to you and not me?"

He could tell she was starting to cry. She was losing it. He didn't answer her question because he knew it would only make it worse.

"Listen to me, Eleanor, we need to keep it together. You have to do this for her. You're there, I'm not."

"What do they want, money?"

"No . . ."

"Then, what?"

Bosch tried to speak calmly, hoping it would be contagious over the phone when the impact of his words came through.

"I think it's a message to me, Eleanor. They're not asking for money. They're just telling me that they have her."

"You? Why? What do they — Harry, what did you do?"

She said the last question in a tone of accusation. Bosch feared it was a question he might be impaled on for the rest of his life.

"I'm on a case involving a Chinese triad. I think —"

"They took her to get to you? How did they even know about her?"

"I don't know yet, Eleanor. I'm working on it. We have a suspect in cust—"

Again she cut him off, this time with another wail. It was the sound of every parent's worst nightmare come to life. In that moment Bosch realized what he was going to do. He lowered his voice further when he spoke.

"Eleanor, listen to me. I need you to pull yourself together. You need to start making calls. I'm coming over. I'll be there before dawn Sunday morning. In the meantime, you have to get to her friends. You have to find out who she was with at the mall and where she went. Anything you can find out about what happened. Do you hear me, Eleanor?"

"I'm hanging up and calling the police."

"No!"

Bosch looked around and saw that his outburst had drawn attention from across the squad room. After the incident in the interview room, he was already the subject of concern across the whole squad. He slid further down into his seat and crouched over his desk so no one could see him.

"What? Harry, we have to—"

"Listen to me first and then you do what you think you need to do. I don't think you should call the police. Not yet. We can't take the chance that the people who have her will know. We might never get her back then."

She didn't respond. Bosch could hear her crying.

"Eleanor? Listen to me! Do you want to get her back or not? Get your shit together. You were an FBI agent! You can do this. I need you to work it like an agent until I get there. I'm going to have the video analyzed. In the video, she kicked at the camera and it moved. I saw a window. They might be able to work with it. I'm taking a plane tonight and will come directly to you when I land. You have all of that?"

There was a long moment before Eleanor responded. When she did, her voice was calm. She had gotten the message.

"I have it, Harry. I still think we have to call the Hong Kong police."

"If that's what you think, then, fine. Do it. Do you know anybody there? Anybody you can trust?"

"No, but they have a Triad Bureau. They've come into the casino."

Almost twenty years removed from her time as an agent, Eleanor was a professional card player. For at least six years she had been living in Hong Kong and working for the Cleopatra Casino in nearby Macau. All the high rollers from the mainland wanted to play against the *gweipo*—the white woman. She was a draw. She played with house money, got a cut of the winnings and no part of the losses. It was a comfortable life. She and Maddie lived in a high-rise in Happy Valley and the casino sent a helicopter to pick her up on the roof when it was time to go to work.

Comfortable until now.

"Talk to your people at the casino," Bosch said. "If there is someone you are told you can trust, then make the call. I need to hang up and get moving here. You'll hear from me before I fly."

She answered as if in a daze.

"Okay, Harry."

"If you come up with something, anything at all, you call me."

"Okay, Harry."

"And Eleanor?"

"What?"

"See if you can get me a gun. I can't take my own over."

"They put you in prison for guns over here."

"I know that, but you know people from the casino. Get me a gun."

"I'll try."

Bosch hesitated before hanging up. He wished he could reach out and touch her, somehow try to calm her fears. But he knew that was impossible. He couldn't even calm his own.

"All right, I'm going to go. Try to stay calm, Eleanor. For Maddie. We stay calm and we can do this."

"We're going to get her back, right, Harry?"

Bosch nodded to himself before answering.

"That's right. We're going to get her back."

19

The digital image unit was one of the subgroups of the Scientific Investigation Division and was still located at the old police headquarters at Parker Center. Bosch traversed the two blocks between the old and new buildings like a man running late for a plane. By the time he pushed through the glass doors of the building where he had spent much of his career as a detective he was huffing and there was a shine of sweat on his forehead. He badged his way past the front desk and took the elevator up to the third floor.

SID was in the process of being readied for the move to the PAB. The old desks and work counters remained in place but the equipment, records and personal effects were being boxed up. The process was carefully orchestrated and was slowing the already plodding march of science in crime fighting.

DIU was a two-room suite in the back. Bosch stepped in and saw at least a dozen cardboard boxes in stacks on one side of the first room. There were no pictures or maps on the walls and a lot of the shelves were empty. He found one tech at work in the rear lab.

Barbara Starkey was a veteran who had jumped around among specialties in SID over nearly four decades in the department. Bosch had met her when he was a rookie cop on post guarding the burned-out remains of a house where police had engaged in a major gun battle with members of the Symbionese Liberation Army. The militant radicals had taken credit for the kidnapping of newspaper heiress Patty Hearst. Starkey at the time was on the forensics team brought in to determine if the remains of Patty Hearst were amid the debris in the smoking shell of the house. Back then the department had a practice of moving female applicants into positions where physical confrontations and the need to carry a weapon were minimal. Starkey had wanted to be a cop. She ended up in the SID and as such had seen firsthand the explosive growth of technology in the use of crime detection. As she liked to tell the rookie techs, when she started in forensics, DNA were just three letters in the alphabet. Now she was an expert in almost all areas of forensics, and her son, Michael, was in the division as well, working as a blood spatter expert.

Starkey looked up from a twin-screen computer workstation where she was looking at grainy video from a bank robbery. On the screens were double images—one more in focus than the other—of a man pointing a gun at a teller's window.

"Harry Bosch! The man with the plan."

Bosch had no time for banter. He approached and got right to the point.

"Barb, I need your help."

Starkey frowned when she noted the urgency in his voice.

"What's up, darling?"

Bosch held his phone up.

"I've got a video on my phone. I need to blow it up and slow it down to see if I can identify location. It's an abduction."

Gesturing toward her screen, Starkey said, "I'm right in the middle of this two eleven in West—"

"My daughter's on it, Barbara. I need your help now."

This time Starkey didn't hesitate.

"Let me see it."

Bosch opened the phone and started the video, then handed it to her. She viewed it wordlessly and kept any other nonprofessional response out of her face. If anything, Bosch saw her posture straighten and an aura of professional urgency emerge.

"Okay, can you send this to me?"

"I don't know. I know how to send it to your phone."

"Can't you send e-mail on here with an attachment?"

"I can send e-mail but I don't know about an attachment. I've never tried."

Starkey walked him through it and he sent Starkey an e-mail with the video as an attachment.

"Okay, now we wait for it to come in."

Before Bosch could ask how long that would be, there was a chime from her computer.

"There it is."

Starkey closed her work on the bank robbery, then opened her e-mail and downloaded the video. Soon she had it playing on the left screen. In full-screen size the image was blurred by the pixel spread. Starkey reduced it to half-screen size and it became clearer. Much clearer and harsher than when Bosch had seen the images on his phone. Harry looked at his daughter and tried hard to stay focused.

"I'm so sorry, Harry," Starkey said.

"I know. Let's not talk about it."

On the screen, Maddie Bosch, thirteen years old, sat tied to a chair. A gag made of bright red cloth cut tightly across her mouth. She wore her school uniform, a blue plaid skirt and white blouse with the school crest above the left breast. She looked at the camera—her own cell phone camera—with eyes that tore Bosch's heart out. *Desperate* and *scared* were only the first words of description that went through his mind.

There was no sound, or rather no one said anything at first on the video. For fifteen seconds the camera held on her and that was enough. She was simply on display for him. The rage came back to Bosch. And the helplessness.

Then the person behind the camera reached into the frame and pulled the gag temporarily loose from Maddie's mouth.

"Dad!"

The gag was immediately replaced, muffling what was yelled after that single word and leaving Bosch unable to interpret it.

The hand then dropped down in an attempt to fondle one of the girl's breasts. She reacted violently, shifting sideways in her bindings and kicking her left leg up at the outstretched arm. The video frame momentarily swung out of control and then was brought back to Maddie. She had fallen over in the chair. For the last five seconds of video the camera just held on her. The screen then went black.

"There's no demand," Starkey said. "They're just showing her."

"It's a message to me," Bosch said. "They're telling me to back off."

Starkey didn't respond at first. She put both her hands on an editing deck attached to the computer's keyboard. Bosch knew that by manipulating the dials, she was able to move the video forward and backward with precise control.

"Harry, I'm going to go through this frame by frame but it's going to take some time," she said. "You've got thirty seconds of video here."

"I can go through it with you."

"I think it would be better if you let me do my job and then I call you the moment I find anything. Trust me, Harry. I know she's your daughter."

Bosch nodded. He knew he had to let her work without breathing down her neck. It would bring the best results.

"Okay. Can we just take a look at the kick and then I'll leave you to it? I want to see if there's something there. He moved the camera when she kicked at him and there was a flash of light. Like a window."

Starkey rolled the video back to the moment Maddie had kicked at her captor. In real time the video at that point had been a blur of sudden movement and light followed by a quick correction back to the girl.

But now in stop-action of frame-by-frame playback, Bosch saw that the camera had momentarily swept left across a room to a window, and then back.

"You're good, Harry," Starkey said. "We may have something here."

Bosch bent down to look over her shoulder and get

closer. Starkey backed up the video and rolled it slowly forward again. Maddie's effort to kick at the outreached arm of her captor made the frame of the video go left and then jog down to the floor. It then came up on the window and corrected to the right again.

The room appeared to be a low-rent hotel room with a single bed and a table and lamp directly behind the chair Maddie was tied to. Bosch noted a dirty beige rug with a variety of stains on it. The wall over the bed was pock-marked with holes left by nails used to hold up wall hangings. The pictures or paintings had possibly been removed to make the location harder to identify.

Starkey backed the video up to the window and froze it there. It was a vertical window with a single pane that opened out like a door. There appeared to be no screen. It had been cranked open in full outward extension and in the glass was a reflection of an urban cityscape.

"Where do you think this is, Harry?"

"Hong Kong."

"Hong Kong?"

"She lives there with her mother."

"Well..."

"Well, what?"

"It's just going to make it harder for us to determine location. How well do you know Hong Kong?"

"I've been going twice a year for about six years. Just clean this up, if you can. Can you make that part bigger?"

Using the mouse, Starkey outlined the window and then moved a copy of that part of the video over to the second screen. She increased its size and then went through some focusing maneuvers.

"We don't have the pixels, Harry, but if I run a program that sort of fills in what we don't have, we can sort of sharpen it. Maybe you'll recognize something in the reflection."

Bosch nodded, even though he was behind her.

On the second screen, the reflection in the window became a sharper image with three different levels of depth. The first thing Bosch noted was that the location of the room was up high. The reflection showed a channel down a city street from at least ten stories up, he judged. He could see the sides of buildings lining the street and the edge of a large billboard or building sign with the English letters *N-O*. There was also a collage of street-level signs with Chinese characters. These were smaller and not as clear.

Beyond this reflection Bosch could see tall buildings in the distance. He recognized one of them by the two white spires on the roof. The twin radio antennas were braced by a crossbar and the configuration always reminded Bosch of football goalposts.

Outlining the buildings was the third level of reflection: a mountain ridgeline broken only by a structure that had a bowl shape supported by two thick columns.

"Is this helping, Harry?"

"Yeah, yeah, definitely. This has to be Kowloon. The reflection goes across the harbor to Central and then the mountain peak behind it. This building with the goalposts is the Bank of China. Very famous part of the skyline. And that is Victoria Peak behind it. That structure you see up on the top through the goalposts is like a lookout spot next to the peak tower up there. So to reflect all of this I'm pretty sure you'd have to be across the harbor in Kowloon."

"I've never been there, so none of this means anything to me."

"Central Hong Kong is actually an island. But there are other islands surrounding it and across the harbor is Kowloon and an area called the New Territories."

"Sounds too complicated for me. But if any of this helps you, then—"

"It helps a lot. Can you print this?"

He pointed to the second screen with the isolated view of the window.

"Sure thing. There's one thing that's sort of weird, though."

"What's that?"

"You see in the foreground this partial reflection of the sign?"

She used the cursor to put a box around the two letters *N* and *O* that were part of a larger sign and word in English.

"Yeah, what about it?"

"You have to remember, this is a reflection in the window. It's like a mirror, so everything is reverse. You understand?"

"Yeah."

"Okay, so all the signs should be backwards but these letters aren't backwards. Of course, with the *O* you can't tell. It's the same forward or backwards. But this *N* is not backwards, Harry. So when you remember this is a reverse reflection, then that means—"

"The sign is backwards?"

"Yes. It would have to be in order for it to show up correctly in a reflection."

Bosch nodded. She was right. It was strange but not something he had the time to dwell on at the moment. He knew it was time to get moving. He wanted to call Eleanor and tell her he thought their daughter was being held in Kowloon. Maybe it would connect with something on her end. It was a start at least.

"Can I get that copy?"

"I'm already printing it. It takes a couple minutes because it's a high-res printer."

"Got it."

Bosch stared at the image on the screen, looking for any other details that would help. Most notable was a partial reflection of the building his daughter was held in. A line of air-conditioning units protruded beneath the windows. That meant it was an older building and that might help him draw a bead on the place.

"Kowloon," Starkey said. "Sounds sort of ominous."

"My daughter told me it means 'Nine Dragons.'"

"See, I told you. Who would name their neighborhood Nine Dragons unless they wanted to scare people away?"

"It comes from a legend. During one of the old dynasties the emperor was supposedly just a boy who got chased by the Mongols into the area that is now Hong Kong. He saw the eight mountain peaks that surrounded it and wanted to call the place Eight Dragons. But one of the men who guarded him reminded him that the emperor was a dragon too. So they called it Nine Dragons. Kowloon."

"Your daughter told you this?"

"Yeah. She learned it in school."

Silence followed. Bosch could hear the printer working

somewhere behind him. Starkey got up and went behind a stack of boxes and pulled the printout of the window reflection out of the high-resolution graphics printer.

She handed it to Bosch. It was a glossy reprint on photo paper. It was as clear as the image on the computer screen.

"Thanks, Barbara."

"I'm not done, Harry. Like I said, I'm going to look at every frame of that video—thirty per second—and if there's something else that will help, I'll find it. I'll also take the audio track apart."

Bosch just nodded and looked down at the printout in his hand.

"You'll find her, Harry. I know you will."

"Yeah, me, too."

20

Bosch called his ex-wife on the speed dial while on the way back to the PAB. She answered the call with an urgent question.

"Harry, anything?"

"Not a lot but we're working on it. I am pretty sure the video I was sent was shot in Kowloon. Does that mean anything to you?"

"No. Kowloon? Why there?"

"I have no idea. But we may be able to find the place."

"You mean the police will?"

"No, I mean you and me, Eleanor. When I come. In fact, I still need to book my flight. Have you called anybody? What have you got?"

"I don't have anything!" she yelled, surprising Bosch. "My daughter is somewhere out there and I don't have anything! The police don't even believe me!"

"What are you talking about? You called them?"

"Yes, I called them. I can't sit here and just wait for you to show up tomorrow. I called the Triad Bureau."

Bosch felt his insides tighten. He couldn't bring himself

to trust strangers, experts though they might be, with his daughter's life.

"What did they say?"

"They put my name into the computer and got a hit. The police have a file on me. Who I am, who I work for. And they knew about the time before. When I thought she was kidnapped and it turned out she was staying at her friend's. So they didn't believe me. They think she ran away again and her friends are lying to me. They said to wait a day and call back if she doesn't show up."

"Did you tell them about the video?"

"I told them but they didn't care. They said if there is no ransom demand, then it was probably staged by her and her friends to get attention. They don't believe me!"

She started crying in frustration and fear but Bosch considered the police reaction and thought it could work in their favor.

"Eleanor, listen to me, I think this is good."

"Good? How could it be good? The police are not even looking for her."

"I told you before, I don't want the police. The people who have her will see the police coming a mile away. But they won't see me."

"This isn't L.A., Harry. You don't know your way like you do there."

"I'll find my way and you'll help me."

There was a long silence before she responded. Bosch was almost back to the PAB.

"Harry, you have to promise me you'll get her back."

"I will, Eleanor," he responded without hesitation. "I promise you. I'm going to get her back."

He walked into the main lobby, holding his jacket open so the badge on his belt could be seen at the fancy new reception counter.

"I gotta go up an elevator now," he said. "I'll probably lose the connection."

"Okay, Harry."

But he stopped outside the elevator alcove.

"I just thought of something," he said. "Was one of the friends you talked to named He?"

"He?"

"Yeah, *H-E*. Maddie said it means 'river.' She told me that was the name of one of the friends she hangs out with in the mall."

"When was this?"

"You mean when did she tell me? Just a few days ago. Must've been Thursday for you. Thursday morning when she was walking to school. I was talking to her and brought up the smoking you mentioned. She—"

Eleanor interrupted by making some kind of sound of disgust.

"What?" Bosch asked.

"That was why she's treated me like shit lately," she said. "You ratted me out."

"No, it wasn't like that. I sent her a photo I knew would bait her into calling me and the smoking would come up. It worked. And when I told her that she better not be smoking, she mentioned He. She said sometimes at the mall He's older brother hangs out to watch over her, and he's the one that smokes."

"I don't know any of her friends named He, or her

brother. I guess that shows how out of touch I am with my own daughter."

"Listen, Eleanor, at a time like this we're both going to be second-guessing everything we ever did or said to her. But it's a distraction from what we need to be focusing on now. Okay? Don't get distracted by what you did or didn't do. Let's focus on getting her back."

"Okay. I'll go back to her friends that I do know. I'll find out about He and her brother."

"Find out if the brother's got any connection to a triad."

"I'll try."

"I've gotta go, but one more thing. Did you find out about that other thing yet?"

Bosch nodded to a couple other RHD detectives who walked by on the way to the elevator. They were from Open-Unsolved, which had its own squad room, and didn't appear to look at him like they knew what was going on. This was good, Bosch thought. Maybe Gandle was keeping it under wraps.

"You mean the gun?" Eleanor asked.

"Yeah, that."

"Harry, it's not even dawn here. I'll get on that when I am not calling people in their beds."

"Right, okay."

"I will call people about He, though. Right now."

"Okay, good. Let's call each other if we get something."

"Good-bye, Harry."

Bosch closed his phone and went into the alcove. The other detectives were gone and he caught the next elevator. On the way up alone he looked at the phone in his hand and thought about it being the predawn hours in Hong Kong. It had been daylight on the video message that had been sent to him. That meant that his daughter could have been abducted as long as twelve hours ago.

There had not been a second message. He pushed the speed dial for her and once again the call went directly to the message. He ended the call and put the phone away.

"She's alive," he said to himself. "She's alive."

He managed to get to his cubicle in RHD without drawing any attention. There was no sign of Ferras or Chu. Bosch pulled an address book out of a drawer and opened it to a page where he listed airlines that flew LAX to Hong Kong. He knew there were choices in airlines but not a lot of play on time. All the flights would leave between 11 P.M. and 1 A.M. and they would land early Sunday morning. Between the fourteen-plus-hour flight and fifteen-hour time difference, all of Saturday would evaporate during the journey.

Bosch first called Cathay Pacific and was able to book a window seat on the first flight out. It would land at 5:25 Sunday morning.

"Harry?"

Bosch swiveled in his seat and saw Gandle standing in the entrance to the cubicle. Bosch signaled him to stand by and finished the call, writing down the record locator code for his ticket. He then hung up.

"Lieutenant, where is everybody?"

"Ferras is still at the courthouse and Chu's booking Chang."

"What's the charge?"

"We're going with murder as planned. But as of now we've got nothing to back it up."

"What about attempting to flee jurisdiction?"

"He added that, too."

Bosch checked the clock on the wall over the bulletin boards. It was two-thirty. With a murder charge and the additional count of attempting to flee, bail would automatically be set at two million dollars for Chang. Bosch knew that it was too late in the day for a lawyer to get him into arraignment court to seek a reduction in bail or to question the lack of evidence for the charge. With the court offices closed over the weekend it was also unlikely Chang would be released without someone putting up the two million in cash. Collateral for a bond could not be verified until Monday. It all added up to meaning that they had until Monday morning to put together the evidence that would make the murder charge stick.

"How'd Ferras do?"

"I don't know. He's still over there and hasn't called in. The question is, how are you doing? Did forensics look at the video?"

"Barbara Starkey is working on it right now. She already got this."

Bosch pulled the printout of the window from his coat pocket and unfolded it. He explained to Gandle what he thought it meant and how it was the only lead so far.

"It sounded like you were booking a flight. When do you go?"

"Tonight. I get there early Sunday."

"You lose a whole day?"

"Yeah, but I gain it coming back. I have all of Sunday

to find her. I then fly back Monday morning and get here Monday morning. We go to the DA and file on Chang. It will work, Lieutenant."

"Look, Harry, don't worry about a day. Don't worry about the case. Just get over there and find her. Stay as long as you need. We'll worry about the case."

"Right."

"What about the police? Your ex call them in?"

"She tried. They're not interested."

"What? Did you send them that video?"

"Not yet. But she told them. They took a pass."

Gandle placed his hands on his hips. He did this when something bothered him or he needed to show his authority in a situation.

"Harry, what's going on?"

"They think she's a runaway and we should wait to see if she turns up. And that's fine with me because I don't want the police involved. Not yet."

"Look, they must have entire units dedicated to the triads. Your ex probably called some dipshit on a desk. You need to bring in some expertise and they have it."

Bosch nodded like he knew all of this already.

"Boss, I'm sure they have their experts. But the triads have survived for more than three hundred years. They've flourished. You don't do that without having lines into the police department. If it was one of your daughters, would you call a bunch of people in you can't trust or would you handle it yourself?"

He knew Gandle had two daughters. Both were older than Maddie. One was back east studying at Hopkins and he worried about her all the time.

"I hear you, Harry."

Bosch pointed at the printout.

"I just want Sunday. I've got a bead on that place and I'm going to go over there and get her back. If I can't find her, I'll go to the police Monday morning. I'll talk to their triad people, hell, I'll even call the local FBI office over there. I'll do whatever is necessary but I want Sunday to find her myself."

Gandle nodded and looked down at the floor. It seemed like he wanted to say something else.

"What?" Harry asked. "Let me guess, Chang's filing a beef on me for trying to choke him out. That's funny because I ended up getting more than I gave in there. That fucker's strong."

"No, no, it's not that. He still won't say a goddamn word. It's not that."

"Then, what?"

Gandle nodded and picked up the printout.

"Well, I was just going to say that if things don't work out on Sunday, you call me. The thing about these fuckers is that they never go straight. You know, another time, another crime. We can always get Chang later."

Lieutenant Gandle was telling Bosch that he was willing to let Chang walk if it would get Harry's own daughter safely home. On Monday, the DA could be informed that evidence would not be presented in support of the murder charge and Chang would be released.

"You're a good man, Lieutenant."

"And, of course, I didn't just say any of that."

"It's not going to come to that, but I appreciate what you didn't just say. Besides, the sad truth is, we may have to kick this guy loose Monday, anyway. Unless we come up with something over the weekend or on the searches."

Bosch remembered that he had promised Teri Sopp that he'd get a copy of Chang's print card to her so she would have it on hand if anything developed during the electro-static enhancement test of the casing recovered from John Li's body. He told Gandle to make sure Ferras or Chu got a card over to her. The lieutenant said he'd get it covered. He handed the printout of the video image back to Bosch and told him what he always told him, to stay in touch. Then he headed back to his office.

Bosch set the printout on his desk and put on his reading glasses. He also took a magnifying glass out of a drawer and began a study of every square inch of the image, looking for anything that might help and that he hadn't seen before. He was ten minutes into it and find-ing nothing new when his cell rang. It was Ferras and he knew nothing about Bosch's daughter being abducted.

"Harry, I got it. We got approval to search the phone, suitcase and car."

"Ignacio, you're a hell of a writer. Still pitching a perfect game."

It was true. So far, in the three years they had been partnered, Ferras had yet to write a search warrant ap-plication that had been turned down by a judge for insuf-ficient cause. He might be intimidated by the streets but he wasn't cowed by the courthouse. He seemed to know just what to put in each search application and what to leave out.

"Thanks, Har."

"You finished over there now?"

"Yeah, I'm coming back."

"Why don't you divert over to the OPG and handle that? I've got the phone and the suitcase right here. I'll dive in now. Chu is booking Chang."

Ferras hesitated. Going to the Official Police Garage to handle the search of Chang's car would stretch the psychological tether to the squad room.

"Uh, Harry? Don't you think I should take the phone? I mean, you just got your first multifunction phone about a month ago."

"I think I can figure it out."

"You sure?"

"Yeah, I'm sure. And I've got it right here. You head over to the garage. Make sure they check the door panels and the air filter. I had a Mustang once. You could fit a forty-five in the filter."

They referred to the staff at the OPG. They would be the ones who tore apart Chang's car while Ferras supervised the search.

"Will do," Ferras said.

"Good," Bosch said. "Call me if you strike gold."

Bosch closed the phone. He didn't see the need to tell Ferras about his daughter's plight yet. Ferras had three young kids of his own and a reminder of how vulnerable he really was wouldn't be helpful at a time when Bosch was counting on his best work.

Harry pushed back from his desk and swiveled the chair to look at Chang's big suitcase on the floor against the cubicle's rear wall. Striking gold meant finding the murder weapon in your suspect's possession or possessions. Bosch knew Chang was heading to a plane, so there would be no gold in the suitcase. If he still possessed the gun that killed John Li, it would likely be in his car or his apartment. Or it would be long gone.

But the suitcase could still yield valuable information and incriminating evidence—a drop of blood from the victim on the cuff of a shirt, for example. They could get lucky. But Bosch turned back to the desk and decided to go with the cell phone first. He would go for gold of a different kind. Digital gold.

21

It took Bosch less than five minutes to determine that Bo-Jing Chang's cell phone would be of little use to the investigation. He easily found the call log but it contained a listing of only two recent calls, both to toll-free numbers, and one incoming call. All three were placed or received that morning. There was no record beyond that. The phone's history had been wiped clean.

Bosch had been told that digital memories lasted forever. He knew a full forensic analysis of the phone could possibly result in the data wiped off the device being rebuilt, but for immediate purposes the phone was a bust. He called the 800 numbers and learned they belonged to Hertz Car Rental and Cathay Pacific Airways. Chang had probably been checking on his itinerary and his plan to drive from Seattle to Vancouver to catch the plane to Hong Kong. Bosch also checked the number from the incoming call in the reverse directory and learned it had come from Tsing Motors, Chang's employer. While it was unknown what the call was about, the number certainly added no new evidence or information to the case.

Bosch had counted on the phone not only adding to the case against Chang but possibly providing a clue to where he was going in Hong Kong, and therefore to Madeline's location. The disappointment hit him hard and he knew he had to keep his mind moving in order to avoid dwelling on it. He shoved the phone back into the evidence bag and then cleared his desk so he could place the suitcase on top of it.

He hoisted the suitcase onto the desk, estimating that it weighed at least sixty pounds. He then used a pair of scissors to cut the evidence tape Chu had placed across the zipper. He found a small padlock was securing the zipper closed. He took out his picks and opened the cheap luggage-store lock in less than thirty seconds. He unzipped the bag and opened it across his desk.

Chang's suitcase was partitioned equally into halves. He started on the left side, unsnapping two diagonal straps that held the contents in place. He removed and examined every item of clothing piece by piece. He stacked everything on a shelf that ran above his desk and which he had not had time to put anything on since moving into the new building.

It looked like Chang had thrown all his possessions into the suitcase. The clothes were bundled tightly together rather than folded as if for use on a trip. At the center of each bundle was a piece of jewelry or other personal possession. He found a watch in one bundle, an antique baby rattle in another. At the center of the last bundle he opened was a small bamboo frame containing a faded photo of a woman. Chang's mother, Bosch presumed.

Chang was not coming back, Bosch concluded after searching only half of the suitcase.

The right side was secured with a divider that Bosch

unsnapped and folded over the empty half. There were more clothing bundles and shoes here, plus a smaller zippered bag for toiletries. Bosch went through the bundles first, finding nothing unusual in the clothing. The first bundle was wrapped around a small jade statue of a Buddha that had a small bowl attached for burning incense or offerings. The second bundle was wrapped around a sheathed knife.

The weapon was a showpiece with a blade that was only five inches long and a handle made of carved bone. The carving was a depiction of a one-sided battle in which men with knives and arrows and axes slaughtered unarmed men who appeared to be praying instead of fighting. Bosch assumed this was the massacre of the Shaolin monks that Chu had told him was the origin of the triads. The shape of the knife was very much like the shape of the tattoo on the inside of Chang's arm.

The knife was an interesting find and possibly proof of Chang's membership in the Brave Knife triad, but it wasn't evidence of any crime. Bosch put it up on the shelf with the other belongings and kept searching.

Soon he had emptied the suitcase. He felt the lining with his hands to make sure there was nothing hidden beneath and came up empty. He lifted the suitcase, hoping that it might feel too heavy to be empty. But it wasn't and he was sure he had not missed anything.

The last thing he looked at were the two pairs of shoes Chang had packed. He had given each shoe an initial look but had then put it aside. He knew the only way to really search a shoe was to pull it apart. It wasn't something he usually relished doing because it rendered them useless, and Bosch didn't like taking away a man's shoes, suspect or not. This time he didn't care.

The first pair he zeroed in on was a pair of work boots he had seen Chang wearing the day before. They were old and worn but he could tell they were well liked. The laces were new and the leather had been oiled on repeated occasions. Bosch pulled the laces out so he could lift the tongue back all the way to look inside. Using the scissors, he pried up the cushioning in the instep to see if it hid any sort of secret compartment in the heel. There was nothing in the first boot but in the second he found a business card had been slipped between two layers of cushioning.

Bosch felt a kick of adrenaline as he put the work boot aside to look at the card. He had finally found something.

It was a two-sided card. Chinese on one side and English on the other. Bosch, of course, studied the English side.

JIMMY FONG

FLEET MANAGER

CAUSEWAY TAXI SERVICE

The card had an address in Causeway Bay and two phone numbers. Bosch sat down for the first time since starting the suitcase search and continued to study the card. He wondered what he had—if he had anything at all. Causeway Bay was not far from Happy Valley and the shopping mall from which his daughter was most likely abducted. And the fact that a business card for a taxi service fleet manager had been hidden in Chang's work boot was cause to ask why.

He flipped the card over and studied the Chinese side.

There were three lines of copy just like on the English side, plus the address and phone numbers in the corner. It appeared that the card said the same thing on both sides.

Bosch made a copy of the card and put the original in an evidence envelope so that Chu could take a look at it. He then moved on to the other pair of shoes. In another twenty minutes he was finished and had found nothing else. He remained intrigued by the business card but disappointed in the lack of returns from the search. He put all the belongings back in the suitcase as close to the way he found it all as he could. He then closed it and pulled the zipper.

After placing the suitcase back on the floor he called his partner. He was anxious to know if the search of Chang's car had gone better than the search of his phone and suitcase.

"We're only about halfway through," Ferras said. "They started with the trunk."

"Anything?"

"Not so far."

Bosch felt his hopes beginning to ebb away. Chang was going to come up clean. And that meant he was going to walk the following Monday.

"Did you get anything out of the phone?" Ferras asked.

"No, nothing. It was wiped. There wasn't much in the suitcase either."

"Shit."

"Yeah."

"Well, like I said, we haven't even gotten inside the car yet. Just the trunk. We'll check the door panels and the air filter, too."

"Good. Let me know."

Bosch closed the phone and then immediately called Chu.

"You still at booking?"

"No, man, I cleared booking a half hour ago. I'm in the courthouse, waiting to see Judge Champagne and get the PCD signed."

After booking a suspect for murder it was required that a judge sign a Probable Cause Detention document, which contained the arrest report and laid out the evidence that led to the suspect's incarceration. The threshold for probable cause to arrest was much lower than the requirement to file charges. Getting a PCD signed was usually routine but nonetheless Chu had made a good move in going back to the judge who had already signed their search warrant.

"Good. I wanted to check on that."

"Got it covered. What are you doing there, Harry? What's going on with your daughter?"

"She's still missing."

"I'm sorry. What can I do?"

"You can tell me about the booking."

It took Chu a moment to make the jump from Bosch's daughter to Chang's booking into the L.A. City Jail.

"There's nothing really to tell. He never spoke a word. He grunted a few times and that was it. He's booked into high power and that's hopefully where he'll stay till Monday."

"He's not going anywhere. Did he call a lawyer?"

"They were going to give him access to the phone after he was inside. So I don't know for sure but I assume he did."

"Okay."

Bosch was just fishing around, looking for anything that might be a direction and would get the adrenaline flowing.

"We got the search warrant," he said. "But there was nothing on the phone and nothing that helps in the suitcase. There was a business card hidden in one of his shoes. It's got English on one side and Chinese on the other. I want to see if they match up. I know you don't read Chinese, but if I faxed it over to the AGU could you have someone there take a look?"

"Yeah, Harry, but do it now. That place is probably clearing out."

Bosch looked at his watch. It was four-thirty on a Friday afternoon. Squad rooms across the city were turning into ghost towns.

"I'll do it now. Call over there and tell them it's coming."

He closed the phone and left the cubicle for the copy office on the other side of the squad room.

Four-thirty. In six hours Bosch had to be at the airport. He knew that once he was on the plane his investigation would go on hold. For the next fourteen-plus hours while in flight, things would continue to happen with his daughter, and with the case, but Bosch would be in stasis. Like a space traveler in the movies who is put into hibernation during the long journey home from the mission.

He knew that he couldn't get on that plane with nothing. One way or another he had to make a break.

After he faxed the business card over to the Asian Gang Unit, he went back to his cubicle. He had left his phone on his desk and he saw that he had missed a call from his ex-wife. There was no message but he called her back.

"You find something?" he asked.

"I've had very long conversations with two of Maddie's friends. This time they were talking."

"He?"

"No, not He. I don't have a full name or a number for her. Neither of the other girls did either."

"What did they tell you?"

"That He and her brother are not from the school. They met up with them at the mall but they're not even from Happy Valley."

"Do they know where they came from?"

"No, but they knew they weren't local. They said Maddie seemed to get really tight with He and that brought her brother into the picture. This is all in the last month or so. Since she came back from her visit with you, in fact. Both girls said she had put some distance between her and them."

"What's the brother's name?"

"All I got was Quick. He said his name was Quick but like with his sister, they never got a last name."

"That's not a lot of help. Anything else?"

"Well, they confirmed what Maddie told you, that Quick was the one who smoked. They said he was sort of rough trade. He has tattoos and bracelets and I guess . . . well, I guess they sort of were attracted to the element of danger."

"They or Madeline?"

"Maddie mostly."

"Did they think she might have gone with him Friday after school?"

"They wouldn't say so but, yes, I think that's what they were trying to say."

"Did you ask if Quick ever talked about triad affiliation?"

"I asked that and they said that never came up. It wouldn't have, anyway."

"Why not?"

"Because you don't talk about that here. The triads are anonymous. They're everywhere but anonymous."

"Okay."

"You know, you haven't really told me what you think is going on. I'm not stupid. I know what you're doing. You're trying not to upset me with the facts but I think I need to know the facts now, Harry."

"Okay."

Bosch knew she was right. If he wanted her best effort, then she had to know all he knew.

"I'm working the murder of a Chinese man who owned a liquor store in the south end. He made regular protection payments to the triad. He was killed on the same day and during the same hour that the weekly payments were always made. That put us onto Bo-Jing Chang, the triad bagman. The trouble is, that's all we've got. No evidence directly connecting him to the murder. Then today we had to take Chang down because he was about to get on a plane and flee the country. We had no choice. So what it comes down to is we have the weekend to get enough evidence to support the charge or we let him walk and he gets on a plane, never to be seen again."

"And how does this connect to our daughter?"

"Eleanor, I'm dealing with people I don't know. The Asian Gang Unit in the LAPD and the Monterey Park Police. Somebody got the word to Chang directly or to the triad that we were onto him and that's why he tried to bolt. They could just as easily have backgrounded me and ze-roed in on Madeline as a way to get to me, to send the message that I need to stand down. I got a call. Somebody told me there would be consequences if I didn't back off Chang. I never dreamed that the consequences would be . . ."

"Maddie," Eleanor said, finishing the thought.

A long silence followed and Bosch guessed that his ex-wife was trying to control her emotions, hating Bosch at the same time she had to rely on him to save their daughter.

"Eleanor?" he finally asked.

"What?"

Her voice was clipped but very obviously filled with dark rage.

"Did Maddie's friends give you an age on this kid Quick?"

"They both said they thought he was at least seventeen. They said he had a car. I spoke to them separately and they both said the same thing about all of this. I think they were telling me what they knew."

Bosch didn't respond. He was thinking.

"The mall opens in a couple hours," Eleanor continued. "I plan to be there with photos of Maddie."

"That's a good idea. There might be video. If Quick was a problem in the past, mall security might have a jacket on him."

"I thought about all of that."

"Sorry, I know."

"What does your suspect say about all of this?"

"Our suspect won't talk and I've just been through his

suitcase and his phone and we're still working on the car. So far nothing."

"What about where he lives?"

"As of now we don't have enough for a search warrant."

That hung out there for a few moments, both of them knowing that with their daughter missing, legal formalities like search warrant approvals were not going to matter to Bosch.

"I should probably get back to it. I have six hours before I have to be at the airport."

"Okay."

"I'll talk to you as soon—"

"Harry?"

"What?"

"I am so upset I don't know what to say."

"I understand, Eleanor."

"If we get her back, you may never see her again. I just need to tell you that."

Bosch paused. He knew she was entitled to her anger and everything else. Anger might make her sharper in her efforts.

"There is no *if*," he finally said. "I'm going to get her back."

He waited for her to respond but got only silence.

"Okay, Eleanor. I'll call you when I know something."

After closing the phone Bosch turned to his desktop computer and pulled up Chang's booking photo. He then sent it over to the color printer. He wanted to have a copy of it with him in Hong Kong.

Chu called back after that and said he had gotten the

PCD signed and was leaving the courthouse. He said he had spoken to an officer at the AGU who had taken Bosch's fax and could confirm that both sides of the business card said the same thing. The card came from a manager of a taxi fleet based in Causeway Bay. Completely innocuous on its face, but Bosch was still bothered by the card being secreted in Chang's shoe and by it being from a business located so close to where his daughter had last been seen by her friends. Bosch had never been a believer in coincidence. He wasn't going to start now.

Bosch thanked Chu and hung up just as Lieutenant Gandle stopped by his cubicle on the way out.

"Harry, I feel like I'm leaving you in the lurch. What can I do for you?"

"There's nothing that can be done that is not already being done."

He updated Gandle on the searches and the lack of solid findings so far. He also reported that there was nothing new on his daughter's whereabouts or abductors. Gandle's face turned sour.

"We need a break," he said. "We really need a break."

"We're working on it."

"When do you leave?"

"In six hours."

"Okay, you have my numbers. Call me anytime, day or night, if you need anything. I'll do whatever I can."

"Thanks, Boss."

"You want me to stay here with you?"

"No, I'm fine. I was about to head over to the OPG and let Ferras go home if he wants to."

"Okay, Harry, let me know when you find something."

"Will do."

"You'll get her back. I know you will."

"I know it, too."

Gandle then awkwardly put his hand out and Bosch shook it. It was probably the first time since they had met three years earlier that they shook. Gandle left then and Bosch surveyed the squad room. It looked like he was the only one left.

He turned and looked down at the suitcase. He knew he had to lug it to the elevator and get it down to evidence lockup. The phone had to be booked into evidence, too. After that, he would leave the building as well. But not for a leisurely weekend at home with the family. Bosch was on a mission. And he would stop at nothing to see it through. Even under Eleanor's last threat. Even if it meant that saving his daughter might mean he'd never see her again.

22

Bosch waited until dark to break into Bo-Jing Chang's home. It was a town house with a shared entry vestibule with the adjoining apartment. This offered him cover as he used his picks to turn the dead bolt and then the doorknob lock. As he worked, he felt no guilt and had no second thoughts about the line he was crossing. The searches of the car, suitcase and phone had all been busts and now Bosch was desperate. He wasn't searching for evidence to make a case against Chang. He was searching for anything that would help him locate his daughter. She was missing for more than twelve hours now and breaking and entering, putting his livelihood and career on the line, seemed like minimal risks compared with what he would face within himself if he didn't get her back safe.

Once the final pin moved into place, he opened the door and moved quickly into the apartment, closing and relocking the door behind him. The search of the suitcase had told Bosch that Chang had packed for good, that he wasn't coming back. But he doubted Chang had fit everything into that one suitcase. He had to have left things behind. Things of less personal meaning to him, but possibly of value to Bosch. Chang had printed his boarding pass out at some point before heading to the airport. Since Chang had been under surveillance, Bosch knew he had made no other stops. He was sure there had to be a computer and printer in the apartment.

Harry waited thirty seconds for his eyes to adjust to the darkness before moving from the door. Once he could see reasonably well, he moved into the living room, banging into a chair and almost knocking over a lamp before managing to find the switch and turn it on. He then stepped quickly to a pair of open drapes and pulled them closed across the front window.

He turned from the window and surveyed the room. It was a small living room and dining room combination with a pass-through window to a kitchen in the back. A stairwell on the right went up to a bedroom loft. On initial view, Bosch saw nothing of a personal nature left behind. No computer, no printer. It was just furniture. He quickly searched the room and then moved into the kitchen. Again, the place was barren of personal effects. The cabinets were bare, not even a cereal box left behind. Under the sink was a trash can but it was empty and freshly lined with a plastic garbage bag.

Bosch moved back into the living room and headed for the stairs. There was a light switch at the bottom of the staircase that had a dimmer and controlled a ceiling light in the loft. He turned it on low and then went back to the living room lamp and turned it off.

The loft was sparely furnished with just a queen-size bed and a bureau. There was no desk and no computer.

Bosch quickly moved to the bureau and opened and closed every drawer, finding each had been cleared out. In the bathroom, the wastebasket was empty and medicine cabinet bare. He lifted the lid off the toilet tank but found nothing hidden there either.

The place had been cleaned out. It must have been after Chang had left, drawing the surveillance away. Bosch thought about the call from Tsing Motors that had been logged on the suspect's phone. Maybe he had given Vincent Tsing the all-clear sign and the apartment had been cleared out and cleaned.

Disappointed and feeling that he had been expertly played, Bosch decided to locate the apartment complex's refuse bin and attempt to find the trash bags that had been taken from the apartment. Maybe they had slipped up and left Chang's trash behind. A thrown-away note or a scribbled phone number would be helpful.

He was three steps down the stairs when he heard a key hit the front door lock. He quickly turned around and moved back up into the loft and hid behind a support column.

Lights below were turned on and the apartment immediately filled with Chinese voices. His back to the column, Bosch counted the voices of two men and one woman. One of the men was dominating the conversation and whenever the other two spoke, they seemed to be asking questions.

Bosch moved to the edge of the column and risked a look down. He saw the dominant male gesturing to the furnishings. He then opened a closet door beneath the staircase and made a sweeping hand movement. Bosch realized he was showing the place to the couple. It was already for rent.

This told him that sooner or later the three people below would be coming up to the loft. He looked at the bed. It was a bare mattress on top of a thick box spring sitting on a frame a foot off the ground. He decided it was the only place he could possibly hide and not be discovered. He quickly got down to the floor and shimmied under the bed, his chest scraping on the underside of the box spring. He moved to the center and waited, tracking the apartment tour by the voices.

Finally, the entourage headed up the steps to the loft. Bosch held his breath as the couple moved around the room and both sides of the bed. He waited for someone to sit on the bed but that never happened.

Bosch suddenly felt a vibration in his pocket and realized that he had not muted his phone. Luckily the man showing the apartment was continuing what was probably the sales pitch about how great the place was. His voice covered any notice of the low-level vibration. Bosch quickly worked his hand into his pocket and pulled the phone to see if the call was from his daughter's phone. He would have to answer such a call, no matter the circumstance.

He reached the phone up into the box spring so he could see it. The call was from Barbara Starkey, the video tech, and Bosch hit the call-decline button. That was a callback he could make later.

Opening the phone to check the call had activated the screen. The dim light illuminated the inside of the box spring and Bosch saw a gun jammed behind one of the wooden slats of the frame.

Bosch's heart kicked its beat up a notch as he stared at the gun. But he decided not to touch it until the apartment was empty again. He closed the phone and waited. Soon he heard the visitors on the staircase going down. It sounded like they took another quick look around the lower level and then left.

Bosch heard the dead bolt being locked from the outside. He then pushed his way out from under the bed.

After waiting a few moments to make sure the rental party was gone for good, he turned the overhead light back on. He moved back to the bed and pushed the mattress off the box spring, leaning it against the rear wall of the loft. He then raised the box spring and leaned it against the mattress. He looked in at the gun, still held in place by the wood framework.

He still could not see it clearly so he pulled his phone again, opened it and used it as a flashlight by holding it in close to the weapon.

"Damn," he said out loud.

He was looking for a Glock, the gun with a rectangular firing pin. The gun hidden under Chang's bed was a Smith & Wesson.

There was nothing here of use to him. Bosch realized that once again he was at ground zero. As if to accentuate this point, a tiny beeping sound came from his watch. He reached to his wrist and turned it off. He had set the alarm earlier so as not to risk missing his flight. It was time for him to head to the airport.

After putting the bed back in place, Bosch turned the light off in the loft and quietly slipped out of the apartment. His plan was to go home first to pick up his passport and lock up his gun. He would not be allowed to carry the weapon into a foreign country without that country's approval — a process that would take days if not weeks. He didn't plan to pack any clothes because he didn't see himself having time to change clothes in Hong Kong. He was on a mission that would begin the moment he stepped off the plane.

He got on the 10 west from Monterey Park and planned on taking the 101 up through Hollywood to his home. He started mulling over a plan for directing police to the gun hidden in Chang's former apartment but as of now there was no probable cause to hit the place. Still, the gun needed to be found and examined. It was of no use to Bosch in the John Li investigation but that didn't mean Chang had used it for good deeds and philanthropy. It had been used for triad business and it could very likely lead to something.

As he was taking the 101 north along the edges of the civic center, Bosch remembered the call from Barbara Starkey. He checked for a message on his phone and heard Starkey tell him to call her as soon as possible. It sounded like maybe she had made a break. Bosch hit the callback button.

"Barbara, it's Harry."

"Harry, yes, I was hoping to get to you before I go home."

"You should've gone home about three hours ago."

"Yeah, well, I told you I would look at this thing."

"Thank you, Barbara. It means a lot. What did you find?"

"A couple things. First of all, I have a printout here that is a little sharper if you want it."

Bosch was disappointed. It sounded like there wasn't much more than what he already had and she just wanted to let him know there was a clearer picture of the view out the window of the room where his daughter was held. Sometimes, he had noticed, when somebody did a favor for you, they really wanted you to know it. But he decided he would just make do with what he had. A jog in off the freeway to pick up the picture would take too much time. He had a plane to catch.

"Anything else?" he asked. "I have to get to the airport."

"Yes, I have a couple other visual and audio identifiers that might help you," Starkey said.

Bosch paid full attention now.

"What are they?"

"Well, one I think might be a train or a subway. Another is a snippet of conversation that is not Chinese. And the last one I think is a silent helicopter."

"What do you mean *silent?*"

"I mean literally silent. I have a flash reflection in the window of a helicopter going by, but I don't have any real audio track to go with it."

Bosch didn't respond at first. He knew what she was talking about. The Whisper Jet helicopters that the rich and powerful used to move over and around Hong Kong. He had seen them. Commuting by helicopter wasn't uncommon but he also knew only a few buildings in each district were allowed to operate landing pads on their roofs. One reason his ex-wife chose the building where she lived in Happy Valley was that it had a helicopter pad on the roof. She could get to the casino in Macau in twenty minutes door-to-door instead of the two hours it would take to leave the building, get to the ferry docks, take a boat across the harbor and then cab or walk from the dock to the casino.

"Barbara, I'll be there in five minutes," he said.

He exited on Los Angeles Street and headed over to Parker Center. Because of the late hour, Bosch had his pick of spaces in the garage behind the old police headquarters. He parked and then quickly crossed the street and entered through the back door. The elevator up seemed to take forever, and when he walked into the mostly abandoned SID lab, it had actually been seven minutes since he had closed the phone.

"You're late," Starkey said.

"Sorry, thanks for waiting."

"I'm just giving you a hard time. I know you're on the run, so let's just look at this thing."

She pointed to one of her screens where there was a frozen image of the window from the phone video. It was what Bosch had printed out. Starkey put her hands on the dials.

"Okay," she said. "Keep your eyes up here at the top of the glass reflection. We didn't see — or hear — this before."

She turned one dial slowly, reversing the tape. In the murky glass reflection Bosch saw what he had not seen before. Just as the aim of the camera started its swing back toward his daughter, a helicopter moved across the top of the reflection like a ghost. It was a small black craft with some sort of unreadable insignia on its side.

"Now here it is in real time."

She backed the video up until the camera was focused on Bosch's daughter and she was kicking at it. Starkey hit a button and it went by in real time. The camera swung toward the window for a split second and then back. Bosch's eyes registered the window but never the reflection of the city, let alone a passing helicopter.

It was a good find and Bosch was excited.

"The thing is, Harry, to be in that window that chopper has to be flying pretty low."

"So it either just took off or it was landing."

"I think it was ascending. It appears to rise slightly as it crosses the reflection. Nothing you can really see with the eye but I measured it. Considering the reflection shows right to left what is occurring left to right, it would have taken off from a location on the opposite side of the street from the building this video was taken in."

Bosch nodded.

"Now when I look for an audio track..."

She switched to the other screen where there was an audiograph showing different isolated streams of audio she had taken from the video.

"...and take out as much of the competing sound as I can, I get this."

She played a track with almost a flatline graph and all Bosch could hear was distant traffic noise that was chopped into waves.

"That's rotor wash," she said. "You don't hear the helicopter itself but it's disrupting the ambient noise. It's like a stealth chopper or something."

Bosch nodded. He had moved a step closer. He now

knew his daughter was held in a building near one of the few rooftop helicopter pads in Kowloon.

"That help?" Starkey asked.

"You better believe it."

"Good. I also have this."

She played another track and it contained a low hissing sound that reminded Bosch of rushing water. It began, grew louder and then dissipated.

"What is it? Water?"

Starkey shook her head.

"This is with maximum amplification," she said. "I had to work at this. It's air. Escaping air. I would say you are talking about an entrance to an underground subway station or maybe a vent through which displaced air is channeled up and out when a train comes into the station. Modern subways don't make a lot of noise. But there is a lot of air displacement when a train comes through the tunnel."

"Got it."

"Your location is up high here. Maybe twelve, thirteen stories, judging by the reflection. So this audio is hard to pinpoint. Could be ground level to this building or a block away. Hard to tell."

"It still helps."

"And the last thing is this."

She played the first part of the video when the camera was holding on Bosch's daughter and just showing her. She brought up the sound and filtered out competing audio tracks. Bosch heard a muffled line of dialogue.

"What is that?" he asked.

"I think it might be outside the room. I haven't been

able to clean it up any better. It's muffled by structure and it doesn't sound Chinese to me. But I don't think that's what is important."

"Then, what is?"

"Listen again to the end of it."

She played it again. Bosch stared at his daughter's scared eyes while concentrating on the audio. It was a male voice that was too muffled to be understood or translated and then it abruptly ended in what sounded like midsentence.

"Somebody cut him off?"

"Or maybe an elevator door closed and that cut him off."

Bosch nodded. The elevator seemed like a more likely explanation because there had been no stress in the tone of the voice before the cutoff.

Starkey pointed at the screen.

"So when you find the building, you'll find this room close to the elevator."

Bosch stared at his daughter's eyes for one last and long moment.

"Thank you, Barbara."

He stood behind her and gave her shoulders a squeeze.

"You got it, Harry."

"I gotta go."

"You said you were heading to the airport. Are you going to Hong Kong?"

"That's right."

"Good luck, Harry. Go get your daughter."

"That's the plan."

• • •

Bosch quickly returned to his car and raced back to the freeway. Rush-hour traffic had thinned out and he made good time as he headed through Hollywood to the Cahuenga Pass and home. He started focusing on Hong Kong. L.A. and everything here would soon be behind him. It would be all about Hong Kong now. He was going to find his daughter and bring her home. Or he was going to die trying.

All his life Harry Bosch believed he had a mission. And to carry out that mission he needed to be bulletproof. He needed to build himself and his life so that he was invulnerable, so that nothing and no one could ever get to him. All of that changed on the day he was introduced to the daughter he didn't know he had. In that moment he knew he was both saved and lost. He would be forever connected to the world in the way only a father knew. But he would also be lost because he knew the dark forces he faced would one day find her. It didn't matter if an entire ocean was between them. He knew one day it would come to this, that the darkness would find her and that she would be used to get to him.

That day was now.

PART TWO:

The 39-Hour Day

23

Bosch got only fitful sleep on the flight over the Pacific. Fourteen hours in the air, pressed against a window in the coach cabin, he never managed to sleep more than fifteen or twenty minutes at a time before thoughts of his daughter and his guilt over her predicament intruded and jarred him awake.

By moving too fast to think during the day, he had kept himself ahead of the fear and guilt, the brutal recriminations. He was able to put it all aside because the pursuit was more important than the baggage he was carrying. But on Cathay Pacific flight 883 he could run no more. He knew he needed to sleep to be rested and ready for the day ahead in Hong Kong. But on the plane he was cornered and could no longer put his guilt and fear aside. The dread engulfed him. He spent most of the hours sitting in darkness, fists balled tightly and eyes staring blankly, as the jet hurtled through the black toward the place where Madeline was somewhere hidden. It made sleep fleeting if not altogether impossible.

The headwinds over the Pacific were weaker than

212   MICHAEL CONNELLY

anticipated and the plane picked up time on the schedule, landing early at the airport on Lantau Island at 4:55 A.M. Bosch rudely pushed around passengers reaching for belongings in overhead bins and made his way to the front of the plane. He carried only a small backpack containing things he thought might help him find and rescue his daughter. When the jet's door opened he moved quickly and soon took over the lead of all passengers heading toward customs and immigration. Fear stabbed at him as he approached the first screening point—a thermoscan designed to identify fever carriers. Bosch was sweating. Had the guilt burning in his conscious manifested itself as a fever? Would he be stopped before he had even begun the most important mission of all?

He glanced back at the computer screen as he passed by. He saw the images of travelers turned to blue ghosts on the screen. No telltale blooms of red. No fever. At least not yet.

At the customs checkpoint an inspector flipped through his passport and saw the entry and exit stamps from the many trips he had made in the past six years. He then checked something on a computer screen Bosch couldn't see.

"You have business in Hong Kong, Mr. Bosch?" the inspector asked.

He had somehow butchered the single syllable of Bosch's last name, making it sound like *Botch*.

"No," Bosch said. "My daughter lives here and I come to visit her pretty often."

He eyed the backpack slung over Bosch's shoulder.

"You checked your bags?"

"No, I just have this. It's a quick trip."

The inspector nodded and looked back at his computer. Bosch knew what was going to happen. Invariably when he arrived in Hong Kong the immigration inspector saw his law enforcement classification on the computer and put him into the search queue.

"Have you brought your weapon with you?" the inspector asked.

"No," Bosch said tiredly. "I know that's not allowed."

The inspector typed something on his computer and then directed Bosch, as expected, into a chute for a search of his bag. It would waste another fifteen minutes but Harry stayed cool. He had gained a half hour on the schedule with his early arrival.

The second inspector carefully went through the backpack and made curious looks at the binoculars and other items, including the envelope stuffed with cash. But none of it was illegal to enter the country with. When he was finished he asked Bosch to step through a metal detector and then he was cleared. Harry headed into the baggage terminal and spotted a money exchange window that was open despite the early hour. He stepped up, pulled the cash envelope out of his backpack again and told the woman behind the glass he wanted to change five thousand U.S. dollars into Hong Kong dollars. It was Bosch's earthquake money, cash he kept hidden in the gun locker in his bedroom. He had learned a valuable lesson back in '94 when an earthquake rocked L.A. and severely damaged his house. Cash is king. Don't leave home without it. Now the money he kept hidden for just such a crisis would hopefully help him overcome another. The exchange rate was a little less than eight to one, and his five thousand American became thirty-eight thousand Hong Kong dollars.

After getting his money he headed to the exit doors on the other side of the baggage terminal. The first surprise of the day came when he saw Eleanor Wish waiting for him in the main hall of the airport. She was standing next to a man in a suit who had the feet-splayed posture of a bodyguard. Eleanor made a small gesture with her hand in case Harry hadn't noticed her. He saw the mixture of pain and hope on her face and had to drop his eyes to the floor as he approached.

"Eleanor. I didn't—"

She grabbed him in a quick and awkward embrace that abruptly ended his sentence. He understood that she was telling him that blame and recriminations were for later. There were more important things now. She then stepped away and gestured to the man in the suit.

"This is Sun Yee."

Bosch nodded but then put out his hand, a gesture he hoped would help him figure out what to call Sun Yee.

"Harry," he said.

The other man nodded back and gripped his hand tightly but said nothing. No help there. He would have to take Eleanor's cue with the name. Bosch guessed Sun Yee was in his late forties. Eleanor's age. He was short but powerfully built. His chest and arms pressed the contours of the silk suit jacket to the limit. He wore sunglasses although it was still before dawn.

Bosch turned to his ex-wife.

"He's driving us?"

"He's helping us," she corrected. "He works in security at the casino."

Bosch nodded. That was one mystery solved.

"Does he speak English?"

"Yes, I do," the man answered for himself.

Bosch studied him for a moment and then looked at Eleanor and saw in her face a familiar resolve. It was a look he had seen many times when they had been together. She wasn't going to allow an argument on this. This man was part of the package or Bosch was on his own.

Bosch knew that if circumstances dictated it, he could split off and make his way alone through the city. It was what he had anticipated doing, anyway. But for now he was willing to go with Eleanor's plan.

"You sure you want to do this, Eleanor? I was planning on working on my own."

"She's my daughter, too. Where you go I go."

"Okay, then."

They started walking toward the glass doors that would lead them outside. Bosch let Sun Yee take the lead so he could talk privately with his ex-wife. Despite the obvious strain playing clearly on her face, she was just as beautiful as ever to him. She had her hair tied back in a no-nonsense manner. It accented the clean line and determined set of her jaw. No matter how infrequently or what the circumstances, he could never look at her without thinking about the could-have-beens. It was an overworked cliché, but Bosch had always believed that they were meant to be together. Their daughter gave them a lifelong connection, but to Bosch it was not enough.

"So tell me what's happening, Eleanor," he said. "I've been in the air for almost fourteen hours. What's new on this end?"

She nodded.

"I spent four hours at the mall yesterday. When you called and left a message from the airport, I must've been in security. I either didn't have a signal or just didn't hear the call."

"Don't worry about it. What did you find out?"

"They have surveillance video that shows her with the brother and sister. Quick and He. It's all from a distance. They're not identifiable on it—except for Mad. I'd be able to pick her out anywhere."

"Does it show the grab?"

"There was no grab. They were hanging out together, mostly in the food court. Then Quick lit up a cigarette and somebody complained. Security moved in and kicked him out. Madeline walked out with them. Voluntarily. And they never came back in."

Bosch nodded. He could see it. It could all have been a plan to lure her out. Quick lit up, knowing all along that he would be ejected from the mall and that Madeline would go out with him.

"What else?"

"That's it from the mall. Quick is familiar to security there but they had no ID or file on him."

"What time was it when they walked out?"

"Six-fifteen."

Bosch did the math. That was Friday. His daughter had walked off the mall videotape almost thirty-six hours ago.

"When's it get dark here? What time?"

"Usually by eight. Why?"

"The video that was sent to me was shot in daylight. So

less than two hours after she walked out of the mall with them she was in Kowloon and they made the video."

"I want to see the video, Harry."

"I'll show you in the car. You said you got my message. Did you find out about helicopter pads in Kowloon?"

Nodding, Eleanor said, "I called the head of client transportation at the casino. He told me that in Kowloon there are seven rooftop helicopter pads available. I have a list."

"Good. Did you tell him why you wanted the list?"

"No, Harry. Give me some credit."

Bosch looked at her and then moved his eyes to Sun, who had now opened up a several-pace lead on them. Eleanor got the message.

"Sun Yee's different. He knows what's going on. I brought him in because I can trust him. He's been my security at the casino for three years."

Bosch nodded. His ex-wife was a valuable commodity to the Cleopatra Resort and Casino in Macau. They paid for her apartment and the helicopter that brought her to and from work at the private tables where she played against the casino's wealthiest clients. Security—in the form of Sun Yee—was part of that package.

"Yeah, well, too bad he wasn't watching over Maddie, too."

Eleanor abruptly stopped and turned toward Bosch. Unaware, Sun kept going. Eleanor got in Harry's face.

"Look, you want to get into this right now? Because I can if you want. We can talk about Sun Yee and we can also talk about you and how your work put my daughter in this . . . this . . ."

She never finished. Instead, she roughly grabbed Bosch by the jacket and started shaking him angrily until she was hugging him and starting to cry. Bosch put his hand on her back.

"*Our* daughter, Eleanor," he said. "*Our* daughter, and we're going to get her back."

Sun noticed they were not with him and stopped. He looked back at Bosch, his eyes hidden behind the dark glasses. Still in Eleanor's grasp, Harry raised a hand to signal him to hold for a moment and keep his distance.

Eleanor finally stepped back and wiped her eyes and nose with the back of her hand.

"You need to keep it together, Eleanor. I'm going to need you."

"*Stop* saying that, okay? I will keep it together. Where do we start?"

"Did you get the MTR map I asked for?"

"Yes, I've got it. It's in the car."

"What about the card from Causeway Taxi? Did you check it out?"

"We didn't have to. Sun Yee already knew about it. Most of the taxi companies are known to hire triad people. Triad people need legitimate jobs to avoid suspicion and keep the police away. Most of them get taxi licenses and work a few shifts here and there as a front. If your suspect was carrying the fleet manager's card, it was probably because he was going to see him about a job when he got over here."

"Did you go to the address?"

"We went by last night but it's just a taxi station. It's

where the cars get refueled and serviced and the drivers are dispatched at the start of shift."

"Did you talk to the fleet manager?"

"No. I didn't want to make a move like that without asking you. But you were in the air and I couldn't ask. Besides, it looked to me like a dead end. This was a guy who was probably going to give Chang a job. That's all. That's what he does for the triads. He wouldn't be involved in an abduction. And if he was involved, he wasn't going to talk about it."

Bosch thought Eleanor was probably right but that the fleet manager would be someone to come back to if other efforts to locate his daughter didn't pan out.

"Okay," he said. "When's it going to be light out?"

She turned to look out the huge glass wall that fronted the main hall, as if to judge her answer by the sky. Bosch checked his watch. It was 5:45 A.M. and he had already been in Hong Kong nearly an hour. It seemed like the time was going by too quickly.

"Maybe half an hour," Eleanor said.

Bosch nodded.

"What about the gun, Eleanor?"

She nodded hesitantly.

"If you're sure, Sun Yee knows where you can get one. In Wan Chai."

Bosch nodded. Of course that would be the place to get a gun. Wan Chai was where the underside of Hong Kong came to the surface. He had not been there since going there from Vietnam on leave forty years before. But he knew that some things and places never changed.

"Okay, let's get to the car. We're losing time."

They stepped through the automatic doors and Bosch was greeted by the warm, wet air. He felt the humidity start to cling to him.

"Where are we going first?" Eleanor asked. "Wan Chai?"

"No, the Peak. We'll start there."

24

It was known as Victoria Peak during colonial times. Now it was just the Peak, a mountaintop that rose behind the Hong Kong skyline and offered stunning vistas across the central district and the harbor to Kowloon. It was accessible by car and funicular tram and was a popular destination with tourists year-round and with locals in the summer months, when the city below seemed to hold humidity like a sponge holds water. Bosch had been there several times with his daughter, often eating lunch in the observatory's restaurant or the shopping galleria built behind it.

Bosch and his ex-wife and her security man made it to the top before dawn broke over the city. The galleria and tourist kiosks were still closed and the lookout points were abandoned. They left Sun's Mercedes in the lot by the galleria and walked down the path that edged the side of the mountain. Bosch had his backpack over his shoulder. The air was heavy with humidity. The pathway was wet and he could tell there had been an overnight shower. Already his shirt was sticking to his back.

"What exactly are we doing?" Eleanor asked.

The question was the first she had spoken in a long time. On the drive in from the airport Bosch had set up the video and handed her his phone. She watched it and Bosch heard her breathing catch. She then asked to watch it a second time and silently handed the phone back after. There was a terrible silence that lasted until they were on the path.

Bosch swung the backpack around and unzipped it. He handed Eleanor the photo print from the video. He then handed her a flashlight from the bag as well.

"That's a freeze-frame from the video. When Maddie kicks at the guy and the camera moves, it catches the window."

Eleanor turned on the flashlight and studied the print while they walked. Sun walked several paces behind them. Bosch continued to explain his plan.

"You have to remember that everything in the window is reflected backwards. But you see the goalposts on top of the Bank of China building? I have a magnifying glass here if you want to use it."

"Yes, I see it."

"Well, between those posts you can see the pagoda down here. I think it's called the Lion Pagoda or the Lion Lookout. I've been up here with Maddie."

"So have I. It's called the Lion Pavilion. Are you sure it's on here?"

"Yeah, you need the glass. Wait till we get up here."

The path curved and Bosch saw the pagoda-style structure ahead. It was in a prominent position, offering one of the better views from the Peak. Whenever Bosch had been here in the past it was crowded with tourists and cameras. In the gray light of dawn it was empty. Bosch stepped through the arched entrance and out to the viewing pavilion. The giant city spread out below him. There were a billion lights out there in the receding darkness and he knew one of them belonged to his daughter. He was going to find it.

Eleanor stood next to him and held the printout under the beam of the flashlight. Sun took a bodyguard's position behind them.

"I don't understand," she said. "You think you can reverse this and pinpoint where she is?"

"That's right."

"Harry..."

"There are other markers. I just want to narrow it down. Kowloon is a big place."

Bosch pulled his binoculars from the backpack. They were powerful magnifiers he used on surveillance assignments. He raised them to his eyes.

"What other markers?"

It was still too dark. Bosch lowered the binoculars. He would have to wait. He thought maybe they should have gone to Wan Chai to get the gun first.

"What other markers, Harry?"

Bosch stepped close to her so he could see the photo print and point out the markers Barbara Starkey had told him about, particularly the portion of the backwards sign with the letters *O* and *N*. He also told her about the audio track from a nearby subway and reminded her of the helicopter, which was not on the printout.

"You add it all up and I think we can get close," he said. "If I can get close, I'll find her."

"Well, I can tell you right now you are looking for the Canon sign."

"You mean Canon cameras? Where?"

She pointed in the distance toward Kowloon. Bosch looked through the binoculars again.

"I see it all the time when they fly me in and out over the harbor. There is a Canon sign on the Kowloon side. It's just the word CANON standing free on top of a building. It rotates. But if you were behind it in Kowloon when it rotated toward the harbor, you would see it backwards. Then in the reflection it would be corrected. That has to be it."

She tapped the *O-N* on the photo print.

"Yeah, but where? I don't see it anywhere."

"Let me see."

He handed her the binoculars. She spoke as she looked.

"It's normally lit up but they probably turn it off a couple hours before dawn to save energy. A lot of the signs are out right now."

She lowered the binoculars and looked at her watch.

"We'll be able to see it in about fifteen minutes."

Bosch took the binoculars back and started searching for the sign again.

"I feel like I'm wasting time."

"Don't worry. The sun's coming up."

Thwarted in his efforts, Bosch reluctantly lowered the binoculars and for the next ten minutes watched the light creep over the mountains and into the basin.

The dawn came up pink and gray. The harbor was

already busy as workboats and ferries crisscrossed paths in what looked like some kind of natural choreography. Bosch saw a low-lying mist clinging to the towers in Central and Wan Chai and across the harbor in Kowloon. He smelled smoke.

"It smells like L.A. after the riots," he said. "Like the city's on fire."

"It is in a way," Eleanor said. "We're halfway through Yue Laan."

"Yeah, what's that?"

"The Hungry Ghost festival. It began last week. It's set to the Chinese calendar. It is said that on the fourteenth day of the seventh lunar month the gates of hell open and all the evil ghosts stalk the world. Believers burn offerings to appease their ancestors and ward off the evil spirits."

"What kind of offerings?"

"Mostly paper money and papier-mâché facsimiles of things like plasma screens and houses and cars. Things the spirits supposedly need on the other side. Sometimes people burn the real things, too."

She laughed and then continued.

"I once saw somebody burning an air conditioner. Sending an air conditioner to an ancestor in hell, I guess."

Bosch remembered his daughter talking about this once. She said she had seen someone burning an entire car.

Bosch gazed down on the city and realized what he had taken as morning mist was actually smoke from the fires, hanging in the air like the ghosts themselves.

"Looks like there's a lot of believers out there."

"Yes, there are."

Bosch raised his gaze to Kowloon and brought up the

binoculars. Sunlight was finally hitting the buildings along the harborside. He panned back and forth, always keeping the goalposts on top of the Bank of China in his field of vision. Finally, he found the Canon sign Eleanor had mentioned. It sat atop a glass-and-aluminum-skinned building that was throwing sharp reflections of light in all directions.

"I see the sign," he said, without looking away.

He estimated the building that the sign was on at twelve floors. The sign sat atop an iron framework that added at least another floor to its height. He moved the binoculars back and forth, hoping to see something else. But nothing grabbed at him.

"Let me see again," Eleanor said.

Bosch handed over the binoculars and she quickly zeroed in on the Canon sign.

"Got it," she said. "And I can see that the Peninsula Hotel is across the street and within two blocks of it. It's one of the helicopter-pad locations."

Bosch followed her line of sight across the harbor. It took him a moment to find the sign. It was now catching the sun full-on. He was beginning to feel the sluggishness of the long flight breaking off. Adrenaline was kicking in.

He saw a wide road cutting north into Kowloon next to the building with the sign on top.

"What road is that?" he asked.

Eleanor kept her eyes at the binoculars.

"It's got to be Nathan Road," she said. "It's a major north–south channel. Goes from the harbor up into the New Territories."

"The triads are there?"

"Absolutely."

Bosch turned back to look out toward Nathan Road and Kowloon.

"Nine Dragons," he whispered to himself.

"What?" Eleanor asked.

"I said, that's where she is."

25

Bosch and his daughter usually took the funicular tram up and back down from the Peak. It reminded Bosch of a sleek and greatly extended version of Angels Flight back in L.A., and at the bottom his daughter liked to visit a small park near the courthouse where she could hang a Tibetan prayer flag. Often the small, colorful flags were strung like laundry on clotheslines across the park. She had told Bosch that hanging a flag was better than lighting a candle in a church because the flag was outside and its good intentions would be carried far on the wind.

There was no time to hang flags now. They got back into Sun's Mercedes and headed down the mountain toward Wan Chai. Along the way, Bosch realized that one route down would take them directly by the apartment building where Eleanor and his daughter lived.

Bosch leaned forward from the backseat.

"Eleanor, let's go by your place first."

"Why?"

"Something I forgot to tell you to bring. Madeline's passport. Yours, too."

"Why?"

"Because this won't be over when we get her back. I want both of you away from here until it is."

"And how long is that?"

She had turned to look back at him from the front seat. He could see the accusation in her eyes. He wanted to try to avoid all of that so that the rescue of his daughter was the complete focus.

"I don't know how long. Let's just get the passports. Just in case there is no time later."

Eleanor turned to Sun and spoke sharply in Chinese. He immediately pulled to the side of the road and stopped. There was no traffic coming down the mountain behind them. It was too early for that. She turned fully around in her seat to face Bosch.

"We'll stop for the passports," she said evenly. "But if we need to disappear, don't think for a minute we will be going with you."

Bosch nodded. The concession that she would be willing to do it was enough for him.

"Then maybe you should pack a couple bags and put them in the trunk, too."

She turned back around without responding. After a moment Sun looked over at her and spoke in Chinese. She responded with a nod and Sun started down the mountain again. Bosch knew that she was going to do what he'd asked.

Fifteen minutes later Sun stopped in front of the twin towers commonly known by locals as "The Chopsticks." And Eleanor, having said not a single word in those fifteen minutes, extended an olive branch to the backseat.

"You want to come up? You can make a coffee while I pack the bags. You look like you could use it."

"Coffee would be good but we don't have—"

"It's instant coffee."

"Okay, then."

Sun stayed with the car and they went up. The "chopsticks" were actually two interlinked and oval-shaped towers that rose seventy-three stories from the midslope of the mountain above Happy Valley. It was the tallest residential building in all of Hong Kong and as such stuck out at the edge of the skyline like two chopsticks protruding from a pile of rice. Eleanor and Madeline had moved into an apartment here shortly after arriving from Las Vegas six years earlier.

Bosch gripped the railing in the speed elevator as they went up. He didn't like knowing that just below the floor was an open shaft that went straight down forty-four floors.

The door opened on a small foyer leading to the four apartments on the floor, and Eleanor used a key to go in the first door on the right.

"Coffee's in the cabinet over the sink. I won't take long."

"Good. You want a cup?"

"No, I'm good. I had some at the airport."

They entered the apartment and Eleanor split off to go to her bedroom while Bosch found the kitchen and went to work on the coffee. He found a mug that said *World's Best Mom* on its side and used that. It had been hand-painted a long time before and the words had faded with each cycle the mug had gone through in the dishwasher.

He stepped out of the kitchen, sipping the hot mixture, and took in the panorama. The apartment faced west and afforded a stunning view of Hong Kong and its harbor. Bosch had only been in the apartment a few times and never tired of seeing this. Most times when he came to visit, he met his daughter in the lobby or at her school after classes.

A huge white cruise ship was making its way through the harbor and steaming toward the open sea. Bosch watched it for a moment and then noticed the Canon sign sitting atop the building in Kowloon. It was a reminder of his mission. He turned toward the hallway leading to the bedrooms. He found Eleanor in their daughter's room, crying as she put clothes into a backpack.

"I don't know what to take," she said. "I don't know how long we'll be away or what she'll need. I don't even know if we'll ever see her again."

Her shoulders trembled as she let the tears fall. Bosch put a hand on her left shoulder but she immediately shrugged it off. She would take no comfort from him. She roughly zipped the backpack closed and left the room with it. Bosch was left to look about the room by himself.

Keepsakes from trips to L.A. and other places were on every horizontal surface. Posters from movies and music groups covered the walls. A stand in the corner had several hats, masks and strings of beads hanging on it. Numerous stuffed animals from earlier years were crowded against the pillows on the bed. Bosch couldn't help but feel like he was somehow invading his daughter's privacy by being in the room uninvited by her.

On a small desk was an open laptop computer, its screen dark. Bosch stepped over and tapped the space bar and after a few moments the screen came alive. His daughter's screen saver was a photograph taken on her last trip to L.A. It showed a group of surfers in a line, floating on their boards and waiting for the next set of waves. Bosch remembered that they had driven out to Malibu to eat breakfast at a place called Marmalade and afterward had watched the surfers at a nearby beach.

Harry noticed a small box made of carved bone next to the computer's mouse. It reminded Bosch of the carved handle of the knife he had found in Chang's suitcase. It looked like something you would keep important things in, like money. He opened it and found that it contained only a small string of carved jade monkeys — see no evil, hear no evil, speak no evil — on red twine. Bosch took it out of the box and held it up to see it better. It was no more than two inches long and there was a small silver ring on the end so that it could be attached to something.

"You ready?"

Bosch turned. Eleanor was in the doorway.

"I'm ready. What is this, an earring?"

Eleanor stepped closer to see it.

"No, the kids hook those things on their phones. You can buy them at the jade market in Kowloon. So many of them have the same phones, they dress them up to be different."

Bosch nodded as he put the jade string back in the bone box.

"Are they expensive?"

"No, that's cheap jade. They cost about a dollar American and the kids change them all the time. Let's go."

Bosch took a last look around his daughter's private domain and on the way out grabbed a pillow and a folded blanket off the bed. Eleanor looked back and saw what he was doing.

"She might be tired and want to sleep," Bosch explained.

They left the apartment and in the elevator Bosch held the blanket and pillow under one arm and one of the backpacks in the other. He could smell his daughter's shampoo on the pillow.

"You have the passports?" Bosch asked.

"Yes, I have them," Eleanor said.

"Can I ask you something?"

"What?"

He acted like he was studying the pattern of ponies on the blanket he was holding.

"How far can you trust Sun Yee? I'm not sure we should be with him after we get the gun."

Eleanor answered without hesitation.

"I told you, you don't have to worry about him. I trust him all the way and he's staying with us. He's staying with me."

Bosch nodded. Eleanor looked up at the digital display that showed the floors clicking by.

"I trust him completely," she added. "And Maddie does, too."

"How does Maddie even—"

He stopped. He suddenly understood what she was saying. Sun was the man Madeline had told him about. He and Eleanor were together.

"You get it now?" she asked.

"Yeah, I get it," he said. "But are you sure Madeline trusts him?"

"Yes, I'm sure. If she told you otherwise, then she was just trying to get your sympathy. She's a girl, Harry. She knows how to manipulate. Yes, her life has been...disrupted a bit by my relationship with Sun Yee. But he has shown her nothing but kindness and respect. She'll get over it. That is, once we get her back."

Sun Yee had the car waiting in the drop-off circle at the front of the building. Harry and Eleanor put the backpacks in the trunk but Bosch took the pillow and blanket with him into the backseat. Sun pulled out and they went the rest of the way down Stubbs Road into Happy Valley and then over to Wan Chai.

Bosch tried to put the conversation from the elevator out of his mind. It wasn't important at the moment because it wouldn't help him get his daughter back. But it was hard to compartmentalize his feelings. His daughter had told him back in L.A. that Eleanor was in a relationship. And he'd had relationships himself since their divorce. But being hit with the reality of it here in Hong Kong was difficult. He was riding with a woman he still loved on some basic level and her new man. It was hard to take.

He was sitting behind Eleanor. He looked over the seat at Sun and studied the man's stoic demeanor. He was no hired gun here. He had more of a stake than that. Bosch realized that could make him an asset. If his daughter could count on and trust him, then so could Bosch. The rest he could put aside.

As if sensing the eyes on him, Sun turned and looked at Bosch. Even with the blackout shades guarding Sun's eyes, Bosch could tell he had read the situation and knew there were no secrets any longer.

Bosch nodded. It wasn't any sort of approval he was giving. It was just the silent message that he now understood they were all in this together.

26

Wan Chai was the part of Hong Kong that never slept. The place where anything could happen and anything could be had for the right price. Anything. Bosch knew that if he wanted a laser sight to go with the gun they were going to pick up, he could get it. If he wanted a shooter to go with the setup, he could probably get that, too. And this didn't even begin to address the other things, like drugs and women, that would be available to him in the strip bars and music clubs along Lockhart Road.

It was eight-thirty and full daylight as they cruised down Lockhart. Many of the clubs were still active, shutters closed against the light but neon burning brightly up above in the smoky air. The street was wet and steamy. Fragmented reflections of neon splashed across it and over the windshields of the taxis lining the curbs.

Bouncers stood on post and female hawkers sat on stools waving down pedestrians and motorists alike. Men in rumpled suits, their steps slowed by a night of alcohol or drugs, were moving slowly on the pavement. Double-parked outside the rows of red taxis the occasional Rolls-

Royce or Mercedes idled, waiting for the money to run out inside and the journey home to finally begin.

In front of almost every establishment was an ash can for burning offerings to the hungry ghosts. Many were alive with flames. Bosch saw a woman in a silk robe with a red dragon on the back standing outside a club called Red Dragon. She was showering what looked like real Hong Kong dollars into the flames leaping from the can in front of her club. She was hedging her bets with the ghosts, Bosch thought. She was going with the real thing.

The smell of fire and smoke mixed with an underlying scent of fried foods got into the car despite the windows being up. Then a harsh odor Bosch couldn't identify, almost like one of the cover-up odors he'd pick up from time to time in the coroner's office, hit him and he started breathing through his mouth. Eleanor flipped down her visor so she could see him in the makeup mirror.

"Gway lang go," she said.

"What?"

"Turtle-shell jelly. They make it around here in the mornings. They sell it in the medicine shops."

"It's strong."

"That's a nice way of putting it. You think the smell's strong, you should actually taste it sometime. Supposed to be the cure for whatever ails you."

"I think I'll pass."

In another two blocks the clubs got smaller and seedier from the outside. The neon signage was more garish and usually accompanied by lighted posters containing photographs of the beautiful women supposedly waiting inside. Sun double-parked next to the taxi that was first in line at the intersection. Three of the corners were occupied by clubs. The fourth was a noodle shop that was open and already crowded.

Sun released his seat belt and opened his door. Bosch did the same.

"Harry," Eleanor said.

Sun turned back to look at him.

"You don't go," he told Bosch.

Bosch looked at him.

"You sure? I have money."

"No money," Sun said. "You wait here."

He got out and closed the door. Bosch closed his door and stayed in the car.

"What's going on?"

"Sun Yee's calling on a friend for the gun. It's not a transaction involving money."

"Then, what does it involve?"

"Favors."

"Is Sun Yee in a triad?"

"No. He wouldn't have gotten the job in the casino. And I wouldn't be with him."

Bosch wasn't so sure about the casino job being off-limits to a triad man. Sometimes the best way to know your enemy is to hire your enemy.

"*Was* he in a triad?"

"I don't know. I doubt it. They don't let you just quit."

"But he's getting the gun from a triad guy, right?"

"I don't know that either. Look, Harry, we are getting the gun you told me you had to have. I didn't think there would be all of these questions. Do you want it or not?"

"Yes, I want it."

"Then, we are doing what needs to be done to get it. And Sun Yee is risking his job and freedom doing it, I might add. Gun laws are very harsh here."

"I understand. No more questions. Just thank you for helping me."

In the silence that followed, Bosch could hear muffled but pulsing music coming from one of the shuttered clubs or maybe from all three of them. Through the windshield he saw Sun approach three men in suits who were standing outside a club directly across the intersection. Like with most of the establishments in Wan Chai, the sign out front was in Chinese and English. The place was called the Yellow Door. Sun spoke briefly with the men and then nonchalantly opened his suit jacket so they could see he was not armed. One of the men did a quick but competent pat-down and Sun was then allowed to enter through the signature yellow door.

They waited for nearly ten minutes. During that time Eleanor said almost nothing. Bosch knew she was fearful about their daughter's situation and angry with his questions, but he needed to know more than he knew.

"Eleanor, don't get upset with me, okay? Let me just say this. As far as we know, we have the element of surprise here. As far as the people who have Maddic know, I'm still in L.A., deciding whether to kick their guy loose or not. So if Sun Yee is going to the triad here to get me a gun, won't he have to tell them where the gun is going and what it might be used for? Won't the guy with the gun then turn around and give the triad guys across the harbor in Kowloon the heads-up? You know, like, look who's in town and, oh, by the way, he's coming your way."

"No, Harry," she said dismissively. "That's not how it works."

"Well, then how does it work?"

"I told you. Sun Yee is calling in a favor. That's it. He doesn't have to provide any information because the guy with the gun owes him the favor. That's how it works. Okay?"

Bosch stared at the club entrance. No sign of Sun.

"Okay."

Another five minutes went by silently in the car and then Bosch saw Sun step back through the yellow door. But instead of heading back to the car, he crossed the street and went into the noodle shop. Bosch tried to track him through the glass windows but the reflecting neon outside was too strong and Sun disappeared from sight.

"Now what, he's getting food?" Bosch asked.

"I doubt it," Eleanor said. "He was probably sent over there."

Bosch nodded. Precautions. Another five minutes went by and when Sun emerged from the noodle shop he was carrying a Styrofoam to-go carton that was secured closed with two rubber bands. He carried it flat, as if trying not to dishevel the plate of noodles within. He returned to the car and got in. Without a word he handed the carton over the seat to Bosch.

Holding the carton low, Bosch took off the rubber bands and opened it as Sun pulled the Mercedes away from the curb. The carton contained a medium-size pistol made of blue steel. There was nothing else. No backup magazine or extra ammunition. Just the gun and whatever was in it.

Bosch dropped the carton to the floor of the car and held the pistol in his left hand. There was no brand name or marking on the bluing. Just serial and model numbers, but the five-point star stamped into the grip told Bosch the weapon was a Black Star pistol manufactured by the government of China. He had seen them on occasion in L.A. They were made by the tens of thousands for the Chinese military and a growing number ended up being stolen and smuggled across the ocean. Many of them obviously stayed in China and were smuggled into Hong Kong.

Bosch held the pistol down between his knees and ejected the magazine. It was double-stacked with fifteen 9 millimeter Parabellum rounds. He thumbed them out and put them into a cup holder in the armrest. He then ejected a sixteenth round from the chamber and put it in the cup holder with the others.

Bosch looked down the sight to focus his aim. He peered into the chamber, looking for any sign of rust, and then studied the firing pin and extractor. He checked the gun's action and trigger several times. The weapon seemed to be functioning properly. He then studied each bullet as he reloaded the magazine, looking for corrosion or any other indication that the ammunition was old or suspect. He found nothing.

He firmly pushed the magazine back into place and jacked the first round into the chamber. He then ejected the magazine again, pushed the last bullet into the opening and once more put the gun back together. He had sixteen rounds and that was it.

"Happy?" Eleanor asked from the front seat.

Bosch looked up from the weapon and saw that they

were on the down ramp to the Cross Harbour Tunnel. It would take them directly to Kowloon.

"Not quite. I don't like carrying a gun I've never fired before. For all I know, the pin on this thing could have been filed and I'll be drawing dead when I need it."

"Well, there's nothing we can do about that. You just have to trust Sun Yee."

Sunday morning traffic was light in the two-lane tunnel. Bosch waited until they passed the low point in the middle and had started up the incline toward the Kowloon side. He'd heard several backfires from taxis along the way. He quickly wrapped his daughter's blanket around the gun and his left hand. He then pulled the pillow over and turned to look out the rear window. There were no cars in sight behind them because the cars back there had not reached the midpoint of the tunnel.

"Whose car is this, anyway?" he asked.

"It belongs to the casino," Eleanor said. "I borrowed it. Why?"

Bosch lowered the window. He held the pillow up and pressed the muzzle into the padding. He fired twice, the standard double pull he employed to check the mechanism of a gun. The bullets snapped off the tunnel's tiled walls.

Even with the wadding around the gun, the two reports echoed loudly in the car. The car swerved slightly as Sun looked into the backseat. And Eleanor yelled.

"What the hell did you do?"

Bosch dropped the pillow to the floor and raised the window. The car smelled like burnt gunpowder but it was quiet again. He unwrapped the blanket and checked the weapon. It had fired easily and without a jam. He was down to fourteen bullets and was good to go.

"I had to make sure it worked," he said. "You don't carry a gun unless you're sure."

"*Are you crazy?* You could get us arrested before we get a chance to do anything!"

"If you keep your voice down and Sun Yee stays in his lane, I think we'll be fine."

Bosch leaned forward and tucked the weapon into his waistband at the small of his back. Its slide was warm against his skin. Up ahead he saw light at the end of the tunnel. They would be in Kowloon soon.

It was time.

27

The tunnel delivered them to Tsim Sha Tsui, the central waterside section of Kowloon, and within a few minutes Sun turned the Mercedes onto Nathan Road. It was a wide, four-lane boulevard lined with high-rise buildings as far as Bosch could see. It was a crowded mix of commercial and residential uses. The first two floors of every building were dedicated to retail and restaurant space, while the floors rising above were residential or office space. The clutter of video screens and signs in Chinese and English was an intense riot of color and motion. The buildings ranged from dowdy midcentury construction to the slick glass-and-steel structures of recent prosperity.

It was impossible for Bosch to see the top of the corridor from the car. He lowered his window and leaned out in an effort to find the Canon sign, the first marker from the photo generated from his daughter's abduction video. He couldn't find it and pulled back into the car. He raised the window.

"Sun Yee, stop the car."

Sun looked at him in the rearview.

"Stop here?"

"Yes, here. I can't see. I have to get out."

Sun looked at Eleanor for approval and she nodded.

"We'll get out. You find a place to park."

Sun pulled to the curb and Bosch jumped out. He'd taken the photo print from his backpack and had it ready. Sun then pulled away, leaving Eleanor and Bosch on the sidewalk. It was now midmorning and the streets and sidewalks were crowded with people. Smoke was in the air and the smell of fire. The hungry ghosts were close. The streetscape was replete with neon, mirrored glass and giant plasma screens broadcasting silent images of jerking motion and staccato edits.

Bosch referred to the photo and then looked up and traced the skyline.

"Where's the Canon sign?" he asked.

"Harry, you're mixed up," Eleanor said.

She put her hands on his shoulders and turned him completely around.

"Remember, everything is backwards."

She pointed almost directly up, her finger drawing a line up the side of the building they were in front of. Bosch looked up. The Canon sign was directly overhead and at an angle that made it unreadable. He was looking at the bottom edge of the sign's letters. It was rotating slowly.

"Okay, got it," he said. "We start from there."

He looked back down and referred to the photo.

"I think we have to go at least another block further in from the harbor."

"Let's wait for Sun Yee."

"Call him and tell him where we're going."

Bosch started off. Eleanor had no choice but to follow.

"All right, all right."

She pulled her phone and started to make the call. As he walked, Bosch kept his eyes high on the buildings, looking for air-conditioning units. A block here was several buildings long. Looking up as he walked, he had a few near misses with other pedestrians. There seemed to be no collective uniformity of walking to your right. People moved every which way and Bosch had to pay attention to avoid collisions. At one point the people moving in front of him suddenly stepped left and right and Bosch almost stumbled over an old woman lying on the pavement, her hands clasped in beseeching prayer above a coin basket. Bosch was able to avoid her and reached into his pocket at the same time.

Eleanor quickly put her hand on his arm.

"No. They say any money you give them is taken by the triads at the end of the day."

Bosch didn't question it. He stayed focused on what was ahead of him. They walked another two blocks and then Bosch saw and heard another piece of the puzzle drop into place. Across the street was an entrance to the Mass Transit Railway. A glass enclosure leading to the escalators down to the underground subway.

"Wait," Bosch said, stopping. "We're close."

"What is it?" Eleanor asked.

"The MTR. You could hear it on the video."

As if on cue the growing whoosh of escaping air rose as a train came into the underground station. It sounded like a wave. Bosch looked down at the photo in his hand and then up at the buildings surrounding him.

"Let's cross."

"Can we just wait a minute for Sun Yee? I can't tell him where to meet us if we keep moving."

"Once we're across."

They hurried across the street on a flashing pedestrian signal. Bosch noticed several ragtag women begging for coins near the MTR entrance. More people were coming up out of the station than were going down. Kowloon was getting more and more crowded. The air was thick with humidity and Bosch could feel his shirt sticking to his back.

Bosch turned around and looked up. They were in an area of older construction. It was almost like having walked through first class to economy on a plane. The buildings on this block and heading further in were shorter—in the twenty-story range—and in poorer condition than those in the blocks closer to the harbor. Harry noticed many open windows and many individual air-conditioning boxes hanging from windows. He could feel the reservoir of adrenaline inside open up.

"Okay, this is it. She's in one of these buildings."

He started moving down the block to get away from the crowding and loud conversations surrounding the MTR entrance. He kept his eyes on the upper levels of the buildings surrounding him. He was in a concrete canyon and somewhere up there in one of the crevices was his missing daughter.

"Harry, stop! I just told Sun Yee to meet us at the MTR entrance."

"You wait for him. I'll be just down here."

"No, I'm coming with you."

Halfway down the block, Bosch stopped and referred to the photo again. But there was no final clue that helped him. He knew he was close but he had reached a point where he needed help or it would be a guessing game. He was surrounded by thousands of rooms and windows. It was beginning to dawn on him that the final part of his search was impossible. He had traveled more than seven thousand miles to find his daughter and he was about as helpless as the ragtag women begging coins from the pavement.

"Let me see the photo," Eleanor said.

Bosch handed it to her.

"There's nothing else," he said. "All these buildings look the same."

"Let me just look."

She took her time and Bosch watched her regress two decades to the time she was an FBI agent. Her eyes narrowed and she analyzed the photo as an agent, not as the mother of a missing girl.

"Okay," she said. "There's got to be something here."

"I thought it would be the air conditioners but they're on every building around here."

Eleanor nodded but kept her eyes on the photo. Just then Sun came up, his face flushed from the exertion of trying to track a moving target. Eleanor said nothing to him but slightly moved her arm to share the photo with him. They had reached a point in their relationship where words weren't necessary.

Bosch turned and looked down the corridor of Nathan Road. Whether it was a conscious move or not, he didn't want to see what he no longer had. From behind he heard Eleanor say, "Wait a minute. There's a pattern here."

Bosch turned back.

"What do you mean?"

"We can do this, Harry. There's a pattern that will lead us right to that room."

Bosch felt a ghost run down his spine. He moved in close to Eleanor so he could see the photo.

"Show it to me," he said, urgency fueling each word.

Eleanor pointed to the photo and ran her fingernail along a line of air conditioners reflected in the window.

"Not every window has an air-conditioning unit in the building we are looking for. Some, like this room, have open windows. So there is a pattern. We only have part of it here because we don't know where this room is in relation to the building."

"It's probably in the center. The audio analysis picked up muffled voices cut off by the elevator. The elevator is probably centrally located."

"That's good. That helps. Okay, so let's say windows are dashes and AC boxes are dots. In this reflection we see a pattern for the floor she is on. You start with the room she is in—a dash—and then you go dot, dot, dash, dot, dash."

She tapped her nail on each part of the pattern on the photo.

"So that's our pattern," she added. "Looking up at the building, we'd be looking for it going left to right."

"Dash, dot, dot, dash, dot, dash," Bosch repeated. "Windows are dashes."

"Right," Eleanor said. "Should we split up the buildings? We know because of the subway that we're close."

She turned and looked up at the wall of buildings that

ran the entire length of the street. Bosch's first thought was to not trust any of the buildings to anybody else. He wouldn't be satisfied until he had scanned each building for the pattern himself. But he held back. Eleanor had found the pattern and made this break. He would ride her wave.

"Let's start," he said. "Which one should I take?"

Pointing, she said, "You take that one, I'll take this one and, Sun Yee, you check that one. If you get done, you leapfrog to the next building. We go till we find it. Start at the top. We know from the photo, the room is up high."

She was right, Bosch realized. It would make the search faster than he'd anticipated. He stepped away and went to work on the building he was assigned. He started on the top floor and worked his way down, his eyes scanning back and forth floor by floor. Eleanor and Sun separated and did the same.

Thirty minutes later Bosch was halfway through scanning his third building when Eleanor called out.

"I've got it!"

Bosch headed back to her. She had her hand raised and was counting up the floors of the building directly across the street. Sun soon joined them.

"Fourteenth floor. The pattern starts just a little to the right of center. You were right about that, Harry."

Bosch counted the floors, his eyes rising with his hopes. He got to the fourteenth level and identified the pattern. There were twelve windows across in all and the pattern fit the last six windows to the right.

"That's it."

"Wait a minute. This is only one incidence of the pattern. There could be others. We have to keep—"

"I'm not waiting. You keep looking. If you find another match for the pattern, call me."

"No, we're not splitting up."

He zeroed in on the window that would have been the one that caught the reflection in the video. It was closed now.

He lowered his eyes to the building's entrance. The first two levels of the building were retail and commercial use. A band of signage, including two large digital screens, wrapped the entire building. Above this the building's name was affixed to the facade in gold letters and symbols:

CHUNGKING MANSIONS

The main entrance was as wide as a double-car garage door. Through the opening Bosch saw a short set of stairs leading to what looked like a crowded shopping bazaar.

"This is Chungking Mansions," Eleanor said, recognition in her voice.

"You know it?" Bosch asked.

"I've never been here but everybody knows about Chungking Mansions."

"What is it?"

"It's the melting pot. It's the cheapest place in the city to stay and it's the first stop for every third- and fourth-world immigrant who comes here. Every couple of months you read about somebody being arrested or shot or stabbed and this is their address. It's like a postmodern Casablanca—all in one building."

"Let's go."

Bosch started across the street in the middle of the block, wading into slow-moving traffic, forcing taxis to stop and hoot their horns.

"Harry, what are you doing?" Eleanor yelled after him.

Bosch didn't answer. He made it across and went up the stairs into Chungking Mansions. It was like stepping onto another planet.

28

The first thing that hit Bosch as he stepped up into the first level of the Chungking Mansions was the smell. Intense odors of spices and fried food invaded his nostrils as his eyes became accustomed to the dimly lit third-world farmers' market that spread before him in narrow aisles and warrens. The place was just opening for the day but was already crowded with shopkeepers and customers. Six-foot-wide shop stalls offered everything from watches and cell phones to newspapers of every language and foods of any taste. There was an edgy, gritty feel to the place that left Bosch casually checking his wake every few steps. He wanted to know who was behind him.

He moved to the center, where he came to an elevator alcove. There was a line fifteen people deep waiting for two elevators, and Bosch noticed that one elevator was open, dark inside and obviously out of commission. There were two security guards at the front of the line, checking to make sure everybody going up had a room key or was with somebody who had a key. Above the door of the one functioning elevator was a video screen that showed its interior. It was crowded to maximum capacity, sardines in a can.

Bosch was staring at the screen and wondering how he was going to get up to the fourteenth floor when Eleanor and Sun caught up to him. Eleanor roughly grabbed him by the arm.

"Harry, enough with the one-man army! Don't run off like that again."

Bosch looked at her. It wasn't anger he saw in her eyes. It was fear. She wanted to be sure she wasn't without him when she faced whatever there was to face on the fourteenth floor.

"I just want to keep moving," Bosch said.

"Then move with us, not away from us. Are we going up?"

"We need a key to go up."

"Then we have to rent a room."

"Where do we do that?"

"I don't know."

Eleanor looked at Sun.

"We have to go up."

That was all she said but the message was transmitted. He nodded and led them away from the alcove and further into the labyrinth of shop stalls. Soon they came to a row of counters with signs in multiple languages.

"You rent the room here," Sun said. "There is more than one hotel here."

"You mean in the building?" Bosch asked. "More than one?"

"Yes, many. You pick from here."

He gestured to the signs on the counters. And Bosch

realized that what Sun was saying was that there were
multiple hotels within the building, all of them competing
for the business of the cut-rate traveler. Some, by virtue of
the language on their signs, targeted travelers from specific countries.

"Ask which one has the fourteenth floor," he said.

"There won't be a fourteenth floor."

Bosch realized he was right.

"Fifteenth, then. Which one has the fifteenth floor?"

Sun went down the line, asking about the fifteenth
floor, until he stopped at the third counter and waved Eleanor and Bosch over.

"Here."

Bosch took in the man behind the counter. He looked
like he had been there for forty years. His bell-shaped
body seemed form-fitted to the stool he sat on. He was
smoking a cigarette attached to a four-inch holder made
of carved bone. He didn't like getting smoke in his eyes.

"Do you speak English?" Bosch asked.

"Yes, I have English," the man said tiredly.

"Good. We want a room on the four—the fifteenth floor."

"All of you? One room?"

"Yes, one room."

"No, you can't one room. Only two persons."

Bosch realized that he meant the maximum occupancy
of each room was two people.

"Then give me two rooms on fifteen."

"You do."

The deskman slid a clipboard across the counter.
There was a pen attached with a string and under the clip
a thin stack of registration forms. Bosch quickly scribbled

his name and address and slid the board back across the counter.

"ID, passport," the deskman said.

Bosch pulled his passport and the man checked it. He wrote the number down on a piece of scratch paper and handed it back.

"How much?" Bosch asked.

"How long you stay?"

"Ten minutes."

The deskman moved his eyes over all three of them as he considered what Bosch's answer meant.

"Come on," Bosch said impatiently. "How much?"

He reached into his pocket for his cash.

"Two hundred American."

"I don't have American. I have Hong Kong dollars."

"Two room, one thousand five hundred."

Sun stepped forward and put his hand down over Bosch's money.

"No, too much."

He started speaking quickly and authoritatively to the deskman, refusing to let him take advantage of Bosch. But Harry didn't care. He cared about momentum, not the money. He peeled fifteen hundred off his roll and threw it on the desk.

"Keys," he demanded.

The deskman disengaged from Sun and swiveled around to the double row of cubbyholes behind him. As he selected two keys from the slots, Bosch looked at Sun and shrugged.

But when the deskman turned back and Bosch put out his hand, he withheld the keys.

"Key deposit one thousand."

Bosch realized he should never have flashed his roll. He quickly pulled it again, this time holding it below the counter, and peeled off two more bills. He slapped them down on the counter. When the man on the stool finally offered the keys, Harry grabbed them out of his hand and started back to the elevator.

The room keys were old-fashioned brass keys attached to red plastic diamond-shaped fobs with Chinese symbols on them and room numbers. They had been given rooms 1503 and 1504. Along the way back to the alcove, Bosch handed one of the keys to Sun.

"You're with him or me," he said to Eleanor.

The line for the elevator had gotten longer. It was now more than thirty men deep and the overhead video showed that the guards were putting eight to ten people on each time, depending on the size of the travelers. The longest fifteen minutes of Bosch's life were spent waiting to go up. Eleanor tried to calm his growing impatience and anxiety by engaging in conversation.

"When we get up there, what's the plan?"

Bosch shook his head.

"No plan. We play it like it lays."

"That's it? What are we going to do, just knock on doors?"

Bosch shook his head and held up the photo of the reflection again.

"No, we'll know what room it is. There is one window in this room. One window per room. We know from this that our window is the seventh down on the side that fronts

Nathan Road. When we get up there, we hit the seventh room from the end."

"Hit?"

"I'm not knocking, Eleanor."

The line moved forward and it was finally their turn. The security guard checked Bosch's key and passed him and Eleanor toward the elevator door, but then put his arm out behind them and stopped Sun. The elevator was at capacity.

"Harry, wait," Eleanor said. "Let's take the next one."

Bosch pushed onto the elevator and turned around. He looked at Eleanor and then at Sun.

"You wait if you want. I'm not waiting."

Eleanor hesitated for a moment and then stepped onto the elevator next to Bosch. She called out something in Chinese to Sun as the door closed.

Bosch stared up at the digital floor indicator.

"What did you say to him?"

"That we'd be waiting on fifteen for him."

Bosch didn't say anything. It didn't matter to him. He tried to compose himself and slow his breathing. He was readying himself for what he might find or be confronted with on fifteen.

The elevator moved slowly. It stunk of body odor and fish. Bosch breathed through his mouth to try to avoid it. He realized he was also a contributor to the problem. The last time he'd showered was on Friday morning in L.A. To him, that seemed like a lifetime ago.

The ride up was more excruciating than the wait down below. Finally, on its fifth stop, the door opened on fifteen. By then the only passengers left were Bosch, Eleanor and two men who had pushed sixteen. Harry glanced at the two men and then ran his finger down the row of buttons below the one marked 15. It meant the elevator would stop multiple times on the way down. He stepped off first, with his left hand behind his hip and ready to go for the gun the moment it was necessary. Eleanor came out behind him.

"I guess we're not going to wait for Sun Yee, are we?" she said.

"I'm not," Bosch said.

"He should be here."

Bosch wheeled around on her.

"No, he shouldn't."

She raised her hands in surrender and stepped back. This wasn't the time for this. At least she knew it. Bosch turned away and tried to get a sense of their bearings. The elevator alcove was in the center of an *H* floor design. He moved toward the hallway to the right because he knew this would be the side of the building fronting Nathan Road.

He immediately started counting doors and came up with twelve on the front side of the hall. He moved to the seventh door, room 1514. He felt his heart hit a higher gear as a charge went through him. This was it. This was what he was here for.

He leaned forward, putting his ear to the door's crack. He listened intently but heard no sounds from within the room.

"Anything?" Eleanor whispered.

Bosch shook his head. He put his hand on the knob and tried to turn it. He didn't expect the door to be unlocked but he wanted a feel for the hardware and how solid it might be.

The knob was old and loose. Bosch had to decide whether to kick the door in and use the element of complete surprise, or to pick the lock and possibly make a sound that would alert whoever was on the other side of the door.

He dropped to one knee and looked closely at the doorknob. It would be a simple pick but there could be a bolt lock or a security chain inside. He thought of something and reached into his pocket.

"Go to our room," he whispered. "Find out if there's a dead bolt or a security chain."

He handed her the key to room 1504.

"Now?" Eleanor whispered.

"Yeah, now," Bosch whispered back. "I want to know what's inside here."

She took the key and hurried down the hall. Bosch pulled his badge wallet out. Before going through airport security he had slid his two best picks behind the badge. He knew the badge would light up on the X-ray but that the two thin metal strips behind it would likely be mistaken for part of the badge. His plan had worked and now he removed the picks and quietly maneuvered them into the doorknob lock.

It took him less than a minute to turn the lock. He held the knob without pushing the door open until Eleanor came hurrying back down the dimly lit hallway.

"There's a security chain," she whispered.

Bosch nodded and stood up, still holding the knob with his right hand. He knew he could easily shoulder the door past a security chain.

"Ready?" he whispered.

Eleanor nodded. Bosch then reached back and under his jacket and pulled the gun. He thumbed off the safety and looked at Eleanor. In unison, they mouthed the words *one, two, three* and he pushed the door open.

There was no security chain in place. The door moved all the way open and Bosch quickly entered the room. Eleanor came in right behind him.

The room was empty.

29

Bosch stepped through the room to the tiny bathroom. He slapped the dirty plastic shower curtain back from a small, tiled shower space but it was empty. He walked back into the room and looked at Eleanor. He said the words he dreaded.

"She's gone."

"Are you sure this is even the room?" she asked.

Bosch was. He had already looked at the pattern of cracks and nail holes on the wall over the bed. He took the folded photo print out of his jacket and handed it to her.

"This is the room."

He put the gun back under his jacket and in the waistband of his pants. He tried to keep the searing sense of futility and dread from engulfing him. But he wasn't sure where to go from here.

Eleanor dropped the photo on the bed.

"There's got to be some sign that she was here. Something."

"Let's go. We'll talk to the guy downstairs. We'll find out who rented the room Friday."

"No, wait. We have to look around first."

She dropped down and looked under the bed.

"Eleanor, she's not under the bed. She's gone and we need to keep moving. Call Sun and tell him not to come up. Tell him to get the car."

"No, this can't be."

She moved from looking under the bed to kneeling next to it, elbows on top, as if she were a child praying before bedtime.

"She can't be gone. We..."

Bosch came around the bed and leaned down behind her. He put his arms around her and pulled her up standing.

"Come on, Eleanor, we have to go. We're going to find her. I told you we would. We just have to keep moving. That's all. We have to stay strong and keep moving."

He ushered her toward the door, but she broke free and headed toward the bathroom. She had to see it empty for herself.

"Eleanor, please."

She disappeared into the room and Bosch heard her pull the shower curtain back. But then she didn't return.

"Harry!"

Bosch quickly crossed the room and entered the bathroom. Eleanor was leaning over the side of the toilet and lifting the wastebasket. She brought it around to him. At the bottom of the basket was a small wad of toilet paper with blood on it.

Eleanor retrieved it with two fingers and held it up. The blood had made a stain smaller than a dime. The size of the stain and the wadding of the tissue suggested it had been held against a small cut or wound to stanch the flow of blood.

Eleanor leaned into Bosch, and Harry knew that she was assuming that they were looking at their daughter's blood.

"We don't know what this means yet, Eleanor."

His counsel was ignored. Her body language suggested a breakdown was coming.

"They drugged her," she said. "They put a needle in her arm."

"We don't know that yet. Let's go downstairs and talk to the guy."

She didn't move. She stared at the blood and tissue like it was a red-and-white flower.

"Do you have something to put this in?"

Bosch always carried a small quantity of sealable evidence bags in his coat pockets. He pulled one out now and Eleanor placed the wad in it. He closed it and put it into his pocket.

"Okay, let's go."

They finally left the room. Bosch had one arm around Eleanor's back and was looking at her face as they entered the hall. He half expected her to break free and run back to the room. But then he saw some sort of recognition flare in her eyes as she focused down the hall.

"Harry?"

Bosch turned, expecting it to be Sun. But it wasn't.

Two men were approaching from the end of the hall. They were walking side by side with purpose. Bosch realized that they were the two men who had been the last passengers with them in the elevator going up. They had been going to sixteen.

The moment the men saw Harry and Eleanor enter the hallway, their hands went inside their jackets to their waistbands. Bosch saw one man close his grip and instinctively knew he was pulling a gun.

Bosch brought his right arm up to the center of Eleanor's back and shoved her across the hall toward the elevator alcove. At the same time, he brought his left hand up behind his back and grabbed his gun. One of the men yelled something in a language Bosch didn't understand and raised his weapon.

Bosch pulled his own gun and brought it around on aim. He opened fire at the same moment shots were fired from one of the men down the hall. Bosch fired repeatedly, at least ten shots, and continued after he saw both men go down.

Holding his aim, he moved forward on them. One was lying on top of the other's legs. One was dead, his eyes staring blankly at the ceiling. The other was still alive and breathing shallowly at the same time he was still trying to pull his gun from his waistband. Bosch looked down and saw that the hammer spur had gotten snagged in the waistband of his pants. He had never gotten the gun out.

Bosch reached down and took the man's hand off the weapon and roughly pulled the gun loose. The man dropped his hand to the floor. Bosch slid the gun across the carpet out of his reach.

There were two wounds in the man's upper chest. Bosch had gone for body mass and his aim was true. The man was bleeding out quickly.

"Where is she?" Bosch said. "Where is she?"

The man made a grunting sound and blood dripped from his mouth down the side of his face. Bosch knew he would be dead in another minute.

Bosch heard a door open down the hallway and then quickly close. He checked but saw no one. Most people in a place like this wouldn't want to get involved. Still, he knew it wouldn't be long before the police stormed the hotel on the report of a shooting.

He turned back to the dying man.

"Where is she?" he repeated. "Where's my—"

He saw that the man was dead.

"Shit!"

Bosch got up and turned back to the alcove and Eleanor.

"They had to have—"

She was on the floor. Bosch rushed to her and dropped down to the floor.

"Eleanor!"

He was too late. Her eyes were open and just as blank as the man's in the hallway.

"No, no, please, no. *Eleanor!*"

He couldn't see any wound but she wasn't breathing and her eyes were fixed. He shook her by the shoulders and got no response. He put one hand behind her head and opened her mouth with the other. He leaned forward to blow air into her lungs. But then he felt the wound. He pulled his hand out of her hair and it was covered in blood. He turned her head and saw the wound in the hairline behind her left ear. He realized she had probably been hit as he had pushed her into the alcove. He had pushed her into the shot.

"Eleanor," he said quietly.

Bosch leaned forward and put his face down on her chest between her breasts. He smelled her familiar fragrance. He heard a loud, awful groan and realized it had come from himself.

For thirty seconds he didn't move. He just held her there. Then he heard the elevator open behind him and finally raised himself up.

Sun stepped off the elevator. He took in the scene and his focus quickly went to Eleanor on the floor.

"Eleanor!"

He rushed to her side. Bosch realized it was the first time he had heard him say her name. He had pronounced it *Eeeleanor*.

"She's gone," Bosch said. "I'm sorry."

"Who did this?"

Bosch started to get up. He spoke in a monotone.

"Over there. Two men fired on us."

Sun looked into the hallway and saw the two men on the ground. Bosch saw the confusion and horror on his face. He then turned back to Eleanor again.

"No!"

Bosch stepped back into the hall and picked up the gun he had pulled from the man's waistband. Without examining it, he tucked the weapon into his own pants and went back to the alcove. Sun was on his knees next to Eleanor's body. He was holding her hand in his.

"Sun Yee, I'm sorry. They took us by surprise."

He waited a moment. Sun said nothing and didn't move.

"I have to do something here and then we have to go. I'm sure the police are on their way."

He put his hand on Sun's shoulder and pulled him back. Bosch knelt next to Eleanor and picked up her right arm. He wrapped her hand around the gun he had gotten from Sun. He fired a shot into the wall next to the elevator. He then carefully placed her arm back down on the floor, her hand still holding the gun.

"What are you doing?" Sun demanded.

"Gunshot residue. Is the gun clean or will it be traced back to whoever gave it to you?"

Sun didn't respond.

"Sun Yee, is the gun clean?"

"It's clean."

"Then let's go. We have to take the stairs. There's nothing we can do for Eleanor now."

Sun bowed his head for a moment and then slowly stood up.

"They came from the stairs," Bosch said, referring to the gunmen. "We'll go that way."

They moved down the hall but Sun suddenly stopped to examine the two men on the floor.

"Come on," Bosch prompted. "We have to go."

Sun finally followed. They hit the stairwell door and started down.

"They're not triad," Sun said.

Bosch was two steps ahead. He stopped and looked back up at him.

"What? How do you know?"

"They're not Chinese. Not Chinese, not triad."

"Then what are they?"

"Indonesian, Vietnamese—I think Vietnamese. Not Chinese."

Bosch started down again and picked up the pace. They had eleven flights of stairs to go. As he moved he thought about this piece of information from Sun and couldn't see how it fit with what was already known.

Sun fell behind the pace. And no wonder, Bosch thought. When he stepped off that elevator, his life irrevocably changed. That would slow anybody down.

Soon Bosch was a whole floor ahead of him. When he got to the bottom, he opened the exit door a crack to get his bearings. He saw that the door opened onto a pedestrian alley that ran between the Chungking Mansions and the building next door. Bosch could hear traffic and sirens close by and knew the exit was very close to Nathan Road.

The door was suddenly pushed closed. Bosch turned and Sun had one hand flat on the door. He pointed angrily at Harry with the other.

"You! You get her killed!"

"I know. I know, Sun Yee. It's all on me. My case brought all of this—"

"No, they not triad! *I told you.*"

Bosch stared at him for a moment, not comprehending.

"Okay, they're not triad. But—"

"You show your money and they rob."

Bosch now understood. He was saying that the two men lying dead on the fifteenth floor with Eleanor had merely been robbers after Bosch's money. But there was something wrong. It didn't work. Harry shook his head.

"They were in front of us in the line for the elevator. They didn't see my money."

"They were told."

Bosch considered this and his thoughts turned to the man on the stool. He had wanted to pay that man a visit already. The scenario Sun had spun made the need more immediate.

"Sun Yee, we need to get out of here. The police are going to close all the exits once they get up there and see what they have."

Sun dropped his hand off the door and Bosch opened it again. It was clear. They stepped out into the alley. Twenty feet to their left was where the alley opened on Nathan Road.

"Where's the car?"

Sun pointed toward the opposite end of the alley.

"I paid a man to watch it."

"Okay, get the car and drive around front. I'm going back inside but I'll be out front in five minutes."

"What will you do?"

"You don't want to know."

30

Bosch walked out of the alley onto Nathan Road and immediately saw the crowd of onlookers gathered to watch the police response to the call inside the Chungking Mansions. Police and fire rescue vehicles were arriving and stopping and causing traffic snarls and confusion. Barricades had not yet been set up, as the arriving officers were probably too busy trying to get up to the fifteenth floor to find out what had happened. Harry was able to join the end of a flow of paramedics carrying a stretcher up the steps and into the first level of the building.

The commotion and confusion had drawn many of the shopkeepers and customers into a crowd around the elevator alcove. Someone was barking orders at the crowd in Chinese but no one seemed to be reacting. Bosch pushed his way through and got to the rear aisle where the hotel desks were. He saw that the diversion had worked in his favor. The aisle was completely empty.

When he got to the desk where he had rented the two rooms, he saw that a security gate had been pulled halfway down from the ceiling, indicating the desk was closed.

But the man on the stool was there with his back turned while he sat at the rear counter, shoving paperwork into a briefcase. It looked like he was getting ready to leave.

Without losing momentum Bosch jumped up and slid over the counter and under the gate, smashing into the man on the stool and knocking him to the floor. Bosch jumped on top of him and hit him twice in the face with his fist. The man's head was on the concrete floor and he absorbed the full impact of the punches.

"No, please!" he managed to spit out between punches.

Bosch quickly glanced back over the counter to make sure it was still clear. He then pulled the gun from behind him and pressed the muzzle into the roll of fat below the man's chin.

"You got her killed, you motherfucker! And I'm going to kill you."

"No, please! Sir, please!"

"You told them, didn't you? You told them I had money."

"No, I have not."

"Don't fucking lie to me or I'll kill you right now. You told them!"

The man lifted his head off the floor.

"Okay, listen, listen, please. I said nobody to get hurt. You understand? I said nobody to—"

Bosch pulled the gun back and brought it down hard on the man's nose. His head snapped back against the concrete. Bosch pushed the barrel into his neck.

"I don't care what you said. They killed her, you fuck! Do you understand that?"

The man was dazed and bleeding, his eyes blinking as

he wavered in and out of consciousness. With his right hand, Bosch slapped his cheek.

"Stay awake. I want you to see it coming."

"Please, no . . . I am very sorry, sir. Please don't—"

"Okay, this is what you're going to do. You want to live, then you tell me who rented room fifteen fourteen on Friday. Fifteen fourteen. You tell me right now."

"Okay, I tell you. I show you."

"Okay, you show me."

Bosch pulled his weight back off him. The man was bleeding from the mouth and nose and Bosch was bleeding from the knuckles of his left hand. He quickly reached up and pulled the security fence all the way down to the counter.

"Show me. Now."

"Okay, it is here."

He pointed to the briefcase he had been loading. He reached into it and Bosch raised the gun and pointed it at his head.

"Easy."

The man pulled out a stack of room registration forms. Bosch saw his own on top. He reached over and grabbed it off the stack and crumpled it into the pocket of his coat. All the while he kept his aim on the man.

"Friday, room fifteen fourteen. Find it."

The man put the stack of forms on the back counter and started going through them. Bosch knew he was taking too much time. The police would come any moment to the hotel desks and find them. It had been at least fifteen minutes since the shootings on fifteen. He saw a shelf under the front counter and put the gun there. If the police caught him with it, he'd go to prison, no matter what.

Looking at the robber's gun as he placed it down prompted the realization that he had left his ex-wife and the mother of his daughter lying dead and alone up there on fifteen. It put a spear through Bosch's chest. He closed his eyes for a moment to try to push the thought and vision away.

"Here it is."

Bosch opened his eyes. The man was turning to him from the rear counter. Bosch heard a distinct metal snap. He saw the man's right arm start to swing around and up from his side and Bosch knew there was a knife before he saw it. In a split-second decision, he chose to block rather than parry the attack. He moved forward and into the man, raising his left forearm to block the knife and driving his right fist toward his attacker's throat.

The knife tore through the sleeve of Bosch's jacket and he felt the blade slice into the inside of his forearm. But that was all the damage he took. His punch to the throat sent the man backwards and he fell on the overturned stool. Bosch dropped on him again, grabbing his knife hand by the wrist and smashing it back repeatedly against the floor until the weapon clattered loose on the concrete.

Bosch raised himself up while still holding the man down by the throat. He could feel blood sliding down his arm from the wound. He thought again about Eleanor lying dead up on fifteen. Her life and everything taken from her before she could even say a word. Before she could see her daughter safe again.

Bosch raised his left fist and struck the man viciously in the ribs. He did it again and again, punching body and face, until he was sure most of the man's ribs and jaw were broken and he'd lapsed into unconsciousness.

Bosch was winded. He picked up the switchblade and folded it closed and dropped it into his pocket. He moved off the man's unmoving body and gathered the fallen registration forms. He then got up and shoved them back into the counterman's briefcase and closed it. He leaned over the counter to look out through the security gate. It was still clear in the aisle, though he could now hear announcements being made through a bullhorn coming from the elevator alcove. He knew that police procedure would have to be to shut the place down and secure it.

He raised the security gate two feet and then grabbed the gun off the shelf and put it into his rear waistband. He climbed over the counter with the briefcase and slid out. After checking to make sure he had left no blood on the counter, he lowered the gate and walked away.

As he moved, Bosch held his arm up to check the wound through the rip in his coat sleeve. It looked superficial but it was a bleeder. He pulled his coat sleeve up to bunch it around the wound and absorb the blood. He checked the floor behind him to make sure he wasn't dripping.

At the elevator alcove the police were herding everybody out to the street and into a cordoned-off area where they would be held for questioning about what they might have heard or seen. Bosch knew he couldn't go through that process. He made a U-turn and headed down an aisle toward the other side of the building. He got to an intersection of aisles and caught a glimpse to his left of two men hurrying in a direction away from the police activity.

Bosch followed, realizing he wasn't the only one in

the building who wouldn't want to be questioned by the police.

The two men disappeared into a narrow passageway between two of the now-shuttered shops. Bosch followed.

The passage led to a staircase down into a basement where there were rows of storage cages for the shopkeepers above, who had such limited public retail space. Bosch followed the men down one aisle and then turned right. He saw them heading toward a glowing red Chinese symbol over a door and knew it had to be an exit. The men pushed through and an alarm sounded. They slammed the door behind them.

Bosch ran toward the door and pushed through. He found himself in the same pedestrian alley he had been in earlier. He quickly walked out to Nathan Road and looked for Sun and the Mercedes.

Headlights flashed from half a block away and Bosch saw the car waiting ahead of the clot of police vehicles parked haphazardly in front of the entrance to Chungking Mansions. Sun pulled away from the curb and cruised up to him. Bosch at first went to the back door but then realized Eleanor wasn't with them anymore. He got in the front.

"You took long time," Sun said.

"Yeah, let's get out of here."

Sun glanced down at the briefcase with Bosch's bleeding knuckles wrapped around the handle. He said nothing. He accelerated and headed away from the Chungking Mansions. Bosch turned in his seat to look back. His eyes rose up the building to the floor where they had left Eleanor. Somehow, Bosch had always thought they would grow old together. Their divorce didn't matter. Other lovers didn't matter. They'd always had an on-and-off relationship but that didn't matter either. It had always been in the back of his mind that the separations were what were temporary. In the long run they would be together. Of course, they had Madeline together and that would always be their bond. But he had believed there would be more.

Now all of that was gone and it was because of the choices he had made. Whether it was because of his case or his momentary lapse in flashing his money didn't really matter. All roads led back to him and he wasn't sure how he was going to live with it.

He leaned forward and put his head in his hands.

"Sun Yee, I'm sorry . . . I loved her, too."

Sun didn't respond for a long time and when he spoke, he brought Bosch out of the downward spiral and back into focus.

"We must find your daughter now. For Eleanor we will do this."

Bosch straightened up and nodded. He then leaned forward and pulled the briefcase onto his lap.

"Pull over when you can. You have to look at this stuff."

Sun made several turns and put several blocks between them and Chungking Mansions before pulling to a stop against the curb. They were across the street from a ramshackle market that was crowded with westerners.

"What's this place?" Bosch asked.

"This is the jade market. Very famous for westerners. You will not be noticed here."

Bosch nodded. He opened the briefcase and handed Sun the unruly stack of hotel registration forms. There were at least fifty of them. Most had been filled out in Chinese and were unreadable to Bosch.

"What do I look for?" Sun asked.

"Date and room number. Friday was the eleventh. We want that and room fifteen fourteen. It's got to be in that stack."

Sun started reading. Bosch watched for a moment and then looked out the window at the jade market. Through the open entry points he saw rows and rows of stalls, old men and women selling their wares under a flimsy roof of plywood and tenting. It was crowded with customers coming and going.

Bosch thought of the jade monkeys on red twine that he had found in his daughter's room. She had been here. He wondered if she had come this far from home on her own or with friends, maybe with He and Quick.

Outside one of the entrances an old woman was selling incense sticks and had a bucket fire going. On a folding table next to her were rows of papier-mâché items for sale to be burned. Bosch saw a row of tigers and wondered why a dead ancestor would need a tiger.

"Here," Sun said.

He held a registration form up for Bosch to read.

"What's it say?"

"Tuen Mun. We go there."

It sounded to Bosch like he had said *Tin Moon*.

"What's Tin Moon?"

"*Tuen Mun*. It is in the New Territories. This man lives there."

"What's his name?"

"Peng Qingcai."

Qingcai, Bosch thought. An easy jump to an Americanized name to use with girls at the mall might be Quick. Maybe Peng Qingcai was He's older brother, the boy Madeline had left the mall with on Friday.

"Does the registration have his age or birth date?"

"No, no age."

It was a long shot. Bosch had not put his birth date down when he had rented the rooms, and the deskman had only taken his passport number, none of the other particulars of identity.

"The address is there?"

"Yes."

"Can you find it?"

"Yes, I know this place."

"Good. Let's go. How long?"

"It is long time in the car. We go north and then west. It will take one hour or more. The train would be faster."

Time was at a premium but Bosch knew the car gave them autonomy.

"No," he said. "Once we find her we'll need the car."

Sun nodded his agreement and pulled the car away from the curb. Once they were on their way, Bosch shrugged off his jacket and rolled up his shirtsleeve to take a better look at the knife wound on his arm. It was a two-inch slash on the upper inside of his forearm. Blood was finally clotting in the wound.

Sun looked over at it quickly and then back at the road.

"Who did this to you?"

"The man behind the counter."

Sun nodded.

"He set us up, Sun Yee. He saw my money and set us up. I was so stupid."

"It was a mistake."

He had certainly backed off his angry accusation in the stairwell. But Bosch wasn't backing off his own assessment. He had gotten Eleanor killed.

"Yeah, but I wasn't the one who paid for it," he said.

Bosch pulled the switchblade out of the jacket pocket and reached to the backseat for the blanket. He cut a long strip off the blanket and wrapped it around his arm, tucking the end underneath. He made sure it wasn't too tight but that it would keep blood from running down his arm.

He rolled his shirtsleeve back down. It was soaked with blood between the elbow and cuff. He pulled his jacket back on. Luckily it was black and the bloodstains weren't readily noticeable.

As they moved north through Kowloon the urban blight and crowding grew exponentially. It was like any large city, Bosch thought. The further you got from the money, the more gritty and desperate the appearances grew.

"Tell me about Tuen Mun," he said.

"Very crowded," Sun said. "Only Chinese. Heavy-duty."

"Heavy-duty triad?"

"Yes. It is not a good place for your daughter to be."

Bosch didn't think it would be. But he saw one thing positive about it. Moving in and hiding a white girl might be hard to do without notice. If Madeline was being held in Tuen Mun, he would find her. *They* would find her.

31

In the past five years, Harry Bosch's only financial contribution to the support of his daughter had been to pay for her trips to Los Angeles, give her spending money from time to time and write an annual check for twelve thousand dollars to cover half her tuition to the exclusive Happy Valley Academy. This last contribution was not the result of any demand by his ex-wife. Eleanor Wish had made a very comfortable living and never once asked Bosch directly or indirectly through legal channels for a dollar of child support. It was Bosch who needed and demanded to be allowed to contribute in some way. Helping to pay for her schooling allowed him wrongly or rightly to feel that he played some sort of integral part in his daughter's upbringing.

Consequently, he grew to have a paternal involvement in her studies. Whether in person on visits to Hong Kong or early every Sunday morning—for him—on their weekly overseas phone call, Bosch's routine was to discuss Madeline's schoolwork and quiz her about her current assignments.

From all of this came an incidental, textbook knowledge of Hong Kong history. He therefore knew that the place he was now heading toward, the New Territories, was not actually new to Hong Kong. The vast geographic zone surrounding the Kowloon peninsula had been added by lease to Hong Kong more than a century ago as a buffer against outside invasion of the British colony. When the lease was up and the sovereignty of all of Hong Kong was transferred from the British back to the People's Republic of China in 1997, the New Territories remained part of the Special Administrative Region, which allowed Hong Kong to continue to function as one of the world's centers of capitalism and culture, as a unique place in the world where East meets West.

The NT was vast and primarily rural but with government-built population centers that were densely crowded with the poorest and most uneducated citizens of the SAR. Crime was higher and money scarcer. The lure of the triads was strong. Tuen Mun would be one of these places.

"Many pirates were here when I grew up," Sun said.

It was the first either he or Bosch had spoken in more than twenty minutes of driving as each man had lapsed into private thoughts. They were just entering the city on a freeway. Bosch saw row after row of tall residential structures that were so plainly uniform and monolithic that he knew they had to be government-built public housing estates. They were surrounded by rolling hills crowded with smaller homes in older neighborhoods. This was no gleaming skyline. It was drab and depressing, a fishing village turned into a massive vertical housing complex.

"What do you mean by that? You're from Tuen Mun?"

"I grew up here, yes. Until I was the age of twenty-two."

"Were you in a triad, Sun Yee?"

Sun didn't answer. He acted like he was too busy engaging the turn signal and making important checks of the mirrors as they exited the freeway.

"I don't care, you know," Bosch said. "I only care about one thing."

Sun nodded.

"We will find her."

"I know that."

They had crossed a river and entered a canyon created by the walls of forty-story buildings lining both sides of the street.

"What about the pirates?" Bosch asked. "Who were they?"

"Smugglers. They came up the river from the South China Sea. They controlled the river."

Bosch was wondering if Sun was trying to tell him something by mentioning this.

"What did they smuggle?"

"Everything. They brought in guns and drugs. People."

"And what did they take out?"

Sun nodded as if Bosch had answered a question rather than asked one.

"What do they smuggle out *now?*"

It was a long moment before Sun answered.

"Electronics. American DVDs. Children sometimes. Girls and boys."

"And where do they go?"

"This depends."

"On what?"

"What they want them for. Some of it is sex. Some is organs. Many mainlanders buy boys because they have no sons."

Bosch thought of the wad of toilet paper with the bloodstain on it. Eleanor had jumped to the conclusion that they had injected Madeline, that they had drugged her to better control her. He now realized that they could have extracted rather than injected, that blood-typing would require a withdrawal of blood from a vein with a syringe. The wad could have been a compress to stop the blood after the needle was removed.

"She would be very valuable, wouldn't she?"

"Yes."

Bosch closed his eyes. Everything changed. His daughter's abductors might not be simply holding her until Bosch kicked Chang loose in Los Angeles. They might be preparing to move her or sell her into a netherworld of dark choices from which she would never return. He tried to push the possibilities out of the way. He looked out the side window.

"We have time," he said, knowing full well he was talking to himself and not to Sun. "Nothing's happened to her yet. They wouldn't do anything until they heard from L.A. Even if the plan was never to give her back, they wouldn't do anything yet."

Bosch turned to look at Sun and he nodded in agreement.

"We will find her," he said.

Bosch reached behind his back and pulled out the gun he had taken from one of the men he had killed in the

Chungking Mansions. He studied it for the first time and immediately recognized the weapon.

"I think you were right about those guys being Vietnamese," he said.

Sun looked over at the weapon and then back at the road.

"Please do not shoot the gun in the car," he said.

Despite everything that had happened, Bosch smiled.

"I won't. I don't need to. I already know how to use this one and I doubt the guy was carrying a gun that didn't work."

Bosch held the weapon in his left hand and looked down the sight to the floor. He then held it up and studied it again. It was an American-made Colt .45, Model 1911A1. He had carried the exact same gun as a soldier in Vietnam almost forty years before. When his job was to drop down into the tunnels and seek out and kill the enemy.

Bosch ejected the magazine and the extra round from the chamber. He had the maximum eight rounds. He checked the action several times and then started to reload the gun. He stopped when he noticed something scratched into the side of the magazine. He held it up closely to try to read it.

There were initials and numbers hand-etched in the black steel siding of the magazine, but time and use — the loading and reloading of the weapon — had nearly worn them away. Angling the surface for better light, Bosch read *JFE Sp4, 27th.*

All at once, Bosch remembered the care and protection all tunnel rats had placed in their weapons and ammunition. When all you went down into the black with was your .45, a flashlight and four extra ammo clips, you checked everything twice and then you checked it again. A thousand feet into a line was not where you wanted to find you had a weapon jam, wet ammo or dead batteries. Bosch and his fellow rats marked and hoarded their clips the way surface soldiers guarded their cigarettes and *Playboy* magazines.

He studied the etching closely. Whoever JFE was, he had been a spec 4 with the 27th Infantry. That meant he could have been a rat. Bosch wondered if the gun he was holding had been left behind in a tunnel somewhere in the Iron Triangle, and whether it had been taken from JFE's cold, dead hand.

"We are here," Sun said.

Bosch looked up. Sun had stopped in the middle of the street. There was no traffic behind them. He pointed through the windshield at a government apartment tower so tall that Bosch had to lean down beneath the visor to see its roofline. Open walkways along the front of every floor offered views of the front doors and windows of what must have been three hundred different dwellings. Laundry hung over the walkway railings at different intervals on almost every floor, turning the drab facade of the building into a colorful mosaic that differentiated it from the duplicate buildings on either side of it. A sign in multiple languages over the tunnel-like entrance at center announced incongruously that the place was called Miami Beach Garden Estates.

"The address is on the sixth floor," Sun said after double-checking the Chungking Mansions registration form.

"Park it and we'll go up."

Sun nodded and pulled past the building. At the next

intersection he made a U-turn and drove back, pulling to the curb in front of a playground that was surrounded by a ten-foot fence and crowded inside with children and their mothers. Bosch knew he had parked there as an edge against having the car stolen or vandalized while they left it alone.

They got out and walked along the fence line until turning left toward the entrance to the building.

The tunnel was lined on both sides with mailboxes, most of which had popped locks and small graffiti insignias scrawled on them. The passageway led to a bank of elevators where two women holding the hands of small children waited. They paid no mind to Sun and Bosch. A security guard sat behind a tiny counter but never looked up from his newspaper.

Bosch and Sun followed the women onto the elevator. One of the women inserted a key at the bottom of the control board and then pushed two buttons. Before she pulled the key Sun quickly reached over and hit the 6 button.

The first stop was on six. Sun and Bosch moved down the walkway to the third door on the left side of the building. Bosch noticed that against the railing in front of the door of the next apartment down was a small altar with an ash can that was still smoking following a sacrifice to the hungry ghosts. The odor of burnt plastic was in the air.

Bosch took a position to the right of the door where Sun had stopped. He swung his arm back underneath his coat and gripped the handgun but didn't pull it. He felt the clotted blood in the wound on his arm break free with the movement. He was going to start bleeding again.

Sun looked at him and Bosch nodded that he was ready. Sun knocked on the door and they waited.

No one answered.

He knocked again. This time louder.

They waited again. Bosch glanced out over the playground to the Mercedes and saw that so far it had been left alone.

No one answered.

Sun finally stepped back away from the door.

"What do you wish to do?"

Bosch looked down at the smoking ash can thirty feet away.

"There's somebody home next door. Let's ask them if they've seen this guy around."

Sun led the way and knocked on the next door. This time it was opened. A small woman of about sixty peeked out. Sun nodded and smiled and spoke to her in Chinese. Soon the woman relaxed and opened the door a little bit wider. Sun kept talking and soon after that she opened it all the way and stood aside so they could enter.

As Bosch stepped over the threshold Sun whispered to him.

"Five hundred Hong Kong dollars. I promised her."

"No problem."

It was a small two-room apartment. The first room served as kitchen, dining room and living room. It was sparely furnished and smelled like hot cooking oil. Bosch peeled five hundred-dollar bills off his roll without taking it out of his pocket. He put the bills under a dish of salt that was on the kitchen table. He then pulled out a chair and sat down.

Sun remained standing and so did the woman. He continued his conversation in Chinese, pointing at Bosch for a moment. Bosch nodded and smiled and acted like he knew what was being said.

Three minutes went by and then Sun broke off the interview so he could summarize for Bosch.

"She is Fengyi Mai. She lives here alone. She said she has not seen Peng Qingcai since yesterday morning. He lives next door with his mother and his younger sister. She has not seen them either. But she heard them yesterday afternoon. Through the wall."

"How old is Peng Qingcai?"

Sun communicated the question and then translated the response.

"She thinks he is eighteen. He doesn't go to school anymore."

"What's his sister's name?"

Another back and forth and then Sun reported that the sister's name was He. But he didn't pronounce it the way Harry's daughter had.

Bosch thought about all of this for a few moments before asking the next question.

"She's sure it was yesterday that she saw him? Saturday morning? What was he doing?"

While Bosch waited for the translation he watched the woman closely. She had maintained good eye contact with Sun during the earlier questions but she began looking away while answering the latest questions.

"She is sure," Sun said. "She heard a sound outside her door yesterday morning and when she opened it, Peng was there, burning an offering. He was using her altar."

Bosch nodded but he was sure there was something the woman had left out or was lying about.

"What did he burn?"

Sun asked the woman. She looked down the whole time she gave her answer.

"She said he burned paper money."

Bosch stood up and went to the door. Outside he turned the ash can over on the walkway. It was smaller than a conventional water bucket. Smoking black ash spread across the walkway. Fengyi Mai had obviously burned a sacrifice within the last hour or so. He grabbed an incense stick from the altar and used it to poke through the hot debris. There were a few pieces of unburned cardboard but for the most part it was all ash. Bosch pushed it around some more and soon uncovered a piece of melted plastic. It was charred black and shapeless. He tried to pick it up but it was too hot.

He went back inside the apartment.

"Ask her when she last used the altar and what it was she burned."

Sun translated the answer.

"She used it this morning. She also burned paper money."

Bosch was still standing.

"Ask her why she's lying."

Sun hesitated.

"Ask her."

Sun asked the question and the woman denied lying. Bosch nodded when he received her answer, then walked over to the table. He lifted the dish of salt off the five bills and put them back in his pocket.

"Tell her we pay nothing for lies, but that I'll pay two thousand for the truth."

The woman protested after hearing Sun's translation but then Sun's demeanor changed and he angrily barked at her, and the woman clearly got scared. She put her hands together as if to beg his forgiveness and then walked into another room.

"What did you tell her?" Bosch asked.

"I told her she must tell the truth or she would lose her apartment."

Bosch raised his eyebrows. Sun had certainly kicked it up a notch.

"She believes I am police officer and you are my supervisor," he added.

"How'd she get that idea?" Bosch asked.

Before Sun could answer, the woman came back carrying a small cardboard box. She went directly to Bosch and handed it to him, then bowed as she backed away. Harry opened it and found the remains of a melted and burnt cell phone.

While the woman gave Sun an explanation, Bosch pulled his own cell phone and compared it to the burnt phone. Despite the damage, it was clear the phone the woman retrieved from her ash can was a match.

"She said Peng was burning that," Sun said. "It made a very foul smell that would be displeasing to the ghosts so she removed it."

"It's my daughter's."

"Are you sure?"

"I bought it for her. I'm sure."

Bosch opened his own phone and went to the photo files. He scrolled through his photos of his daughter until he found one of her in her school uniform.

"Show her this. See if she's seen her with Peng."

Sun showed the phone to the woman and asked the question. The woman shook her head as she responded, putting her hands together in prayer to underline that she was telling the truth now. Bosch didn't need the translation. He stood up and pulled out his money. He put two thousand Hong Kong dollars on the table—less than three hundred American—and headed to the door.

"Let's go," he said.

32

They knocked on Peng's door once again but got no answer. Bosch knelt down to untie and retie his shoe. He studied the lock on the doorknob as he did so.

"What do we do?" Sun asked after Bosch stood back up.

"I have picks. I can open the door."

Bosch could see reluctance immediately cloud Sun's face, even with the sunglasses.

"My daughter could be in there. And if she isn't, there might be something that tells us where she is. You stand behind me and block anyone's view. I'll get us in in less than a minute."

Sun looked out at the wall of duplicate buildings surrounding them like giants.

"We watch first," he said.

"Watch?" Bosch asked. "Watch what?"

"The door. Peng could come back. He could lead us to Madeline."

Bosch looked at his watch. It was half past one.

"I don't think we have time. We can't go static here."

"What is 'static'?"

"We can't stand still, man. We have to keep moving if we are going to find her."

Sun turned from the view and looked directly at Bosch.

"One hour. We watch. If we come back to open the door, you don't take the gun."

Bosch nodded. He understood. Getting caught breaking and entering was one thing. Getting caught breaking and entering with a gun was about ten years of something else.

"Okay, one hour."

They went down the elevator and out through the tunnel. Along the way Bosch tapped Sun on the arm and asked him which one of the mailboxes had Peng's apartment number on it. Sun found the box and they saw that the lock had long been punched out. Bosch glanced back through the tunnel to the security guard reading the paper. He opened the mailbox and saw two letters.

"Looks like nobody got Saturday's mail," Bosch said. "I think Peng and his family have split."

They returned to the car and Sun said he wanted to move it to a less noticeable spot now that they were back in it. He drove up the street, turned around and then parked by a containment wall that surrounded the trash bins for the building across the street and down one. They still had a view of the sixth-floor walkway and the door to Peng's apartment.

"I think we're wasting our time," Bosch said. "They're not coming back."

"One hour, Harry. Please."

Bosch noted it was the first time Sun had called him by his name. It didn't placate him.

"You're giving him another hour's lead time, that's all."

Bosch pulled the box out of his jacket pocket. He opened it up and looked at the phone.

"You watch the place," he said. "I'm going to work on this."

The plastic hinges on the phone had melted and Bosch struggled to open it. Finally, it broke in two when he applied too much pressure. The LCD screen was cracked and partially melted. Bosch put that part aside and concentrated on the other half. The battery compartment cover was melted, its seams fused together. He opened his door and leaned out. He struck the phone on the curb three times, harder each time, until the impacts finally cracked the seams and the compartment cover fell off.

He pulled back in and closed the door. The phone's battery appeared to be intact but again the deformed plastic made it difficult to remove. This time he pulled his badge case and removed one of his picks. He used it to pry the battery out. Beneath it was the cradle for the phone's memory card.

It was empty.

"Shit!"

Bosch threw the phone down into the foot well. Another dead end.

He looked at his watch. It had only been twenty minutes since he had agreed to give Sun the hour. But Bosch couldn't remain still. All of his instincts told him he had to get into that apartment. His daughter could be in there.

"Sorry, Sun Yee," he said. "You can wait here, but I can't. I'm going in."

He leaned forward and pulled the gun out of his waistband. He wanted to leave it outside the Mercedes in case they were caught in the apartment and the police connected them with the car. He wrapped the gun in his daughter's blanket, opened the door and got out. He walked through an opening in the containment wall and put the bundle on top of one of the overfull trash bins. He would easily be able to retrieve it when he got back.

When he stepped out of the containment area, he found Sun out of the car and waiting.

"Okay," Sun said. "We go."

They started back to Peng's building.

"Let me ask you something, Sun Yee. Do you ever take those shades off?"

Sun's answer came without explanation.

"No."

Once again the security guard in the lobby never looked up. The building was big enough that there was always somebody with a key waiting for an elevator. In five minutes they were back in front of Peng's door. While Sun stood at the railing as a lookout and visual block, Bosch went down to one knee and worked the lock. It took him longer than expected—almost four minutes—but he got it open.

"Okay," he said.

Sun turned away from the railing and followed Bosch into the apartment.

Before he had even closed the door Bosch knew they would find death in the apartment. There was no overpowering odor, no blood on the walls, no physical indication at all in the first room. But after attending more than five hundred murder scenes over the years as a cop, he had developed what he considered a sense for blood. He had no scientific backing to his theory, but Bosch believed that spilled blood changed the composition of air in an enclosed environment. And he sensed that change now. The fact that it could be his own daughter's blood made the recognition dreadful.

He held up his hand to stop Sun from entering further into the apartment.

"You feel that, Sun Yee?"

"No. Feel what?"

"Somebody's dead. Don't touch anything, and follow in my steps if you can."

The apartment layout was the same as the unit next door. A two-room dwelling, this one shared by a mother with her two teenage children. There was no sign of any disturbance or danger in the first room. There was a sofa that had a sleeping pillow and sheet haphazardly tossed on it and Bosch assumed the boy slept on the couch while the sister and mother took the bedroom.

Bosch moved across the room and into the bedroom. A curtain was drawn across the window and the room was dark. With his elbow Bosch pushed up the wall switch and a ceiling light over the bed came on. The bed was unmade but empty. There was no sign of struggle or disturbance or death. Bosch looked to his right. There were two more doors. He guessed one led to a closet and the other led to a bathroom.

He always carried latex gloves in his coat pocket. He pulled a pair out and put a glove on his left hand. He opened the door on the right first. It was a closet that was packed tightly with clothes on hangers and in stacks on the floor. The overhead shelving was crowded as well with boxes that had Chinese writing on them. Bosch backed up and moved to the second door. He opened it without hesitation.

The small bathroom was awash in dried blood. It had been splashed over the sink, the toilet and the tiled floor. There were spatter and drip lines on the back wall and on the dirty white plastic shower curtain with flowers on it.

It was impossible to step into the room without stepping on one of the blood trails. But Bosch didn't worry about it. He had to get to the shower curtain. He had to know.

He quickly moved across the room and yanked the plastic back.

The shower stall was tiny by American standards. It was no bigger than the old phone booths outside Du-Par's in the Farmers Market. But somehow someone had managed to pile three bodies on top of one another in there.

Bosch held his breath as he leaned over and in to try to identify the victims. They were fully clothed. The boy, who was the biggest, was on top. He was facedown atop a woman of about forty—his mother—who was sitting slouched against a wall. Their positioning suggested some sort of Oedipal fantasy that probably was not the killer's intention. Both of their throats had been savagely cut from ear to ear.

Behind and partially underneath the mother—as if hiding—was the body of a young girl. Her long dark hair was covering her face.

"Ah, God," Bosch called out. "Sun Yee!"

Soon Sun came in behind him and he heard the sharp intake of his breath. Bosch started putting on the second glove.

"There's a girl on the bottom and I can't tell if it's Maddie," he said. "Put these on."

He pulled another pair of gloves from his pocket and handed them to Sun, who quickly snapped them on. Together they pulled the body of the dead boy out of the shower stall and lowered it to the floor beneath the sink. Bosch then gently moved the mother's body until he could see the face of the girl on the tile beneath. She, too, had been slashed across the throat. Her eyes were open and looked fearfully at death. It tore Bosch's heart to see that look, but it wasn't his daughter's face.

"It's not her," he said. "It's gotta be her friend. He."

Harry turned away from the carnage and squeezed past Sun. He went out to the bedroom and sat down on the bed. He heard a bumping sound from the bathroom and guessed that Sun was putting the bodies back as they had found them.

Bosch exhaled loudly and leaned forward, arms folded across his chest. He was thinking about the girl's frightened eyes. He almost fell forward off the bed.

"What happened here?" he asked in a whisper.

Sun stepped out of the bathroom and adopted his bodyguard stance. He said nothing. Harry noticed that there was blood on his gloved hands.

Bosch stood up and looked around the room as if it might hold some explanation for the scene in the bathroom.

"Could another triad have taken her from him? Then killed them all to cover the tracks?"

Sun shook his head.

"That would have started a war. But the boy is not triad."

"What? How do you know that?"

"There is only one triad in vertical Tuen Mun. Golden Triangle. I looked and he did not have the mark."

"What mark?"

Sun hesitated for a moment, turning toward the bathroom door but then turning back to Bosch. He pulled off one of his gloves, then reached up to his mouth and pulled down his lower lip. On the soft, inside skin was an old and blurred black-ink tattoo of two Chinese characters. Bosch assumed they meant Golden Triangle.

"So you are in the triad?"

Sun released his lip and shook his head.

"No more. It has been more than twenty years."

"I thought you can't just quit a triad. If you leave, you leave in a box."

"I made a sacrifice and the council allowed me to leave. I also had to leave Tuen Mun. This is how I went to Macau."

"What kind of sacrifice?"

Sun looked even more reluctant than when he'd shown Bosch the tattoo. But slowly he reached up to his face again, this time removing his sunglasses. For a moment Bosch noticed nothing wrong, but then he realized that Sun's left eye was a prosthetic. He had a glass eye. There was a slightly noticeable scar hooking down from the outside corner.

"You had to give up a fucking eye to quit the triad?"

"I do not regret my decision."

He put his sunglasses back on.

Between Sun's revelations and the horror scene in the bathroom, Bosch was beginning to feel like he was in some sort of medieval painting. He reminded himself that his daughter wasn't in the bathroom, that she was still alive and out there somewhere.

"Okay," he said, "I don't know what happened here or why, but we have to stay on the trail. There's got to be something in this apartment that will tell us where Maddie is. We've got to find it and we're running out of time."

Bosch reached into his pocket but it was empty.

"I'm out of gloves, so be careful what you touch. And we probably have blood on the bottom of our shoes. No sense in transferring it around the place."

Bosch removed his shoes and cleaned the blood off them in the sink in the kitchenette. Sun did the same thing. The men then searched the apartment, beginning in the bedroom and working their way toward the front door. They found nothing that was useful until they got to the small kitchen and Bosch noticed that, like the apartment next door, there was a dish of salt on the table. Only the salt was piled higher on this plate and Bosch could see finger trails left by someone who had built the granules into a mound. He ran his own fingers through the pile and displaced a small square of black plastic that had been buried in salt. Bosch immediately recognized it as the memory card from a cell phone.

"Got something."

Sun turned from a kitchen drawer he had been looking through. Bosch held up the memory card. He was sure it was the card missing from his daughter's cell phone.

"It was in the salt. Maybe he hid it just as they came."

Bosch looked at the tiny plastic card. There was a reason Peng Qingcai removed it before burning his daughter's phone. There was a reason he had then tried to hide it. Bosch wanted to go to work on those reasons right away but decided that for Sun and him to extend their stay in an apartment with three bodies in the shower was not a smart move.

"Let's get out of here," he said.

Bosch moved to the window next to the door and looked down through the curtain to the street before giving the all-clear sign. Sun opened the door and they quickly exited. Bosch pulled the door closed before stripping off his gloves. He glanced behind him as he stepped away and saw that the old woman next door was on the walkway, kneeling in front of her altar and burning another sacrifice to the ghosts. Bosch did a double-take when he saw that she was using a candle to light one of the real hundred-dollar bills he had given her.

Bosch turned and walked quickly down the walkway in the opposite direction. He knew he was in a world beyond his understanding. He only had to understand his mission to find his daughter. Nothing else mattered.

33

Bosch retrieved the gun but left the blanket behind. As soon as he was back in the car, he took out his phone. It was an exact duplicate of his daughter's that he'd bought as part of a package deal. He opened the rear compartment and removed the battery and memory card. He then slid the card from his daughter's phone into the cradle. He replaced the battery, closed the compartment and switched the phone on.

While they waited for the phone to boot, Sun pulled the car away from the curb and they headed away from the building where the family had been massacred.

"Where are we going?" Harry asked.

"To the river. There is a park. We go there until we know where we are going."

In other words, there was no plan yet. The memory card was the plan.

"That stuff you told me about the pirates when you were a kid, that was the triad, wasn't it?"

After a moment Sun nodded once.

"Is that what you did, smuggle people in and out?"

"No, my job was different."

He said nothing else and Bosch decided not to press it. The phone was ready. He quickly went to the call records. There were none. The page was blank.

"There's nothing on here. No record of any calls."

He went to the e-mail file and again found the screen empty.

"Nothing transferred with the card," he said, agitation growing in his voice.

"This is common," Sun said calmly. "Only permanent files go on the memory card. Look to see if there are any videos or photos."

Using the little ball roller in the middle of his phone's keyboard, Bosch went to the video icon and selected it. The video file was empty.

"No videos," he said.

It began to dawn on Bosch that Peng might have pulled the card from Madeline's phone because he believed it held a record of all uses of the phone. But it didn't. The last, best lead was looking like a bust.

He clicked on the photo icon and here he found a list of stored JPEG photos.

"I've got photos."

He started opening the photos one by one, but the only shots that seemed recent were the photos of John Li's lungs and ankle tattoos that Bosch had sent her. The rest were photos of Madeline's friends and from school trips. They were not specifically dated but did not appear to be in any way related to her abduction. He found a few photos from her trip to the jade market in Kowloon. She had taken photos of small jade sculptures of couples in Kama Sutra positions of sexual intercourse. Bosch wrote these off as teenage curiosity. Photos that would be sure to provide uneasy giggles among the girls at school.

"Nothing," he reported to Sun.

He kept trying, moving across the screen and clicking on icon after icon in hopes of finding a hidden message. Finally, he found that Madeline's phone book was also on the card and had been transferred to his phone.

"Her phone book's on here."

He opened the file and saw the list of contacts. He didn't know all of her friends and many were simply listed by nicknames. He clicked on the listing for *Dad* and got a screen that had his own cell and home numbers but nothing else, nothing that shouldn't be there.

He went back to the list and moved on, finally finding what he thought he might be looking for when he got to the *T*s. There was a listing for Tuen Mun that contained only a phone number.

Sun had pulled into a long, thin park that ran along the river and under one of the bridges. Bosch held the phone out to him.

"I found a number. It was listed under Tuen Mun. The only number not listed under a name."

"Why would she have this number?"

Bosch thought for a moment, trying to put it together.

"I don't know," he said.

Sun took the phone and studied the screen.

"This is a cell number."

"How do you know?"

"It begins with a nine. This is a cell designation in Hong Kong."

"Okay, so what do we do with it? It's labeled Tuen Mun. It might belong to the guy who has my daughter."

Sun stared out the windshield at the river, trying to come up with an answer and a plan.

"We could text him," he said. "Maybe he will respond to us."

Bosch nodded.

"Yeah, try to deke him. Maybe we get a location from him."

"What is 'deke'?"

"Decoy him. Fake him out. Act like we know him and set up a meet. He gives us his location."

Sun pondered this while continuing to watch the river. A barge was slowly making its way south toward the sea. Bosch started thinking of an alternate plan. David Chu back in L.A. might have the sources that could run down the name and address attached to a Hong Kong cell number.

"He may recognize that number and know it is a deke," Sun finally said. "We should use my phone."

"You sure?" Bosch asked.

"Yes. I think the message should be sent in traditional Chinese. To help with the deke."

Bosch nodded again.

"Right. Good idea."

Sun pulled his cell phone out and asked for the number Bosch had found. He opened up a text field but then hesitated.

"What do I say?"

"Well, we need to put some urgency into it. Make it seem like he has to respond, and then has to meet."

They talked about it back and forth for a few minutes and finally came up with a text that was simple and direct. Sun translated and sent it. Written in Chinese, the message said, *We have a problem with the girl. Where can we meet?*

"Okay, we wait," Bosch said.

He had decided not to bring Chu into this unless he had to.

Bosch checked his watch. It was 2 P.M. He had been on the ground in Hong Kong for nine hours and he was no closer to his daughter than when he had been thirty-five thousand feet over the Pacific. In that time he had lost Eleanor Wish forever and now was playing a waiting game that allowed thoughts of guilt and loss to enter his imagination with nothing to deflect them. He glanced over at the phone in Sun's hand, hoping for a quick return to the message.

It didn't come.

Minutes of silence went by as slowly as the boats on the river. Bosch tried to concentrate his thoughts on Peng Qingcai and on how the abduction of Bosch's daughter had gone down. There were things that didn't make sense to him without having all the information, but there was still a chronology and a chain of events that he could put together. And as he did so, he knew that everything led back to his own actions.

"This all comes back to me, Sun Yee. I made the mistake that allowed all of this to happen."

"Harry, there is no reason to—"

"No, wait. Just hear me out. You need to know all of this because you might see something I don't."

Sun said nothing and Bosch continued.

"It all starts with me. I was working a case with a triad suspect in L.A. I couldn't get any answers, so I asked my daughter to translate the Chinese markings on a tattoo. I sent her a photo. I told her it was a triad case and she couldn't show the tattoo or talk about it with anybody. But that was my mistake. Telling that to a thirteen-year-old was like announcing it to the world—her world. She'd been hanging out with Peng and his sister. They were from the other side of the tracks. She probably wanted to impress them. She told them about the tattoo and the case and that's where this all started."

He looked over at Sun but couldn't read his face.

"What tracks?" he asked.

"Never mind, it's just an expression. They weren't from Happy Valley, that's all that means. And like you said, Peng wasn't part of any triad in Tuen Mun but maybe he knew people, maybe he wanted to get in. He was hanging out all the way across the harbor in Happy Valley. Maybe he knew somebody and thought this might be his ticket in. He told someone what he had heard. They put it together with L.A. and told him to grab the girl and send me the message. The video."

Bosch stopped there for a moment as thoughts of his daughter's situation distracted him again.

"But from there, something happened. Something changed. Peng took her to Tuen Mun. Maybe he offered her to the triad up here and they took her. Only they still didn't take him. Instead, they killed him and his family."

Sun shook his head slightly and finally spoke. There

was something about Bosch's storyline that didn't make sense to him.

"But why would they do this? Kill his whole family."

"Look at the timing, Sun Yee. The lady next door heard the voices through the wall in the late afternoon, right?"

"Yes."

"By then I was on the plane. I was coming and they somehow knew it. They couldn't risk that I would find Peng or his sister or mother. So they eliminated the threat and tied it off right there. If it wasn't for the memory card Peng hid, where would we be? At a dead end."

Sun incisively zeroed in on something Bosch had left out.

"How did they know you were coming on the plane?"

Bosch shook his head.

"Good question. From the start there's been a leak in the investigation. But I thought I was at least a day ahead of it."

"In Los Angeles?"

"Yeah, back in L.A. Somebody tipped the suspect that we were onto him and that made him try to split. That was why we had to arrest him before we were ready and why they grabbed Maddie."

"You don't know who?"

"Not for sure. But when I get back I'll find out. And I'll take care of it."

Sun read more into that than Bosch had intended.

"Even if Maddie is safe?" he asked.

Before Bosch could respond, the phone in Sun's hand vibrated. He had received a text. Bosch leaned over to look as Sun read. The message, in Chinese, was short.

"What's it say?"

"Wrong number."

"That's it?"

"He did not accept the deke."

"Shit."

"What now?"

"Send another message. Tell him we meet or we go to the police."

"Too dangerous. He might decide just to get rid of her."

"Not if he has a buyer lined up. You said she's valuable. Whether it was for sex or organs, she's valuable. He won't get rid of her. He might hurry up the deal and that's the chance we take, but he won't get rid of her."

"We don't know if this is even the right person. This is just a phone number on your daughter's list."

Bosch shook his head. He knew Sun was right. Shooting messages into the dark was too risky. His thoughts took him back to David Chu. The AGU detective might very well be the leak in the investigation that got Bosch's daughter abducted. Did he risk calling him now?

"Sun Yee, do you have anybody in casino security who could run this number down and get us a name and billing address?"

Sun considered the question for a long moment and then shook his head.

"No, this is not possible with my associates. There will be an investigation because of Eleanor . . ."

Bosch understood. Sun had to do what he could to limit the blowback on his company and the casino. That tipped the scale toward Chu.

"Okay. I think I might know someone."

Bosch opened his phone to go to his contact list but then realized the card from his daughter's phone was still in place. He started through the process of replacing his own card and returning the phone to his settings and contacts.

"Who will you call?" Sun asked.

"A guy I was working with. He's in the Asian Gang Unit and has contacts over here."

"Is he the man you think could be the leak?"

Bosch nodded. Good question.

"I can't rule him out. But it could have been anyone in his unit or another police department we were working with. At the moment, I don't see where we have any choice."

When he had the phone rebooted, he went to his contact list and found Chu's cell number. He made the call and checked his watch. It was almost midnight Saturday night in Los Angeles.

Chu answered after one ring.

"Detective Chu."

"David, it's Bosch. Sorry to call so late."

"Not late at all. I'm still working."

Bosch was surprised.

"On the Li case? What's happening?"

"Yes, I spent a good part of the evening with Robert Li. I am trying to convince him to cooperate with a prosecution of Chang for extortion."

"Is he going to?"

There was a pause before Chu answered.

"So far no. But I have till Monday morning to work on him. You're still in Hong Kong, right? Have you found your daughter?"

Chu's voice picked up an urgent tone as he asked about Madeline.

"Not yet. But I have a line on her. That's where I need your help. Can you run down a Hong Kong cell number for me?"

Another pause.

"Harry, the police there are much more capable of this than I am."

"I know, but I am not working with the police on this."

"You're not."

It wasn't a question.

"I can't risk the potential for a leak. I'm close. I've tracked her all day and it's down to this number. I think it belongs to the man who has her. Can you help me?"

Chu didn't respond for a long moment.

"If I help you, my source on this will be within the Hong Kong police, you know that, right?"

"But you don't have to tell them the reason you need the information or who you are going to give it to."

"But if things blow up over there, it could come back to me."

Bosch began to lose his patience but tried to keep it out of his tone as he bluntly gave voice to the nightmare he knew was unfolding.

"Look, there isn't a lot of time. Our information is that she is being sold. Most likely today. Maybe right now. I need this information, Dave. Can you get it for me or not?"

This time there was no hesitation.

"Give me the number."

34

Chu said he would need at least an hour to run the cell number down through his contacts in the Hong Kong police. Bosch hated the idea of giving up so much time when every minute could be the minute his daughter changed to the next set of hands, but he had no choice. He believed that Chu well understood the urgency of the situation. Bosch closed the phone call by telling Chu not to share his request with anyone inside the department.

"You still think there's a leak, Harry?"

"I know there is but now's not the time to talk about it."

"What about me? You trust me?"

"I called you, didn't I?"

"I don't think you trust anybody, Harry. You called me because there was no one else."

"You know what? Just work that number and get back to me."

"Sure, Harry. Whatever you say."

Bosch closed the phone and looked at Sun.

"He said it might take as long as an hour."

Sun remained impassive. He turned the key and started the car.

"You should get food while we wait."

Bosch shook his head.

"No, I can't eat. Not with her out there and ... what happened. My stomach ... I couldn't keep anything down."

Sun turned the car back off. They would wait there for Chu's callback.

The minutes went by very slowly and felt very costly. Bosch reviewed his moves going back to the moments he crouched behind the counter at Fortune Liquors and examined the body of John Li. He came to fully realize that his relentless pursuit of the killer had put others in jeopardy. His daughter. His ex-wife. A whole family in faraway Tuen Mun. The burden of guilt he would now carry would be the heaviest of his life and he was not sure he was up to it.

For the first time he put *if* into the equation of his life. *If* he got his daughter back he would find a way to redeem himself. *If* he never saw her again, there could be no redemption.

All things would end.

These realizations made him physically shudder and he turned and opened the car door.

"I'm going to take a walk."

He stepped out and closed the door before Sun could ask him a question. There was a path that went along the river and he started walking it. He had his head down, his mind on dark thoughts and he did not notice the people who passed him on the path or the boats that moved swiftly by him on the river.

Eventually, Bosch realized he wasn't helping himself or his daughter by dwelling on things he could not control. He tried to shake off the dark shroud that was coming down on him and focus on something useful. The question about the memory card from his daughter's phone was still open and bothersome. Why had Madeline stored the cell number marked Tuen Mun on her phone?

After grinding the question down he finally saw an answer that had escaped him earlier. Madeline had been abducted. Therefore, her phone would have been taken away from her. So it was probably her abductor, not Madeline, who had stored the number on her phone. This conclusion led to a cascade of possibilities. Peng had taken the video and sent it to Bosch. So he was in possession of the phone. He could very well have been using it rather than his own phone to complete the abduction and set up the exchange of Madeline for whatever he had bartered her for.

He probably saved the number to the card. Either because he was using it a lot in the negotiations or because he simply wanted to leave a trail just in case something happened. And this would be why he hid the card in the salt. So somebody would find it.

Bosch turned around to take his new conclusion back to Sun. He was a hundred yards away and could see Sun already standing outside the car, excitedly waving him back. Bosch looked down at the phone in his hand and checked the screen. He had not missed a call and there was no way Sun's excitement could be related to his call to Chu.

Bosch started trotting back.

Sun dropped back into the car and closed the door. Bosch soon jumped in beside him.

"What?"

"Another message. A text."

Sun held up his phone to show Bosch the message, even though it was in Chinese.

"What's it say?"

"It says, 'What problem? Who is this?'"

Bosch nodded. There was still a lot of deniability in the message. The sender was still feigning ignorance. He didn't know what this was about, yet he had sent this text unbidden, and this told Bosch that they were closing in on something.

"How do we respond?" Sun asked.

Bosch didn't answer. He was thinking.

Sun's phone started to vibrate. He looked at the screen.

"This is a call. It's him. The number."

"Don't answer," Bosch said quickly. "That could blow it. We can always call back. Just see if he leaves a message first."

The phone stopped vibrating and they waited. Bosch tried to think of the next move to make in this very delicate and deadly game. After a while, Sun shook his head.

"No message. It would have alerted me by now."

"What's your outgoing message say? Do you give your name on it?"

"No, no name. I use the robot."

That was good. A generic outgoing message. The caller was probably hoping to pick up a name or a voice or some other sort of intel.

"Okay, send him back a text. Say, no talking on phones or text because it's not safe. Say you want to meet in person."

"That's it? They ask what the problem is. I don't answer?"

"No, not yet. String it along. The longer we keep this going, the more time we give Maddie. You see?"

Sun nodded once.

"Yes, I see."

He typed in the message Bosch had suggested and sent it.

"Now we wait again," he said.

Bosch didn't need the reminder. But something told him the wait would not be long. The deke was working and they had someone on the other end of the text on the hook. He had no sooner come to this conclusion than another text came in on Sun's phone.

"He wants to meet," Sun said, looking at the screen. "Five o'clock at Geo."

"What's that?"

"A restaurant at the Gold Coast. Very famous. It will be very crowded on a Sunday afternoon."

"How far is the Gold Coast?"

"Almost an hour's drive from here."

Bosch had to consider that the person they were dealing with was playing them, sending them an hour out of the way. He checked his watch. It had been almost an hour since he had talked to Chu. Before committing to the Gold Coast meeting, he first needed to check on what Chu had come up with. As Sun started the car and headed out of the park, Bosch called Chu's number again.

"Detective Chu."

"It's Bosch. It's been an hour."

"Not quite but I'm still waiting. I made the call and haven't heard back."

"Did you talk to somebody?"

"Uh, no, I left a message with my guy over there. I guess because it's so late he might not be—"

"It's not late, Chu! It's late there, not here. Did you make the call or not?"

"Harry, please, I made the call. I just got mixed up. It's late here, it's Sunday over there. I think maybe because it's *Sunday,* he isn't as tied to his phone as he normally is. But I made the call and I will call you as soon as I have something."

"Yeah, well, it might be too late by then."

Bosch closed the phone. He was sorry he had trusted Chu in the first place.

"Nothing," he said to Sun.

They got to the Gold Coast in forty-five minutes. It was a resort on the western edge of the New Territories that catered to travelers from the mainland as well as Hong Kong and the rest of the world. A tall, gleaming hotel rose above Castle Peak Bay and open-air restaurants crowded the promenade that edged the harbor.

The Geo was wisely chosen by the text contact. It was sandwiched between two similar open-air restaurants and all three were heavily crowded. An arts and crafts show on the promenade doubled the number of people in the area and the places from which an observer could hide from view. It would make identifying someone who didn't want to be identified extremely hard to do.

In accordance with the plan Bosch and Sun hatched on the drive, Bosch was dropped at the entrance to the Gold Coast. The two men synchronized their watches and then Sun drove on. As he walked through the hotel, Bosch stopped in the gift shop and bought sunglasses and a baseball-style hat with the hotel's golden emblem on it. He also bought a map and a throwaway camera.

By ten of five, Bosch had made his way to the entrance of a restaurant called Yellow Flower, which was next to and afforded a full view of the seating area of Geo. The plan was simple. They wanted to identify the owner of the phone number Bosch had found in his daughter's contact list and follow him when he left Geo.

Yellow Flower, Geo and a third restaurant on the other side, Big Sur, were crowded with tables under white canopies. The sea breeze kept the patrons cool and the canopies aloft. As he waited to be seated, Bosch alternately checked his watch and surveyed the crowded restaurants.

There were several large parties, whole families joined together for a Sunday afternoon meal. These tables were easy for him to discount in looking for the cell phone contact because Bosch didn't expect their man to be part of a large party. But even so, he quickly realized how daunting the task of spotting the contact would be. Just because the supposed meeting was set for Geo did not mean the person they were looking for was in the restaurant. He could be in any of the three restaurants doing exactly what Bosch and Sun were doing — looking to surreptitiously identify the other contact.

Bosch had no choice but to continue with the plan. He held up one finger to the hostess and was led to a bad table in a corner that had a view of all three restaurants but no glimpse of the sea. It was a bad table they passed off on singles and that was just what he had hoped for.

He checked his watch again and then spread the map out on the table. He weighted it with the camera and took his hat off. It had been cheaply made and was ill fitting, anyway. He was glad to take it off.

He made one more survey of the restaurants before five o'clock but did not see any likely candidates for the contact. No one like him, sitting by himself or with other mysterious men, wearing sunglasses or any other sort of disguise. He began to think the deke hadn't worked. That the contact had gotten wise to their charade and had deked them instead.

He checked his watch just as the second hand swept toward the twelve and it would be five o'clock. The first text from Sun would go out exactly at five.

Bosch looked out across the restaurants, hoping to see a quick movement, somebody glancing at a text on their phone. But there were too many people and he saw nothing as the seconds ticked by.

"Hello, sir. Just one?"

A waitress had come up to the side of his table. Bosch ignored her, his eyes moving from person to person at the tables in Geo.

"Sir?"

Bosch answered without looking at her.

"Can you bring me a cup of coffee for now? Black."

"Okay, sir."

He could feel her presence move away. Bosch spent another minute with his eyes on the crowd. He expanded the search to include Yellow Flower and Big Sur. He saw a woman talking on a cell phone but nobody else using a phone.

Bosch's own phone buzzed in his pocket. He pulled it out and answered, knowing it would be Sun.

"He answered the first text. He said, 'I am waiting.' That's all."

The plan had been for Sun to send a text at exactly five o'clock that said he was caught in traffic and would be late. He had done that and the message was received and responded to.

"I didn't see anyone," Bosch said. "This place is too big. He picked the right place."

"Yes."

"Where are you?"

"At the bar at the back of Big Sur. I didn't see anyone."

"Okay, ready for the next one?"

"Ready."

"We'll try again."

Bosch closed the phone as a waitress brought his coffee.

"Ready to order?"

"No, not yet. I have to look at the menu."

She went away. Bosch took a quick sip of the hot coffee and then opened the menu. He studied the listings while keeping his right hand on the table so he could see his watch. At 5:05 Sun would send the next text.

The waitress came back and once more asked Bosch to order. The hint was clear. Order or move on. They needed to turn the table.

"Do you have *gway lang go?*"

"That is turtle-shell gelatin."

She said it in a tone suggesting he had made a mistake.

"I know. The cure for whatever ails you. Do you have it?"

"Not on menu."

"Okay, then just bring me some noodles."

"Which noodle?"

She pointed to the menu. There were no pictures on the menu so Bosch was lost.

"Never mind. Bring me fried rice with shrimp in it."

"That all?"

"That's all."

He handed her the menu so she would go away.

The waitress left him and he checked the time again before resuming his watch on the restaurants. The next text was going out. He scanned from table to table quickly. Again he picked up nothing that fit. The woman he had noticed before took another call and spoke briefly to someone. She was sitting at a table with a little boy who looked bored and uncomfortable in his Sunday clothes.

Bosch's phone vibrated on the table.

"Got another response," Sun said. "'If you're not there in five minutes, the meeting is off.'"

"And you didn't see anybody?"

"Nothing."

"Did you send the next one?"

"I will at five-ten."

"Okay."

Bosch closed the phone and put it down on the table. They had designed the third text as the one that would finally draw the contact out. The message would say that

Sun was canceling the meeting because he had spotted a tail and believed it was the police. He would urge the unknown contact to leave Geo immediately.

The waitress came and put down a bowl of rice. The shrimp on top were whole, their distended eyes cooked white. Bosch pushed the bowl away.

His phone buzzed. He checked his watch before answering it.

"You already sent it?" Bosch asked.

At first there was no response.

"Sun Yee?"

"Harry, it's Chu."

Bosch checked his watch again. It was time for the last text.

"I gotta call you back."

He closed the phone and once more looked out across the tables of three restaurants, hoping for the needle-in-the-haystack moment that would reveal the contact. Somebody reading a text, maybe typing a response.

Nothing came. He saw no one pull a phone and glance at the screen. There were too many people to cover at the same time and the futility of the plan began to open a hollow in his chest. His eyes moved to the table where the woman and boy had sat and he saw that they were gone. He swept the restaurant and saw them leaving. The woman was moving fast, dragging the boy by the hand. In her other hand she carried her cell phone.

Bosch opened his phone and punched in a call to Sun. He answered immediately.

"The woman and the boy. They're coming your way. I think it might be her."

"She got the text?"

"No, I think she was sent to make the contact. The texts went offsite. We have to follow the woman. Where's the car?"

"Out front."

Bosch stood up, put three hundred-dollar bills down on the table and headed toward the exit.

35

Sun was already in the car waiting out front of the Yellow Flower. As Bosch was opening the door, he heard a voice calling from behind him.

"Sir! Sir!"

He turned and it was the waitress coming after him, holding out his hat and the map. She had also brought the change from his tab.

"You forgot these, sir."

Bosch grabbed the items and said thanks. He pushed the change back toward her.

"You keep that," he said.

"You did not enjoy your shrimp rice," she said.

"You got that right."

Bosch ducked into the car, hoping that the momentary delay would not cost them the tail on the woman and the boy. Sun immediately pulled away from the restaurant and into traffic. He pointed through the windshield.

"They are in the white Mercedes," he said.

The car he pointed at was a block and a half ahead, moving in light traffic.

"Is she driving?" Bosch asked.

"No, she and the boy got into a waiting car. A man was driving."

"Okay, you got them? I need to make a call."

"I have them."

As Sun followed the white Mercedes, Bosch called Chu back.

"It's Bosch."

"Okay, I got some information through HKPD. But they were asking me a lot of questions, Harry."

"Give me the information first."

Bosch pulled out his notebook and pen.

"Okay, the phone number you gave me is registered to a company. Northstar Seafood and Shipping. Northstar is one word. It's located in Tuen Mun. That's up in the New—"

"I know. You have the exact address?"

Chu gave him an address on Hoi Wah Road and Bosch repeated it out loud. Sun nodded his head. He knew where it was.

"Okay, anything else?" Bosch asked.

"Yes. Northstar is under suspicion, Harry."

"What's that mean? Suspicion of what?"

"I couldn't get anything specific. Just of illegal shipping and trade practices."

"Like human trafficking?"

"It could be. Like I said, I could not get specific information. Just questions about why I was tracing the number."

"What did you tell them?"

"That it was a blind trace. The number was found on a

piece of paper in a homicide investigation. I said I didn't know the connection."

"That's good. Is there any name associated with this phone number?"

"Not directly to the number, no. But the man who owns Northstar Seafood and Shipping is Dennis Ho. He is forty-five years old and that's all I could get without making it seem like I was working something specific. Does it help?"

"It helps. Thanks."

Bosch ended the call and then updated Sun on what he knew.

"Have you heard of Dennis Ho?" he asked.

Sun shook his head.

"Never."

Bosch knew they had to make a major decision.

"We don't know if this woman has anything to do with this," Bosch said, pointing ahead at the white Mercedes. "We could be just spinning our wheels here. I say we break off of this and go directly to Northstar."

"We don't need to decide yet."

"Why not? I don't want to waste time on this."

Sun nodded in the direction of the white Mercedes. It was about two hundred yards ahead.

"We are already heading toward the waterfront. They may be going there."

Bosch nodded. Both angles of investigation were still in play.

"How's your gas?" Bosch asked.

"Diesel," Sun replied. "And we are fine."

• • •

For the next half hour they edged the coastline on Castle Peak Road, staying a good distance behind the Mercedes but always keeping it in sight. They drove without speaking to each other. They had reached a point where they knew time was short and there was nothing else to say. Either the Mercedes or Northstar would lead them to Maddie Bosch or it was likely they would never see her again.

As the vertical buildup of housing estates in Central Tuen Mun appeared ahead of them, Bosch saw the turn signal on the Mercedes engage. The car was turning left, away from the waterfront.

"They're turning," he warned.

"That's a problem," Sun said. "The industrial waterfront is ahead. They are turning toward residential neighborhoods."

They were both silent for a moment, hoping a plan would materialize or maybe the driver of the Mercedes would realize they needed to go straight and correct the car's course.

Neither happened.

"Which way?" Sun finally asked.

Bosch felt a tearing inside. His choice here could mean his daughter's life. He knew that he and Sun could not split up with one following the car and the other going to the waterfront. Bosch was in a world he did not know and would be useless on his own. He needed Sun with him. He came to the same conclusion he had reached after the call from Chu.

"Let her go," he finally said. "We go to Northstar."

Sun kept going straight and they passed the white

Mercedes as it took the left on a road marked Tsing Ha Lane. Bosch glanced out the window at the car as it slowed down. The man driving glanced back at him but only for a second.

"Shit," Bosch said.

"What is it?" Sun asked.

"He looked at me. The driver. I think they knew we were following them. I think we had it right—she's part of this."

"Then this is good."

"What? What are you talking about?"

"If they knew we were following, then their turning away from the waterfront could be an effort to lead us away from Northstar. You see?"

"I see. Let's hope you're right."

Soon they entered an industrial waterfront area filled with ramshackle warehouses and packing plants lined along the wharfs and piers. There were river barges and medium-size seafaring boats docked up and down, sometimes two and three abreast. All of it seemed abandoned for the day. No work on Sunday.

Several fishing boats were moored out in the harbor, all safe behind a typhoon shelter created by a long concrete pier that formed the outer perimeter of the harbor.

Traffic thinned and Bosch began to worry that the casino's slick black Mercedes would be too noticeable as they made the approach to Northstar. Sun must have been thinking the same thing. He pulled into the parking lot of a closed food shop and stopped the car.

"We are very close," he said. "I think we leave the car here."

"I agree," Bosch said.

They got out and walked the rest of the way in, holding tight against the warehouse facades and scanning in all directions for forward spotters. Sun led the way and Bosch was right behind him.

Northstar Seafood and Shipping was located on wharf 7. A large green warehouse with Chinese and English printing on its side fronted the dockside and a pier extended out into the bay beyond it. Four seventy-five-foot net boats with black hulls and green pilothouses were tied up on either side of the pier. Docked at the end was a bigger boat with a large crane jutting skyward.

From his viewpoint at the corner of a warehouse on wharf 6, Bosch could see no activity. The loading bay doors of the Northstar warehouse were all rolled down and the docks and boats looked buttoned up for the weekend. Bosch was beginning to think he had made a terrible mistake in not keeping the tail on the white Mercedes. Then Sun tapped his shoulder and pointed down the length of the pier to the crane boat at the end.

His aim was high and Bosch followed it to the crane. The steel arm extended from a platform that sat atop a rail system fifteen feet over the deck of the boat. The crane could be moved up and down the length of the boat depending upon which ship's hold was being filled with cargo. The boat was obviously designed to go out to sea and relieve smaller net boats of their catch so that they could continue to harvest. The crane was controlled from a small booth on the upper platform that protected the operator from the wind and other elements at sea.

It was the tinted windows of the booth that Sun was

pointing at. With the sun in the sky beyond the boat, Bosch could see the silhouette of a man in the booth.

Bosch pulled himself back around the corner with Sun.

"Bingo," he said, his voice already tightening with the sudden blast of adrenaline. "Do you think he saw us?"

"No," Sun said. "I saw no reaction."

Bosch nodded and thought about their situation. He now believed with complete conviction that his daughter was somewhere on that boat. But getting to the boat without the lookout spotting them seemed impossible. They could wait for him to come down for a meal or bathroom break or a changing of the watch, but there was no telling when that would be or if it would even happen. Waiting defied the urgency that was growing in Bosch's chest.

He checked his watch. It was almost six. It would be at least two hours before total darkness. They could wait and then make a move. But two hours could be too long. The text messages had put his daughter's abductors on notice. They could be about to make some sort of move with her.

As if to drive this possibility home, the deep throb of a marine engine suddenly sounded from the wharf. Bosch stole a glimpse around the corner and saw exhaust rising from the stern of the crane boat. And now he saw movement behind the windows of the pilothouse.

He ducked back.

"Maybe he saw us," he reported. "They started the boat."

"How many did you see?" Sun asked.

"At least one inside the pilothouse and one still up on the crane. We need to do something. Now."

To accent the need to move, he reached behind his back and pulled the gun. He was tempted to move around the corner and go down the wharf shooting. He had a fully loaded .45 and liked his chances. He'd seen worse in the tunnels. Eight bullets, eight dragons. And then there would be him. Bosch would be the ninth dragon, as unstoppable as a bullet.

"What's the plan?" Sun asked.

"No plan. I go in and I get her. If I don't make it, I'll make sure none of them do either. Then you go in and get her and put her on a plane out of here. You've got her passport in your trunk. That's the plan."

Sun shook his head.

"Wait. They will be armed. This plan is not good."

"You got a better idea? We can't wait for dark. That boat's about to go."

Bosch moved to the edge and took another look. Nothing had changed. The lookout was still up in the booth and there was somebody in the pilothouse. The boat was rumbling on idle but still tied to the end of the pier. It was almost as if they were waiting for something. Or someone.

Bosch ducked back and calmed himself. He considered everything around him and what was available to use. Maybe there was something other than a suicide run at this. He looked at Sun.

"We need a boat."

"A boat?"

"A small boat. We can't go down the pier without being seen. They'll be watching for it. But with a small boat we could create a distraction on the other side. Enough for somebody to go down the pier."

Sun moved past Bosch and looked around the corner. He surveyed the end of the pier and then ducked back.

"Yes, a boat could work. You want me to get the boat?"

"Yeah, I've got the gun and I'm going down the pier to get my daughter."

Sun nodded. He reached into his pocket and pulled out the car keys.

"Take the keys. When you have your daughter, you drive away. Don't worry about me."

Bosch shook his head and pulled out his phone.

"We'll get someplace nearby but safe and then I'll call you. We'll wait for you."

Sun nodded.

"Good luck, Harry."

He turned to go.

"And good luck to you," Bosch said.

After Sun left, Bosch kept his back against the front wall of the warehouse and prepared to wait. He had no idea how Sun would commandeer a boat but he trusted that somehow he'd get his part done and then would create the distraction that allowed Bosch to make his move.

He also thought about finally making the call to the Hong Kong police, now that he had located his daughter, but he quickly discarded that idea as well. Police swarming the pier was no guarantee of his daughter's safety. He'd stick with the plan.

He turned to look around the corner of the warehouse and make another check of activities on the Northstar boat, when he saw a car approaching from the south. He noted the familiar styling of the front grille of a Mercedes. The car was white.

Bosch slid down the wall to make himself less noticeable. Nets that had been hung to dry from the rigging of two boats between him and the approaching car also gave him camouflage. He watched as the car slowed and turned onto wharf 7 and then headed down the pier toward the crane boat. It was the car they had followed from the Gold Coast. He caught a glimpse of the driver and identified him as the same man who had returned his look earlier.

Bosch did some quick computing and concluded that the man behind the wheel was the man whose phone number had been placed by Peng in the contact list on his daughter's phone. He had sent the woman and child—probably his wife and son—inside Geo as decoys that would help him identify the person who had been texting him. Spooked by the last message sent by Sun, he had driven them home or to some other safe spot, dropped them and then driven to wharf 7, where Bosch's daughter was being held.

It was a lot to string together, considering the few known facts he had, but Bosch believed he was on target and that something was about to happen that wasn't part of the Mercedes man's original plan. He was deviating. Hurrying things up or moving the merchandise or doing something worse—getting rid of the merchandise.

The Mercedes stopped in front of the crane boat. The driver jumped out and quickly moved across a gangway onto the boat. He yelled something to the man up in the booth but did not break stride as he quickly headed to the pilothouse.

For a moment, there was no further movement. Then Bosch saw the man step out of the crane booth and start climbing down from the platform. After reaching the deck, he followed the Mercedes man into the pilothouse.

Bosch knew that they had just committed a strategic error that gave him a momentary advantage. This was his chance to move down the pier unseen. He pulled his phone again and called Sun. The phone rang and then went to message.

"Sun, where are you? The Mercedes man is here and they left the boat unguarded. Never mind the distraction, just get back here and be ready to drive. I'm going in."

Bosch pocketed the phone and stood up. He checked the crane boat one last time and then bolted from cover. He crossed the wharf to the pier and began moving toward the end. He held the gun in a two-handed grip, up and ready.

36

Stacks of empty crates on the pier afforded Bosch partial cover but the last twenty yards to the gangway of the crane boat were wide open and exposed. He picked up his speed and quickly covered the distance, ducking at the last moment behind the Mercedes idling next to the gangway. Bosch noted the distinctive sound and smell of the diesel engine. He peeked over the line of the trunk and saw no reaction to his moves coming from the boat. He jumped from cover, moved quickly and quietly across the gangway and then picked his way between six-foot-wide hatch covers on the deck. He finally slowed his pace as he reached the pilothouse. He pressed himself against the wall next to the door.

Harry slowed his breathing and listened. He heard nothing over the sound of the throbbing engines other than the wind through the rigging of the boats on the pier. He turned to look in through a small square window in the door. He saw no one inside. He reached to the handle and quietly opened the door and entered.

The room was the operation center of the boat. Besides the wheel, Bosch saw glowing dials, double radar screens, twin throttles and a large gimbaled compass. Against the back wall of the room was a chart table next to a set of built-in bunks with curtains that could be pulled for privacy.

On the floor on the forward left was an open hatch with a ladder leading down into the hull. Bosch moved over and crouched next to the opening. He heard voices down below but the language spoken was Chinese. He tried to separate them and count how many men were down there but the echo effect of the hull made this impossible. He knew at a minimum there were three men in the hull. He did not hear his daughter's voice, but he knew she was down there, too.

Bosch moved to the boat's control center. There were several different dials and switches but all were marked in Chinese. Finally, he zeroed in on two side-by-side switches with red button lights above them. He turned one switch off and immediately heard the hum of the engines decrease by half. He had killed an engine.

He waited five seconds and turned the other switch, killing the second engine. He then moved to the rear corner of the room and onto the lower bunk. He pulled the curtain closed halfway and crouched and waited. He knew he would be in a blind spot for anyone coming up the ladder from the hull. He returned his gun to his belt and took the switchblade out of his coat pocket. He quietly opened the blade.

Soon he heard running steps from below. This told him the meeting of the men below was in the forward section of the hull. He counted only one set of approaching steps. That would make it easier.

A man began to rise through the hatch, his back to the bunks and his eyes on the control center. Without looking around he moved quickly to the controls and looked for a reason for the double engine stall. He found nothing wrong and went through procedures to restart the engines. Bosch quietly crawled out of the bunk and moved toward him. The moment the second engine trundled to life, he put the point of the switchblade against the man's spine.

Grabbing him by the back collar, Bosch pulled him away from the control center and whispered in his ear.

"Where's the girl?"

The man said something in Chinese.

"Tell me where the girl is."

The man shook his head.

"How many men are below?"

The man said nothing and Bosch roughly yanked him out through the door onto the deck. He moved him over to the rail and bent him over the side. The water was twelve feet below.

"Can you swim, asshole? Where's the girl?"

"No . . . speak," the man managed to say. "No speak."

Keeping the man down over the rail, Bosch looked around for Sun—his translator—but didn't see him. Where the hell was he?

The momentary distraction allowed the man to make a move. He swung an elbow backwards into Bosch's ribs. It was a direct impact and Bosch was knocked back into the sidewall of the pilothouse. The man then spun around and raised his hands to attack. Bosch prepared to cover but it was the man's foot that came up first, kicking Bosch's wrist and knocking the knife into the air.

The man didn't bother tracking the flight of the knife. He quickly waded into Bosch with both fists, striking with short, powerful impacts to the midsection. Bosch felt the air explode out of his lungs just as another kick came up and hit him below the chin.

Bosch went down. He tried to shake off the impact but his eyesight started to close into tunnel vision. His attacker calmly stepped away and Bosch heard the switchblade scrape on the deck as he picked it up. Struggling for consciousness, Bosch reached behind his back for the gun.

As the attacker approached, he spoke in clear English. "Can you swim, asshole?"

Bosch pulled the gun from behind his back and fired twice, the first shot only ticking the man's shoulder as he narrowed his aim and the second catching him in the center left of the chest. He went down with a look of surprise on his face.

Harry slowly pulled himself up onto his hands and knees. He saw a line of blood and saliva dripping from his mouth to the deck. Using the wall of the pilothouse, he started to get to his feet. He knew he had to move quickly. The gunshots would have been heard by the men in the boat.

Just as he got to his feet, a riot of gunfire erupted from the direction of the bow. Bullets zinged over his head and ricocheted off the steel wall of the pilothouse. Bosch ducked around the corner and behind the pilothouse. He came up and found a line of sight through the windows of the structure. He saw a man on the bow advancing toward the stern with pistols in each hand. Behind him was the open hatch through which he had climbed out of the front hold.

Bosch knew he had six rounds left and had to assume the approaching gunman had started with full clips. Ammunition-wise, Harry was outnumbered. He needed to go on the offensive and take the gunman out quickly and efficiently.

He looked around for an idea and saw a row of rubber docking bumpers secured along the rear gunwale. He put the gun into his waistband and then grabbed one of the bumpers out of its receptacle. He edged back to the rear window of the pilothouse and looked through the structure again. The gunman had chosen the port side of the pilothouse and was preparing to move to the stern. Bosch stepped back, raised the three-foot-long bumper over his head with two hands, and hurled it high and over the top of the pilothouse. While it was still in the air he started moving down the starboard side, pulling his gun out as he moved.

He got to the front of the pilothouse just as the gunman was ducking away from the flying bumper. Bosch opened fire, hitting the man repeatedly until he went down on the deck without getting off a single shot.

Bosch moved in and made sure the man was dead. He then threw his empty .45 over the side and picked up the dead man's weapons—two more Black Star semiautomatics. He stepped back into the pilothouse.

The room was still empty. Bosch knew at least one more man was below in the hold with his daughter. He popped the magazines on both guns and counted eleven bullets between the two.

He stuck them in his belt and took the ladder down like a fireman, locking his feet around the vertical bars and sliding into the hull. At the bottom he dropped and rolled, pulling his weapons and expecting to be fired upon, but no more bullets came his way.

Bosch's eyes adjusted to the dim light and he saw that he was in an empty bunk room that opened on a central passageway running the length of the hull. The only light came from the overhead hatch all the way down in the bow. Between Harry and that point were six compartment hatches—three on each side—going down the length of the passageway. The last hatch down on the left was standing wide open. Bosch got up and stuck one of the guns back in his belt so he would have a free hand. He started to move, the remaining gun up and ready.

Each hatch had a four-point locking system for storing and sealing the catch. Arrows stenciled on the rusting steel told Bosch which way to turn each handle to unlock and open the compartment. He moved down the passageway, checking the compartments one by one, finding each empty but obviously not used recently to haul fish. Steel-walled and windowless, each chamber was filled with a ground layer of detritus of cereal and other food boxes and empty gallon water containers. Wooden crates overflowed with other trash. Fishnets—refashioned as hammocks—hung on hooks bolted to the walls. There was a putrid smell in each compartment that had nothing to do with the catch the vessel once hauled. This boat carried human cargo.

What bothered Bosch most were the cereal boxes. They were all the same brand, and smiling from the front of the package was a cartoon panda bear standing on the brim of a bowl that held a treasure of rice puffs sparkling with sugar. It was cereal for kids.

The last stop in the passageway was the open hatch. Bosch crouched low and moved into the compartment in one fluid stride.

It too was empty.

But it was different. There was no trash here. A battery-powered light hung from a wire attached to a hook on the ceiling. There was an upturned shipping crate stacked with unopened cereal boxes, packs of noodles and gallon jugs of water. Bosch looked for any indication that his daughter had been kept in the room, but there was no sign of her.

Bosch heard the hinges on the hatch behind him screech loudly. He turned just as the hatch banged shut. He saw the seal on the upper right corner turn into locked position and immediately saw that the internal handles had been removed. He was being locked in. He pulled the second gun and aimed both weapons at the hatch, waiting for the next lock to turn.

It was the lower right. The moment the bolt started to turn Bosch aimed and fired both guns repeatedly into the door, the bullets piercing metal weakened by years of rust. He heard someone call out as if surprised or hurt. He then heard a banging sound out in the hallway as a body hit the floor.

Bosch moved to the hatch and tried to turn the bolt on the upper right lock with his hand. It was too small for his fingers to find purchase. In desperation, he stepped back a pace and then threw his shoulder into the door, hoping to snap the lock assembly. But it didn't budge and he knew by the feel of the impact on his shoulder that the door would not give way.

He was locked in.

He moved back close to the hatch and tilted his head to listen. There was only the sound of the engines running now. He banged the heel of one of the guns loudly on the metal hatch.

"Maddie?" he called out. "Maddie, are you here?"

There was no response. He banged again on the hatch, this time even louder.

"Give me a sign, baby. If you're here, make some noise!"

Again there was no response. Bosch pulled his phone and opened it to call Sun. But he saw he had no signal. He tried the call anyway and got no response. He was in a metal-lined room and his cell phone was useless.

Bosch turned and banged one more time on the door and called out his daughter's name.

There was no response. Harry leaned his sweating forehead against the rusty hatch in defeat. He was stuck in the metal box and trapped with the realization that his daughter wasn't even on the boat. He had failed and had gotten what he deserved, what he had earned.

A physical pain shot across his chest, matching the pain in his mind. Sharp, deep and unrelenting. He started breathing heavily, and turned his back against the hatch. He opened his collar another button and slid down the rusting metal until he was sitting on the floor with his knees up. He realized he was in a place as claustrophobic as the tunnels he had once inhabited. The battery on the overhead light was dying and soon he would be left in darkness. Defeat and despair overtook him. He had failed his daughter and he had failed himself.

37

Bosch suddenly looked up from his contemplation of failure. He had heard something. Above the drone of the engines, he'd heard a banging sound. Not from above. It had come from down in the hull.

He jumped up and turned back to the hatch. He heard another banging sound and knew somebody was checking the compartments in the same way he had.

He pounded on the hatch with the heels of both guns. He yelled above the clanging echo of steel on steel.

"Sun Yee? Hey! Down here! Somebody! Down here!"

There was no response, but then the bolt of the upper right seal turned. The door was being unlocked. Bosch stepped back, wiped his face with his sleeves, and waited. The bottom left seal was turned next and then the hatch door slowly began to open. Bosch raised the guns, unsure how many bullets he had left to fire.

In the dim light of the passage he saw Sun's face. Bosch moved forward and pushed the hatch all the way open.

"Where the fuck you been?"

"I was looking for a boat and—"

"I called you. I told you to come back."

Once he was in the passageway, Bosch saw the Mercedes man lying facedown on the floor a few feet from the hatch. He quickly moved to him, hoping to find him still alive. Harry turned him over, rolling him into the slop of his own blood.

He was dead.

"Harry, where is Madeline?" Sun asked.

"I don't know. Everybody's dead and I don't know!"

Unless . . .

One final plan began to work into Bosch's brain. One final chance. The white Mercedes. Gleaming and new. The car would have all the extras, including a navigation system, and the first address in its stored data would be the Mercedes man's home.

They would go there. They would go to the home of the Mercedes man and Bosch would do what was necessary to find his daughter. If he had to hold a gun to the head of that bored little boy he had seen at Geo, he would do it. And the wife would tell. She would give Bosch back his daughter.

Harry studied the body in front of him. He presumed he was looking at Dennis Ho, the man behind Northstar. He patted the dead man's pockets, looking for car keys, but he found none and just as quickly as his plan had formed, Bosch began to feel it disappear. Where were the keys? He needed that computer to tell him where to go and how to find his way.

"Harry, what is it?"

"His keys! We need his keys or we—"

He suddenly stopped. He realized he had missed

something. When he had made his run on the pier and
ducked for cover behind the white Mercedes, he had
heard and smelled the car's diesel engine. The car had
been left running.

At the time it meant little to Bosch because he was
sure his daughter was on the crane boat. But now he
knew different.

Bosch stood up and started moving down the passageway toward the ladder, his mind racing far ahead of him.
He heard Sun following behind him.

There was only one reason why Dennis Ho would have
left his car running. He intended to come back to it. Not
with the girl, because she was not on the boat. But to *get*
the girl once the storage compartment in the hull was
ready and it was safe to transfer her.

Bosch charged out of the pilothouse and crossed the
gangway to the pier. He ran to the driver's door of the
white Mercedes and flung it open. He checked the backseat and found it empty. He then studied the dashboard,
looking for a button that would open the trunk.

Finding none, he turned the car off and grabbed the keys.
Moving to the back of the car, he pushed the trunk button
on the ignition key.

The trunk lid lifted automatically. Bosch moved in,
and there lying on a blanket inside the compartment was
his daughter. She was blindfolded and gagged. Her arms
were pinned to her body with several wrappings of duct
tape. Her ankles were taped together as well. Bosch cried
out at the sight of her.

"Maddie!"

He almost jumped into the trunk with her as he quickly pulled the blindfold up and went to work on the gag.

"It's me, baby! It's Dad!"

She opened her eyes and started blinking.

"You're safe now, Maddie. You're safe!"

As the gag came loose, the girl let out a shriek that pierced her father's heart and would stay with him always. It was at once an exorcism of fear, a cry for help and the sound of relief and even joy.

"Daddy!"

She started to cry as Bosch reached in and lifted her out of the trunk. Sun was suddenly there and helping.

"It's going to be okay now," Bosch said. "It will all be okay."

They stood the young girl up and then Bosch used the teeth of one of the keys to start cutting through the tape. He noticed that Madeline was still wearing her school uniform. The moment her arms and hands were free, she grabbed Bosch around the neck and squeezed with all her life.

"I knew you would come," she said between gasping sobs.

Bosch didn't know if he had ever heard words that meant more to him. He held her just as tightly in his own arms. He turned his face down to whisper in her ear.

"Maddie?"

"What, Dad?"

"Are you hurt, Maddie? I mean, physically hurt. If they hurt you we need to get you to —"

"No, I'm not hurt."

He pushed back from her and put his hands on her shoulders as he studied her eyes.

"You sure? You can tell me."

"I'm sure, Dad. I'm fine."

"Okay. Then, we need to go."

He turned to Sun.

"Can you get us to the airport?"

"No problem."

"Then, let's go."

Bosch put his arm around his daughter and they started to follow Sun off the pier. She held on to him the whole way and it wasn't until they got to the car that she seemed to acknowledge the meaning of Sun's presence and asked the question Harry had been dreading.

"Dad?"

"What, Maddie?"

"Where's Mom?"

38

Bosch didn't answer her question directly. He simply told his daughter that her mother could not be with them at the moment but had packed a bag for her and that they needed to get to the airport to leave Hong Kong. Sun said nothing and picked up his pace, moving in front of them and removing himself from the discussion.

The explanation seemingly bought Harry some time to consider how and when he would give the answer that would alter the rest of his daughter's life. When they got to the black Mercedes, he put her in the backseat before going to the trunk to grab the backpack. He didn't want her to see the bag Eleanor had packed for herself. He checked the compartments of Eleanor's bag and found his daughter's passport. He put it in his pocket.

He got in the front passenger seat and handed the backpack to her. He told her to change out of her school uniform. He then checked his watch and gave Sun a nod.

"Let's go. We've got a plane to catch."

Sun started driving, proceeding out of the waterfront area at a brisk but not attention-getting pace.

"Is there a ferry or train you can drop us at that will get us there direct?" Bosch asked.

"No, they closed the ferry route and you would have to switch trains. It would be better if I take you. I wish to."

"Okay, Sun Yee."

They drove for a few minutes of silence. Bosch wanted to turn and talk to his daughter, putting his eyes on her to make sure she was okay.

"Maddie, are you changed?"

She didn't answer.

"Maddie?"

Bosch turned and glanced back at her. She had changed clothes. She was leaning against the door behind Sun, staring out through the window while hugging her pillow to her chest. There were tears on her cheeks. It did not appear that she had noticed the bullet hole through the pillow.

"Maddie, you all right?"

Without answering or looking away from the window, she said, "She's dead, isn't she?"

"What?"

Bosch knew exactly who and what she was talking about but was trying to stretch time, put off as long as possible the inevitable.

"I'm not stupid, you know. You're here. Sun Yee's here. She should be here. She would be here but something's happened to her."

Bosch felt an invisible punch hit him square in the chest. Madeline was still hugging the pillow in front of her and looking out the window with tear-filled eyes.

"Maddie, I'm sorry. I wanted to tell you but this wasn't the right time."

"When is the right time?"

Bosch nodded.

"You're right. Never."

He reached back and put his hand on her knee but she immediately pushed it away. It was the first sign of the blame he would always carry.

"I'm so sorry. I don't know what I can say. When I landed this morning your mother was there at the airport, waiting for me. With Sun Yee. She only wanted one thing, Maddie. To get you home safe. She didn't care about anything else, including herself."

"What happened to her?"

Bosch hesitated but there was no other way to respond but with the truth.

"She got shot, baby. Somebody was shooting at me and she got hit. I don't think she even felt it."

Madeline put her hands over her eyes.

"It's all my fault."

Bosch shook his head, even though she wasn't looking at him.

"Maddie, no. Listen to me. Don't ever say that. Don't even think that. It's not your fault. It's my fault. Everything here is my fault."

She didn't respond. She hugged the pillow closer and kept her eyes on the roadside as it passed by in a blur.

An hour later they were at the drop-off curb at the airport. Bosch helped his daughter out of the Mercedes and then turned to Sun. They had said little in the car. But now it was time to say good-bye and Bosch knew his daughter could not have been rescued without Sun's help.

"Sun Yee, thank you for saving my daughter."

"You saved her. Nothing could stop you, Harry Bosch."

"What will you do? The police will come to you about Eleanor, if not everything else."

"I will handle these things and make no mention of you. This is my promise. No matter what happens, I will leave you and your daughter out of it."

Bosch nodded.

"Good luck," he said.

"Good luck to you, too."

Bosch shook his hand and then stepped back. After another awkward pause, Madeline stepped forward and hugged Sun. Bosch saw the look on his face, even behind the disguise of the sunglasses. No matter their differences, Bosch knew Sun had found some sort of resolve in Madeline's rescue. Maybe it allowed him to find refuge in himself.

"I am so sorry," Madeline said.

Sun stepped back and broke the embrace.

"You go on now," he said. "You have a happy life."

They left him standing there and headed into the main terminal through the glass doors.

Bosch and his daughter found the first-class window at Cathay Pacific and Harry bought two tickets on the 11:40 P.M. flight to Los Angeles. He got a refund for his intended flight the next morning but still had to use two credit cards to cover the overall cost. But he didn't care. He knew that first-class passengers were accorded special status that moved them quickly through security checks and first onto planes. Airport and airline staff and security were less likely to concern themselves with first-class travelers, even if they were a disheveled man with blood on his jacket and a thirteen-year-old girl who couldn't seem to keep tears off her cheeks.

Bosch also understood that his daughter had been left traumatized by the past sixty hours of her life, and while he couldn't begin to know how to care for her in this regard, he instinctively felt that any added comfort couldn't hurt.

Noting Bosch's unkempt appearance, the woman behind the counter mentioned to him that the first-class waiting lounge offered showering facilities to travelers. Bosch thanked her for the tip, took their boarding passes and then followed a first-class hostess to security. As expected, they breezed through the checkpoint on the power of their newfound status.

They had almost three hours to kill and though the previously mentioned shower facility was tempting, Bosch decided that food might be a more pressing need. He couldn't remember when and what he had last eaten and he assumed his daughter had been equally deprived of nourishment.

"You hungry, Mads?"

"Not really."

"They fed you?"

"No, uh-uh. I couldn't eat, anyway."

"When did you last eat something?"

She had to think.

"I had a piece of pizza at the mall on Friday. Before…"

"Okay, we've got to eat, then."

They took an escalator up to an area where there were a variety of restaurants overlooking the duty-free shopping mecca. Bosch chose a sit-down restaurant in the center of the concourse that had good views of the shopping level. His daughter ordered chicken fingers and Bosch ordered a steak and french fries.

"You should never order a steak at an airport," Madeline said.

"Why's that?"

"You won't get good quality."

Bosch nodded. It was the first time she had said something more than one or two words in length since they had said good-bye to Sun. Harry had been watching her slowly collapse inward as the release of fear that followed her escape wore off and the reality of what she had been through and what had happened to her mother sank in. Bosch had feared she might be going into some form of shock. Her odd observation about the quality of steak in an airport seemed to indicate that she was in a dissociated state.

"Well, I guess I'll find out."

She then jumped the conversation to a new place.

"So am I going to live in L.A. with you now?"

"I think so."

He studied her face for a reaction. It remained unchanged—blank stare over cheeks streaked with dried tears and sadness.

"I want you to," Bosch said. "And last time you were over, you said you wanted to stay."

"But not like this."

"I know."

"Will I ever go back to get my things and say good-bye to my friends?"

Bosch thought for a moment before responding.

"I don't think so," he finally said. "I might be able to get your things sent. But you're probably going to have to e-mail your friends, I guess. Or call them."

"At least I'll be able to say good-bye."

Bosch nodded and was silent, noting the obvious reference to her lost mother. She soon spoke again, her mind like a balloon caught in the wind, touching down here and there on unpredictable currents.

"Are we, like, wanted by the police here?"

Bosch looked around to see if anyone sitting nearby had heard the question, then leaned forward to answer.

"I don't know," he said quietly. "We could be. I could be. But I don't want to find out here. It will be better to deal with all of this from L.A."

After a pause she asked another question and this one hit Bosch between the numbers.

"Dad, did you kill those men that had me? I heard a lot of shooting."

Bosch thought about how he should answer — as a cop, as a father — but didn't take too long.

"Let's just say that they got what they deserved. And that whatever happened was brought on by their own actions. Okay?"

"Okay."

When the food came they stopped talking and ate ravenously. Bosch had chosen the restaurant, the table and his seat so that he would have a good view of the shopping area and the security gate beyond. As he ate, he kept a vigilant watch for any unusual activity involving the airport's security staff. Any movement of multiple personnel or search activity would cause him concern. He had no idea if he was even on any police radar yet but he had cut a deadly path across Hong Kong and had to remain alert to it catching up to him.

"Are you going to finish your french fries?" Maddie asked.

Bosch turned his plate so she could reach the fries.

"Have at it."

When she reached across the table her sleeve pulled back and Bosch saw the bandage in the crook of her elbow. He thought of the bloodstained tissue Eleanor had found in the wastebasket in the room at Chungking Mansions.

Bosch pointed at her arm.

"Maddie, how did you get that? Did they take your blood?"

She put her other hand over the wound as if that could stop all consideration of it.

"Do we have to talk about this now?"

"Can you just tell me one thing?"

"Yes, Quick took my blood."

"I was going to ask something else. Where were you before you were put in the trunk and taken to the boat?"

"I don't know, some kind of hospital place. Like a doctor's office. I was locked in a room the whole time. Please, Dad, I don't want to talk about it. Not now."

"Okay, sweetheart, we'll talk about it when you want."

After the meal, they headed down to the shopping area. Bosch bought a complete set of new clothes in a men's store and a pair of jogging shoes and arm sweatbands in a sports shop. Maddie declined the offer of new clothing and said she'd stick with what was in her backpack.

Their next stop was a general store and Maddie picked out a stuffed panda bear she said she wanted to use as a pillow and a book called *The Lightning Thief*.

They then headed to the airline's first-class lounge and signed up to use the shower facilities. Despite a long day's buildup of blood, sweat and grime, Bosch showered quickly because he didn't want to be separated from his daughter for very long. Before getting dressed he checked the wound on his arm. It was clotted and beginning to scab over. He used the armbands he had just bought as a double bandage over the wound.

Once he was dressed he took the top off the trash can that was next to the sink in the shower room. He bundled his old clothes and shoes together and buried them under the paper towels and other debris in the can. He didn't want anyone to spot his belongings and retrieve them, especially the shoes in which he had trod across the bloody tiles in Tuen Mun.

Feeling somewhat refreshed and ready for the long flight ahead, he stepped out and looked around for his daughter. He didn't see her anywhere in the lounge and went back to wait for her near the entrance to the women's shower room. After fifteen minutes and no sign of Madeline, he started getting worried. He waited another five and then went to the reception desk and asked the woman behind the counter to send an employee into the shower room to check on his daughter.

The woman said she would do it herself. Bosch

followed and then waited when she went into the shower room. He heard the shower running when the door was opened. He then heard voices and soon the woman from the front desk stepped out.

"She's still in the shower and she said everything is fine. She said she was going to be a while longer."

"Okay, thanks."

The woman went back to her position and Bosch checked his watch. The boarding of their flight would not start for at least a half hour. There was time. He went back to the lounge and sat in a chair nearest to the hallway leading to the showers. He kept watch the whole time.

He couldn't imagine where Madeline's thoughts were. He knew she needed help and that he was completely un-equipped to provide it. His governing thought was sim-ply to get her back to Los Angeles and to go from there. He already had in mind who he would call in to counsel Maddie once he got her there.

Just as the boarding of their flight was announced in the lounge, Madeline came down the hallway, her dark hair slicked back and wet. She was wearing the same clothes she had changed into in the car but had added a hooded sweatshirt. Somehow she was cold.

"Are you all right?" Bosch asked.

She didn't answer. She just stopped in front of Bosch with her head down.

"I know, stupid question," Harry said. "But are you ready to fly? They just called our flight. We need to go."

"I'm ready. I just wanted a long, hot shower."

"I understand."

They left the lounge and made their way to the gate,

and while approaching, Bosch saw no more than the usual gathering of security. Their tickets were taken, their passports checked and they were allowed to board.

The plane was a large double-decker with the cockpit on the upper level and the first-class cabin right below in the nose of the craft. A flight attendant informed them that they were the only ones flying first class and that they could pick their seats. They took the two seats in the front row and it felt like they had the plane to themselves. Bosch wasn't planning on taking his eyes off his daughter until they were in Los Angeles.

As the loading of the plane neared completion, the pilot came on the speaker and announced that they would spend thirteen hours in the air. That was shorter than the flight over because the winds would be with them. However, they would be flying back against the grain of time. They would land in Los Angeles at 9:30 Sunday night, two hours before they had taken off in Hong Kong.

Bosch did the math and knew that it would add up to a thirty-nine-hour day before it was over. The longest day of his life.

Eventually, the big plane was cleared for an on-time takeoff and it trundled down the runway, picked up speed and climbed loudly into the dark sky. Bosch breathed a little easier as he looked out the window and saw the lights of Hong Kong disappear below the clouds. He hoped never to be back again.

His daughter reached across the space between their seats and grabbed his hand. He looked over and held her eyes. She had started to cry again. Bosch squeezed her hand and nodded.

"It's going to be all right, Maddie."

She nodded back and held on.

After the plane leveled off, the flight attendant came around and offered them food and drink but both Bosch and his daughter declined. Madeline watched a movie about teenage vampires and then folded her seat down flat—one of the perks of first class—and went to sleep.

Soon she was soundly asleep and he envisioned some sort of internal healing process taking place. The armies of sleep charging through her brain and attacking the bad memories.

He bent down and kissed her lightly on the cheek. As the seconds, minutes and hours moved backwards, he watched her sleep and wished for the impossible, that time would move backwards far enough for him to begin the whole day again. That was the fantasy. The reality was that his life was almost as significantly altered as hers was. She was with him now. And he knew that no matter what he had done or caused to happen until this point in his life, she would be his ticket to redemption.

If he could protect and serve her, he had the chance to make up for everything. For all of it.

His plan was to keep watch on her through the night. But his exhaustion eventually defeated him and he closed his eyes as well. Soon he dreamed of a place by a river. There was an outdoor table with a white tablecloth ruffled by the wind. He sat across the table from both Eleanor and Madeline and they smiled at him. It was a dream of a place that had never been and would never be.

PART THREE:

To Protect and Serve

39

The last hurdle was customs and immigration in Los Angeles. The agent at the entry booth swiped their passports and was ready to routinely stamp them when something on the computer caught his eye. Bosch held his breath.

"Mr. Bosch. You were in Hong Kong for less than a day?"

"That's right. I didn't even need to pack a bag. I just went to pick up my daughter."

The agent nodded as though he understood and had seen it before. He stamped the passports. He looked at Madeline and said, "Welcome to L.A., young lady."

"Thank you," she said.

It was almost midnight by the time they got to the house on Woodrow Wilson Drive. Bosch carried the backpack into the guest room and his daughter followed. She was familiar with the room, having used it on several visits.

"Now that you'll be living here full-time, we can fix up this room any way you want," Bosch said. "I know you had a lot of posters and stuff back in Hong Kong. You can do whatever you want here."

There were two cardboard boxes stacked in the corner that contained old case files Bosch had copied.

"I'll get these out of here," he said.

He moved them one at a time into his bedroom. He continued to talk to her as he moved up and down the hall.

"I know you don't have a private bathroom but the guest bathroom in the hall is all yours. I don't get many guests here, anyway."

After moving the boxes, Bosch sat down on the bed and looked at his daughter. She was still standing in the middle of the room. The look on her face cut Bosch deeply. He could see the reality of the situation hitting her. It didn't matter that she had repeatedly voiced a desire to live in L.A. She was now here permanently and grasping that fact was a daunting task.

"Maddie, I just want to tell you something," he said. "I'm used to being your father four weeks a year. That was easy. This is going to be hard. I am going to make mistakes and I'm going to need you to be patient with me while I learn. But I promise you I will do the best I can."

"Okay."

"Now, what can I get you? Are you hungry? Tired? What?"

"No, I'm fine. I guess I shouldn't have slept so much on the plane."

"Doesn't matter. You needed the sleep right then. And sleep is always good. It heals."

She nodded and looked awkwardly around the room.

It was a basic guest room. A bed, bureau and a table with a lamp.

"Tomorrow we'll get you a TV to put in here. One of those flat screens. And also a computer and a desk. We'll need to go shopping for a lot of things."

"I think I need a new cell phone. Quick took mine."

"Yeah, we'll get you a new phone, too. I have your memory card from the old one, so you won't lose your contacts."

She looked over at him and he realized he had made a mistake.

"You have the card? Did you get it from Quick? Was his sister there?"

Bosch held his hands up in a calming gesture and shook his head.

"I never met Quick or his sister. I found your phone but it was broken. All I got was the memory card."

"She tried to save me. She found out that Quick was going to sell me and tried to stop it. But he kicked her out of the car."

Bosch waited for her to say more but that was it. He wanted to ask her many questions about the brother and sister and everything else but his role as father overtook his role as cop. Now wasn't the right time. He had to get her calmed and situated. There would be time later to be a cop, to ask about Quick and He and to tell her what happened to them.

He studied her face and she seemed to be drained of emotion. She still looked tired, even after all the sleep on the plane.

"Everything's going to be okay, Maddie. I promise."

She nodded.

"Um, do you think I can just be alone for a little while in here?"

"Sure you can. It's your room. I think I should make some calls, anyway."

He got up and headed to the door. He hesitated as he was closing it behind him and looked back at her.

"You'll tell me if you need anything, right?"

"Yes, Dad. Thanks."

He closed the door and went out to the living room. He pulled his phone and called David Chu.

"It's Bosch. Sorry to call so late."

"No problem. How is it going over there?"

"I'm back in L.A."

"You're back? What about your daughter?"

"She's safe. What's the status on Chang?"

There was a hesitation before Chu answered. He didn't want to be the messenger.

"Well, he walks in the morning. We don't have anything to file on him."

"What about the extortion?"

"I took a last run at Li and Lam today. They won't file a formal complaint. They're too scared of the triad. Li said somebody called already and threatened him."

Bosch thought for a moment about the threatening call he had received on Friday. He assumed it was the same caller.

"So Chang walks out of the DDC in the morning and heads to the airport," he said. "He gets on a plane and we never see him again."

"Looks like we lost this one, Harry."

Bosch shook his head, his rage boiling over.

"Goddamn those motherfuckers."

Bosch realized his daughter might be able to hear him. He opened one of the living room sliders and stepped out onto the rear deck. The sound from the freeway traffic down in the pass would help muffle his conversation.

"They were going to sell my kid," he said. "For her organs."

"God," Chu said. "I thought they were just trying to intimidate you."

"Yeah, well, they took her blood and she must've matched somebody with a lot of money because the plan changed."

"Well, they could've tested her blood to make sure she was clean before they ..."

He stopped, realizing the alternate scenario wasn't comforting. He changed directions.

"Is she back here with you, Harry?"

"I told you, she's safe."

Bosch knew that Chu would read his indirect answer as a lack of trust, but what was new? He couldn't help it after the day he'd had. He tried to change the subject.

"When was the last time you talked to Ferras or Gandle?"

"I haven't talked to your partner since Friday. I talked to the lieutenant a couple hours ago. He wanted to know where things stood as well. He's pretty pissed off about it, too."

It was almost midnight on a Sunday and yet the freeway down below was packed, all ten lanes across. The air was crisp and cool, a welcome change from Hong Kong.

"Who's supposed to tell the DA's office to kick him loose?" Bosch asked.

"I was going to call over there in the morning. Unless you want to."

"I'm not sure I'll be there in the morning. Why don't you handle it, but wait until ten to make the call."

"Sure, but why ten?"

"It will give me time to get over there and say good-bye to Mr. Chang."

"Harry, don't do something you'll regret."

Bosch briefly considered the past three days.

"It's too late for that."

Bosch ended the call with Chu and stood against the railing, looking out at the night. There was certainly something safe about being home but he couldn't help thinking about what had been lost and left behind. It was like the hungry ghosts of Hong Kong had followed him across the Pacific.

"Dad?"

He turned. His daughter stood in the open doorway.

"Hey, baby."

"Are you all right?"

"Sure, why?"

She stepped out onto the deck and stood next to him at the rail.

"It sounded like you were mad when you were on the phone."

"It's about the case. It's not going well."

"I'm sorry."

"Not your fault. But listen, in the morning, I have to take a quick run downtown. I'll make some calls and see if I can get somebody to watch you while I'm gone. And then when I get back we'll go to the store, like I was saying before. Okay?"

"You mean like a babysitter?"

"No . . . I mean, yeah, I guess so."

"Dad, I haven't had a babysitter or a nanny since I was, like, twelve."

"Yeah, well, that was only a year ago."

"I think I will be all right by myself. I mean, Mom lets me go to the mall after school by myself."

Bosch noted her use of the present tense. He was tempted to tell her that the plan to allow her to go to the mall by herself didn't work out so well, but he was smart enough to save that for another time. The bottom line was that he had to consider her safety ahead of everything else. Could the forces that grabbed her in Hong Kong find her all the way over here in his home?

It seemed unlikely but even if there was a small percentage chance, he couldn't risk leaving her alone. The problem with that was he didn't really know who he could call in. He wasn't plugged into the neighborhood. He was the resident cop who got called when there was a problem. But otherwise he had never socialized with people on his street, or with anyone for that matter other than cops. He didn't know who would be safe or any different from a complete stranger chosen from the child-sitter ads in the phone book. Bosch was at a loss and it was beginning to dawn on him that he had no business raising his own daughter.

"Maddie, listen, this is one of those times when I said you were going to have to be patient with me. I don't want you left alone. Not yet. You can stay in your room if you want—you'll probably still be asleep because of jet lag. But I want an adult in the house with you. Somebody I can trust."

"Whatever."

Thinking about being the resident cop in the neighborhood suddenly pushed another idea into his brain.

"Okay, I'll tell you what. If you don't want a sitter, then I have another idea. There's a school down at the bottom of the hill. It's a public middle school. I think classes started last week because I saw all the cars on my way to work. I don't know if it's where you'll end up going or if we'll try to get you into a private school, but I could take you down there and you could look around and check it out. Maybe sit in on a class or two and see what you think while I go downtown. How would that be? I know the assistant principal and I trust her. She'll take care of you."

His daughter hooked a strand of hair behind her ear and stared out at the view for a few moments before answering.

"I guess that would be okay."

"Okay, good, then we'll do that. I'll call in the morning and set it up."

Problem solved, Bosch thought.

"Dad?"

"What, baby?"

"I heard what you said on the phone."

He froze.

"I'm sorry. I will try not to use that kind of language anymore. And never around you."

"No, I don't mean that. I mean when you were out here. About what you said about them selling me for my organs. Is that true?"

"I don't know, darling. I don't know what their exact plan was."

"Quick took my blood. He said he was going to send it to you. You know, so you could run DNA and know that I was really kidnapped."

Bosch nodded.

"Yeah, well, he was lying to you. The video he sent was enough to convince me. The blood wasn't necessary. He was lying to you, Mad. He betrayed you and he got what he deserved."

She immediately turned toward him and Bosch realized he had slipped again.

"What do you mean? What happened to him?"

Bosch didn't want to go down the slippery slope of lying to his daughter. He also knew that his daughter obviously cared about Quick's sister, if not for Quick himself. She probably still didn't understand the depth of his betrayal.

"He's dead."

Her breath caught in her throat and she brought her hands to her mouth.

"Did you..."

"No, Maddie, I didn't do it. I found him dead at the same time I found your phone. I guess you somehow liked him, so I'm sorry. But he betrayed you, baby, and I have to tell you, I might have done the same thing to him if I had found him alive. Let's go in now."

Bosch turned from the railing.

"What about He?"

Bosch stopped and looked back at her.

"I don't know about He."

He moved to the door and went inside. There, he had lied to her for the first time. It was to save her from some grief, but it didn't matter. He could already feel that he was beginning to slide down the slope.

40

At 11 A.M. Monday, Bosch was waiting outside the Downtown Detention Center for the release of Bo-Jing Chang. He wasn't sure what he was going to do or say to the murderer when he stepped through the door as a free man. But he knew he couldn't let the moment pass. If Chang's arrest had been the trigger that resulted in all that had happened in Hong Kong, including the death of Eleanor Wish, then Bosch would not be able to live with himself if he didn't confront the man when he had the chance.

His phone buzzed in his pocket and he was tempted not to answer it and risk missing Chang, but he saw on the screen that it was Lieutenant Gandle calling. He took the call.

"I hear you're back."

"Yeah, I was going to call you."

"You got your daughter?"

"Yeah, she's safe."

"Where?"

Bosch hesitated but not for too long.

"She's with me."

"And her mother?"

"She's still in Hong Kong."

"How's that going to work?"

"She'll live with me. For a while, at least."

"What happened back there? Anything I need to worry about?"

Bosch wasn't sure what to tell him. He decided to put it off.

"I'm hoping there's no blowback. But you never know."

"I'll let you know what I hear. Are you coming in?"

"Uh, not today. I need to take a couple days to get my daughter situated and in school and stuff. I want to get her some counseling."

"Is this white time or vacay days? I need to put it down."

Comp time was called "white time" in the LAPD, after the blank white form on which supervisors kept track of it.

"Doesn't matter. I think I have the white time."

"Then I'll go with that. Are you okay, Harry?"

"I'm fine."

"I guess Chu told you about Chang getting kicked."

"Yeah, he told me."

"His prick lawyer was already here this morning to pick up his suitcase. I'm sorry, Harry. There's nothing we could do. The case isn't there and those two wimps up in the Valley won't help us hold him on the extortion."

"I know."

"Didn't help that your partner stayed home all weekend. Claimed he was sick."

"Ycah, well..."

Bosch had reached the end of his patience with Ferras but that was between him and his partner. He wouldn't discuss it with Gandle yet.

The door to the release office opened and Bosch saw an Asian man in a suit step out, carrying a briefcase. It wasn't Chang. The man held the door with his body and waved up the street to a waiting car. Bosch knew this was it. The man in the suit was a well-known defense attorney named Anthony Wing.

"Lieutenant, I gotta go. Can I call you back?"

"Just call me when you decide how many days you're taking and when I can put you back on the schedule. Meantime, I'll find something for Ferras to do. Something inside."

"I'll talk to you later."

Bosch closed the phone just as a black Cadillac Escalade cruised up and Bo-Jing Chang stepped through the jail's release door. Bosch moved into the path between him and the SUV. Wing then stepped between Bosch and Chang.

"Excuse me, Detective," Wing said. "You are impeding my client's path."

"Is that what I'm doing, 'impeding'? What about him impeding John Li's life?"

Bosch saw Chang smirk and shake his head behind Wing. He heard a car door slam behind him and Wing's attention moved over Harry's shoulder.

"Make sure you get this," he commanded.

Bosch looked behind him and saw that a man with a video camera had gotten out of the big SUV. The lens of the camera was pointed at Bosch.

"What is this?"

"Detective, if you touch or harass Mr. Chang in any way, it will be documented and offered to the media."

Bosch turned back to Wing and Chang. Chang's smirk had turned into a satisfied smile.

"You think this is over, Chang? I don't care where you go, this isn't over. You and your people made it personal, asshole, and I don't forget that."

"Detective, move aside," Wing said, clearly playing to the camera. "Mr. Chang is leaving because he is innocent of the charges you tried to concoct against him. He is returning to Hong Kong because of LAPD harassment. Because of you, he is unable to continue enjoying the life he has known here for several years."

Bosch stepped out of their way and let them pass to the car.

"You are full of shit, Wing. Take your camera and shove it up your ass."

Chang got into the backseat of the Escalade first, then Wing signaled the cameraman to get into the front seat.

"We have your threat on film now, Detective," Wing said. "Remember that."

Wing got in next to Chang and closed the door. Bosch stood there and watched the big SUV glide off, probably taking Chang directly to the airport to complete his legal escape.

• • •

When Bosch got back to the school, he went to the assistant principal's office to check in. Sue Bambrough had agreed that morning to allow Madcline to audit eighth-grade classes and see if she liked the school. When he stepped in, Bambrough asked him to sit down and then proceeded to tell him that his daughter was still in class and assimilating quite well. Bosch was surprised. She had been in L.A. a little more than twelve hours after losing her mother and spending a harrowing weekend in captivity. Bosch had feared that the drop-off at the school might be disastrous.

Bosch already knew Bambrough. A couple of years earlier, a neighbor who had a child attending the school asked him to speak to the kid's class about police work and crime. Bambrough was a bright, hands-on administrator who had interviewed Bosch at length before allowing him to address any students. Bosch had rarely been grilled so thoroughly by defense attorneys in court. She had taken a hard line on the quality of police work in the city but her arguments were well thought out and articulate. Bosch respected her.

"Class ends in ten minutes," Bambrough said. "I'll take you to her then. There is something I would like to talk to you about first, Detective Bosch."

"I told you last time, call me Harry. What is it you want to talk about?"

"Well, your daughter's quite a storyteller. She was overheard during the midmorning break telling other students that she just moved here from Hong Kong because her mother was murdered and she got kidnapped. My concern is that she's self-aggrandizing in order to—"

"It's true. All of it."

"What do you mean?"

"She was abducted and her mother was killed trying to rescue her."

"Oh, dear God! When did this happen?"

Bosch regretted not telling Bambrough the whole story when they had talked that morning. He had simply told her that his daughter was going to be living with him and wanted to check the school out.

"Over the weekend," he answered. "We arrived from Hong Kong last night."

Bambrough looked like she had taken a punch.

"Over the weekend? Are you telling me the truth?"

"Of course I am. She's been through a lot. I know it might be too soon to put her in school, but this morning I had . . . an appointment I couldn't avoid. I'll take her home now and if she wants to come back in a few days, I'll let you know."

"Well, what about counseling? What about a physical examination?"

"I'm working on all of that."

"Don't be afraid to get her help. Children like to talk about things. It's just that sometimes it's not to their parents. I have found that children have an innate ability to know what they need in order to heal themselves and survive. Without her mother and with you being new at full-time parenting, Madeline may need an outside party to talk to."

Bosch nodded at the end of the lecture.

"She'll get whatever she needs. What would I need to do if she wants to go to school here?"

"Just call me. You're in the district and we have the space. There will be some minor paperwork for enrollment and we'll have to get her transcript from Hong Kong. You'll need her birth certificate and that's about it."

Bosch realized that his daughter's birth certificate was probably back in the apartment in Hong Kong.

"I don't have her birth certificate. I'll have to apply for one. I think she was born in Las Vegas."

"You think?"

"I, uh, didn't meet her until she was already four. At the time, she lived with her mother in Las Vegas and I assume she was born there. I can ask her."

Bambrough looked even more puzzled.

"I have her passport," Bosch offered. "It'll say where she was born. I just haven't looked at it."

"Well, we can make do with that until you get the birth certificate. I think the important thing now is to take care of your daughter psychologically. This is a terrible trauma for her. You need to get her talking to a counselor."

"Don't worry, I will."

A chime sounded the change of classes and Bambrough stood up. They left the office and walked down a main hallway. The campus was long and narrow because it was built on the hillside. Bosch saw Bambrough still trying to absorb the idea of what Madeline had just been through and survived.

"She's a strong kid," he offered.

"She'll have to be after an experience like that."

Bosch wanted to change the subject.

"What classes has she been in?"

"She started in math and then had a short break before

social studies. They then went to lunch and now she just finished Spanish."

"She was learning Chinese in Hong Kong."

"I'm sure this is just one of the many difficult changes she'll be going through."

"Like I said, she's tough. I think she'll make it."

Bambrough turned and smiled as she walked.

"Like her father, I assume."

"Her mother was tougher."

Children were crowding the hallway as they changed classes. Bambrough saw Bosch's daughter before he did.

"Madeline," she called.

Bosch waved. Maddie had been walking with two girls and somehow seemed to be already making friends. She said good-bye to them and rushed over.

"Hi, Dad."

"Hey, how'd you like it?"

"It was all right, I guess."

Her voice was reserved and Bosch didn't know if that was because the assistant principal was standing right there with them.

"How was Spanish?" Bambrough asked.

"Um, I was kind of lost."

"I heard you were learning Chinese. It's a much more difficult language than Spanish. I think you'd pick up Spanish very quickly here."

"I guess."

Bosch decided to save her from the small talk.

"Well, are you ready, Mad? We're going to go shopping today, remember?"

"Sure, I'm ready."

Bosch looked at Bambrough and nodded.

"Thank you for doing this, and I'll be in touch."

His daughter chimed in with her own thanks and they left the school. Once they got in the car, Bosch started up the hill to their house.

"So, now that we're alone, what did you really think, Mad?"

"Uh, it was okay. It's just not the same, you know?"

"Yeah, I know. We can look at some private schools. There's a few nearby on the Valley side."

"I don't want to be a Valley girl, Dad."

"I kind of doubt you'll ever be a Valley girl. It's not about where you go to school, anyway."

"I think that school will be fine," she said after some thought. "I met some girls there and they were pretty nice."

"You sure?"

"I think so. Can I start tomorrow?"

Bosch looked over at her and then back at the curving road.

"That's sort of fast, isn't it? You just got here last night."

"I know, but what am I supposed to do? Sit up in that house and cry all day?"

"No, but I thought if we took things kind of slow, it might—"

"I don't want to fall behind. School started last week."

Bosch thought for a few moments about what Bambrough had said about kids knowing what they need to heal. He decided to trust his daughter's instincts.

"Okay, if you feel it's right. I'll call Mrs. Bambrough

back and tell her you want to enroll. By the way, you were born in Las Vegas, right?"

"You mean you don't know?"

"Yeah, I know. I just wanted to make sure because I have to apply for a copy of your birth certificate. For the school."

She didn't respond. Bosch pulled into the carport next to the house.

"So, Vegas, right?"

"Yes! You really didn't know, did you? God!"

Before he could work up a response, Bosch was saved by his phone. It buzzed and he pulled it out. Without looking at the screen, he told his daughter he had to take it.

It was Ignacio Ferras.

"Harry, I hear you're back and your daughter's safe."

He sure was late getting the news. Bosch unlocked the kitchen door and held it open for his daughter.

"Yeah, we're good."

"You're taking off a few days?"

"That's the plan. What are you working on?"

"Oh, just a few things. Writing up some summaries on John Li."

"What for? That one's over. We blew it."

"I know but we need to keep the file complete and I need to file the search warrant returns with the court. That's sort of why I'm calling. You bugged out Friday without leaving any notes on what you found on the searches of the phone and the suitcase. I already wrote up the car search."

"Yeah, well, I didn't find anything. That's one reason why we didn't have a case to file, remember?"

Bosch threw his keys on the dining room table and watched his daughter go down the hall to her room. He felt a growing annoyance with Ferras. At one point he had embraced the idea of mentoring the young detective and teaching him the mission. But he was now finally accepting the reality that Ferras would never recover from being wounded in the line of duty. Physically, yes. Mentally, no. He would never be the full package again. He would be a paper pusher.

"So put down zero returns?" Ferras asked.

Bosch momentarily thought of the business card from the taxi service in Hong Kong. It had been a dead end and wasn't worth putting into the search warrant return that had to go back to the judge.

"Yeah, zero returns. There was nothing."

"And nothing on the phone."

Bosch suddenly realized something but also knew in the same instant that it was probably too late.

"Nothing *on* the phone, but did you guys go to the company for the records?"

Chang might have wiped all call records off his phone but he wouldn't have been able to touch the records kept by his cellular service carrier. There was a pause before Ferras answered.

"No, I thought—you had the phone, Harry. I thought you contacted the phone company."

"I didn't, because I was heading to Hong Kong."

All phone companies had established protocols for receiving and accepting search warrants. It usually amounted to faxing the signed search warrant to the legal affairs office. It was a simple thing to do but it had fallen through the cracks. Now Chang had been kicked loose and was probably long gone.

"Goddamnit," Bosch said. "You should've been on that, Ignacio."

"Me? You had the phone, Harry. I thought you did it."

"I had the phone but you were on point with the warrants. You should have checked it off before you left Friday."

"That's bullshit, man. You're going to blame me for this?"

"I'm blaming us both. Yeah, I could've done it, but you *should've* made sure it was done. You didn't because you left early and you let it slide. You've been letting the whole job slide, partner."

There, he had said it.

"And you are full of shit, partner. You mean because I'm not like you, losing my family to the job and then *risking* my family to the job, that I'm letting it slide? You don't know what you're talking about."

Bosch was stunned silent by the verbal shot. Ferras had hit him right in the spot where he had been living for the past seventy-two hours. Finally, he shook it off and came back.

"Ignacio," he said calmly. "This isn't working. I don't know when I will be back into the squad this week, but when I get in there, we're gonna talk."

"Fine. I'll be here."

"Of course you will. You're always in the squad. I'll see you then."

Bosch closed the phone before Ferras could protest his final shot. Bosch was sure Gandle would back him when he asked for a new partner. He went back into the kitchen to grab a beer and take the edge off the conversation. He opened the refrigerator and started to reach in but stopped. It was too early and he was going to be driving his daughter around the Valley shopping for the rest of the afternoon.

He closed the refrigerator and walked down the hallway. The door to his daughter's room was closed.

"Maddie, you ready to go?"

"I'm changing. I'll be out in a minute."

She had answered in a clipped don't-bother-me tone. Bosch wasn't sure what to make of it. The plan was to go to the phone store first and then to get clothing and furniture and a laptop computer. He was going to get his daughter whatever she wanted and she knew it. Yet she was being short with him and he wasn't sure why. One day on the job as a full-time father and he already felt like he was lost at sea.

41

The next morning Bosch and his daughter set to work assembling some of the purchases of the day before. Maddie was not in school yet because her enrollment would take an additional day to wind through public school bureaucracy — a delay Bosch welcomed because it gave them more time together.

First in line for assembly was the computer desk and chair they had bought at the IKEA store in Burbank. They had gone on a four-hour shopping spree, accumulating school supplies, clothes, electronics and furniture, completely filling Bosch's car and leaving him with a feeling of guilt that was new to him. He knew that buying his daughter everything she pointed at or asked for was a form of trying to buy her happiness — and the forgiveness that would hopefully come with it.

He had moved the coffee table out of the way and spread the parts of the prefabricated desk out on the floor of the living room. The instructions said it could be completely assembled with only one tool — a small Allen wrench that came with it. Harry and Madeline sat cross-legged on the floor, trying to understand the assembly map.

"It looks like you start by attaching the side panels to the desktop," Madeline said.

"You sure?"

"Yes. See, everything that is marked 'one' is part of the first step."

"I thought that just meant you have one of those parts."

"No, because there are two side panels and they're marked 'one.' I think it means step one."

"Oh."

A phone rang and they looked at each other. Madeline had gotten a new phone the day before and it was once again a match to her father's. The trouble was, she had not selected an individual ring tone, so both phones sounded the same. She had received a series of calls throughout the morning from friends in Hong Kong whom she had sent messages to, saying she had moved to Los Angeles.

"I think that's you," she said. "I left mine in my room."

Bosch slowly climbed to his feet, his knees aching after being rescued from his cross-legged position. He made it over to the dining room table to grab the phone before the caller hung up.

"Harry, it's Dr. Hinojos, how are you?"

"Plugging away, Doc. Thanks for the callback."

Bosch opened the slider and stepped out onto the deck, closing the door behind him.

"I'm sorry I didn't get back until today," Hinojos said. "Mondays are always brutal here. What's up?"

Hinojos ran the department's Behavioral Science Section, the unit that offered psychiatric services to the rank and file. Bosch had known her almost fifteen years, ever since she had been a frontline counselor assigned to evaluate him after he'd had a physical altercation with his supervisor at Hollywood Division.

Bosch kept his voice low.

"I wanted to ask if you would do something for me as a favor."

"Depends on what it is."

"I want you to talk to my daughter."

"Your daughter? Last you talked to me about her she lived with her mother in Vegas."

"They moved. She's been living in Hong Kong for the past six years. Now she's with me. Her mother's dead."

There was a pause before Hinojos responded. Bosch got a call-waiting beep in his ear but ignored the second call and waited her out.

"Harry, you know that we see police officers only here, not their families. I can give you a referral for a child practitioner."

"I don't want a child shrink. I've got the yellow pages here if I wanted that. That's where the favor comes in. I want her to talk to you. You know me, I know you. Like that."

"But Harry, it doesn't work like that here."

"She got abducted over there in Hong Kong. And her mother got killed trying to get her back. The kid's got baggage, Doc."

"Oh, my God! How long ago did this happen?"

"Last weekend."

"Oh, Harry!"

"Yeah, not good. She needs to talk to somebody besides me. I want it to be you, Doctor."

Another pause and again Bosch let it play out. There wasn't much sense in pushing it with Hinojos. Bosch knew that from firsthand experience.

"I guess I could meet her off campus. Has she asked to talk to anyone?"

"She didn't ask but I told her I wanted her to. She didn't object. I think she'll like you. When could you meet with her?"

Bosch was pushing it, he knew. But it was for a good cause.

"Well, I have some time today," Hinojos said. "I could meet her after lunch. What is her name?"

"Madeline. What time?"

"Could she meet me at one?"

"No problem. Should I bring her there, or will that be a problem?"

"I think it will be fine. I won't record it as an official session."

Bosch's phone beeped again. This time he pulled it away from his ear to check the caller ID. It was Lieutenant Gandle.

"Okay, Doc," Bosch replied. "Thank you for this."

"It will be good to see you, too. Maybe you and I should have a conversation. I know your ex-wife still meant a lot to you."

"Let's take care of my daughter first. Then we can worry about me. I'll drop her with you and then get out of the way, maybe walk over to Philippe's or something."

"See you then, Harry."

He hung up and checked to see if Gandle had left a message. There was none. He headed back inside and saw that his daughter had already assembled the main structure of the desk.

"Wow, girl, you know what you're doing."

"It's pretty easy."

"Didn't seem that way to me."

He had just gotten back down on the floor when the landline started to ring from the kitchen. He got up and hustled to get it. It was an old wall-mounted phone with no caller ID screen.

"Bosch, what are you doing?"

It was Lieutenant Gandle.

"I told you I was taking a few days."

"I need you to come in, and bring your daughter."

Bosch was looking down into the empty sink.

"My daughter? Why, Lieutenant?"

"Because there are two guys from the Hong Kong Police Department sitting in Captain Dodds's office and they want to talk to you. You didn't tell me that your ex-wife is dead, Harry. You didn't tell me about all the dead bodies they say you left in your wake over there."

Bosch paused as he considered his options.

"Tell them I'll see them at one-thirty," he finally said.

Gandle's response was sharp.

"One-thirty? What do you need three hours for? Get down here now."

"I can't, Lieutenant. I'll see them at one-thirty."

Bosch hung the phone up and then pulled his cell from his pocket. He had known that the Hong Kong cops would eventually come, and he had already made a plan for what to do.

The first call he made was to Sun Yee. He knew it was late in Hong Kong but he couldn't wait. The phone rang eight times and then went to message.

"It's Bosch. Call me when you get this."

Bosch hung up and stared at his phone for a long moment. He was concerned. It was one-thirty in the morning in Hong Kong, not a time when he would have expected Sun Yee to be away from his phone. Unless it wasn't by his choice.

He next scrolled through the contact list on his phone and found a number he had not used in at least a year.

He called the number now and this time got an immediate answer.

"Mickey Haller."

"It's Bosch."

"Harry? I didn't think I'd —"

"I think I need a lawyer."

There was a pause.

"Okay, when?"

"Right now."

42

Gandle came charging out of his office the moment he saw Bosch enter the squad room.

"Bosch, I told you to get in here forthwith. Why haven't you been answering your—"

He stopped when he saw who entered behind Bosch. Mickey Haller was a well-known defense attorney. There wasn't a detective in the RHD who didn't know him on sight.

"This is your lawyer?" Gandle said with disgust. "I told you to bring your daughter, not your lawyer."

"Lieutenant," Bosch said, "let's get something straight from the start. My daughter is not part of this equation. Mr. Haller is here to advise me and help me explain to the men from Hong Kong that I committed no crimes while I was in their city. Now, do you want to introduce me to them or should I do it myself?"

Gandle hesitated and then relented.

"This way."

Gandle led them to the conference room off Captain Dodds's office. Waiting there were the two men from

Hong Kong. They stood up upon Bosch's arrival and handed him business cards. Alfred Lo and Clifford Wu. They both were from HKPD's Triad Bureau.

Bosch introduced Haller and handed the cards to him.

"Do we need a translator, gentlemen?" Haller asked.

"That is not necessary," Wu said.

"Well, that's a start," Haller said. "Why don't we sit down and hash this big old thing around."

Everyone, including Gandle, took a seat around the conference table. Haller spoke first.

"Let me start things off here by saying that my client, Detective Bosch, is not waiving any of his constitutionally guaranteed rights at this time. We are on American soil here and that means he doesn't have to speak to you gentlemen. However, he is also a detective and he knows what you two men are up against on a daily basis. Against my advice he is willing to talk to you. So the way we will work this is that you can ask him questions and he'll try to answer them if I think he should. There will be no recording of this session but you can take notes if you like. We hope to end this conversation with you two fellows leaving with a greater understanding of the events of this past weekend in Hong Kong. But one thing that is for certain is that you will not be leaving with Detective Bosch. His cooperation in this matter ends when this meeting ends."

Haller punctuated his opening salvo with a smile.

Before coming into the PAB, Bosch had met with Haller for nearly an hour in the back of Haller's Lincoln Town Car. They were parked at the dog park near Franklin Canyon and were able to watch Harry's daughter walk around and pet the sociable dogs while they talked. After they were finished, they took Maddie to her meeting with Dr. Hinojos and then drove over to the PAB.

They were not operating in complete agreement but had forged a strategy. A quick Internet search on Haller's laptop had even provided some backup material. They had come in ready to make Bosch's case to the men from Hong Kong.

Being a detective, Bosch was walking a thin line. He wanted his colleagues from across the Pacific to know what had happened, but he wasn't going to put himself, his daughter or Sun Yee in jeopardy. He believed that all his actions in Hong Kong were justified. He told Haller he had been in kill-or-be-killed situations initiated by others. And that included his encounter with the hotel manager at Chungking Mansions. In each case he had emerged victorious. There was no crime in that. Not in his book.

Lo took out a pen and notebook and Wu asked the first question, revealing that he was the lead man.

"First, we would ask, why did you go to Hong Kong on such short trip?"

Bosch shrugged like the answer was obvious.

"To get my daughter and bring her back here."

"On Saturday morning your former wife, she report the daughter missing to police," Wu said.

Bosch stared at him for a long moment.

"Is that a question?"

"Was she missing?"

"My understanding is that she was indeed missing but on Saturday morning I was thirty-five thousand feet over the Pacific. I can't speak to what my ex-wife was doing then."

"We believe your daughter was taken by someone named Peng Qingcai. Do you know him?"

"Never met him."

"Peng is dead," Lo said.

Bosch nodded.

"That doesn't make me unhappy."

"Mr. Peng's neighbor, Mrs. Fengyi Mai, she recall speaking with you at her home Sunday," Wu said. "You and Mr. Sun Yee."

"Yes, we knocked on her door. She wasn't much help."

"Why is this?"

"I guess because she didn't know anything. She didn't know where Peng was."

Wu leaned forward, his body language easy to read. He thought he was zeroing in on Bosch.

"Did you go to Peng's apartment?"

"We knocked on the door but nobody answered. After a while we left."

Wu leaned back, disappointed.

"You acknowledge that you were with Sun Yee?" he asked.

"Sure. I was with him."

"How do you know this man?"

"Through my ex-wife. They met me at the airport Sunday morning and informed me that they were looking for my daughter because the police department there did not believe she had been abducted."

Bosch studied the two men for a moment before continuing.

"You see, your police department dropped the ball. I hope you will include that in your reports. Because if I'm dragged into this, I certainly will. I'll call every news-paper in Hong Kong—doesn't matter what language— and tell them my story."

The plan was to use the threat of international em-barrassment to the HKPD to make the detectives move cautiously.

"Are you aware," Wu said, "that your ex-wife, Eleanor Wish, died of gunshot wound to the head on fifteenth floor of Chungking Mansions, Kowloon?"

"Yes, I am aware of that."

"Were you present when this happened?"

Bosch looked at Haller and the attorney nodded.

"I was there. I saw it happen."

"Can you tell us how?"

"We were looking for our daughter. We didn't find her. We were in the hallway about to leave and two men started to fire at us. Eleanor was hit and she . . . got killed. And the two men were hit, too. It was self-defense."

Wu leaned forward.

"Who shot these men?"

"I think you know that."

"You tell us, please."

Bosch thought of the gun he had put into Eleanor's dead hand. He was about to tell the lie when Haller leaned forward.

"I don't think I'm going to allow Detective Bosch to get into who-shot-whom theories," he said. "I am sure your fine police department has tremendous forensic capabili-ties and has already been able to determine through fire-arm and ballistic analysis the answer to that question."

Wu moved on.

"Was Sun Yee on the fifteenth floor?"

"Not at that time."

"Can you give us more detail?"

"About the shooting? No. But I can tell you something about the room where my daughter was held. We found tissue with blood on it. Her blood had been drawn."

Bosch studied them to see if they reacted to this information. They showed nothing.

There was a file on the table in front of the men from Hong Kong. Wu opened it and took out a document with a paper clip on it. He slid it across the table to Bosch.

"This is statement from Sun Yee. It has been translated into English. Please read and acknowledge for accuracy."

Haller leaned in next to Bosch and they read the two-page document together. Bosch immediately recognized it as a prop. It was their investigative theory disguised as a statement from Sun. About half of it was correct. The rest was assumption based on interviews and evidence. It attributed the murders of the Peng family to Bosch and Sun Yee.

Harry knew they were either trying to bluff him into telling what really happened or had arrested Sun and forced him to sign his name to the story they preferred, namely that Bosch had been responsible for a bloody rampage across Hong Kong. It would be the best way to explain nine violent deaths on one Sunday. The American did it.

But Bosch remembered what Sun had said to him at the airport. *I will handle these things and make no mention of you. This is my promise. No matter what happens, I will leave you and your daughter out of it.*

"Gentlemen," Haller said, completing his read of the document first. "This document is —"

"Total bullshit," Bosch finished.

He slid the document back across the table. It hit Wu in the chest.

"No, no," Wu said quickly. "This is very real. This is signed by Sun Yee."

"Maybe if you held a gun to his head. Is that how you do it over there in Hong Kong?"

"Detective Bosch!" Wu exclaimed. "You will come to Hong Kong and answer these charges."

"I'm not going anywhere near Hong Kong ever again."

"You have killed many people. You have used firearms. You placed your daughter above all Chinese citizens and—"

"They were blood-typing her!" Bosch said angrily. "They took her blood. You know when they do that? When they're trying to match organs."

He paused and watched the growing discomfort on Wu's face. Bosch didn't care about Lo. Wu was the power and if Bosch got to him, he would be safe. Haller had been right. In the back of the Lincoln, he had set the subtle strategy for the interview. Rather than focus on defending Bosch's actions as self-defense, make clear to the men from Hong Kong what would be brought to the international media stage should they pursue any sort of case against Bosch.

Now was the time to make that play and Haller took over and calmly moved in for the kill.

"Gentlemen, you can hang on to your signed statement there," he said, a seemingly permanent smile playing on his face. "Let me summarize the facts that are supported by the actual evidence. A thirteen-year-old American girl was abducted in your city. Her mother dutifully called the police to report this crime. The police declined to investigate the crime and then—"

"The girl had run away before," Lo interjected. "There was no reas—"

Haller held up a finger to cut him off.

"Doesn't matter," he said, now a tone of contained outrage in his voice and the smile gone. "Your department was told an American girl was missing and chose, *for whatever reason,* to ignore the report. This forced the girl's mother to look for her daughter herself. And the first thing she did was call in the girl's father from Los Angeles."

Haller gestured to Bosch.

"Detective Bosch arrived and together with his ex-wife and a friend of the family, Mr. Sun Yee, they began the search that the Hong Kong police had determined they would not be involved in. On their own, what they found was evidence that she had been kidnapped for her organs. This American girl, they were going to sell her for her organs!"

His outrage was growing and Bosch believed it was not an act. For a few moments Haller let it float over the table like a thundercloud before continuing.

"Now, as you gentlemen know, people got killed. My client isn't going to get into the details with you about all of that. Suffice it to say that, left alone in Hong Kong without any help from the government and police, this mother and father trying to find their daughter encountered some very bad people and there were kill-or-be-killed situations. There was *provocation!*"

Bosch saw the two Hong Kong detectives physically lean back as Haller shouted the last word. He then continued in a calm and well-modulated courtroom voice.

"Now, we know you want to know what happened and you have reports that need to be filled out and supervisors who need to be informed. But you have to seriously ask yourself, is this the proper course to take?"

Another pause.

"Whatever happened in Hong Kong occurred because your department failed this young American girl and this family. And if you are now going to sit back and analyze what actions Detective Bosch took because your department failed to act properly—if you are looking for a scapegoat to take back with you to Hong Kong—then you won't find one here. We won't be cooperating. However, I do have someone here whom you *will* be able to talk to about all of this. We can start with him."

Haller pulled a business card out of his shirt pocket and slid it across the table to them. Wu picked it up and studied it. Haller had shown it to Bosch earlier. It was the business card of a reporter from the *Los Angeles Times*.

"Jock Meekeevoy," Lo read. "He has information about this?"

"That's Jack McEvoy. And he has no information now. But he would be very interested in a story like this."

This was all part of the plan. Haller bluffing. The truth was, and Bosch knew, that McEvoy had been laid off by the *Times* six months earlier. Haller had dug the old card out of a stack of business cards he kept wrapped in a rubber band in his Lincoln.

"That's where it will start," Haller said calmly. "And I think it will make a great story. Thirteen-year-old American girl kidnapped in China for her organs and the police do nothing. Her parents are forced into action and the mother is killed trying to save her daughter. From there it will go international for sure. Every paper, every news channel in the world, will want a part of this story. They'll make a Hollywood movie out of it. And Oliver Stone will direct it!"

Haller now opened his own file that he had carried into the meeting. It contained the news stories he had printed in the car following his Internet search. He slid a set of printouts across the table to Wu and Lo. They moved closer together to share.

"And finally, what you have there is a package of news articles that I will be providing to Mr. McEvoy and any other journalist who makes an inquiry of me or Detective Bosch. These articles document the recent growth of the black market in human organs in China. The waiting list in China is said to be the longest in the world, with some reports of as many as a million people waiting for an organ at any given time. Doesn't help that a few years back and under pressure from the rest of the world, the Chinese government banned the harvesting of organs from executed prisoners. That only heightened the demand and value of human organs on the black market. I am sure you will be able to see from those stories from very credible newspapers, including the *Beijing Review,* where Mr. McEvoy will be going with his story. It's up to you now to decide if that is what you want to happen here."

Wu turned so he could whisper in rapid-fire Chinese directly into Lo's ear.

"No need to whisper, gentlemen," Haller said. "We can't understand you."

Wu straightened himself.

"We would like to make private telephone call before continuing the interview," he said.

"To Hong Kong?" Bosch asked. "It's going on five in the morning there."

"This does not matter," Wu said. "I must make the call, please."

Gandle stood up.

"You can use my office. You'll have privacy."

"Thank you, Lieutenant."

The Hong Kong investigators stood up to go.

"One last thing, gentlemen," Haller said.

They looked at him with *what now?* written on their faces.

"I just want you and whoever it is you are calling to know that we are also very concerned about the disposition of Sun Yee in this matter. We want you to know that we'll be getting in touch with Mr. Sun and if we can't reach him or if we learn that he has encountered any sort of impediment to his personal freedom, we plan to bring that issue up before the court of public opinion as well."

Haller smiled and paused before continuing.

"It's a package deal, gentlemen. Tell your people that."

Haller nodded, keeping the smile going the whole time, his demeanor contradicting the obvious threat. Wu and Lo nodded that they understood the message and followed Gandle out of the room.

"What do you think?" Bosch asked Haller when they were alone. "Are we in the clear?"

"Yeah, I think so," Haller said. "I think this thing just ended. What happens in Hong Kong stays in Hong Kong."

43

Bosch decided not to wait in the conference room for the Hong Kong detectives to return. He remained bothered by the verbal altercation he'd had with his partner the day before and went into the squad room to try to find Ferras.

But Ferras was gone and Bosch wondered if he had intentionally gone to lunch in order to avoid further confrontation. Harry stepped into his own cubicle to check the desk for interoffice envelopes and other messages. There were none, but he saw a blinking red light on his phone. He had a message. He was still getting used to the practice of having to check his phone line for messages. In the squad room at Parker Center, things were antiquated and there was no personal voice mail. All messages went to a central line, which the squad secretary monitored. She then wrote out message slips that went into mailboxes or were left on desks. If the call was urgent the secretary personally tracked the detective down by pager or cell phone.

Bosch sat down and typed his code into the phone. He

had five messages. The first three were routine calls about other cases. He made a few notes on a desk pad and erased the messages. The fourth had been left the night before by Detective Wu of the HKPD. He had just landed and checked into a hotel and wanted to set up an interview. Bosch erased it.

The fifth message was from Teri Sopp in latent prints. It had been left at 9:15 that morning, just about the time Bosch was opening the flat box that contained his daughter's new computer desk.

"Harry, we did the electrostatic enhancement test on the casing you gave me. We pulled a print off it and everybody around here's pretty excited. We got a match on the DOJ computer, too. So give me a call as soon as you get this."

As he called latents, Bosch looked up over the wall of his cubicle and saw Gandle escorting the two HKPD detectives back to the conference room. He waved his arm at Bosch, signaling him to come back as well. Bosch held up a finger, telling him that he needed a minute.

"Latents."

"Let me speak to Teri, please."

He waited another ten seconds, excitement growing. Bo-Jing Chang might have been kicked loose and might already be back in Hong Kong for all Bosch knew, but if his fingerprint was on the casing of one of the bullets that killed John Li, then that was a game changer. It was direct evidence linking him to the murder. They could charge him and seek an extradition warrant.

"This is Teri."

"It's Harry Bosch. I just got your message."

"I was wondering where you were. We got a match on your casing."

"That's wonderful. Bo-Jing Chang?"

"I'm in the lab. Let me go to my desk. It was a Chinese name but not the one on the print card your partner gave me. Those prints didn't match. Let me put you on hold."

She was gone and Bosch felt a fissure suddenly form in his assumptions about the case.

"Harry, are you coming?"

He looked up and out of the cubicle. Gandle had called from the door of the conference room. Bosch pointed to the phone and shook his head. Not satisfied, Gandle stepped out of the conference room and came over to Bosch's cubicle.

"Look, they are folding on this," he said urgently. "You need to get in there and finish it off."

"My lawyer can handle it. I just got the call."

"What call?"

"The one that changes—"

"Harry?"

It was Sopp back on the line. Bosch covered the mouthpiece.

"I have to take this," he said to Gandle. Then, dropping his hand and speaking into the phone, he said, "Teri, give me the name."

Gandle shook his head and went back toward the conference room.

"Okay, it's not the name you mentioned. It's Henry Lau, *L-A-U*. DOB is nine-nine-eighty-two."

"What's he in the computer for?"

"He was pulled over on a deuce two years ago in Venice."

"That's all he's got?"

"Yeah. Other than that he's clean."

"What about an address?"

"The address on his DL is eighteen Quarterdeck in Venice. Unit eleven."

Bosch copied the information into his pocket notebook.

"Okay, and this print you pulled, it's solid, right?"

"No doubt, Harry. It came up glowing like Christmas. This technology is amazing. It's going to change things."

"And they want to use this as the test case for California?"

"I wouldn't jump the gun on that just yet. My supervisor wants to first see how this plays in your case. You know, whether this guy is your shooter and what other evidence there is. We're looking for a case where the technology is an integral piece in the prosecution."

"Well, you'll know it when I know it, Teri. Thanks for this. We're going to move on it right now."

"Good luck, Harry."

Bosch hung up. He first looked over the cubicle wall at the conference room. The blinds were down but open. He could see Haller gesturing toward the two men from Hong Kong. Bosch checked his partner's cubicle once more but it was still empty. He made a decision and picked up the phone again.

David Chu was in the AGU office and took Bosch's call. Harry updated him on the latest piece of information to come out of latent prints and told him to run Henry Lau's name through the triad files. In the meantime, Bosch said, he was heading over to pick Chu up.

"Where are we going?" Chu asked.

"To go find this guy."

Bosch hung up and headed to the conference room, not to take part in whatever was being discussed, but to inform Gandle of what appeared to be a major breakthrough in the case.

When he opened the door, Gandle put his it's-about-time look on his face. Bosch signaled him to step out again.

"Harry, these men still have questions for you," Gandle said.

"They'll have to wait. We've caught a break on the Li case and I need to move on it. Now."

Gandle got up and started toward the door.

"Harry, I think I can handle this," Haller said from his seat. "But there's one question you need to answer."

Bosch looked at him and Haller nodded, meaning the remaining question was a safe one.

"What?"

"Do you want your ex-wife's body transported to Los Angeles?"

The question gave Bosch pause. The immediate answer was yes, but the hesitation was in measuring the consequences for his daughter.

"Yes," he finally said. "Send her to me."

He let Gandle step out and then closed the door.

"What happened?" Gandle asked.

Chu was waiting out front of the AGU building when Bosch pulled up. He was holding a briefcase, which made

Bosch think that he had found some information on Henry Lau. He hopped in and Bosch took off.

"We're starting in Venice?" Chu asked.

"That's right. What did you find on Lau?"

"Nothing."

Bosch looked over at him.

"Nothing?"

"As far as we know, he's clean. I could not find his name anywhere in our intelligence files. I also talked to some people and made some calls. Nothing. By the way, I did print out his DL photo."

He leaned down and opened his briefcase and pulled out the color printout of Lau's driver's license photo. He handed it to Bosch, who stole quick glances at it as he drove. They got on the Broadway entrance to the 101 and took it up to the 110. The freeways were congested downtown.

Lau had smiled at the camera. He had a fresh face and a stylish cut to his hair. It was hard to connect the face with triad work, particularly the cold-blooded murder of a liquor store owner. The address in Venice didn't fit well either.

"I also checked with ATF. Henry Lau is the registered owner of a nine-millimeter Glock Model Nineteen. Not only did he load it, he owns it."

"When did he buy it?"

"Six years ago, the day after he turned twenty-one."

To Bosch that meant they were getting warm. Lau owned the right gun and his purchase of the weapon as soon as he was of legal age most likely indicated that he had had a long-term desire to acquire a weapon. That made him a traveler in the world Bosch knew. His connection to John Li and Bo-Jing Chang would become apparent once they had him in custody and started taking apart his life.

They connected to the 10 and headed west toward the Pacific. Bosch's phone buzzed and he answered without looking, expecting the caller to be Haller with news about the meeting with the Hong Kong detectives being over.

"Harry, it's Dr. Hinojos. We're waiting for you."

Bosch had forgotten. For more than thirty years he had simply moved with an investigation when it was time to move. He had never had to think about anybody else.

"Oh, Doctor! I'm so sorry. I completely—I'm on my way to pick up a suspect."

"What do you mean?"

"We got a break and I had to—is there any way that Maddie could stay with you a little while longer?"

"Well, this is...I suppose she could stay here. I really just have administrative work the rest of the day. Are you sure this is what you want to do?"

"Look, I know this is bad. It looks bad. She just got here and I left her with you and forgot. But this case is the reason she's here. I have to ride it out. I'm going to grab this guy if he's home and come back downtown. I'll call you then. I'll come get her then."

"Okay, Harry. I could use the extra time with her. You and I are also going to need to find time to talk. About Maddie and then about you."

"Okay, we will. Is she there? Can I speak to her?"

"Hold on."

After a few moments Maddie got on the line.

"Dad?"

With one word she imparted all of the messages: surprise, disappointment, disbelief, terrible letdown.

"I know, baby. I'm sorry. Something's come up and I need to go with it. Go with Dr. Hinojos and I will be there as fast as I can."

"All right."

A double helping of disappointment. Bosch feared it would not be the last time.

"Okay, Mad. I love you."

He closed the phone and put it away.

"I don't want to talk about it," he said before Chu could ask a question.

"Okay," Chu said.

The traffic opened up and they made it into Venice in less than a half hour. Along the way Bosch took another call, this one the expected one from Haller. He told Harry that the Hong Kong police would bother him no further.

"That's it, then?"

"They'll be in touch about your ex-wife's body, but that's it. They're dropping any inquiry into your part in this."

"What about Sun Yee?"

"They claim he is being released from questioning and that he faces no charges. You will need to contact him, of course, to confirm."

"Don't worry, I will. Thank you, Mickey."

"All in a day's work."

"Send me the bill."

"No, we're even, Harry. Instead of billing you, why

don't you let my daughter meet your daughter? They're almost the same age, you know."

Bosch hesitated. He knew that Haller was asking for more than a visit between the two girls. Haller was Bosch's half brother, though they had never met as adults until they crossed paths on a case just a year before. Hooking up the daughters meant hooking up the fathers, and Bosch wasn't sure he was ready for that.

"When the time is right we'll do it," he said. "Right now, she's supposed to start school tomorrow and I've got to get her settled in here."

"Sounds good. You be safe, Harry."

Bosch closed the phone and concentrated on finding Henry Lau's residence. The streets that made up the neighborhoods at the south end of Venice were gridded in alphabetical order and Quarterdeck was one of the last before the inlet and Marina del Rey.

Venice was a bohemian community with uptown prices. The building where Lau resided was one of the newer glass-and-stucco structures that were slowly crowding out the little weekend bungalows that had once lined the beach. Bosch parked in an alley off Speedway and they walked back.

The building was a condominium complex and there were signs out front advertising two units for sale. They entered through a glass door and stood in a small vestibule with an inner security door and a button panel for calling up to individual units. Bosch didn't like the idea of pushing the button for unit 11. If Lau knew police were at the building entrance, he could escape through any fire exit in the building.

"What's the plan?" Chu said.

Bosch started pushing the buttons for the other units. They waited and finally a woman answered one of the calls.

"Yes?"

"Los Angeles police, ma'am," Bosch said. "Can we speak with you?"

"Speak to me about what?"

Bosch shook his head. There was a time when he would not have been questioned. The door would have been immediately opened.

"It's about a homicide investigation, ma'am. Can you open the door?"

There was a long pause and Bosch wanted to buzz her again but he realized he was not sure which of the buttons he had pushed was the one she had responded to.

"Can you hold your badges to the camera, please?" the woman said.

Bosch had not realized there was a camera and looked around.

"Here."

Chu pointed to a small aperture located at the top of the panel. They held up their badges and soon the inner door buzzed. Bosch pulled it open.

"I don't even know what unit she was in," Bosch said.

The door led to a common area that was open to the sky. There was a small lap pool in the center and the building's twelve townhomes all had entrances here, four each on the north and south sides and two each on the east and west. Eleven was on the west side, which meant the unit had windows facing the ocean.

Bosch approached the door to number 11 and knocked on it and got no answer. The door to number 12 opened and a woman stood there.

"I thought you said you wanted to speak to me," she said.

"We're actually looking for Mr. Lau," Chu said. "Do you know where he is?"

"He might be at work. But I think he said he was shooting at night this week."

"Shooting what?" Bosch asked.

"He's a screenwriter and he's working on a movie or a TV show. I'm not sure which."

Just then the door to number 11 cracked open. A man with bleary eyes and unkempt hair peered out. Bosch recognized him from the photo Chu had printed.

"Henry Lau?" Bosch said. "LAPD. We need to ask you some questions."

44

Henry Lau had a spacious home with a back deck that was ten feet over the boardwalk and had a view of the Pacific across the widest stretch of Venice beach. He invited Bosch and Chu in and asked them to sit down in the living room. Chu sat down but Bosch remained standing, positioning his back to the view so that he would not be distracted during the interview. He wasn't getting the vibe he was expecting. Lau seemed to take their knocking on his door as routine and expected. Harry hadn't counted on that.

Lau was wearing blue jeans, sneakers and a long-sleeved T-shirt with a silk-screened image of a long-haired man wearing sunglasses, and a caption that said, THE DUDE ABIDES. If he had been sleeping, he had slept in his clothes.

Bosch pointed him to a square black leather chair with armrests a foot wide.

"Have a seat, Mr. Lau, and we'll try not to take up too much of your time," he said.

Lau was small and catlike. He sat down and brought his legs up onto the chair.

"Is this about the shooting?" he asked.

Bosch glanced at Chu and then back at Lau.

"What shooting is that?"

"The one out there on the beach. The robbery."

"When was this?"

"I don't know. A couple weeks back. But I guess that's not why you're here if you don't even know when it was."

"That's correct, Mr. Lau. We are investigating a shooting but not that one. Do you mind talking to us?"

Lau hiked his shoulders up.

"I don't know. I don't know about any other shootings, Officers."

"We're detectives."

"Detectives. What shooting?"

"Do you know a man named Bo-Jing Chang?"

"Bo-Jing Chang? No, I don't know that name."

He looked genuinely surprised by the name. Bosch signaled Chu and he pulled a printout of Chang's booking photo from his briefcase. He showed it to Lau. While he studied it, Bosch moved to another spot in the room to get another angle on him. He wanted to keep moving. It would help keep Lau off guard.

Lau shook his head after looking at the photo.

"No, don't know him. What shooting are we talking about here?"

"Let us ask the questions for now," Bosch said. "Then we'll get to yours. Your neighbor said you're a screenwriter?"

"Yes."

"You write anything I might have seen?"

"Nope."

"How do you know?"

"Because I've never had anything that actually got made until right now. So there's nothing out there you could've seen."

"Well, then who pays for this nice pad on the beach?"

"I pay for it. I get paid to write. I just haven't had anything hit the screen yet. It takes time, you know?"

Bosch moved behind Lau and the young man had to turn in his comfortable seat to track him.

"Where did you grow up, Henry?"

"San Francisco. Came down here to go to school and stayed."

"You were born up there?"

"That's right."

"You a Giants or Dodgers man?"

"Giants, baby."

"That's too bad. When was the last time you were in South L.A.?"

The question came from left field and Lau had to think before answering. He shook his head.

"I don't know, five or six years at least. Been a while, though. I wish you could tell me what this is about because then I might be able to help you."

"So if somebody said they saw you down there last week, they'd be lying?"

Lau smirked like they were playing a game.

"Either that or they were just mistaken. You know what they say."

"No, what do they say?"

"That we all look alike."

Lau smiled brightly and looked to Chu for confirmation. Chu held his ground and just returned a dead-eyed stare.

"What about Monterey Park?" Bosch asked.

"You mean, have I been there?"

"Yes, that's what I mean."

"Uh, I went out there a couple times for dinner, but it's really not worth the drive."

"So you don't know anyone in Monterey Park?"

"No, not really."

Bosch had been circling, asking general questions and locking Lau in. It was time to circle closer now.

"Where's your gun, Mr. Lau?"

Lau put his feet down on the floor. He looked at Chu and then back at Bosch.

"This is about my gun?"

"Six years ago you bought and registered a Glock Model Nineteen. Can you tell us where it is?"

"Yeah, sure. It's in the lockbox in a drawer next to my bed. Where it always is."

"Are you sure?"

"Okay, I get it, let me guess. Mr. Asshole in unit eight saw me holding it out there on the deck after the beach shooting and he made a complaint?"

"No, Henry, we haven't spoken to Mr. Asshole. Are you saying that you had the gun with you after the shooting on the beach?"

"That's right. I heard shots out there and a scream. I was on my own property and am entitled to protect myself."

Bosch nodded to Chu. Chu opened the slider and stepped out onto the deck, closing the door behind him. He pulled his phone to make a call about the beach shooting.

"Look, if somebody said I fired it, they are full of shit," Lau said.

Bosch looked at him for a long moment. He felt like there was something missing, a piece of the conversation he didn't know about yet.

"As far as I know, nobody's said that," he said.

"Then, please, what is this all about?"

"I told you. It's about your gun. Can you show it to us, Henry?"

"Sure, I'll go get it."

He sprang up from the chair and headed toward the stairs.

"Henry," Bosch said. "Hold it there. We're going to go with you."

Lau looked back from the stairs.

"Suit yourself. Let's get this over with."

Bosch turned back to the deck. Chu was coming through the door. They followed Lau up the stairs and then down a hallway that cut back to the rear of the unit. Framed photographs, movie posters and diplomas lined both sides. They passed an open door to a bedroom that was used as a writing office and then entered the master bedroom, a grand room with twelve-foot ceilings and ten-foot windows looking out over the beach.

"I called Pacific Division," Chu said to Bosch. "The shooting was on the night of the first. They have two suspects in custody on it."

Bosch flipped back through the calendar in his mind. The first was the Tuesday one week before the killing of John Li.

Lau sat down on the unmade bed next to a two-drawer side table. He opened the bottom drawer and pulled out a steel box with a handle on the top.

"Hold it right there," Bosch said.

Lau put the box on the bed and stood up, hands up.

"Hey, I wasn't going to do anything, man. You asked to see it."

"Why don't you let my partner open the box," Bosch said.

"Suit yourself."

"Detective."

Bosch pulled a pair of latex gloves from his coat pocket and handed them to Chu. He then stepped over to Lau so that he was within arm's reach if necessary.

"Why'd you buy the gun, Henry?"

"Because I was living in a complete shithole at the time and the bangers were all over the place. But it's funny. I paid a million fucking dollars for this place and they're still right out there on the beach, shooting the place up."

Chu snapped the second glove on and looked at Lau.

"Do you give us permission to open this box?" he asked.

"Sure, go ahead. I don't know what this is about but why the hell not? Just open it. The key is on a little hook on the back side of the table."

Chu reached behind the bed table and found the key. He then used it to open the box. A black felt gun bag sat on some folded papers and envelopes. There was a passport and a box of bullets as well. Chu carefully lifted the bag out and opened it, producing a black semiautomatic pistol. He turned it and examined it.

"One box of Cor Bon nine-millimeter bullets, one Glock Model Nineteen. I think this is it, Harry."

He popped the gun's magazine and studied the bullets through the slot. He then ejected the round from the chamber.

"Fully loaded and ready to go."

Lau took a step toward the door but Bosch immediately put his hand on his chest to stop him and then backed him against the wall.

"Look," Lau said, "I don't know what this is about but you people are freaking me out here. What the fuck is going on?"

Bosch kept his hand on his chest.

"Just tell me about the gun, Henry. You had it the night of the first. Has it been out of your possession at any time since then?"

"No, I . . . right there is where I keep it."

"Where were you last Tuesday, three o'clock in the afternoon?"

"Um, last week I was here. I think I was here, working. We didn't start shooting until Thursday."

"You work here alone?"

"Yes, I work alone. Writing is a solitary pursuit. No, wait! Wait! Last Tuesday I was at Paramount all day. We had a read-through of the script with the cast. I was over there all afternoon."

"And there will be people who will vouch for you?"

"At least a dozen. Matthew fucking McConaughey will vouch for me. He was there. He's playing the lead."

Bosch made a jump then, hitting Lau with a question designed to keep him off balance. It was amazing what fell out of people's pockets when they were being knocked back and forth by seemingly unrelated questions.

"Are you associated with a triad, Henry?"

Lau burst out laughing.

"What? What the fuck are you—look, I'm out of here."

He slapped Bosch's hand away and pushed off the wall in the direction of the door again. It was a move Harry was ready for. He grabbed Lau by the arm and spun him around. He clipped his ankle with a kick and threw him facedown on the bed. He then moved in, kneeling on his back while he cuffed him.

"This is fucking crazy!" Lau yelled. "You can't do this!"

"Calm down, Henry, just calm down," Bosch said. "We're going to go downtown and straighten all of this out."

"But I've got a movie! I have to be on the set in three hours!"

"Fuck the movies, Henry. This is real life and we're going downtown."

Bosch pulled him up off the bed and pointed him toward the door.

"Dave, you got all of that secured?"

"Got it."

"Then, lead the way."

Chu left the room, carrying the metal box containing the Glock. Bosch followed, keeping Lau in front of him and keeping one hand on the chain between the cuffs.

They moved down the hall, but when they got to the top of the stairs, Bosch pulled the cuffs like the reins on a horse and stopped.

"Wait a minute. Back up here."

He walked Lau backwards to the middle of the hall. Something had caught Bosch's eye as they had passed but it didn't register until they got to the stairs. Now he looked at the framed diploma from the University of Southern California. Lau had graduated with a liberal arts degree in 2004.

"You went to SC?" Bosch asked.

"Yeah, the film school. Why?"

Both the school and graduation year matched the diploma Bosch had seen in the back office at Fortune Fine Foods & Liquor. And then there was the Chinese connection as well. Bosch knew that a lot of kids went to USC and several thousand graduated every year, many of them of Chinese descent. But he had never trusted coincidences.

"Did you know a guy at SC named Robert Li— spelled *L-I?*"

Lau nodded.

"Yeah, I knew him. He was my roommate."

Bosch felt things suddenly begin to crash together with an undeniable force.

"What about Eugene Lam? Did you know him?"

Lau nodded again.

"I still do. He was my roommate back then, too."

"Where?"

"Like I told you, a shithole down in gangland. Near the campus."

Bosch knew that USC was an oasis of fine and

expensive education surrounded by hardscrabble neighborhoods where personal safety would be an issue. A few
years back a football player on the practice field had even
been hit with a stray round from a nearby gang shooting.

"Is that why you bought the gun? For protection
down there?"

"Exactly."

Chu had realized he had lost them and came hurrying
back up the stairs and down the hallway.

"Harry, what's up?"

Bosch held up his free hand to signal Chu to hang back
and be quiet. He spoke to Lau again.

"And those guys knew you bought the gun six years
ago?"

"We went together. They helped me pick it out. Why
are you—"

"Are you still friends? You stay in touch?"

"Yeah, but what's this got to do with—"

"When was the last time you saw one of them?"

"I saw them both last week. We play poker almost
every week."

Bosch glanced over at Chu. The case had just broken
wide open.

"Where, Henry? Where do you play?"

"Most of the time right here. Robert still lives with his
parents and Huge has a tiny place in the Valley. I mean,
come on, I've got the beach here."

"What day did you play last week?"

"It was Wednesday."

"You sure?"

"Yeah, because I remember it was the night before my

shoot was going to start and I didn't really want to play. But they showed up and we played for a little bit. It was a short night."

"And the time before that? When was that?"

"The week before. Wednesday or Thursday, I can't remember."

"But it was after the shooting on the beach?"

Lau shrugged.

"Yeah, pretty sure. Why?"

"What about the key to the box? Would one of them have known where the key was?"

"What did they do?"

"Just answer the question, Henry."

"Yeah, they knew. They used to like to get the gun out sometimes and play around with it."

Bosch pulled his keys out and uncuffed Lau. The screenwriter turned and started to massage his wrists.

"I always wondered what that felt like," he said. "So I could write about it. The last time I was too drunk to remember."

He finally looked up and saw Bosch's intent stare.

"What's going on?"

Bosch put a hand on his shoulder and turned him toward the stairs.

"Let's go back down to the living room and talk, Henry. I think there is a lot you can tell us."

45

They waited for Eugene Lam in the alley behind Fortune Fine Foods & Liquor. There was a small employee lot squeezed between a row of trash bins and the stacks of baled cardboard. It was Thursday, two days after they had visited Henry Lau, and the case had come together. They had used the time to work on evidence gathering and testing, and to prepare a strategy. Bosch had also used the time to enroll his daughter in the school at the bottom of the hill. She had started classes that morning.

They believed Eugene Lam was the shooter but also the weaker of the two suspects. They would bring him in first, then Robert Li second. They were locked and loaded and as Bosch watched the parking lot, he felt certain that the killing of John Li would be understood and resolved by the end of the day.

"Here we go," Chu said.

He pointed to the mouth of the alley. Lam's car had just turned in.

• • •

They put Lam in the first interview room and let him cook for a while. Time always favored the interviewer, never the suspect. In RHD, they called it "seasoning the roast." You let the suspect marinate in time. It always made him more tender. Bo-Jing Chang had been the exception to this rule. He hadn't said a word and had held up like a rock. Innocence gave you that resolve, and that was something Lam didn't have.

An hour later, after conferring with a prosecutor from the district attorney's office, Bosch entered the room carrying a cardboard box containing the case evidence and sat down across the table from Lam. The suspect looked up with scared eyes. They always did after a period of isolation. What was just an hour on the outside was an eternity inside. Bosch put the box down on the floor, then folded his arms on the table.

"Eugene, I'm here to explain the facts of life to you," he said. "So listen closely to what I tell you. You have a big choice to make here. The fact of the matter is that you are going to prison. There's no doubt about that. But what you are going to decide here in the next few minutes is how long you go for. It can be until you are a very old man or until they stick the needle in your arm and put you down like a dog...

"Or you can leave yourself a chance at getting your freedom back one day. You're a very young man, Eugene. I hope you make the right choice."

He paused and waited but Lam didn't react.

"It's sort of funny. I've been doing this a long time and I've sat across a table like this with a lot of men who have killed. I can't say they were all bad or evil men. Some had reasons and some were manipulated. They got led down the path."

Lam shook his head in a show of bravado.

"I told you people, I want a lawyer. I know my rights. You can't ask me any questions once I ask for a lawyer."

Bosch nodded in agreement.

"Yeah, you're right about that, Eugene. Absolutely right. Once you've invoked your rights we can't question you. Not allowed. But, see, that's why I'm not asking you anything here. I'm just telling you how it is going to be. I'm telling you that you have a choice to make here. Silence is certainly a choice. But if you choose silence, you'll never see the outside world again."

Lam shook his head and looked down at the table.

"Please leave me alone."

"Maybe it would help you if I summarized things and gave you a clearer picture of where you're at here. You see, I am perfectly willing to share with you, man. I'll show you my whole hand because, you know what? It's a royal flush. You play poker, right? You know that's the hand that can't be beat. And that's what I've got here. A royal fucking flush."

Bosch paused. He could see curiosity in Lam's eyes. He couldn't help but wonder what they had on him.

"We know you did the dirty work on this thing, Eugene. You went into that store and you shot Mr. Li dead in cold blood. But we're pretty sure it wasn't your idea. It was Robert who sent you in there to kill his father. And he's the one we want. I've got a deputy district attorney sitting in the other room and he's ready to make you a deal—fifteen to life if you give us Robert. You'll do the fifteen for sure, but after that, you get a shot at freedom. You convince a parole board you were just a victim, that you got manipulated by a master, and you walk free...

"It could happen. But if you go the other way, you roll the dice. If you lose, you're done. You're talking about dying in prison in fifty years—if the jury doesn't decide to stick the needle in your arm first."

Lam quietly said, "I want a lawyer."

Bosch nodded and responded with resignation in his voice.

"Okay, man, that's your choice. We'll get you a lawyer."

He looked up at the ceiling where the camera was located and raised an imaginary phone to his ear.

He then looked back at Lam and knew he wasn't going to be convinced by words alone. It was show-and-tell time.

"All right, they're making the call. If you don't mind, while we're waiting here I'm going to tell you a few things. You can share them with your lawyer when he gets here."

"Whatever," Lam said. "I don't care what you say as long as I get the attorney."

"Okay, then, let's start with the crime scene. You know, there were a few things about it that bothered me from the beginning. One was that Mr. Li had the gun right there under the counter and never got the chance to pull it. Another was that there were no head wounds. Mr. Li was shot three times in the chest and that was it. No shot to the face."

"Very interesting," Lam said sarcastically.

Bosch ignored it.

"And you know what all of that told me? That said that

Li probably knew his killer and hadn't felt threatened. And that this was a piece of business. This wasn't revenge, this wasn't personal. This was purely a piece of business."

Bosch reached down to the box and removed the lid. He reached in for the plastic evidence bag that held the bullet casing taken from the victim's throat. He tossed it on the table in front of Lam.

"There it is, Eugene. You remember looking for that? Coming around the counter, moving the body, wondering what the fuck happened to that casing? Well, there it is. There's the one mistake that brought it all down on you."

He paused while Lam stared at the casing, fear permanently lodging in his eyes.

"You never leave a soldier behind. Isn't that the shooter's rule? But you did, man. You left that soldier behind and it brought us right to your door."

Bosch picked up the bag and held it up between them.

"There was a fingerprint on the casing, Eugene. We raised it with something called electrostatic enhancement. EE, for short. It's a new science for us. And the print we got belonged to your old roommate Henry Lau. Yeah, it led us to Henry and he was very cooperative. He told us the last time he fired and then reloaded his gun was at a range about eight months ago. His fingerprint was sitting on that shell all that time."

Harry reached down to the box and removed Henry Lau's gun, still in its black felt bag. He took it out of the bag and put the weapon down on the table.

"We went to Henry and he gave us the weapon. We had it checked out by ballistics yesterday, and sure enough, it's our murder weapon, all right. This is the gun that killed John Li at Fortune Liquors on September eighth. The problem was that Henry Lau has a solid alibi for the time of the shooting. He was in a room with thirteen other people. He's even got Matthew McConaughey as an alibi witness. And then on top of that, he told us he hadn't given his gun out to anybody to borrow."

Bosch leaned back and scratched his chin with his hand, as if he were still trying to figure out how the gun ended up being used to kill John Li.

"Damn, this was a big problem, Eugene. But then, of course, we got lucky. The good guys often get lucky. You made us lucky, Eugene."

He paused for effect and then brought down the hammer.

"You see, whoever used Henry's gun to kill John Li cleaned it up after and then reloaded it so Henry wouldn't ever know his gun had been borrowed and used to kill a man. It was a pretty good plan, but he made one mistake."

Bosch leaned forward across the table and looked at Lam eye to eye. He turned the gun on the table so that its barrel was pointing at the suspect's chest.

"One of the bullets that were replaced in the magazine had a nice readable thumbprint on it. Your thumbprint, Eugene. We matched it to the print they took when you traded in your New York driver's license for a California DL."

Lam's eyes slowly dropped away from Bosch's and down to the table.

"All of this, it means nothing," he said.

There was little conviction in his voice.

"Yeah?" Bosch responded. "Really? I don't know

about that. I happen to think it means a lot, Eugene. And the prosecutor on the other side of that camera is thinking the same thing. He says it sounds like a prison door slamming, with you standing there on the wrong side of it."

Bosch picked up the gun and the bag with the casing in it and put them back in the box. He grabbed the box with both hands and stood up.

"So that's where we're at, Eugene. You think about all of that while you're waiting for your lawyer."

Bosch slowly moved toward the door. He hoped Lam would tell him to stop and come back, that he wanted to make the deal. But the suspect said nothing. Harry put the box under one arm, opened the door and walked out.

Bosch carried the evidence box back to his cubicle and dropped it heavily on his desk. He looked over at his partner's cubicle to make sure it was still empty. Ferras had been left behind in the Valley to keep an eyeball on Robert Li. If he figured out that Lam was in police custody and possibly talking, he might make a move. Ferras hadn't liked the babysitting assignment but Bosch didn't really care. Ferras had moved himself to the periphery of the investigation and that was where he was going to stay.

Soon Chu and Gandle, who had been watching Bosch's play with Lam from the other side of the camera in the AV room, came to the cubicle.

"I told you it was a weak play," Gandle said. "We know he's a smart kid. He had to have been wearing gloves when he reloaded the gun. Once he knew you were playing him, you lost."

"Yeah, well," Bosch said. "I thought it was the best we had."

"I agree," Chu said, showing his support for Bosch.

"We're still going to have to kick him loose," Gandle said. "We know he had the opportunity to take the gun but we have no proof that he actually did. Opportunity is not enough. You can't go to court with just that."

"Is that what Cook said?"

"That's what he was thinking."

Abner Cook was the deputy DA who had come over from the CCB to observe in the AV room.

"Where is he, anyway?"

As if to answer for himself, Cook called Bosch's name from across the squad room.

"Get back here!"

Bosch straightened up and looked over the cubicle partition. Cook was frantically waving from the door of the AV room. Harry got up and started walking toward him.

"He's calling for you," Cook said. "Get back in there!"

Bosch picked up speed as he moved toward the interview room door, then he slowed and composed himself before opening the door and calmly stepping back in.

"What is it?" he said. "We called your lawyer and he's on the way."

"What about the deal? Is it still good?"

"For the moment. The DA's about to leave."

"Bring him in. I want the deal."

Bosch stepped all the way in and closed the door.

"What are you giving us, Eugene? If you want the deal, I've got to know what you're going to give me. I'll bring in the DA when I know what's on the table."

Lam nodded.

"I'll give you Robert Li...and his sister. The whole thing was their plan. The old man was stubborn and wouldn't change. They needed to close that store and open another in the Valley. One that made money. But he said no. He always said no and finally Rob couldn't take it anymore."

Bosch slid back into his seat, trying to hide his surprise about Mia's involvement.

"And the sister was part of this?"

"She was the one who planned it. Except..."

"Except what?"

"She wanted me to hit them both. The mother and father. She wanted me to show up early and hit 'em both. But Robert told me no. He didn't want his mother hurt."

"Whose idea was it to make it look like a triad hit?"

"That was her idea and then Robert sort of planned it. They knew the police would go for it."

Bosch nodded. He hardly knew Mia but knew enough about her story to feel sad about the whole thing.

He glanced up at the overhead camera, hoping his stare would send the message to Gandle that he needed to put somebody on locating Mia Li so arrest teams could move in simultaneously.

Bosch brought his eyes back down to Lam. He was staring down dejectedly at the table.

"What about you, Eugene? Why'd you get involved in this?"

Lam shook his head. Bosch could read the regret in his face.

"I don't know. Robert said he was going to lay me off

because his father's store was losing too much money. He told me I could save my job... and that when they opened the second store in the Valley it would be mine to run."

It was no more pitiful an answer than any other Bosch had heard over the years. There were no surprises left when it came to motivations for murder.

He tried to think of any loose ends he should try to cover before Abner Cook came in and sealed the deal.

"What about Henry Lau? Did he give you the gun or did you take it without him knowing?"

"We took it—I took it. We were playing poker one night at his place and I said I had to go to the bathroom. I went into the bedroom and got it. I knew where he kept the key to the box. I took it and then I put it back afterward—the next time we played. It was part of the plan. We didn't think he'd ever know."

That seemed entirely plausible to Bosch. But Harry knew that once the deal was formally struck and signed off on by Cook and Lam, he would be able to question Lam in more detail about all things pertaining to the case. He just had one last aspect to cover before bringing Cook in.

"What about Hong Kong?" he asked.

Lam looked confused by the question.

"Hong Kong?" he asked. "What about it?"

"Which one of you had the connection over there?"

Lam shook his head in bewilderment. It seemed real to Bosch.

"I don't know what you mean. My family is in New York, not Hong Kong. I have no connection there and as far as I know, neither does Robert or Mia. Hong Kong wasn't mentioned."

Bosch thought about this. Now he was confused. Something didn't connect here.

"You're saying that as far as you know, neither Robert nor Mia made any calls to anyone over there about the case or any of the investigators involved?"

"Not as far as I know. I really don't think they know anybody."

"What about Monterey Park? The triad Mr. Li was paying off."

"We knew about them and Robert knew when Chang came to collect every week. That's how he planned it. I waited and when I saw Chang leave the store I went in. Robert told me to take the disc out of the machine but to leave the other discs there. He knew one had Chang on it and the police would see it as a clue."

A nice bit of manipulation on Robert's part, Bosch thought. And he had gone for it, just as planned.

"What did you two tell Chang when he came to the store the other night?"

"That was part of the plan, too. Robert knew he would come to collect from him."

He looked down and away from Bosch's eyes. He seemed embarrassed.

"So what did you say to him?" Bosch prompted.

"Robert told him that the police had shown us his photo and that they told us that he committed the murder. He told him the police were looking for him and would arrest him. We thought that would make him run. He would leave town and it would look like he had done the crime. If he went back to China and disappeared, it would help us."

Bosch stared at Lam as the meaning and ramifications of the statement slowly sank into the dark blood in his heart. He had been totally manipulated every step of the way.

"Who called me?" he asked. "Who called and told me to back off the case?"

Lam slowly nodded.

"That was me," he said. "Robert wrote a script for me and I made that call from a pay phone downtown. I'm sorry, Detective Bosch. I didn't want to scare you but I had to do what Robert told me to do."

Bosch nodded. He was sorry too, but not for the same reasons.

46

An hour later Bosch and Cook emerged from the interview room with a full confession and agreement of cooperation from Eugene Lam. Cook said he would be filing charges immediately against the young killer as well as Robert and Mia Li. Cook said there was more than enough evidence to proceed with arrests of the sister and brother.

Bosch gathered with Chu, Gandle and four other detectives in the conference room to discuss the arrest procedures. Ferras was still watching Robert Li but Gandle said that a detective sent to the Li home in the Wilshire District had reported back that the family car was gone and there appeared to be no one home.

"Do we wait for Mia to show up or do we take Robert down now, before he starts wondering about Lam?" Gandle asked.

"I think we've got to move," Bosch said. "He already has to be wondering where Lam is. If he starts getting suspicious, he might run."

Gandle looked around the room for objections. There were none.

"Okay, then let's mount up," he said. "We take down Robert in the store and then we go find Mia. I want these people booked before the end of the day. Harry, check with your partner and confirm Robert's location. Tell him we're on the way. I'll ride up with you and Chu."

It was unusual for the lieutenant to want to leave the office. But the case had transcended routine. He apparently wanted to be there when it was closed by arrest.

Everybody stood up and started to file out of the conference room. Bosch and Gandle lagged behind. Harry pulled his phone and hit a speed dial button for Ferras. At last check-in, he was still in his car, watching Fortune Fine Foods & Liquor from across the street.

"You know what I still don't get, Harry?" Gandle asked.

"No, what don't you get?"

"Who took your daughter? Lam claims he doesn't know anything about it. And at this point he has no reason to lie. Do you still think it was Chang's people, even though we now know he was clear on the killing?"

The call was answered before Bosch could respond to Gandle.

"Ferras."

"It's me," Bosch said. "Where's Li?"

He held a finger up to Gandle, holding him while he took the call.

"He's in the store," Ferras said. "You know, we need to talk, Harry."

Bosch could tell by the tension in his partner's voice that it wasn't Robert Li that Ferras wanted to talk about. While he was sitting there in his car alone all morning, something was festering in his brain.

"We'll talk later. Right now we have to move. We turned Lam. He gave us everything. Robert *and* his sister. She was part of this. Is she in the store?"

"Not that I saw. She dropped off the mother but then she drove off."

"When was this?"

"About an hour ago."

Tired of waiting and needing to get ready to join the arrest teams, Gandle headed off toward his office and Bosch was left thinking that he was safe for the time being from having to answer the lieutenant's question. Now he just had to deal with Ferras.

"Okay, sit tight," he said. "And let me know if anything changes."

"You know what, Harry?"

"What, Ignacio?" he responded impatiently.

"You didn't give me a chance, man."

There was a whining tone in his voice that set Bosch on edge.

"What chance? What are you talking about?"

"I'm talking about you telling the lieutenant you wanted a new partner. You should've given me another chance. He's trying to move me to autos, you know. He said *I'm* not dependable, so I'm the one who has to go."

"Look, Ignacio, it's been two years, okay? I've given you two years of chances. But now's not the time to talk about this. We'll do it later, okay? In the meantime, just sit tight. We're on our way."

"No, you sit tight, Harry."

Bosch paused for a moment.

"What's that supposed to mean?"

"It means, I'll handle Li."

"Ignacio, listen to me. You're by yourself. You don't go in that store until you have an arrest team with you. You understand? You want to put the cuffs on him, fine, you can do that. But you wait until we get there."

"I don't need a team and I don't need you, Harry."

Ferras disconnected. Bosch hit redial as he started moving toward the lieutenant's office.

Ferras didn't pick up and the call went direct to voice mail. When Bosch entered Gandle's office, the lieutenant was buttoning his shirt over a Kevlar vest he had donned for the field trip.

"We've got to move," Bosch said. "Ferras is going off the map."

47

After returning from the funeral, Bosch took off his tie and grabbed a beer out of the refrigerator. He went out on the deck, sat back on the lounge chair and closed his eyes. He thought about putting on some music, maybe a little Art Pepper to bounce him out of the blues.

But he found himself unable to move. He just kept his eyes closed and tried to forget as much as he could about the two weeks that had just passed. He knew this was an unattainable task but it was worth a try and the beer would help, if only on a temporary basis. It had been the last one in the refrigerator and he had vowed that it would be the last one for him as well. He had his daughter to raise now and he would need to be the best he could be with her.

As if thoughts of her conjured her presence, he heard the sliding door open.

"Hey, Mads."

"Dad."

In only the one word her voice sounded different, troubled. He opened his eyes and squinted in the afternoon sunlight. She had already changed out of her dress and was wearing blue jeans and a shirt that had come from the bag her mother had packed for her. Bosch had noticed she wore more of the few things her mother had put into the backpack in Hong Kong than all of the clothes they had shopped for together.

"What's up?"

"I wanted to talk to you."

"Okay."

"I'm really sorry about your partner."

"Me, too. He made a bad mistake and paid for it. But I don't know, it just doesn't seem like the punishment fit the crime, you know?"

Bosch's mind momentarily shifted to the ghastly scene he'd encountered inside the manager's office of Fortune Fine Foods & Liquor. Ferras facedown on the floor, shot four times in the back. Robert Li cowering in the corner, shaking and moaning, staring at his sister's body near the door. After killing Ferras she had turned the gun on herself. Mrs. Li, the matriarch of this family of killers and victims, was standing stoically in the doorway when Bosch got there.

Ignacio had not seen Mia coming. She had dropped her mother off at the store and then driven away. But something made her come back, sneaking down the alley in her car and parking in the back lot. It was speculated afterward in the squad room that she had spotted Ferras on his surveillance and knew that the police were about to close in. She had driven home, retrieved the gun her murdered father had kept below the front counter at his store, and then gone back to the store in the Valley. It was unclear and would always remain a mystery what her plan was. Perhaps she was looking for Lam or her mother. Or maybe she was just waiting for the police. But she returned to the store and came in through the employee entrance in the back at approximately the same time Ferras entered through the front door to single-handedly attempt to arrest Robert. She watched Ferras enter her brother's office and then came up behind him.

Bosch wondered what Ignacio's final thoughts were as the bullets ripped through his body. He wondered if his young partner was amazed that lightning could strike twice, the second time finishing the job.

Bosch pushed the vision and the thoughts away. He sat up and looked at his daughter. He saw the burden in her eyes and knew what was coming.

"Dad?"

"What is it, baby?"

"I made a bad mistake, too. Only I'm not the one who paid for it."

"What do you mean, sweetheart?"

"When I was talking to Dr. Hinojos, she said I have to unburden. I have to tell what's bothering me."

Tears started to flow now. Bosch sat sideways on the lounge chair and took his daughter by the hand and guided her to a seat right next to him. He put his arm across her shoulders.

"You can tell me anything, Madeline."

She closed her eyes and held a hand over them. She squeezed his hand with the other.

"I got Mom killed," she said. "I got her killed and it should've been me."

"Wait a minute, wait a minute. You're not respons—"

"No, wait, listen to me. Listen to me. Yes, I am. I did it, Dad, and I need to go to jail."

Bosch pulled her into a crushing hug and kissed the top of her head.

"You listen to me, Mads. You're not going anywhere. You're staying right here with me. I know what happened but it doesn't make you responsible for what other people did. I don't want you thinking that."

She pulled back and looked at him.

"You know? *You know* what I did?"

"I think you trusted the wrong person...and the rest, all the rest, is on him."

She shook her head.

"No, no. The whole thing was my idea. I knew you would come and I thought maybe you'd make her let me go with you back here."

"I know."

"How do you know?" she demanded.

Bosch shrugged.

"It doesn't matter," he said. "What matters is that you couldn't have known what Quick would do, that he would take your plan and make it his."

She bowed her head.

"Doesn't matter. I killed my mother."

"Madeline, no. If anybody is responsible, it's me. She got killed in something that had nothing to do with you. It was a robbery and it happened because I was stupid, because I showed my money in a place I should never have shown it. Okay? It's on me, not you. I made the mistake."

She could not be calmed or consoled. She shook her head violently and the force threw tears into Bosch's face.

"You wouldn't have even been there, Dad, if we didn't send that video. I did that! I knew what it would do! That you would be on the very next plane! I was going to escape before you landed. You would get there and everything would be all right but you would tell Mom it wasn't safe for me there and you would take me back with you."

Bosch just nodded. He had put roughly the same scenario together a few days before, when he realized Bo-Jing Chang had nothing to do with the murder of John Li.

"But now Mom is *dead!* And they're *dead!* And everybody's *dead* and it's all *my* fault!"

Bosch grabbed her by the shoulders and turned her in toward him.

"How much of this did you tell Dr. Hinojos?"

"None."

"Okay."

"I wanted to tell you first. You have to take me to jail now."

Bosch pulled her into another hug and held her head against his chest.

"No, baby, you're staying here with me."

He gently caressed her hair and spoke calmly.

"We all make mistakes. Everybody. Sometimes, like with my partner, you make a mistake and you can't make up for it. You don't get the chance. But sometimes you do. We can make up for our mistakes here. Both of us."

Her tears had slowed. He heard her sniffle. He thought maybe this was why she had come to him. For a way out.

"We can maybe do some good and make up for the things we did wrong. We'll make up for everything."

"How?" she said in a small voice.

"I'll show you the way. I'll show you and you'll see that we can make up for this."

Bosch nodded to himself. He hugged his daughter tightly and wished he never had to let her go.

Acknowledgments

This book could not have been written without the help of Steven Vascik and Dennis Wojciechowski. Steve showed me whatever I needed in Hong Kong and Wojo found whatever I needed on the Internet. I will always be grateful.

Also of tremendous help to me were Asya Muchnick, Bill Massey, Michael Pietsch, Shannon Byrne, Jane Davis, Siu Wai Mai, Pamela Marshall, Rick Jackson, Tim Marcia, Michael Krikorian, Terrill Lee Lankford, Daniel Daly, Roger Mills, Philip Spitzer, John Houghton and Linda Connelly. Many thanks to you all.

Special thanks to William J. Bratton, LAPD chief of police 2002–2009, for opening so many doors for me and Harry Bosch.

About the Author

Michael Connelly is a former journalist and the author of the #1 bestsellers *The Scarecrow, The Brass Verdict,* and *The Lincoln Lawyer,* the bestselling series of Harry Bosch novels, and the bestselling novels *Chasing the Dime, Void Moon, Blood Work,* and *The Poet. Crime Beat,* a collection of his journalism, was also a *New York Times* bestseller. He spends his time in California and Florida.